Praise for
Club Sandwich

"*Club Sandwich* is a *Please Don't Eat the Daisies* of commitment and hope—a funny, bittersweet look at seasons of change and challenge, in which belief is the one thread that does not fray. It makes a case for the practical virtue of sustaining faith in which even a dissenter can find joy."

—JACQUELYN MITCHARD, author of *The Deep End of the Ocean* and *The Breakdown Lane*

"Forget trying to be evangelically correct: *Club Sandwich* serves up the messy, crazy truth of living a life of faith in twenty-first-century suburbia, sandwiched between endless responsibilities, fleshly temptations, and one wildly dysfunctional family. When it comes to speaking the truth in love, Lisa Samson is the Real Deal."

—LIZ CURTIS HIGGS, author of *Thorn in My Heart*

"In a Lisa Samson novel, I expect wit and wisdom with vibrant characters that live next door to me, and *Club Sandwich* is no exception. But it is more. The character's thoughts move like lasers of insight onto the page. 'I'm still careening to the right on the Snow Emergency Route of faith,' says Ivy of her faith journey. Or in describing the distance between Ivy and her father she says, 'An arbitrary melody in our lives, he sang his own descant at will, leaving the true composing to my mother.' Lisa defines that aching place so many women know, as their parents age while their children potty train, and they and their spouses pursue career goals that often separate them from each other. These women hope to do the best they can for their families without losing themselves in the process. I'm a member of Club Sandwich. I'm telling my friends about this book because Lisa's story both satisfies and gives us hope."

—JANE KIRKPATRICK, author of *A Land of Sheltered Promise*

"*Club Sandwich* is like a slice of my life—and Lisa Samson definitely gets it. With her intelligent wit, she takes us beneath the complicated layers of generational relationships as she unfolds a delicious tale of relevance and redemption. Lisa's best one yet!"

—MELODY CARLSON, author of *Crystal Lies, Finding Alice,* the True Colors series, and *Diary of a Teenage Girl*

"*Club Sandwich* offers us a warm slice of life peppered with the kind of panache only Lisa Samson can dish up. She's truly an original voice—refreshing and honest. Sit back and enjoy the meal."

—ROBERT ELMER, author of *The Duet* and *The Celebrity*

Club Sandwich

Club Sandwich

a novel

lisa samson

WATERBROOK
PRESS

CLUB SANDWICH
PUBLISHED BY WATERBROOK PRESS
2375 Telstar Drive, Suite 160
Colorado Springs, Colorado 80920
A division of Random House, Inc.

Scriptures are quoted or paraphrased from the *King James Version.*

ISBN 1-57856-885-4

Library of Congress Cataloging-in-Publication Data
Samson, Lisa, 1964–
    Club sandwich / Lisa Samson.— 1st ed.
        p. cm.
    ISBN 1-57856-885-4
    1. Parent and adult child—Fiction. 2. Mothers and daughters—Fiction.
3. Female friendship—Fiction. 4. Single mothers—Fiction. I. Title.
    PS3569.A46673C58 2005
    813'.54—dc22

                                                    2004030852

Printed in the United States of America
2005—First Edition

10 9 8 7 6 5 4 3 2 1

———

To my youngest, Gwynneth:

My beetlebug, my baby, my spirit. May your zest for life never be quenched. May your God-given gifts be used for the good of all humankind.

I love you.

Acknowledgments

A heartfelt thank you to Lori York, who suggested that a book on the sandwich generation would help a lot of people. And to Kathy Kreyling, for entering those blasted changes from hard copy!

To all my family members, friends, and fellow journeyers, thanks for making it special.

A special thanks to Lori, Leigh, Jef, Heather, Chris, Marty and Bob, Miss Gloria, Mom and Dad S., Val; Claudia, Don, Dudley, Erin, Laura; the guys at Main Street Cigar; the blogosphere writer-friends, especially Jules, Mary, Michael, Claudia, Marilyn and Katy; Jim, Angie, Jack, Liz, Melody, and the Chi Libris family.

To Will, Ty, Jake, and Gwyn, for all you are. Thank You, Jesus, for the dust on Your sandals and the love in Your eyes.

And finally, thank you lovely readers! Email me at lesamson@ hotmail.com or visit my Web site at www.lisasamson.com.

No one's ever accused me of being balanced.

If childhood maps our future beliefs and actions, it's no wonder I veer to the right when walking down the sidewalk. If I spin, I twirl right. If I dance, my right foot leads. Perhaps my left-handedness dictates this bent, but I know better. I even look like a conservative with my understated pageboy, my Keds, and my sundresses. Now if I chose orthopedic sandals, I'd look like a member of PETA. And dreadlocks on this stark white woman? That might land me a delegate position to the Democratic National Convention.

My kitchen could well serve as a stopping point for Captain America between missions. Years ago, when I began collecting flag-themed items, my friends and family latched on to it like suckers to wool socks. The Schneider house now holds 179 flags and flag knickknacks. After eighty items, I told them I had enough. Apparently they hadn't. And who can blame them? Finding the right gift for someone proves enough of a chore. Collections narrow the field. Well, it could be worse. I might have launched an endless parade of pigs or roosters. Or cows. At least flags don't contract crazy diseases or curly parasites. Sometimes they attract the matches of malcontents. But not in my kitchen.

My most vivid childhood memories still frighten me. I entered life in the thick of the cold war. Nineteen sixty-four. JFK's assassination found me curled safely within my mother's womb. Had nature's resolve not eclipsed my mother's, I might still reside there, "the way things are going these days," as she always said. Does the unborn child assume its mother's emotions? If so, fear began to embroider a repeating pattern upon my heart well before the day I emerged with one fist clamped onto my own ear and ripping it halfway off. The uterus in which I grew from two cells to four to eight "and so on and so on and so on" nested inside a card-carrying member of the John Birch Society and the Towson Republican Club. Conservatism entwined with my DNA, enriched my blood cells, oxygenated my brain and—God bless the USA—the flag, the Constitution, and the death penalty. And all God's people said, "Amen!"

Leavened by Mom's Christian fundamentalism, my fear rose like a sourdough sponge in a greenhouse. Fear joggled and popped about our congregation like Mexican jumping beans and escorted us just about as far. In Mom's circles, the cold war forever remained a hot topic. And the Soviet Union? "Let's face the truth now, Sister Starling, the USSR has probably infiltrated even our own congregation with a 'change agent' we've been duped into thinking really loves the Lord!"

Yes, we believed in an all-powerful, all-knowing, and everywhere-present God, but we acted like He'd totally lost control over the good old US of A, and if we failed to win it back, He'd be up a creek. Poor God. Imagine His thankfulness for churches like ours, willing to fight His political battles for Him, to "contend for the faith which was once delivered unto the saints." Somehow, I doubt battling Communism entered the apostle Jude's mind the day he penned that phrase.

In 1973, a film I viewed at church informed me that in less than two years the Communists would assume complete control of the US government. Graphic depictions of torture, designed to light a fire of terror beneath the derrières of God-fearing, law-abiding citizens, bloodied the screen. A sandy-haired, freckle-faced boy regurgitated as a soldier burst his eardrums with a bamboo stick. Other soldiers tied ropes around the four limbs of a father and repeatedly lowered him onto pitchforks while his children watched, screaming. Even now, the nationality of these people eludes me, but Asian faces flicker across my memory.

I believed it real footage of a real event, spots and spatters and lines marring the celluloid like an old newsreel. Yet today I wonder whether actors performed a macabre script. Either way, I guess the purveyors of the film deemed "snuff in the name of freedom" acceptable. "Violence porn" they call it these days.

I'll never forget standing at the back of the church afterward, shaking uncontrollably from a fear that, having crawled inside of me, proceeded to gnaw away at my innocence, upon which no real value had been placed. The fear tinted my soul the clear red of blood mixed with water and dug sharp roots into the lining of my spirit. Should a nine-year-old possess a working knowledge of the Trilateral Commission and the Illuminati?

"This is a John Birch church," Betty Christopher said when the pastor suggested maybe congregants advanced matters toward the extreme. And believe me, if my pastor, who considered *left* a four-letter word, supposed things went too far, they really had slid right off the edge of the rational world. We resided in suburban Baltimore, for heaven's sake, in a blue-collar neighborhood of people who worked hard and merely wanted to abide in peace. Well, Betty eventually left the church, taking others with her, because that unknown change agent had worked his magic on our ideology. She dubbed us members of the vast left-wing conspiracy, members of the aforementioned Trilateral Commission who also secreted pink cards in our wallets and pocketbooks.

Mom didn't cry about it. "Good riddance. She was nothing but a troublemaker anyway. What a paranoid."

I can happily report Mom calmed down eventually. In fact, she's perfectly lovely and serene and rests in a much stronger, more normal faith these days. My personal theory? The whole thing tired her out, and she believes she paid her dues in full. She's right. I paid mine by the time I was fifteen, when I picketed an abortion clinic out on Bel Air Road and was declared a particularly foul name for a female dog by a passerby. On that freezing cold Saturday morning, the wind swung down the street with such force it immediately froze my hands to the picket-sign post. Hardly a great reward after giving myself a stiletto-sized splinter while making my sign. The only consolation any of us has on the matter is that at least the babies live with Jesus now. I guess in heaven nobody's considered an inconvenience.

I have to give my pastor credit, though. He loved us kids. In fact, during church picnics at Muddy Run Park, it was my pastor who swam with us, let us dunk him, and threw us high in the air so we could flip, dive, and cannonball ourselves into exhaustion.

Okay, time to stop the mental rumination before the snooze alarm goes off again. I slide the lever of the clock before it bleeps, pick up the bedside phone, and call Mom.

"Hello, dear!"

Her voice comforts more than a down quilt.

"Hi Mom. Have a good night?"

"Fine. Your brother brought me up some dinner, some kind of baked flounder. I always sleep well after fish."

She's always so happy to hear from me. I'm one of the few weird women who actually like being with her mom. I extend all the credit to her. I was a mouthy brat between ages thirteen and sixteen. She persevered. That's Mom, though.

"Good. Can I drop Trixie off a little early this morning?"

"Of course, dear. Why?"

"Persy cut his hair last night, and I want to get him to the barber before school."

"How bad is it?"

"Let's just put it this way: his bangs look like Milton Berle took a bite out of them."

I wanted to say Steven Tyler, but Mom's no Aerosmith fan.

"Oh my. I think every little boy does it at least once."

"This is the eighth time, Mom."

"Eighth? Are you sure?"

"That isn't something a mother forgets."

"My goodness. You'll have to start hiding the scissors."

"I've been hiding the scissors. He did it with his bowie knife."

"Oh my!" She laughs. Low and a bit scratchy. Mom had thyroid cancer at the untested age of twenty-one. They scraped her vocal cords to make sure they'd removed it all.

"Better go wake them up. Love you, dear."

"I love you too. Oh wait—bring Trixie in her pajamas. I bought the cutest little outfit for her the other day at the Hecht Company."

Of course, they started calling it plain-old *Hecht's* years ago. Mom takes a while to align her vernacular with the times.

———

I possess a fantasy. Ad gurus love to think they know about a woman's fantasies. Of course, theirs involve strawberries, silk scarves, and sweat. I fantasize about marriage to a man who says bedtime prayers with the kids so I can take a nice hot bath.

That's about it.

———

The day I walked in the March for Victory, my Easter outfit hugged my skinny body. Well, it was the seventies. While millions (or so they say) of students protested the Vietnam War, our church group marched down the streets of Philadelphia in support of the troops. I held one end of a banner for WTOW, a religious AM radio station, feeling pretty darned important, not to mention stylish, in my navy polyester-knit dress and coat with white buttons and a patent-leather belt. The white vinyl knee-high go-go boots positively puffed me proud.

I don't regret those times of my childhood. My friends and I thought such activities more fun than the Professor Kool show on channel 2. Which, to be honest, I actually didn't care for. But I was realistic enough to know the general population frowned on our cause. And to this day, other than my best friend, Lou, and the kids I churched around with, I know no other children who participate in marches, then or now. I still support the troops, by the way.

So here: if you're looking for a story about someone who grew up in extreme conservatism and ended up a liberal or, God help me, a moderate, shut the book now. I am who I am, and if you can't read about somebody who thinks different than you, you're not the liberal you think. Conversely, if you're reading this for affirmation, go read something by Dave Eggers or Gore Vidal, then think for yourself. But by all means, finish this book, then go tell your friends to buy a copy because, as you'll see, I need the cash more than ever.

Money is why I still write a column for our local paper, a strip of rhetoric dedicated to the proposition that there isn't a person alive I cannot anger or offend. It lets me do the blabbering for a change, instead of those annoying Hollywood types who live in mansions and have garages full of Bentleys, closets full of Prada originals, boxes full of Harry Winston jewels, and noses full of high-grade cocaine. Who are they to talk about social justice because they gave ten grand to the Democratic gubernatorial candidate? (Which, in truth, would be the same as me sending in a check for ten bucks.)

The newspaper columnist in me explains my verbose asides. Believe it or not, I don't always write about national and local politics in my column. Sometimes I write about domestic—as in behind the front door of your house—politics.

Today I will write about making lemonade out of lemons. I have coronated myself the empress of lemonade-making. I pride myself on my lemonade. I mean, when you're married to a man who's gone eighty percent of the time and you're still together, that's lemonade. That might even qualify as hard lemonade.

All part of womanhood.

Oh sure, the activists tell me we've advanced miles and miles. But nobody's gained more from our liberation than men. Now, not only do they have less responsibility for the household budget, they can get sex more easily before a household even exists. And even most of the married ones don't lift a finger at home. Who packs the lunches, helps with homework, makes sure somebody's home for the cable man? We do, that's who.

Let me tell you, there's not a man alive, other than single or stay-at-home dads, who have a clue whether there's enough clean underwear in the kids' drawers for tomorrow. If I'm wrong, I'll be the first one to applaud.

Now, I may be mistaken, but I don't expect even the Jesus my old church worshiped would leave all the vacuuming to one person, or that He'd push back from the supper table and hop right on His computer.

It's not that I don't like men. I love men. I just think we women have created monsters and then blamed the monsters. It's time now to liberate the men, to teach them not to merely view us as equals, but to raise us up on the pedestals we deserve, to adore us, to admire us, and at the very least do fifty percent of the housework without our having to ask. Shoot, even dishes three nights a week would be nice. Straightening the den now and again? Putting a new roll on the toilet paper holder? Okay, putting the cap back on the toothpaste! How about that?

I'm a little mad right now. I haven't heard from my husband, Rusty, in three days. Granted he's busy singing tenor for a traveling gospel barbershop quartet, Heavenly Harmonies, but would it be so hard to turn on the blinkin' cell phone before the concert begins and just say hi?

Frankly, I'll take anger over fear any day. At least anger buffs you up.

Lemons out of lemonade. Hmm. Well, let's see now. Three days incommunicado may just equal that new light fixture I want for the front porch. Oh yeah. Drink up, Rusty. I just won this one.

God, I'd hate myself to really think of that as a victory. I never for a moment imagined this life. Just bedtime prayers and a bath.

It's 5:00 a.m. I fire up my computer, Old Barbara by name, and set out to write my column. We women must learn the art of the deal and utilize it whenever possible. Especially with our kids. I'm doing all I can to spread the word.

Don't let me fool you. Yeah, I sound like I'm all that, but if any of them saw how my son's hair turned out at the barber's yesterday, they'd see me for the freak I really am! Trixie, in her smart new Hecht's romper, did nothing but point and laugh at her brother all the way home, and soft-hearted me decided to show her, and I let Persy eat chocolate-chip cookies for dinner while she ate spinach and dried-out chicken breast.

She kicked up such a fuss I swear fresh vocal nodules accompanied her to bed.

2

Young, pregnant movie stars always tear at the lining of my heart. Their taut bellies contrast with their tight butts like a splash of red paint on a black canvas. They don't seem to know what the rest of us know: that they inhabit an Alpo world and that someday so many bites will be chewed from them, their marriage, their families, and even their own self-awareness. They'll retreat to their Hollywood Hills homes, spinning down to L.A. only for plastic surgery. Martinis, muumuus, and pool boys will frame their days.

It's why I love to hear about a solid Hollywood marriage. I want to stand up and yell, "Hooray for you! You did it, darn it! You did it."

Paul Newman and Joanne Woodward come to mind. Paul and Lynda McCartney, too.

I should've married a guy named Paul.

———

I'll never forget the face of the young guy who was first to *ma'am* me. What started out as a typical convenience-store jaunt landed me in a rite of passage. Only twenty-five at the time, I thought my khaki shorts and camp shirt youthful enough. No crow's-feet then, no dark circles or bony knuckles, no drooping triceps. No baby straddled my hip that day. And this *boy*, probably at least twenty-one years old, separated me socially from himself with nary a beat.

Did he possibly realize the import of his words? Did he understand that in proclaiming me one of "them," he stripped away all my excuses? Well, it's been downhill ever since. And each year I live engraves two years upon my face.

Never more aware of that than tonight, I ready myself for my twentieth high-school reunion. Now, the ten-year reunion means nothing. Still babies then. Late twenties? Pah. Sure, the expectation to achieve some measure of responsibility followed us into the school gym. Maybe a kid or two. A barely established career. Or if not a career, serious grad school rated acceptable. I measured up fine then with a husband and one child. I helped Mom and Grandpa run a successful if homey restaurant, and Rusty not only looked handsome, he enjoyed a good job as the music director of a hoity-toity United Methodist church down on Charles Street. Hardly rich and living out in the county, we nevertheless enjoyed our life in a city apartment near church, paid off our car two years early, and ate sushi every Friday night. An exciting city life, strolling around Hopkins U. in the evenings, playing tennis on the lighted courts with bright-eyed baby Lyra looking on from her car seat. The fact that she turned fourteen last year makes me ill.

They snapped our pictures the night of that reunion, everyone closely resembling their senior picture, if a bit more substantial either in body or expression. In line I turned to Lou, my best friend then and still my best friend now. Eight months pregnant, she clad herself in a close-fitting black gown and a turban. A turban on a twenty-eight-year-old. And she pulled it off! I laid a hand on her belly. "The next one will really show the difference, won't it? We'll all be pushing forty."

She rubbed her back and grimaced. "Yeah, except for Glynn Spicer. She'll still look perky, won't she?" Lou possesses no clue of the deep well of artsiness and svelteness and gorgeousness she taps with every single outfit. Every single one! I should be jealous of her, but I've known Lou since we were eight, and some of her faults are doozies! For one thing, her spelling is atrocious, and she gets gas all the time. Poor thing has cornered the market on Mylanta.

We voted Glynn "Most Beautiful." I got "Cutest," which pretty much says it all. The category should be called, "Pretty but with Slightly Irregular Features." O that the years had been more kind to me. We voted Lou "Funniest" and "Best Dressed." Our friend Mitch, the third leg of our high-school threesome, ended up "Most Likely to Succeed."

I hope he comes tonight. Last I heard he moved overseas or something and married a former supermodel. No wonder he hasn't kept in contact. He's moved on like real people do, and here I sit, Ivy Schneider, mother of three, hometown newspaper columnist whose acne still flares up around her period. And my hair? Man oh man.

I wanted my hairdresser to paint in some highlights, but why kid myself? I need a complete dye job. They call this blond, but I know how faded it is, how much white mixes in with the mouse, how pretty it used to be back in those days. But Trixie started running a fever last night, and I had to cart her to the doctor this morning after I canceled my appointment. They seem so fragile through age four. I even clipped out a photo of a cute, sexy cut, but here I stand before the mirror, scraping back from my wide face hair I chopped off myself. Oh man, I look like a spinster kindergarten teacher. A marm, ma'am, a marm.

Ma'am.

Thanks a lot, store boy. He's probably at least thirty-five now, balding and working to support a family.

Remind me to throw out my Keds when I get home.

I shake my head at my reflection as I spray the ornery wisps into place. Look at the hollows under my eyes. No cosmetics company out there manufactures a cover-up, at my budget, capable of camouflaging these dark circles or hiding these bags that could double as change purses.

I look ten years older than I am, and Rusty's to blame. He set his musical self on the singing road three years ago when the Methodist church decided they wanted somebody more hoity-toity than Rusty. No other job option materialized in Baltimore, and God alone knows how much I tried praying one into existence. Rusty refused to budge toward the middle, and so did I, basically because some situations have no middle.

Lou calls. Thank goodness. I couldn't stand looking at myself for another minute. "I'm really sorry I can't come."

"I know, Lou. It's okay. And I owed you one anyway."

"Huh?"

"Remember when I forgot to pick you up at the train station last year?"

"Okay. Then I won't feel extremely guilty."

Good. That train thing's hung over my head for way too long. I'm glad to let it go.

"And the fact of the matter is, Rusty should be here. Even if you could have come, it begs the question."

"I'd like to see you give him a good reason to stay away."

I love Lou.

"So what do I say? 'Oh, my husband travels most of the time with Heavenly Harmonies Gospel Barbershop Quartet.' I mean, if the Gaither Vocal Band had hired him, at least I could save face. But no, not only am I not woman enough to keep a man by my side, I can't even compete with some second-tier gospel act like Heavenly Harmonies. A gospel barbershop quartet, for heaven's sake!"

"Maybe it's better that he's not here, Ive. You can just say he's a musician and he's out of town, so he couldn't come."

"His weight embarrasses me now too. I can't imagine ever feeling desire for him again this way. Isn't that terrible?"

"Nope. But I don't think it's the merely the weight. It's his absence more than anything."

Uh, ya think, Lou? "He's been out of our lives so long, I don't know if I really do want him back. I stopped knowing him a long time ago. Man, do I wish divorce for reasons like this was biblical."

Of course, she offers up the fact that he is unfaithful. Only music is his mistress.

Yak, yak. We've had this conversation at least fifty times, and we'll have it fifty more.

I tell her how happy I am for her that she's missing this. She offers more condolences and we ring off.

This nightmare of an activity doesn't actually deserve my presence, does it? And why do I feel compelled to show up? The only people I care about from school are Lou, who's not coming, and Mitch, who's disappeared. I mean some of them—like Lara Pierce, Phillip Barlow, and Jana Josefoweski, who all made fun of me in the cafeteria because I brought leftovers from the restaurant—deserve not one glance. Jamie Standish and Eve Davis thought my thrift-store clothing hilarious! Well, they weren't voted "most" anything, so it just goes to show.

Back to the bathroom mirror.

"Maybe I should just stay home." My reflection agrees.

My daughter Lyra, fourteen and lithe, with long tan limbs and skin stretched in a smooth sheet over her pert little features, enters the bathroom. "You've got to go, Mom. You'll end up having a good time. Can I watch you get ready?"

"Surely you have something less gruesome to observe."

"Mo-om."

"Suit yourself. Have a seat."

She closes the lid on the commode and sits down, hugging her knees to her chest. Her toenails are dark blue with white, pearly moons on them, her fingernails photo negatives of their southern cousins. "I like the dress."

"Thanks. Do you think it's too much?"

"Mom, it's brown. Seriously. But it's cool. Hey, would I lead you wrong?"

"No." I really should listen to Lyra more often. I have no shape really. There's no time to work out or grab a decent meal these days. And while a lot of women yearn to be thin, I don't imagine they picture this androgynous figure I own, or the hunched look I walk around with. I have no boobs, no butt, no defined waistline—nothing but big hands, elbows, and knees. And feet. Size 10 feet. I am a tie box with a head and appendages. I hate what I've become. I'm not a woman anymore. Not at all.

But then, is it necessary these days? With Rusty always gone, it's not like sexiness matters; it's not like my pitiful 34AA bra size means anything anymore. Maybe I should buy one of those tubs of breast-enhancement cream.

The kicker is that Rusty's such a nice guy. He lost it with me only one time…one single time. And honestly, after waiting in twenty-degree weather for thirty minutes wearing nothing but galoshes and an overcoat, I'd have yelled at me too. That's a story that deserves a venue all its own.

Lyra stands up. "Here, let me do your makeup. That eye shadow is all wrong."

"Fabulous. I'm so nervous I can't even hold the applicator." I turn toward her. "Do what you can. But believe me, I don't expect miracles."

"Oh, stop it, Mom. You're so pretty."

But I know she speaks as a daughter who entered the world with a sweet young mother and fails to notice the change.

She roots through my makeup case. "Mom, when was the last time you bought eye shadow? Look at this CoverGirl stuff. There must be twelve different colors in this thing. Do they even make this kind of thing anymore?"

"Oh please, Lyr, I hate to throw out good makeup."

"It's not good makeup, Mom. It's probably full of creepy-crawly bacteria. I just read an article about that in *Seventeen,* and it said…"

I tune out the infomercial. I'm going to be late. I hate this. I'm always late these days. "Can you hurry, sweets? It starts at six."

"Let me get my stuff. You shouldn't be wearing blues and purples and greens anyway. Neutrals are best at your age."

Great. Render me even more insignificant than my present state. But hey, that might ward off further mental monologues about Rusty.

Wait.

Did she really say, "at your age"? Another passage across yet another river crisscrossing the aging process. Man.

Lyra returns. She does what she can. Not nearly enough, but honestly, nothing short of a face transplant would suffice. Still, the feel of her fingertips against my skin… Well, nothing, absolutely nothing comes close to the touch of your child. I know some perfectly fertile people choose to forgo parenthood, and what can I say to that? However, if they felt what I'm feeling right now, they'd conceive in a heartbeat, career or what have you be cursed.

I praise Lyra's heroic efforts. The doorbell rings. She runs out of the room hollering, "I'll get it!"

Trixie yells from downstairs, "No! Me!"

"I said I'll get it!" Yep, still a kid. She tromps down the steps three at a time. Trixie's little feet thump at steam-engine speed from the kitchen where I set her up with some Play-Doh.

Persy, nine years old and all boy, couldn't care less who gets the door. Biologically attached to the GameCube, that one.

"Winky!" Both girls yell my mother's grandma name in unison. Winky. It's horrible, but Lyra started it, and it never evolved to a proper Grandma, Granny, Gran, or Nanny. And Mom likes being a little different. Not a lot different, just a little.

I hurry down. I'll apply my lipstick in the car. "Mom!"

She looks up from where she stands just inside the door. "Hello, dear!" And she smiles like Debbie Reynolds before everybody found out she was so self-centered. Mom's never once greeted me with anything other than that smile.

The late-afternoon light, pale gold and jangly from the fluttering leaves of the maple beside the pathway, softens her age lines, and in this moment I remember her young. The way she'd wing open the car door with such force it would spring back and hit her hip. The way she'd always laugh at that and say, "One of these days I'm gonna learn!"

Still spry, she bends over without so much as a groan and plucks up the diaper Trixie's just dropped. My youngest stands there with her little tush shining brighter than a harvest moon beneath her pajama top. She jumps up and down, arms stretched toward her grandmother.

But Mom embraces me first. I feel little again. It's wonderful.

Then she hugs her grandchildren, Trixie first.

I turn to Trixie, full name Bellatrix. We named all our children after constellations or stars. Wacky, I know. But Rusty got the idea, and I failed to speak up. "Go get me a diaper." Trixie climbs away.

Mom presses the wrinkles out of her pantsuit with the palms of her hands. She kicks off her high heels and places them on the steps. Unfortunately for me, Mom's fashion sense skipped a generation and went straight to my Lyra. "I'll take care of Trixie. If you don't leave soon, you'll be late. Brian will be in in a minute. He's talking to his latest paramour on his car phone."

"Did you remember your insulin?"

She hits her forehead with the heel of her hand. "I'll get your brother to run back."

I reach for my wrap and slide my feet into new pumps. Five dollars on the clearance rack at The Shoe Nook. "Hey, how're you feeling today? Any dizzy spells?"

"Just one. Got out of bed too quickly. But I didn't fall."

"Good." I keep waiting for "the fall." Anyone with an aging parent does. But thankfully it's still future tense. "Okay everybody, give your mother a kiss!"

Lyra reaches out first. I really don't deserve this child. When Rusty left to sing with Heavenly Harmonies, God knew I needed a companion, and He appointed Lyra. I've never cut down Rusty in front of the children, and they deem him a celebrity of sorts, because they've actually seen him on some religious cable network. Personally it's all a little too Lawrence Welk for my British Invasion taste, but it helps pay the bills and keeps me from worrying about sex ten months of the year. He mostly sings before audiences of Sunday-dressed seniors, warbling numbers like "Just a Little Talk with Jesus" and "Mansion over a Hilltop," eating meals at places like Denny's, IHOP, and Chili's, and smiling that show-biz smile. My life, however, consists of changing diapers and arranging menus, driving to lacrosse games, and wiping crumbs off countertops while filling out permission slips and popping multiplication flashcards in Persy's face. But the verbal photograph of Rusty I hand to the kids each day as I read them his e-mail is always covered by a soft-focus lens. It would only hurt them to complain, to voice my loneliness and my fears and my disgust with both of us, with him for leaving, with me for waving him off with a brave smile. And yet I long to tell it like it is, to hold him accountable to his own children.

I kiss Persy and Trixie and tell them to be good for Winky and Uncle Brian. Trixie and I rub our kisses in.

My brother meets me on the doorstep. A very polished male. I think he showers at least twice a day. Wears leather jackets in the winter and watches all the latest films from France and Bollywood. We share hair color and eye color and not much more. Today he's dressed in easygoing khaki pants and a moss-colored, heavy-weave T-shirt that fits as perfectly as a paper band around a stack of crisp bills.

"Hi Bri."

He kisses my cheek and removes his cap. "Ivy, darlin'. You ready for this?"

"Nope. But hey, I'm curious enough to want to see what's happened to everyone."

"Yeah. Know what you mean. At mine, I couldn't believe how some of those girls turned out. But then, you know I like them older anyway."

I don't want to hear about my brother's meanderings among the fairer sex. He's forty and acts like he's still in college. One day, his private parts are going to fall off, and he'll come crying to me, and I won't have a thing to say. I'll just go up to the medicine cabinet, pluck out some Neosporin, and tell him to keep the tube. The kicker is, he looks ten years younger than his age, possesses an athletic grace, and has hair thicker than a yeti's.

So much for clean living. Maybe I should give his lifestyle a try.

"Anyway. There are chicken breasts in the fridge and some snow peas. I bought a nice bottle of Chardonnay, too. Do your magic."

He runs his scarred fingers through his dirty blond hair. "Sure thing. Got some rice?"

I nod.

"Basmati?"

"Actually, yes. Just the Mahatma kind."

"That'll work."

One time I left supper already cooked, and my brother, a trained chef who runs our restaurant, reamed me out—pulp, seeds, and pith—with such vigor I wouldn't dare make *that* mistake again.

"If there's any left, I'll save it for you."

"Thanks. You know reception food. I'll probably be starving by the time I get home."

He pulls a face as he slides past me at the doorway and into the house.

Certainly the same old buffet fare will unroll the length of the table, punctuated by curly endive and carrot curl garnish. Roast beef, baked chicken, some kind of dried-out fish with paprika on it. Green beans almondine, California medley, maybe an overcooked ratatouille. Tossed salad mostly consisting of iceberg lettuce, and some sort of confetti rice concoction complete with wrinkled peas and cubed canned-soup-worthy carrots. Buttered new potatoes with rosemary and parsley? Your choice of carrot cake or chocolate torte for dessert. Some kind of pie. Iced tea, coffee. Cash bar. The flier warned us there'd be a cash bar.

I may just go straight for the dessert. After watching Glynn Spicer enter the room as though a red carpet supports her fabulous footwear, I'm sure my appetite will flee quicker than Rusty after the singing bug bit him.

Oh man. Tomorrow's trash day.

I head out to the side of the house and wheel the can toward the street. The driveway needs a new coat of asphalt. Is that a pansy planted right smack in the middle? Persy did that. I know it.

"Ivy!"

My neighbor. Mr. Zachary Moore.

"Hi Mr. Moore!" He's doing the same thing I am. But with his arthritis, it'll take five times longer. I hurry over. "Let me."

"Now, child. You don't have to be doin' those things for me." His deep brown eyes crinkle in his deep brown face. I rub my hand along his sweatered arm. Hard bone under knit.

"Course I don't have to. But I want to. Is that okay?"

"Well, I surely wouldn't want to deprive you of a blessing."

Mr. Moore loves Jesus.

I walk slowly, letting him keep pace. The reunion can definitely wait.

"Now where you headin' all dressed up so fine?"

"My high-school reunion."

"Lord bless you."

"I know. Can't say I'm looking forward to it much. Just curious, I guess."

"You know what curiosity done for that cat."

"That's what I'm afraid of."

We chuckle together. I love Mr. Moore. He took care of his own mother for years and years and still found time to bring over soup and bread and whatever else he cooked up in his kitchen when my grandma got so sick. He's an incredible bridge player. Had his master's points by the time he was thirty.

"Well, you have yourself a good time anyway."

"If it's possible."

He scratches his bushy eyebrow. "Oh, it's always possible, Ivy. Just not probable. I guess we decide which way we want to go. As for me, two tables of bridge right here tonight would make me a happy camper. I do miss your grandparents. Fine card players. Shame the way life never stops changing."

"All you can do is go with the flow."

He chuckles. "I do believe we've just gone and contradicted each other!"

"Somehow it worked, Mr. Moore."

I kiss his wrinkled cheek.

Oh really, why not?

I kiss the other one, too.

He raises his brows. "Child, you're even more nervous than I thought."

———

I start the engine of my Blazer, remembering when Rusty and I purchased it over three years ago. And why did we like brown? I mean, yeah, it was a loaner model, five thousand dollars off the bottom line, only two thousand miles on the engine. Who wouldn't like brown?

Well, at least it matches my new dress and shoes.

Did I actually comfort myself with *that?*

Rusty probably comforts himself with the fact that a reliable car sits in our driveway. But he also left me with car payments and baby Trixie on my hip. I couldn't talk him out of leaving. He told me this was the opportunity of a barbershop quartet tenor's lifetime, but where would Mom be? I mean really, she worked at that restaurant from dawn to dusk every day after my father left us, put my sister and me through college and my brother through culinary school. She only laid a finger on us when we sassed her. And even then it didn't hurt. She wore the same five dresses for twenty years, simply classic, of course, resoled the same two pairs of high-heeled pumps for eternity. I'm telling you, my mother would have handled the depression with finesse. I know oldsters who say, "Shoot, I didn't even realize we were poor."

I didn't either. Until my fifteenth year, when my mom said we couldn't afford braces.

I still hate my teeth.

Fabulous. Just the thought I needed on my way to a class reunion. And I forgot to brush them too! I drag my tongue down the front of my teeth. Like that's going to do a thing.

Glynn Spicer was blessed with pretty teeth, white and straight and on the large side. Sexy on her. There wasn't anything less than sexy on Glynn Spicer.

Now if the dictionary needed an illustration for the word *unsexy,* my picture would fit the bill. No wonder Rusty refused to hang around. Who'd stay for this? I can't believe he went without us. I can't believe I didn't give him an ultimatum.

At least we moved out of the city well before he left. We now abide in Grandma and Grandpa's old house in east Towson, half a mile from the restaurant. Mom, who lives in the apartment over the restaurant, rented it out after her parents passed on. But now we're the lessees and free to decorate it how we please. Actually, we don't pay much rent, just enough to cover the taxes. My brother and sister never let me forget how much I rely on the family largesse, even though they never wanted the place.

Whatever, as Lyra says.

No traffic snarls braid the beltway today, and every light dips its green at me in the wind. While not wanting to be late, I didn't want to be one of the early losers either. So I park the car at the Hunt Valley Marriott and head for the bar.

At a small corner table, I lay my purse on the bench, fold my wrap, and place it on top. This feels weird. I haven't sooloed in a lounge in years. An older couple sits a few tables away. The ice in their drinks makes more noise than they do as they while away the minutes before heading off to someplace more official. Or maybe not. Honestly, right now I don't possess enough energy or goodwill to lob into their court. I begin imagining the evening ahead. Lots of artificial laughter and perfectly manicured fingers fiddling with expensive necklaces. Darn, I forgot jewelry. And I haven't put on the lipstick either. Could I appear more bland?

A throat clears.

A cocktail waiter stands before me, a young guy with too many gold chains, including an odd crucifix with Jesus suffering on an anchor instead of a cross. What's that about?

"What can I get for you, ma'am?"

Ma'am? Go soak your head.

"Red wine."

"Merlot? Cabernet?"

"Shiraz." So there.

"Great. I'll be right back."

Wonder what everybody will be like now? I remember the kids from the clubs I joined. Drama, chorus, debate. Oh yes, Ivy Starling, all-American girl. Salvation Army trendsetter. Popular but kind, down to earth. The girl sophomores went to for advice. And now? I can't even remember to put on lipstick.

Could I have regressed any further?

Count your blessings, Ive. Think about your great kids, the restaurant (though unglamorous and not at all akin to the life Michelle Pfeiffer led in *Tequila Sunrise*). You know how it is in movies, how the owners always sit at the end of the bar in the morning with the newspaper, a cup of coffee, and a cigarette, and it's quiet and comforting with the soft clink of cutlery and china emanating from the kitchen, murmuring voices and a transistor radio eking a soft burble from somewhere in the back.

Ha!

Here I go again. Lemonade out of lemons? Who am I kidding?

The wine arrives as well as the tab.

Five fifty?

I sip. Not even that good. I probably paid for the entire bottle.

A group files in. Tut-tut. Bling-bling. Flutter-flutter. Chuckle-chuckle. Must be reunion bound. One man looks like Will Stanton, but without hair. Oh wow, yeah. I imagine we'll notice big changes in hairlines this time.

Two women spark no recognition. Must be wives. That's nice. Mates to cling to during this dark hour and all that.

One of the men points toward me and a discussion ensues. He breaks free, and as he approaches I recognize him. I can't remember his name, but he was on the basketball team, varsity, for three years. Man, that guy could jump. He also would bark at the ugly girls. I'm glad he's going bald. Working on a nice paunch there too, slick.

"Excuse me. Miss Stein?"

Miss Stein? Miss Stein?

The science teacher?!

"No. I'm sorry. I'm Mrs. Schneider."

"Oh, what did you teach?"

Teach?

I want to toss the wine in his face. I mean, he's not looking any younger either. This proves the vast difference between men and women as they view themselves in the mirror.

Men: *Dang, you still got it!*

Women: *I'm fat.*

Men: *Lookin' good.*

Women: *I'm old.*

Men: *Knock 'em dead today, dude!*

Women: *I'm fat and old.*

I shake my head, going for confused instead.

He apologizes. "We're here for a reunion, and I thought you were one of our teachers."

I bestow a tight-lipped smile on him. "No problem."

"Sorry again."

He turns away and joins the others.

What a dummy. Miss Stein must be seventy years old by now.

I leave the wine, the bar, and the reunion to sit in my car and cry.

I'm a crier. I admit it. Whenever Lyra and I sit down to a movie after the others go to bed, I see her eyes steal over in my direction when something poignant occurs. I almost never disappoint, and sometimes I cry even when she doesn't suspect it.

She doesn't always know why. She doesn't see the loneliness I see in the eyes of the actor, for sometimes even when someone plays out a comedic scene, craziness alight on the screen, something deeper in the player betrays him. I see emptiness and solitude, a gaping hole that even Hollywood fame and money failed to fill. I see quiet desperation. I see joy flown. (Unless of course it's Jeff Bridges, who just looks like a nice, dependable, happy guy no matter what movie he's in.) I see the beginnings of a really good story that only I can write!

If only someone would give me a contract. Man, some of the drivel I read out there today! And here I sit, with no connections to a publishing house. Well, and nobody knows this, I did send off a proposal to my agent, though no one knows I have one. See, I *have* written a novel, a short one, I admit, but it's got all the earmarks of a hit. It really does. Drama, emotion, intensity, a great premise—high concept. I sent it off a month ago and haven't heard word one. But I hear it takes time, that publishers and glaciers move at about the same speed. I'm giving the agent, Candace Frost, another month, and then I'll buzz off an e-mail. I've told no one. I mean, you expose enough of yourself on the pages of the work without having to let other people in on the true torture of it all. What if I have no luck? I'd hate enduring all the well-meaning condolences.

And why do these thoughts ramble around as I sit here ruined by the reunion wrecking ball? At least I spared myself the humiliation of talking to Glynn Spicer. Thank You, God, for that! You know, she probably didn't even come. I mean really. The highly successful, busy people don't take time out for a stupid high-school reunion at the Marriott. Not at all. The only success stories that show are the unpopular ones. They hope to rub everyone's nose in their achievements, and I don't blame them one bit.

Oh, how tables can turn.

A tap at the window.

Huh? Oh, a guy. I push the button. "Yeah?"

Fabulous, I'm blotchy and tear-stained. As if I didn't look bad enough. I must resemble a plucked chicken with sunburn now.

"Ivy!"

The streetlight shines on his back, casting his face in the shadow. "Hi."

"I can't believe I caught you out here, you babe you!"

Oh yeah!

It can only be one person. Mr. Babe himself, not to mention the nicest guy in the world.

"Mitch Sullivan! Oh my gosh!"

I open the door, and he swings out of the way, then hugs me, with a hoist-the-breath-from-the-bottommost-portion-of-the-lungs, feet-off-the-ground hug! Our own laughter hangs above our heads. Mitch Sullivan, my best guy friend since third grade. Oh yeah, me and Mitch and Lou. We pull apart.

"Where have you been, Mitch?"

"Japan!"

"No wonder I haven't heard from you in years."

"Hey, you got married first, Ive. That put a damper on things. How is Rusty?"

"Gone."

His eyes grow. "As in *gone* gone?"

"No. As in, traveling all over kingdom come with a barbershop quartet."

"No kidding?"

"Does that sound like something I'd make up?"

"Wow. So, you heading in?"

I shake my head and shrug. "Nah. Remember that dork on the basketball team, the one that Sheila Barber broke up with because he was coming on too strong, and then he told everyone he broke up with her because she was a tramp? Remember him?"

"Joe Bisbee?"

"Yes! That guy! He actually thought I was Miss Stein!"

"The science teacher?!"

"Yes!" And can we just shout a little louder please?

"You don't look anything like Miss Stein, Ivy. My gosh, she was fifty-five at least when we graduated. The guy's a dip-wad."

See? Now here's a smart man.

"Now *there's* an expression I haven't heard in years."

"It sure is easy to slip back into the vernacular, isn't it?"

I smile. "Man, it is so good to see you."

"You said it. Look, I don't really want to go in there either. I just came to catch up with you and Lou. Is she coming?"

"No. Her father's heading off to Africa tonight, and she had to take him to the airport. He's big into missions work over there now. Practical missions, like well-digging, medicine, and things."

"Well, how about we just go get a meal together? My treat."

"Oh, you don't have to."

"Shoot, Ive. I disappeared for ten years. The least I can do is buy you dinner while I tell you my sad story."

What could it hurt? This is so great. "Let's go."

"My car's over there. Let's ride together." He points to an old Jaguar.

"Pretty car."

"Fixed it up myself over the last year. Needed something to do after work."

"Part of your story?"

"You know it. Anyway, the car helped a lot. And you remember Dad and me and cars."

"Oh, that '69 Mustang."

"Three-ninety cubic inch. Man, that baby blew!"

He opens the door, and I slide in. Nice.

"How's your dad, Mitch?"

"He died five years ago. Mom remarried a wonderful guy last year."

"I should have known that."

"How? You're not the one that disappeared."

I'll bet Mitch would say bedtime prayers with his kids.

Well, I can see him a little better now that we're in the restaurant, a little place we used to frequent in our teens after bowling or going to the Orioles game. The Towson Diner. Lots of fake stonework and ceiling beams, a little faux wrought-iron lamp by the register.

All the awkward news I should have heard but didn't has been told.

I don't even look at the menu. The beef stroganoff special on the board sounds good enough to make me forget being mistaken for Miss Stein. For now, anyway. "You look almost the same, Mitch. More mature, though. Filled out, like a man-sized guy."

He puffs his chest and pats it, feigns a bass. "Yep, that happens."

Intriguing, the changes in him. His russet hair, still curly and soft, is mixed with white. His eyes, still a deep brown, aren't afraid to look at the world—or me, for that matter—straight on. I guess he's gained a little weight, sure, but nothing like Rusty, who's at least a hundred pounds heavier since he went on the road. And he's still sweet and hangs on every word I say. Just like the old days. He wears himself well. We talk and talk and talk, just like the old days too.

He actually listens to me.

My mom wanted us to marry each other, but Mitch went out of state to college, and I stayed in town and met Rusty, and here we sit. I'd better not think about what life would have been like had it gone according to Mom's plans. Of course, right now she'd be by herself, worrying about my brother and sister. She'd be up to her eyes in anxiety. Life works out for the best, I suppose. On the other hand, what isn't glorious about living in a glitzy apartment in Tokyo, shopping at all those wonderful stores, employing a maid and a cook, and traveling all over the world with my husband?

Without Lyra, Persy, or Trixie.

Well, that puts things into perspective, doesn't it?

We're the last customers to leave.

I lie to everyone about the reunion. Tell them all I had a great time at the Marriott, made new friends from old acquaintances, got potential business for Brian if indeed he fires up a catering arm of the restaurant. Er, bistro. Sorry.

And they believe me.

My grandpa always said that for every lie you tell, a wrinkle appears.

Maybe that's my problem. Maybe living this lie, that I am strong and fine and capable and supportive of Rusty and his singing career, explains these gullies. I should've told them about dinner with Mitch. It was innocent, after all. We sat and chatted about my sorry life and his divorce from what sounded like a horrible woman name Pam. Excuse me, Pamela. Dahling.

"That's the thing about trophy wives, Ive," Mitch had said, forking up some salad. "They don't do anything but sit there looking pretty, taking up useful space and spending money they don't even appreciate. I paid her to be thin and beautiful, is what the marriage boiled down to. She hated sex too."

Well, at least she was beautiful. So the supermodel rumor was truth, and doesn't that beat all? Why would Mitch want to sit with a thirty-eight-year-old crone like Ivy Schneider when he could have a model on his arm?

Oh, that's right. She hated sex.

Ha!

Sex? What's that?

So now the quiet of the house echoes in my ears. Brian dropped Mom off at her apartment and zoomed over to Schooner's to rustle up a bimbo. The kids sleep, and I log on for Rusty's daily e-mail. It's the same. He asks what's going on. How are the kids? He relates all the minutiae of his daily doings. And in one e-mail out of fifty he expressly asks me, "So how are *you* doing, Ivy?"

I know I'm whining. I try keeping it to a minimum, but tonight my complaints actually register against the stillness. If I can't admit reality, maybe I'll fade away completely. I can't lie to myself, can I?

I answer his questions, lie more about the reunion, act like I'm having all the fun in the world without him. Fifteen minutes later, I slip between the sheets and cry some more.

3

Maybe I could have played my hand differently. Rusty suggested we sell the house, buy a luxury RV, and all travel together. But I couldn't get past the obvious: sharing a closet-sized bathroom, turning a dinette into a bed every night, having the kids crawling all over me twenty-four hours a day. And Mom would probably die during the duration, cheating me of the final years of her life. She doesn't drive anymore, so I drive her. Doctor appointments galore. The foot specialist, the kidney specialist, the dentist, the optometrist, the family practitioner. Grocery shopping as well, and Mom buys only from individual food purveyors: the greengrocer, the butcher, the baker, the seafood shop. And then there's the pharmacist, who knows us by name: prescriptions, prescriptions, prescriptions.

As useless as Styrofoam scissors, Brian can't be relied upon.

My sister, Brett, weighed down with two spoiled teenagers, a dress shop, and a workaholic husband, consumes herself with her own responsibilities.

That leaves me.

I simply said, "No Rusty, I won't go. I can't."

"But Ivy, this is something I've wanted all my life. Traveling, entertaining, bringing joy to thousands of people through song."

Excuse me, but I've read the brochure, thanks.

"But what about me? How can you ask me to give up my entire life? And what about the kids? What about their education?"

"We can homeschool them!"

"Oh please! You mean *I* can homeschool them."

"No. I'd help. It would be fun. On the road, town to town. Think of what they'd see, what they'd learn. All the sites we could take them to!" Oh, the eagerness in his eyes, how brightly they sparkled, like blue-tinted Ray-Bans in full sun.

He let it go for a little while, but then he began bugging me, and bugging me and bugging me. When he wasn't bugging me, he pestered me. He left brochures around the house for RVs, RV parks, historical parks, monuments. Great for the kids' education! Imagine seeing this stuff firsthand and all, Ivy! Theme parks—you know how much you love a scary roller coaster, Ivy! The clock is ticking, hon. They need to know in two weeks, one week, five days, three days, tomorrow!

Tomorrow!

Tomorrow!

And I did a stupid thing. I suggested he go alone. That we'd all be fine.

Fine, fine, fine!

And darn it, he took me up on it. And he reminds me again and again this was *my* idea. So not only is he gone, but he feels justified, even vindicated, and when he's at his most lonely—the victim.

I honestly never thought he'd jump on my idea. What husband chooses his own ambitions over his family?

"Why not wait until Mom's gone?" I'd ask.

"She's not exactly at death's door, hon, and besides, they need a tenor now, for the new tour. Oh, Ivy, thanks, doll-baby. Thanks for giving me this chance. You're not going to regret it."

No. Thank *you*. Thanks for manipulating me, for leaving me with no options. I should've been better at the game.

And then his excitement swelled like a spider bite, and I prayed and tried to go along with the revised plan with vigor. After all, God would supply our needs. And maybe He'd make my husband see sense. If I nagged Rusty, he'd only be glad to go.

We'd lay out on the hammock together, and he'd speak his dreams. "We can get out of this cramped house, Ive. Maybe buy something in Ocean City and live at the beach year-round! This could be big, baby-doll. Big money. Exposure. I can finally treat you like you deserve."

I'll never forget the evening he informed me the deal was final, the contract signed, and hey, the salary wasn't at all bad. Not what he'd hoped for, but we'd make out just fine. The clock said 7:11.

Now, the numbers 7 and 11 hold a significance in my life. My high-school boyfriend, Tom Webber, wore number 7 for soccer season and 11 for basketball. We sure were the couple back then. He, tall and blond and coordinated. Me, honey-blond and a cheerleader and an alto in the choir. He spread my heart across his history like Persy spreads peanut butter on crackers. Persy's birthday is 7/11, and Trixie was born at 7:11 a.m.

Anyway, there Rusty went, and here I stay. He's entertaining an audience, and I'm entertaining bitterness. How lovely. Yes, I know I choose my own emotions.

The alarm clock buzzes: 7:11. I reach out, turn it off, and another day begins.

Morning and I have never tangoed well. I'd rather rush us around than miss a second's sleep. Sleep is my six-pack, my chocolate, my hot bubble bath. Just wish I got more of it.

I crank on the shower and make the rounds while it heats up. Beginning with Lyra. She wakes up great. Gathers her clothes and runs into the bathroom to shower first.

Persy next.

Oh, my little Perseus Jacob Schneider, the affectionate one who sidles up and kisses me on his own. I slide his comforter down. His hair sticks out like quills all over his head. A definite improvement on the disastrous cut. He pulls the blanket back over his head, and I yank it down again and kiss all over his face. "Time for school, bud. Please put on clean underwear today, okay?"

He blinks his sleepy blue eyes at me.

"When was the last time you had a bath?"

"I don't know."

"Shoot. Me either. Well, we'll get one tonight. Remind me, okay?"

And how stupid a request is that? Persy revels in a boyish overlay of dirt, evidence he played his heart out the day before and that he is, indeed, a wild man. I like that about him.

He rolls out of his covers, and I leave the room, still taking pleasure in the bright primary-colored walls I painted during the winter. Trixie, who sleeps in a crib in Lyra's room, looks deader than road chops. I won't wake her yet. She's awful in the morning. Why deal with her any longer than necessary?

She needs her dad. That's what I tell myself. She sees Rusty four times a year, for two weeks a pop.

How does he stand it?

He blames me, that's how. I can hear his mind: *If Ivy would come on the road, I could be a father to my own children, but no.*

And the kicker is, she's crazy about him! No wonder there. He's better than the Cat in the Hat at Six Flags, Robin Williams on a trampoline, and would I want him to be anything else considering the circumstances? No way.

Man oh man. I am so trapped.

Three years later, and I still haven't wrapped my mind around this. Am I wrong not to leave a failing old woman? Or is he wrong to leave his family?

Well, yes, he is, but shouldn't I be the supportive wife and literally go along for the ride, let him lead the family, and trust God to take care of Mom?

So where does that leave a conservative Christian woman who believes her husband is wrong?

If I could answer that with certainty, I could write one of those inspirational how-to books and make a million dollars. "Proper" Christian motherhood. What a myth!

What to wear today. Let's think about that instead.

I hurry down the hall to my closet. Well, at least Rusty doesn't need his half anymore.

Ouch!

Thanks for leaving that LEGO there, Perse.

I figure it will be in the midseventies today, a typical early June day in Baltimore. I rub my foot. Bed sounds good.

So, tank top and long burlap-weave sundress. I do like my arms. Knees are knobby. Need the length on the dress. Keds. Gotta keep the feet comfy at the restaurant. Oh, that's right, I'm getting rid of my Keds. I pull out a pair of huaraches.

Persy finds me just as I take my nightgown off. I mean really. "Persy, close your eyes." I fold my arms across my chest. A mother can't even change a tampon alone.

"I know, you're undecent."

"Indecent."

"That's what I said."

"No, you said... Oh, who cares. Just close your eyes, okay?"

"I just wanted to know where my tennis shoes are."

I give up. I grab my sundress off the hanger and hold it up

against myself. "They're in the kitchen in the middle of the floor. I almost tripped over them last night."

"Okay."

And off he goes looking like he stayed in the dryer too long after it stopped. I learned to stop pressing his pants long ago. Maybe I still can learn a few things. I hear the metallic scrape as Lyra pushes back the shower curtain. Great. Hurry, Ivy. Slip on the clean underwear before she comes out. I rush over to the chest of drawers, whip out some briefs, and swap underpants. Of course, the waistband takes on a life of its own, jumping around like a rubber ball on concrete flooring. I can't seem to face it outward. It slips out of one hand, and Lyra's singing one of those Good Charlotte songs, which means any second her hand will find the doorknob.

Hurry up, Ivy.

Sit down on the bed. Yeah, much better than full frontal nudity. I plop down just as she opens the door.

"Oh. Sorry, Mom."

"That's okay." My back is toward her, thank goodness.

She runs out, and I can't help it, but I feel so embarrassed at my nakedness.

I quickly slip on the panties and my tank top. Love the built-in bras these days. Now, if anybody enters uninvited, at least nothing scary is on display.

Of course, nobody does.

Motherhood.

When a babe slips out of your body, your dignity leaves with it. Along with your whittled waistline, pert breasts, high-heeled shoes, romantic dinners, long showers, and cups of coffee drunk without at least three zaps in the microwave. Not to mention sex without an ear cocked in the kids' direction.

After dressing, combing my hair, and trying once again to cover up the obsidian crescents beneath my eyes, darn them, I decide it's time to get Trixie up. Even dealing with Miss Baby Hellion 2002 holds more charm than looking at Ms. Stretch Mark of the Millennium in the mirror.

To fortify myself, I try to picture anything that can go wrong: a crib painted with poop, a red little screaming face, the sheets lying in a puddle on the floor, the wallpaper peeled off in strips. I can't remember the last time I thought a morning would afford me a pleasant surprise.

There she sleeps, innocence and wonder and potential in God-made stillness.

I caress her rounded cheek. "Trixie." Singsong. "Trixie-girl." Oh, sweet baby.

———

"Come on, Trix!"

Five minutes later I'm still trying to change her diaper. I swear some imp came in and greased her up, the way she's slipping out of my grasp. And as much as I adore Lyra, I know better than to ask for her help. She and Trixie go together like salsa and ice cream.

I promise Trixie the world. Cookies for breakfast and a trip to the bowling alley. *SpongeBob* during dinner. I even perform a mean imitation of that porous little sea creature's giggle.

Nothing doing.

Patrick's stupid sayings are next, then Sandy the Squirrel's song about Texas. Squidward's clarinet. Mr. Crab's pirate accent.

Nope.

Just as red-faced. Just as squirmy. And whoops, there's the jutting lip.

That does it!

"Okay, missy. If you don't sit still and let me change that diaper, you'll be coming up to your crib as soon as we get home this afternoon. And you'll stay there until you fall asleep for bedtime."

"What about supper at the bowling alley?"

"No pizza at the bowling alley now. It'll be saltines right here. You blew it, honey."

Let the screams begin.

I should send a parenting-book proposal to *The Worst-Case Scenario Survival Guide* people.

Fact is, I wouldn't know what to advise. I lost my motherly instincts with this child, and she will drag my ineptness like a third leg into adulthood, the spoiled freak nobody wants to socialize with. All because her mother stretched herself as thin as cellophane and had no bulk to teach her even how to be nice.

"Oh, she'll be fine! Just fine!" Mom always says. The thing is, she really believes that.

Now if Trixie's potty habits matched her verbal skills, we'd be set as beautifully as a table at the Ritz at teatime.

"Come down when you're ready to be nice, Trix."

I gather up her outfit and head downstairs.

A dresser drawer scrapes open. "Way to go, Trixie," Lyra says. "You're such a brat."

"Lyra!" I hate it when she does this. Undermines all I'm trying to accomplish with Trixie.

"It's true, Mom!"

"And it'll stay true as long as you keep telling her that."

Now. Breakfast. I meant to pack lunches last night but started reworking that novel and drowned all my good intentions. Which doesn't help my patience level today. Maybe I should promise my*self* some pizza at the bowling alley for being nicer.

Call me whatever you want, but I love to bowl. We haven't all gone to the bowling alley since Rusty hit the road.

———

"Ivy Schneider!"

"Mr. Moore! How are you this morning?"

"Doin' fine. I clipped a funny little comic strip out for you this mornin'." He stands on his porch, dressed as usual in gray chinos and a plaid shirt. "But you're in a hurry, so it'll keep."

"I'll come by this evening. We're having halibut for a special tonight. Can I bring you some?"

He kneads the top of his cane. "You know I never turn down a good piece of fish, child. You have yourself a good day. I still got you on my prayer list. Every day!" He waves a bumpy old hand.

I just love that man.

Mr. Moore never married. He taught high-school science, then took care of his mother after he retired. And he loves his life. I could learn more than a lesson or two from that man about the glory of a simple life well lived.

———

I drop the older two off at their schools and head to the restaurant.

What a great night last night turned out to be. Maybe I'll run into Mitch again soon now that he plans to call Baltimore his town again.

He's still the same.

Mitch and I met in third grade, and although other friends came and went, he, Lou, and I remained a group. In high school we always sat together on the game bus, and one time, just once, I made out with him behind Tom Webber's back. Even then his kisses felt sweeter than Tom's, but Tom and I were *the* couple. How could I turn my back on that?

Those kisses promised a world of care. I knew Mitch loved me. But at that age, what girl ever desires what's really good for her? I allow myself to soak in that lovely memory for a few seconds. Just a few.

———

Mom's still wearing her robe. Highly unusual for this time of day. She swings the door wide. "Come on in! Hi Trixie-baby! Come to Winky!"

Trixie runs forward. She and my Mom have a thing. "Winky!"

"*Hey Arnold!* is ready to go. I taped it for you last night. Go on ahead."

I wish Mom wouldn't let her watch so much television. And *Hey Arnold!?* Trixie's slipped on the shoes of the mean girl, Helga, not nice, sweet Arnold, friend in adversity, child with helping hands, a pure heart, and a football head. My in-depth knowledge of children's television frightens me.

Bottom line: she doesn't charge me for day care, so who am I to complain?

"Can you stay for coffee, dear?"

"I can't. I've got to get downstairs and open up the bistro." Did I actually just call it that? I must be flustered!

She shakes her head. "The bistro. Your grandparents would laugh themselves silly at that."

Our bistro, epitome, with no capital letter (which seems oxymoronic to me, but what do I know, I was just a journalism major), specializes in crazy sandwiches, soups and fish with odd names, curly greens, and olive oil. It began its days in the thirties as the Towson County Restaurant, specializing in regular old sandwiches, pot roast, chicken croquettes with egg sauce, meat loaf, and rice pudding and homemade pies.

I grew up making my own sandwiches behind the counter, pulling up the stainless steel lid that protected the lunchmeats, mayo, mustard, and toppings like lettuce, tomato, and sliced onion. Ham on rye with mustard and mayo mixed, a red ripe tomato slice, and a hank of lettuce satisfied me more than any other combination. Man, I miss that. When Brian removed the long counter and the grill and work area behind it, I wanted to strangle him for vandalizing my memories. He might as well have removed my liver or my left arm.

But Towson turned around a couple of decades ago and became tony and smart, and Brian felt the need to follow suit. I actually have to give my brother credit. With L & N Seafood, Paolo's, and other glitzy places across the street at the Towson Commons, we'd have gone under for sure. But he could have consulted with me about the name change. I work as many hours as he does. I do the books, seat customers, wait tables when necessary, and pay the bills. He could have called me from where I sat poolside at one of Lyra's swim meets and checked to see if I liked the name. Instead, he ordered an expensive sign, knowing I'd just go along rather than spend more money on something we could agree to. He's a sneaky twit.

But he always remembers the kids' birthdays.

Mom's apartment over the restaurant simplifies my life. And though we spent a fortune redecorating the business—chrome this, linen that—Mom's two floors remain exactly as they were when she moved us in after Harry bugged out. The front room, the living room, still glows a sea-foam green, and everything sits properly in its place. Unless of course you look into her hall closet, which is messier than a presidential impeachment. Thank goodness she's never been fond of vinyl slipcovers, because the couch, of heavy green-and-white plaid upholstery, uglies up the room enough on its own. She loves this couch, the first large-ticket item she ever bought for herself.

I kiss her cheek, head back down the outside stairs, and slip my key into the restaurant's back door.

Already I anticipate that fresh pot of coffee, the newspaper, and an ample strip of sunlight unfurling across the page, transforming newsprint to parchment. I enjoy watching people scuttle by on their way to work, although some of them depress me. So put together and confident. Women with bouncy hair and fine leather pumps and stylish briefcases. Men sporting good haircuts and pressed clothing and those can-do attitudes I don't think I've ever felt for more than thirty seconds. Others, well, they make me feel pretty good about myself. It would be mean to say why.

A sticky bun completes the scenario. Got to have a sticky bun.

I grab the copy of the monthly inspirational booklet I stash behind the register. It's all I can manage these days. Never one to study Scripture, in all honesty, I've never wanted to be, which says something negative. Take your pick: lazy, unspiritual, apathetic, cold, hard, prone to procrastination. Which one I assign to myself depends upon the day. Today, as the coffee drips, I'm leaning toward the apathetic. The most menacing by far.

But the devotional encourages me. Talks about the enduring

qualities of God's love, about how He bases His fatherly affection not on our performance but upon His heart. After what my father did to us, I need that.

The coffee's done, praise God from whom all blessings flow. I remember the days a fresh pot awaited me on the kitchen counter, courtesy of Rusty. We always got along so well.

Mitch and I always got along so well. That thought lasts awhile.

I tried to rejoice in my husband's accomplishments when he first went on the road. I even possessed the energy for excitement back then, or at least what it took to fool myself into some semblance of enthusiasm. But I'm worn down like a brook stone. I need a pep pill. Whatever those are. Didn't people in the forties and fifties take them?

After the paper and the sticky bun I head to the small office in the very back of the restaurant, turn on the computer, and look over the present state of epitome's finances. Not good. We took out a loan for the improvements, and how each month we pay for that and our staff remains a matter of prayer. These numbers foreshadow some belt-tightening. I have a feeling I'm going to have to start waiting tables soon.

Man oh man. I'll bet Mitch's ex-wife never worried about having to wait tables, dahling.

I reach into my briefcase, slip out the floppy disk that holds my novel, and decide to edit for a bit. Did I say I was depressed before? But the books soon call me back, and I begin the tedious process of entering all our expenses. Nothing but red ink. We can only hang on like this a couple of months more. Maybe.

Brian and a hangover stumble in at ten.

"Hi Ive." He winces, the words probably scraping around in his head like grinding gears.

I swivel around in the old wooden office chair Grandpa used to use. "Hey Bri." I consider screaming in his ear, *"How are you this fine morning?"* but decide to exhibit a little grace. He fits into the category of the pathetic sort, after all. Good-looking, talented, and totally unfit for relating to women in a meaningful way. Unable to learn from mistakes, if he even sees them as mistakes in the first place.

Am I like that?

Dear God, don't answer that.

"Let's sit in the dining room."

I pour him a cup of coffee and place it in his hand.

"You are a gift from heaven, Ivy."

It's the same every morning. Sometimes it goes like this (especially when he's late):

"You're wonderful, old Ivy dear."

"Save it for your washed-up tarts, Bri."

"Hey, I can get any woman I want."

"Yeah, as long as they're tarts."

After idolizing a high-school friend for the past two hours, I'm glad that conversation isn't happening today.

He'll hold up his hand. "Can we have this conversation later when my headache clears?"

"Sure. Or we can pretend we did. It's always the same anyway. I posit you have an inherent disrespect for women, and you end up telling me I'm judgmental, and then I have nothing to say to that."

He'll shake his head and fish in the cabinet under the register for some pain reliever. I'll say, "So was it worth it?" But of course I say that almost every morning, so since we're skipping the verbiage today, I decide to start filling salt shakers instead.

I first saw Rusty at the restaurant back before Brian tore down my beloved long counter and pie case. He tumbled in five minutes to closing time on a Saturday night. Now you can't help but notice Rusty. Even then, at a mere hundred and fifty pounds, he somehow took up more space than anyone in the room. While the rest of us rubber helium balloons float around the world, Mylar Rusty tumbles among us, rendering us transparent and feeling a little silly, realizing our helium will be gone well before he's even begun to pucker.

The bell slammed against the glass door, and he apologized.

His dark auburn hair, very thick, swung around his forehead like a British actor's hair. His caramel eyes took in the room, including me, at a single glance. We both blushed. Not that he was embarrassed or anything. He told me later the first thought he had upon seeing me: "Now, that is what I call a woman!" He said his breath caught in his throat, and he felt so lacking. That lacking pushed him forward, for Rusty liked challenges even then, if only to prove he possessed more oomph than his older brother ever gave him credit for. Ten minutes later, he and I sat alone at a table for two, talking about musicians and poets.

His fingers resting on the table, raised up slightly in time to the songs, trumpet miming. Energy buzzed about him, his eyes like sparklers—so bright it hurt to look; so lively and intriguing I couldn't look away.

I felt strange and almost desperate sitting next to this guy, but Tom Webber had broken up with me for the eighth time three weeks before, and…well, this guy loved more than sports. He didn't use lingo. He said he liked my glasses. He told me my hair was the most intriguing shade of blond he'd ever seen. He told his roommate to go on home, he'd catch him later.

I accompanied him to church the next day and watched him play percussion. He became so thoroughly enveloped in the rhythm of the songs it mesmerized me. And then, when he sang a solo written by Phil Keaggy, a man I knew nothing about at the time, I felt my heart lurch forward toward him and God. That voice watered some spot in my heart that no one had ever touched. Not Mitch, not Tom. Not Pastor Kincaid. Not Chuck Swindoll. Nobody. Afterward, we took a walk by the waters of Loch Raven. I laughed at his jokes and self-deprecating stories. We sat on the banks of the reservoir, and he pulled out a Far Side book, and we laughed ourselves silly at that, too. He didn't kiss me, but he held my hand and told me he'd never yet met a girl who laughed as much as I did.

The next morning he showed up at the restaurant before his first class at Towson State. We served breakfast back in those days. In his hand a dozen pink roses bobbed. Pink. Not the typical red. Good, an individual. We strolled together again, this time down the streets of Towson, sat on the lip of the dry fountain in the sterile square of the new courthouse, and drank coffee. And I felt comfortable and more like myself than ever before. All soft and open and maybe even a little sweet. Tom Webber made me nervous, always wondering when he'd break my heart again.

I didn't laugh much that day with Rusty, for a different atmosphere pervaded, something silent and profound, but I smiled all the way down, especially when he told me his parents were still together, still strong and loving, twenty-five years post "I do." I promised myself I'd never let him go.

Oh great. My father, Harry Starling, just walked by the front window.

Harry's a schmo. No other way around it. And I guess because he deserted us with such glibness, the sight of him hones Rusty's departure to a more exquisite point.

Mom, bearing the heavy load of hindsight, said lots of warning signals flashed, even during the dating months: the times he stood her up, the way money slipped through his fingers and she'd have to pay for their nights out. The way his eye wandered. But she loved him, she said. She loved his bright, good looks, his slim physique, the way he turned everyday life into a party. He ran with a wild crowd, sure, drag racing, clubbing, smoking like Robert Mitchum, but she was the woman to tame him, yes sir. Not to mention she was twenty-eight and couldn't make babies by herself.

Even at ten years old I noticed the way he looked women up and down. And choosy? No, no, no! It didn't matter the hair color or the build, whether a skirt hung from her hips or pants stretched tight, she demanded a look-see. I didn't realize my mother noticed until I was twelve. Some fuse blew inside me then. Never Daddy's girl in the first place—that was Brett's position—I realized he'd never sit close to my heart. After that I found myself on "Mom's side," though no one ever demanded a choice from me. Even then I pitched my tent in the camps of "all" and "nothing" and never the fragile space in between.

My brother Brian takes after Harry, but he's smart enough to pitch his tent in the singles' camp, whereas Harry just kept sneaking into other people's tents. I guess he can at least thank Harry for the gift of a negative role model.

At least Harry has the courtesy to appear after the lunch rush for his meal. We feel compelled to offer up a freebie—he's our dad—but he always orders expensive items.

We perform the obligatory greeting song-and-dance, and Brian appears from the kitchen.

"Whatchya got in the back, Brian?" And before Brian can answer, reporting only salmon or tenderloin, Harry heads to the back like he still belongs and discovers the jumbo lump crabmeat in the refrigerator. "How about one of your crab cakes, son?"

"Well, Dad, we're planning on just using it in the pasta special—"

"Oh, come on. Make a crab cake for your old man!"

I puff out my chest. "Harry, we don't have enough crab. Did you not hear your son?"

"Ivy, that's no way to talk to your—"

"Old man. Yeah, maybe. Now listen, we have a business to run here. The specials are set. Maybe you can squirrel Brian into this, but not me. Now do you want a burger or a club sandwich?"

"How about a steak sandwich?"

The old coot. "Okay."

"Don't forget to grill the onions, son. You know how much I like them grilled, right?"

Pathetic. He's Willie Loman without the right to be noticed.

He pushes the swinging door and heads back into the dining room.

Brian opens the fridge. "Man, he makes me mad. Thanks."

"What are little sisters for? He's such a loser."

Yeah, that sounds like something Jesus would say. I should treat him like any other wanderer in need of God's grace. But my contest with the flesh rages like thunder, and the flesh is about to spike the ball and do a victory dance in the end zone. My flesh even knows how to break dance, it's so good at winning the skirmish.

I walk back out to the front. My father sits at one of the window tables smoking a cigar. Oh man!

"Harry, put that out. You know it's not allowed."

"Oh, come on, Ivy. Nobody's here."

I cross my arms. "Harry, please. We can't afford the fines."

"Okay." He stubs it out on a bread plate.

"Thanks." I remove it and stride toward the wait station.

"That was a Cuban."

"Oh please." Under my breath.

"Are you mumbling?"

"Darn straight. Today's paper is under the register." I should offer to bring it to him. I should honor my father so my days may be long in the land the Lord my God giveth me, even though my life is hardly the Promised Land. Land of the Lost is more like it.

"Man, you're a piece of work, Ivy."

"I've learned from the best." I march back into the kitchen.

Brian throws onions on the grill. "He makes me sick."

"I know."

"At least I don't drag a wife and kids through my exploits."

What can I say?

He shakes his head and gently works the ground sirloin into a patty. He's a pro, right? Personally, I'd work the thing down to the seventh circle of hell and back, ensuring the most unsatisfactory hamburger on York Road. "No matter how bad I feel about myself and my life, Dad always puts me to shame."

And Mom thought surely she'd be the one to bring Harry Starling to Jesus. Missionary daters possess the best of intentions, don't they? Sometimes it works out, and sometimes others bear the fallout. Like me and Brian. And Brett. For crying out loud, I don't have enough time to start thinking about my sister, who messes up just about everything she touches. And it's never her fault. Maybe she just touches the wrong things.

She's working on marriage number two, and the fog alarms are beginning to blare. Marcus is okay, if you like plastic men. He actually gets pedicures and waxing: brows, chest, and back. Can't blame him for the back.

I've got it good compared to my siblings. But they have no idea how hard it is to be the responsible one without truly major issues. I get no easy outs.

"Did he forget your birthday last week, Bri?"

"Of course."

"He forgot mine in May."

"Figures."

I head back out to the dining room, praying with fervor that more diners have materialized during my absence. No such luck for Ivy Schneider.

"Ivy, come on over and talk to your old man."

He never uses the word *father* or *dad* with me. Maybe even he realizes he shouldn't assume.

"I'm busy."

"Oh, come on. There's nobody here."

One of our waitresses arrives. Unfortunately, the boot will find her first as the kitty dwindles. "Hi Flannery!"

"Hi Ivy! Gorgeous day, isn't it?"

"Couldn't ask for better!"

I love Flannery. She always wears trendy hairstyles, cool jewelry, and hand-painted clothing. She's an art student married to an oceanographer—isn't that the hippest combo imaginable? And she's one of those naturally happy people. I love that about her. She comes from big-time money through her grandmother, but you can't tell.

Harry taps the table. "See, kid? Reinforcements have arrived."

Nothing else to be done. I sit opposite him, place my chin in my hand. "What do you want to talk about?"

He never asks me about my life. He only talks about himself. Gee, who does that sound like?

"You can congratulate me for starters, Ive. I'm getting married next month."

"Oh."

"Yep, a real sweetheart. Reminds me of your mother."

"Don't even go there."

"You're not happy for your old man?"

"It's number four."

"Hey, the last two were not my fault. Now, I admit, I ruined it with your mother, but I was young, and we messed up." He shrugs. "What can I say? I won't make excuses for myself."

How about an apology? Even one.

"So, Harry, got any more contracts?"

"Oh yeah. Lots of brickwork down in Canton these days."

Brian sets down his plate. "Enough to pay for a sirloin burger?" He turns around right away.

Three ladies with shopping bags enter. God bless you, girls.

"Gotta seat these customers, Harry. Eat up."

Dear God, let him leave soon.

4

People wonder how I can be so sure of Rusty all the time, with him traveling all over the place, hanging around lonely women who flirt and make sweeping hints that usually begin with talk of "a cup of coffee." It amazes me here in America we initiate so many of our mating rituals with "a cup of coffee." I mean, it yellows our teeth, makes our hands quiver like a ninety-year-old's, and gives us dog breath. But for many of us, it's our first date. Well, it's a sure-fire method of avoiding kisses you'd rather keep to yourself.

You'd assume Rusty's obesity would be a deterrent. But you'd be about as close to the truth as Tim Robbins to a speaking engagement at the Baseball Hall of Fame. Think about men like Orson Welles, or even that Meatloaf guy. He doesn't seem to have a problem with the ladies, although I could be wrong. Or maybe he's actually a nice guy with a sweet wife who realizes the thing that pays the bills is only his schtick. He probably gets in the shower right away and washes all that grease out of his hair. And I'll bet Meatloaf's wife doesn't mind *his* concert tours. I'll bet Meatloaf's wife goes with him everywhere she can!

I'll also bet some women out there watch my husband sing and think to themselves, "I'd follow that man to the ends of the earth," as if a great singing voice provides for all needs. My mother always said, "You can't live on love." Well, you can't live on a fabulous tenor voice, either.

Women throw themselves at Rusty. Married or not. He performs solo concerts at churches from time to time when he can arrange the gig. And those ladies are the worst. Anybody who says adultery isn't alive and well in the North American church is about as wrong as low-rise jeans on Hillary Clinton. I mean, consider my own thoughts since the class reunion. And honestly, a lot of church people out there don't want to admit the sinning that runs rampant in the holy hallways. But sometimes dirty laundry needs airing. If nobody did that, it would molder and fester and rot. And these ladies, or should I say women, would love to generate some dirty laundry with my husband. I know, it makes me sick too.

So how do I cope? With this: Rusty says he looks at the prettiest woman and thinks, "No matter how good she looks, some guy somewhere is tired of putting up with her junk."

That is plain truth, Rusty style. Now I know he puts off these women with as much gentleness and Christian charity as he can muster, but every once in a while he lets someone have it: "Lady, if you're this desperate, there isn't a man alive who'd have you if he knew the truth." And then he'll tell me all about it.

I'm sitting at Persy's lacrosse game musing about this because, well, times like these I miss Rusty the most, and a good muse always benefits the column. Rusty would be so proud of Persy just because he's Persy. He wouldn't get all over Persy because he fails to run as fast as the other boys. He wouldn't sit here a bundle of nerves. He'd be encouraging and fatherly and good. That God gave him such a phenomenal tenor voice is a blessing as well as a curse. Perhaps I should gladly share him with the world, but man oh man, I just wish the world would share him with us.

I can think of no other activity I'd less rather attend at eight thirty on a Saturday morning—except maybe a recital of first-year violinists or a full-body wax. I thought about stopping at Starbucks on the way, but the sports complex has no Porta Potti toilets, and I knew my bladder wouldn't last through the game. You know little things like this bug me about womanhood. Here I've gifted the world with three beautiful citizens (and every single one of them weighed in at over eleven pounds) to redeem some bad things over to the good side, and what reward do I get for carrying them to term? The lovely ability to pee when I laugh and the privilege of using the bathroom twice as often as I did at twenty-two. No coffee at soccer games. No sodas on trips. No water before bed. Life is not fair. Didn't God know mothers need coffee to manage early morning rec council games? I comfort myself with a handful of Dove chocolate candies.

Lou walks toward me. "Hey Ive-O."

Her nickname for me since we were three. She put *o's* on the end of everything. "Lou!" Her name is actually Jean-Louise, like the girl in *To Kill a Mockingbird.* Her father, a high-school literature teacher, named her after that character. He actually wanted to call her Scout, but Mrs. Lybeck refused. It took the likes of Demi Moore and Bruce Willis to have the guts for that. And I applaud them. Besides, Bruce is a Republican.

She *plonks* open a folding chair. A gorgeous one, of course, displaying a classy floral pattern. "Lyra told me I'd find you here." She folds her body into a fluid, dark line, leaning back like a bored actress. The eyes, bright and curious, convey a different narrative, though.

"Where else would I be? Thank goodness Lyra hates sports and Trixie's still too little. What are you up to today?"

"Just running around looking for fabric for my living-room and dining-room curtains."

"Again?"

"I just didn't take to the cortez gold like I thought I would. I had the walls repainted blackberry wine."

"When?"

"Yesterday. I'll do some texturing next week." Lou solves interior-design dilemmas all over the county. My patriotic kitchen, a design predicament if there ever was one, makes her all but retch.

"Want a Dove?"

"No, thanks."

What willpower. "More for me."

"Well, you have the luck of a racecar metabolism. Us regular women have to starve."

Like I feel so sorry for her! "So when are you going to come help me with my house?"

"When you tell me I have free rein. I'm not going to make the dramatic change of painting your white walls cream. You can do that on your own."

She tells me I possess no creative imagination. And she's right. I mean, white walls complement everything, don't they? It matches all my furniture, and while we're not exactly poor, some things you can't justify—like buying a new couch just because you're sick of the old one. Hardly good money management. But didn't Persy say he felt a sharp spring the other day? I definitely can't endanger my children, and the couch is older than my marriage.

"Well, okay then. I'm tired of fighting it. Have your way. I need a new couch, so pick that out for me, and go from there."

"A new couch?"

"Yeah, I guess so. It's beginning to poke." Or at least I think so.

"I'm on it, mama."

Well, then, here we go. The whirlwind begins. The Jean-Louise cyclone of transformation. Without her I'd molder away. And eat more candy.

I pull out another chocolate and place it on my tongue.

———

Mr. Moore offers me his little wave. I shut the car door and run over.

"Thanks for that fish the other day. Your brother cooks up a fine halibut."

"He sure does. How's the arthritis?"

"Oh, it has its good days and its bad days. The bad days I just put 'eat popcorn' and 'watch old movies' on my list of chores, and it suits me just fine."

"I need to remember that. Adjust my to-do list to fit my needs."

"That sure is right. Makes for a lot less trouble, in my view."

"I think you're onto something there."

And my next column begins.

———

When I was little, eight times out of ten we didn't shut the car door tightly.

"Mom, the car door's not shut tight!" we'd yell.

And Mom would slow down a bit, just a bit, mind you, and we'd open the car door, feel the slight thrill of fear as the asphalt whizzed by beneath our gaze and the road line blinked on and off like a neon beer sign. Then we'd heave with all our might, ensuring a fully engaged latch, and we'd sit back in our seat without a seat belt holding us in.

We possessed good reflexes back then. One slight tip of the

brakes, and both hands and one foot automatically found their way to the seat back or dashboard in front of us. Yep, mighty good reflexes.

They stand me in good stead right now as I place a hand on Persy's chest and curve my arm around his waist as he walks by my kitchen chair. "You are not going for the candy bowl, bud."

"I wasn't—"

"Oh yes you were. Get a granola bar from the drawer."

"Okay." He swings his head down and turns from my arms.

"Hey, at least there's sugar in it."

My son could ingest five pounds of sugar at a sitting and still want more. I know he gets it from me, and who knows what else he's inherited from the Starlings? Poor kid.

A granola bar. Yep, we're not living in the same old world, folks.

5

School's out for summer! That's my anthem right now, despite its birth in the bloodstained mouth of Alice Can-You-Believe-He's-a-Minister's-Son Cooper. Now I ask you, how in the world does *that* happen? An aside to those with theological knowledge: if cases like these don't furnish you with a full belief in total depravity, I don't know what does!

My church sure had a lot to say about Alice Cooper, let me tell you! He was going to turn all the teenagers of America into satanic minions. And where is he now? I'm sure VH1 assembled a *Behind the Music* on that guy, but I haven't seen it yet, even though—and I hate to admit it—I'm quite fond of the show. That, and *I Love the 80s*. But God didn't let him go. He's rocking hard and praying hard these days. And I'm not about to tell him he can't do both.

No one anticipates the end of the school year more than I do. Of course, for two and a half months my house deteriorates faster than a pop princess's reputation. Nutrition hides under a rock, and the television? Well, let's just say all motherly intentions go the way of nutrition. But so will sports games, school projects, permission slips, and my inability to say no to room-mothers' requests for cookies on a stick, planning the Valentine's party, or sitting the class rat or goldfish for the weekend. They claim to teach the kids responsibility, but who ends up feeding the darn animals—or buying a twin replacement?

And Rusty's coming home. When push comes to shove, I do still love the guy. I made a promise all those years ago. A fact of which I'm painfully aware.

Some writer, probably Shakespeare, said, "To err is human, to forgive, divine." So I've got a little work to do before his plane lands. God, help me be a great actress. Even if only for the kids' sake. Knowing Rusty, he'll disembark and say the right thing, and I'll truly be glad to see him. I hate that.

So as we drive to the airport to pick him up, we sing "I've Been Working on the Railroad" over and over, our very own summer anthem.

Dinah, won't you blow your horn!

We haven't seen him since Easter. He could have driven back this way with the group, but we sprang for the plane ticket.

We park in the garage at BWI and sigh with gratitude as the air conditioning of the terminal hits us full on and begins to evaporate our perspiration. I have no luck when it comes to the Blazer's AC, even though I'm so faithful with the coolant. I was tempted to leave the windows rolled down, but airport garages aren't exactly *Mayberry RFD*.

Lyra almost skips with excitement. Daddy's girl. Knowing how a teen girl gains her sexual identity from her father at this time of her life, I do all I can to hide my feelings about my husband from her. I want her to love him purely in response to how he treats her, then translate that in light of how he treats me so that someday, when choosing a mate, her standards will rise every bit to the level she deserves. She wears new khaki shorts and a pink tank top. She's anticipating evening walks after the others go to bed, and trips to Friendly's Ice Cream twice a week. And Rusty won't disappoint her.

Me, I'm looking forward to hearing Rusty humming around

the house. "In Times Like These" finds its way out of Rusty's lips more than anything.

"In times like these, you need a Savior. In times like these, you need an anchor. Be very sure, be very sure, your anchor holds, and grips the solid rock." I need that anchor. It's what keeps me from drifting so far off center I don't recognize who I am in the eyes of God. So here's the thing, Lord, help me not to waste this visit with bickering, because Rusty will leave and the hurtful words will remain, hanging all about the house, shaking their finger at me saying, "Now what good did that do?"

"Can we go up to the gate this time?" Persy jangles with excitement.

"Not anymore."

"Is that ever going to change, Mom?" Lyra.

"Nope."

"Oh, okay."

Isn't that acceptance sad? The world looks so different, and they don't even realize it. Don't worry. I won't go into my opinions on homeland security other than to say I'm not comfortable with the privacy invasions. Unfortunately I have no good alternatives to offer, so I'll keep my mouth shut.

We check the flight board and head toward Pier C. Thank goodness the flight is on time. "Only about five minutes, gang."

They know better than to worry that we'll miss him. Nobody misses Rusty.

Trixie's squirming in the stroller already. She's a wire that can slip loose from almost any constraint. But I've already run interference, as losing your child in an airport is way too scary. I tightened the belt to the point of circulation loss and promised her a trip to Toys "R" Us if she stays put until we see Daddy. In times like these

I'm glad she's not yet potty trained, because you can bet your engagement ring, your farm, and your firstborn she'd have had me in the bathroom at least twice by now. Lyra trained by two. Persy on his third birthday. If Trixie's out of diapers by four, I'll buy the world a drink. I'm sure she's used up half the amount of diapers Lyra did anyway, so we're even on that point. In those days, I changed the slightest dampness. Now, if those silicone balls haven't made an appearance, she's still good to go.

Those poor third children. No wonder they're so pushy. They need to be.

"There he is!" Persy's off and running.

"Daddy! Daddy!" Trixie pulls against her restraints.

As I free her, I feel a smile stretch my face, and I wave my arms. I have no backbone. I don't want to encourage him, but I can't help myself, I'm glad to see him, maybe because he's so glad to see us.

Rusty hugs all three kids at once, and when he pulls me close he whispers, "Saved the best for last." He kisses me on the mouth, and before I can compute my feelings about it, Trixie scampers away. The race is on.

———

"Brian's planning a family dinner tonight at the restaurant. Is that okay?"

Rusty sits out back on the deck in a pair of Bermuda shorts and a button-down with the sleeves rolled up. He always looks nice, dresses properly for every occasion in clean, pressed, traditional clothing. He's a neat freak, too. When Rusty's home the house stays picked up. Is it any wonder I want him home more often?

"Sounds great. What's he making?"

"Don't know. I took off today to pick you up, and I wasn't about to call in."

"Good girl. Have a seat, hon."

"I'll get us some iced tea first."

In the kitchen, Lyra's making up a pan of her famous brownies. That's what she calls them, "my famous brownies." A Ghirardelli mix. But her claim to fame doesn't bother me at all. Let's face it: she recognized the best mix and is known by the church people as one fantastic brownie maker. She also knows exactly when to remove them from the oven so they're still gooey and immediately disintegrate on your palate. A box can't tell you how to do that.

"I thought maybe I could take these over to the restaurant to serve as dessert."

Brian would have a fit if anyone other than Lyra made the offer. But he claims her as his legacy. "Cool. Just call Uncle Brian and let him know before he spends an hour on something else."

I pour the tea and head back to the deck. So far, so good.

Rusty's already placed the pad on the cedar lounger next to his. A hammock hangs between two maples in the small yard. I often wish we could lie there together as we did years ago, but these days, once Rusty got in, chances are he might not make it out without breaking something. I hand him the drink.

"Thanks, Ive. Man, it's great to be home."

I settle on the lounger. The sun warms my knees, and a couple of birds splash in the hanging birdbath by the back fence, their flutters spangling the air with diamonds of water. "Sing me a song, Rust."

He sips his tea. "What'll it be?"

"In Times Like These."

And Rusty begins. I've waited two months for this. My eyes close on their own, and I feel like a bit of grace is mine for the taking, that I'll enjoy this time with him as much as I possibly can. Perhaps it isn't good for me in the long run, but right now, there's only now, and I choose it.

———

I run the comb through Persy's hair one last time. "Let's go couch shopping tomorrow night, Rust."

"I'm up for that. Last time I sat on that thing I was feeling the springs for a week."

That settles it, then.

The kids all cheer, and Lyra promises to surf the Internet to print out all the latest styles. But we have to leave. Dinner at the restaurant beckons.

God, give me strength.

———

It's amazing how much a younger kid actually absorbs. The race riots in Baltimore took place in April, I know now. But for years I only remembered that it wasn't cold outside. I knew little about TheReverendDoctorMartinLutherKingJunior. But I remember snippets of television news items, and I recall being scared. Which isn't surprising, is it?

For years and years I was afraid of African Americans, until I entered high school and played volleyball. Twilah Marcus could spike a ball like nobody's business, and she always sat with me on the bus to games. I thought, "Twilah wouldn't hurt anybody."

One day, back when the races mixed even less than they do now, Baltimore further cemented its reputation as a violent town.

Nowadays our mile-high homicide rate continues the tradition. And heroin? We do heroin like crazy in this city.

Well, it was right after the death of Dr. King that the race riots began, leaving a burning Monument Street in their wake. Dad drove to his office downtown with a Colt handgun on the seat next to him. I was scared for him and for me. What if he got shot before he could pick it up? What if angry people surrounded the car and pulled him out and executed him right there in front of his optometry practice? Shot him in the head? Or in the stomach, which took longer to kill you?

Maybe I'd never see him again. My heart would thunder, and my mouth would dry out like an old sponge, and I'd hug him and hug him and hug him.

After my father—Harry—left us and optometry, and Mom settled into the apartment over the restaurant to make ends meet, I came upon the gun. I had remembered it as shiny and turquoise with a white bone handle. Are there even guns that look like that? But there it lay in its case, black and streamlined and ugly. I don't think he ever took it out after 1968. I think maybe those days scared him, too. But he had appointments to keep.

Maybe he just got tired of keeping appointments.

I have to give my father credit. He examined the eyes of all races, and no sign saying "No Coloreds" ever besmirched the windows of his practice. I guess he didn't have to deal with any of those decisions once he became a bricklayer. He sure was glad to lay aside the malpractice insurance, too. But don't get me started on lawyers! God knows I could write a lifetime of columns on them alone.

6

We try to have these family meals at least once a month, and for the life of me I don't always know why. Brian constantly looks at his watch, waiting impatiently to begin his next conquest. Brett does nothing but complain, and she hardly ever smiles these days. I tell you, I hate looking at her anymore. And to try and give her advice? Whoa. Just don't. Mom's okay when we're all together, treats us all the same, but she unwittingly pits us against each other in private. When I'm with her, all she can talk about is Brett; when Brett's with her, she goes on and on about me. Brian's her baby boy. She talks about him to him. No wonder he's a selfish pig. Don't get me wrong, I love him. I really do. I even like him, when I don't start adding up his vices and shortcomings. I just want to wring his neck because he never seems to learn. How is it some people keep making the same mistake over and over again and never learn?

Tonight we're dressing up. Lyra requested it, and my sister loves an excuse to spend money on a new outfit. Rusty wears khaki pants, a blue button-down, and loafers. I pull on my brown reunion dress. The kids flit about in light, summery clothes: Lyra, blond perfection in a paisley sundress, Trixie in floral bloomers, and Persy in plaid shorts and a light yellow polo shirt.

We file in the back door of the restaurant. Rusty makes the

huggy-kissy rounds and settles in the dining room with the little kids to keep them out of the way. Mom pours him a glass of wine, and she sips hers while they chat like the chums they are. Those two can converse for thirty minutes about nothing but nothing.

Brian's jerking saucepans at the range. "Hey sis."

"Hi Bri. What's cooking?"

"Soft crabs, veal, asparagus, grilled endive."

"What's our starch?"

"Just bread. Made it after lunch. I'm grilling that too, with a little olive oil and a garlic rub."

"Mmm. Sounds good."

"Naturally."

I wrap myself inside an apron. "What can I do?"

"Clean the endive and cut them in half. Spread on a little extra virgin."

"Got it."

We work side by side in silence, listening to the dining-room murmur. Rusty's laugh resounds, and I notice a smile creep onto Bri's face.

"I'll bet you're glad to have him home."

"The kids are beside themselves."

"He's a good dad. You found a good one, Ivy."

Bri's always saying that about Rusty.

When I compare Rusty to Brian and Harry, I actually thank God for him. "Lord knows this family needed him."

He adds more butter to the beurre blanc. "You said it. Brett's husband is such a twit."

"What makes you say that?"

A shrug. "Never mind, I've just never liked the guy, is all."

It's more than that. I can tell. But I'll let it slide for now.

New voices mingle with the others. Brian sighs. "Well, trouble's arrived. I wonder which of the evil twins Brett coaxed into coming?"

"Does it matter?"

Brett birthed two daughters. Ashley and Margeaux. If that doesn't beat all. They're not twins, actually, but just a year apart and as spoiled as a twenty-year-old jar of herring, they more than deserve the nickname. I listen. They're both out there.

Brian removes the sauté pan from the heat. "Wonder what they're wearing tonight?"

"Something highly inappropriate, I'm sure."

"I can't understand why Brett lets them dress the way they do. I mean, an exposed butt crack isn't attractive on any woman."

I purposely fail to remind him that he consistently dates women who dress just like that.

He checks the soft crabs in the oven. "Now Lyra, there's a class act just waiting in the wings."

"She does have a tasteful flair, doesn't she?"

We're going to be so disillusioned when she turns into a typical teen. And yet I hope. Every so often a girl stays sweet. And she is fourteen. Surely we'd already be traveling a rough road if things were going to go that way.

Now with Trixie, I anticipate awful. Awful, awful. Slammed-doors, sneaking-out-of-the-house, profanity-filled-IMs awful.

Brian wraps the bread in some foil. "Maybe they'll stay out there awhile longer."

"It's a safe bet." My sister and her girls never help out at these things.

"Would you get out the serving pieces when you're done, Ive?"

"Sure thing." I brush the oil on the last of the endive. "These are ready for the grill. Table set yet?"

"No. Shoot. Would you?"

"Lyra!"

She peeks her head in. "Yeah, Mom?"

"Would you get the table set?"

"Most definitely."

She disappears back into the fray. She'll know better than to ask her cousins for help. These things you learn young. I hear her bossing Persy, though, in fabulous big-sister fashion. Poor Persy! I'm sure he's rolling his eyes right now. But he's obeying her, regardless.

I don't scold her, classifying this incident as noncritical. You see, Lyra was born blue. That moment made any fear I'd ever experienced unravel into insignificance. The medical staff tried procedure after procedure, my throat constricting more tightly with each excruciating second until I thought my heart would stop. The threat of a communist takeover and of subsequent torture is nothing compared to watching your own baby suffocate. And then Rusty grabbed her from the doctor's arms and belted out the "Hallelujah Chorus" in her ear. On the fourth "hallelujah" that little thing gasped and began to breathe, turning bright red, the most beautiful color I've ever seen. It's been her favorite song ever since, and her life has become a living hallelujah. I gave her to God right then and there. I mean completely to Him, in a way I can't quite explain. I knew I could trust Him no matter what, and that trust went so far as to know He'd make something special out of Lyra.

I peep through the small, diamond-shaped window in the swinging door, careful not to let anyone see me. Lyra sets out the cutlery at express-train speed, sure of herself. I grieve a bit as I take in my sister and her two girls dressed in beautiful designer clothing. Lyra's outfit, one she made herself and worked so hard on this spring, simply can't compare. And I'd like to say she is like Cinderella among the wicked stepsisters, those ugly things dressed up like birthday cakes, their faces bulbous and lacking compared to Cinderella's loveliness. However, Ashley and Margeaux resemble perfect pop princesses. Flat stomachs stretched between sharp hipbones peeping above their low, slender miniskirts, gold belts twinkling in the spotlights. They're tanned and fit from working out at the country club and playing tennis. Just gorgeous. Life really isn't fair when playing by the rules of the world.

But Lyra plays by different, more lasting rules, and when I picture these three in the future, I see only one with the ability to invest herself in others and so live fulfilled. Lyra will probably feel plain around them for years to come, possibly forever, but they will feel shallow and without purpose. There. Having bashed two young girls and proclaimed them deficient, I feel better.

Really, I do. I'm a twit. But I'm an honest twit.

Brett's dressed in slimming black silk-crepe pants and a long gold-brocade jacket with a mandarin collar. Her hair's always perfect too. Dark brown with subtle streams of gold, cut with a deft razor in face-and-neck-brushing wisps at a tony salon down in Mount Washington. She bugs me every time she sees me to do something with mine, but never offers to pay for a trip to the salon. She could. She's loaded. It's not that I want a handout, but if it's so important to her, she needs to either put up or shut up. *Shut up* would work just fine for me. If anyone knows she's not the gal she used to be, it's me.

Brian turns off the final burner. "Okay, sis, let's fill the platters."

You know, they could at least offer to help, those girls. At the very least, they could poke their heads in to say hi.

Brian and I work quickly, in our usual swinging rhythm much like a cadence sung by Old Blue Eyes. The sound system fires up some Tony Bennett.

"Well that's good," I say.

"Oh yeah."

"Let's try to keep this nice, Bri."

"I'll try, but sometimes Brett makes that thoroughly impossible. Ready?"

"Is that a serious question?"

At least Rusty's here to tame the horde, God bless him.

———

Rusty stands to his feet as I enter the room, arms full. What a gentleman. "Let the feast begin!" The benediction accompanies a reach for one of my platters.

Mother and Lyra clap, and Lyra hurries back into the kitchen and reappears with the bowl of asparagus and the platter of endive as Brian and I lay down our platters. The veal smells gorgeous, and the soft crabs, well, I'm not going to be shy there! There's two for each, but I'm counting on Persy to eat only one, so that's three for me.

After we line up the food along the center of the table, we sit down, and Rusty does the honors of saying grace. We hold hands, Lyra squeezing mine, her warmth lending me some strength for the conversation that lies ahead.

Amen.

"Amen!"

Unfortunately Brett has enthroned herself on my left.

She rests a hand on my thigh. "Is that veal?"

"Oh yes. Brian really splurged."

"And soft crabs."

"Aren't they gorgeous?"

"Well, this leaves my girls out, Ivy. They hate seafood and positively won't eat veal."

"What?"

"Frankly I'm surprised you'd serve that meat, the way those poor calves are raised."

"It's not like that. This is free-range veal."

"Still. Poor baby cows."

"There's endive and asparagus, too."

"Oh please. Girls! Just eat the vegetables and bread. Obviously you all weren't taken into consideration when this meal was planned. But then what's new?"

Where's Mo with his backhand when you really need it? I shake my head slightly at Brian, who's turning a charming shade of magenta across the table. *Don't say a word, bro,* I vibe.

She puffs. "On second thought, why don't you girls go over to Paolo's and get something you can eat?"

"You *will* eat." Did I really just murmur that?

"What did you say, Ivy?"

"Nothing."

"I'm choosing to let that go."

Lyra jumps up. "I'll go grill up a couple of chicken breasts." Before I can stop her, she's gone.

She doesn't deserve this role, but at least she can handle it. And she does grill a great chicken breast.

She pokes her head back out the door. "Wine sauce, guys?"

"Absolutely." Ashley nods. She's the nicer of the two. She folds her arms across her bare stomach.

"Plain for me," Margeaux orders—yes *orders*—as she flips through a magazine.

Club Sandwich

Brett: "See? Perfect! You know, Ivy, you could learn a lesson or two from your daughter. That child is an angel."

At least she adores Lyra. It keeps me from disowning her and her tedious offspring.

Rusty raises his glass. "Time for a toast!"

"Hear! Hear!" Mother does the same.

"To family. Related, no matter what!"

"Cheers!" we all say and clink our glasses. Well, almost all of us. Margeaux's reading her horoscope. I'm glad we got the uncomfortable stuff out of the way early.

———

We sit at a table for two now. Just my sister and me. A candle cuts the gloom of the empty restaurant.

I love her. When all the sludge is pumped away, she's my sister and I love her. Her marriage is falling apart. The time-honored adultery story. I forgive every miffy remark she made earlier. I'm surprised she showed up at all. I'm not surprised, however, that I made no attempt to give her the benefit of the doubt. I'm a boob.

Bottom line: I wouldn't trade places with Brett for one second, not even for a million dollars or a week on a desert isle with Ralph Fiennes.

She's crying. "I thought this would be the good one. I really thought this one would work."

Marriage number three, fifteen years in length, and despite her golden baubles and her golden glow, she feels like she's not enough for anyone right now. I'm glad Lyra cooked the chicken breasts for my nieces. They've spent their lives with adults who spend their lives trying to make up for their mistakes, and always in the wrong way, with clothing, jewelry, parties, and good schools. No wonder they measure affection in terms of what they can get from a person.

And now, another divorce, and perhaps a trip to Europe or Tahiti to ease the pain. Marcus will leave and probably try to continue to see the girls—I mean they were four and five when he married their mother—but Brett won't let him, and the girls will suffer more than anyone. She'll spend half her divorce settlement attempting to purchase their mental health from places like Neiman Marcus and Club Med, or whatever resort spa rates these days.

I feel so sorry for them.

If Rusty hadn't come along, this could have been me. Sure, he's absent most of the time, but we are a pair. No. We're a unit, he and I. I can't imagine life any other way. It's why his absence pains me so much. I guess the day I should really begin to worry is the day it stops hurting.

"When did you find out about her?"

"Last night."

"How?"

"An anonymous phone call. My gosh, it's so typical!"

"Did he deny it?"

"No. He was actually relieved."

"As if he deserved that."

"Exactly. Way to go, Brett, you did that creep a favor! Perfect!" I pour more water into her glass. "So what's next?"

"He says he wants to work things out, but—"

"The trust is broken."

"You got it."

"Is it the first time? The first woman?"

"I didn't ask. I'm not ready to hear the answer."

"Do you know who called?"

"It was a man."

"Maybe the other woman's husband?"

"No, her father."

"Eww. How old is she?"

"I'm not about to ask." She taps her fingers on the tabletop. "I can't believe I didn't see it myself. He's been working late way too much lately. And you know, Ivy, I'm not the type to check up on him."

"Well, why would you be?"

"Exactly. He's suggesting we go away together to patch things up. As if it will be so easy."

"I'll check up on the girls."

She shakes her head. "They'll be fine, and I haven't agreed to anything yet."

"Good girl." I'm trying very hard not to offer any advice. Brett's going to do what she's going to do anyway. "We're here for you. You know that."

"Thanks."

"Keep me posted, though, would you?"

She purses her lips, and I grab her hand. "What I mean is, whatever you need, okay? I know we don't always get along like maybe we should, but I love you."

Her lips relax.

I don't know what more Marcus could want in a wife. Brett is a golden goddess. Toned. Smooth. Glittering like a fairy.

"Brett, I'm not here to judge you, and I don't want you to think I'm going to sit around and compare our lives. I mean really, you're a successful, beautiful woman." (I take a deep breath for the building-up speech.) "You look ten years younger than you are. You run a thriving shop, your children are gorgeous, and they're getting great grades in college. You've made a beautiful home. Frankly, Marcus must be a fool to jeopardize all that. You are a great lady, and you *will* get through this. I promise."

"I wish I felt like that woman right now."

I lean over to her and fold her into my arms. She smells like Chanel; I smell like kitchen. She looks like an actress; I look like a tired mom. She wears silk; I wear rayon. She's got the drive to succeed; I possess the drive to survive. And together we'll see this thing through.

We have to. She's my sister. And we own a bond that only sisters can own.

———

Mr. Moore's house wins the award for Most Cheerful on the street. A few years ago, before his mother died, he painted it her favorite colors, yellow and rose. Moss-green shutters tie it into the landscape and render my plain old white house more boring than a lecture on cell division. It always gives my heart a lift.

He doesn't sleep much, so I know he'll welcome my ten o'clock knock.

"Ivy Jane! Come on in!"

He steps aside as I amble into the entryway. He painted much of the interior in peaceful shades of blue.

"I brought you some leftovers from our family dinner. A soft crab, some veal." I hold out the takeout container.

"Oh my goodness. This'll sure beat the Manwich I made tonight." He takes the box. "Hold on while I put this in the fridge. You got a minute?"

"Always got time for you, Mr. Moore."

"I'll make us some tea. Have a seat in the living room."

I was hoping he'd invite me in. Mr. Moore doesn't know it, but he's my confessor, my wise man. On second thought, maybe he does know it but doesn't mind.

No couches congregate in the living room, only comfy chairs that don't match. Two florals, a plaid, a book-binding pattern, two solids, and somehow it all works. Built-in bookcases testify to my friend's interests. Planes and seafaring vessels and the history thereof, gardening, gemstones, Civil War, theology. I choose a floral chair, swivel around, and grab a book about eschatology, something in which I have very little knowledge and very little interest. I leaf through the pages reading nothing, thinking only about Brett.

"Ivy, dear! Could you come help me carry this tray?"

"I'm coming."

A minute later, he relaxes in the plaid chair, feet up on a plain green ottoman, and we sip the brew. An antique plate of Pepperidge Farm cookies goes uneaten by both of us.

"Thanks for inviting me in."

"You had that look on your face. What happened?"

I tell him all about Brett.

He shakes his old head. "Now, I never did get married, which saved me from a lot of life's ills, but kept me from a lot of joy, too."

"I don't know what to tell her."

He thinks on that, and I slurp in anticipation. I look down at the book on my lap. The word *preterism* jumps off the page. Preterism? What's preterism?

"Does it matter, in the end, what you say?"

"I guess not."

"I remember your sister when she was a little girl and she used to visit your grandparents. My guess is she's one who has to find her own way no matter how thorny the path."

That sure is the truth.

He adds, "But she has a good heart tucked inside there."

"That's true, Mr. Moore."

"And she knows God."

I nod.

"So we'll just pray for her, and when she asks for your help, you'll be there to lend a hand."

I set my tea on the side table. "I just wish I could make life easier for her."

He waves a hand. "Life is never easy, Ivy. All you can do is know your resources and use them the best you know how. In fact"—he points at me—"that's something you might start doing yourself."

7

Something's wrong. As I helped Rusty ready the kids for their trip down to the King's Dominion theme park, my gut started knotting up. I had called Mom to remind her she wouldn't have to watch Trixie and Persy today, and the phone rang and rang. Darn it, but I just can't convince the woman to employ an answering machine! I even bought one for her for Christmas several years ago. When I asked her about it, she said, "I'm saving it for when I really need it." What's that supposed to mean? And she never leaves messages on mine either. God bless caller ID is all I can say, or I'd never know when she needs me.

I called again after the kids were dressed. Yet again after I set out the cereal bowls and finally just before I left.

Three calls, ten rings apiece. Surely one of those would have awakened her. My stomach vibrates. But I'm on my way to the restaurant, and now I speed dial her on my cell phone.

Nothing.

I step on the gas and call Brett.

She answers on the first ring. "Hey Ivy."

"Hi sweetie. I can't get an answer at Mom's."

"I called earlier. I didn't get one either."

"I'm on my way. Hopefully she's volunteering down at St. Joe's or something and forgot to tell me."

"Call me."

"I will. How are you doing this morning?"

"Okay. You know. Didn't sleep much last night. I can't even get in the bed with him."

"Who can blame you?"

"Exactly. Listen, I gotta go. Call me later, okay?"

"Sure thing."

I tear down York Road, seeing a ticket in my future, but no policemen lurk. The closest parking space sits a block away from the restaurant. I screech in. Dear God, don't let anyone hit the tail end of my car!

I dash down the sidewalk, fishing in my purse for the keys, because, of course, I automatically dropped the ring inside when I stopped the car. And the ring automatically dove to the bottom. Of course.

As I try to shove the key into the lock, it begins slipping from my grasp. Calm down, Ivy. Slow down. Remember, she's probably volunteering at the hospital or at bridge with some of her friends. She probably forgot to tell you she was going, and surely a woman her age doesn't have to report her every move to her daughter.

I finally open the door and hear a moan.

"Mom!" I run inside, multiple "Oh noes" opening and closing my mouth.

"Ivy…" She moans again.

The kitchen.

She lays on the floor. No, no, no. Her leg, angled askew, lies like a broken branch still attached to the tree. Her skin glows with the same pallor as the linoleum.

"I'm here, Mom."

"Fell. Last night."

Last night. I rush to the phone in the living room and dial 911.

I've made my way through life relatively pain free. Other than bearing children, I remember only a few times intense pain beat me blue. The day I put ear-cleaning solution in my left ear not knowing my eardrum was ruptured tops the list. Brett was there, hopping behind me where I bent over the sink, grabbing my ear. She was freaking out in a good way because I realized even amid the fiery pain how much she cared. "Should I call an ambulance? Should I call an ambulance?" she said to Mom, who remained calm.

The second was the day some stranger in a mask extracted my tonsils.

I was three.

I remember a blue sky, the yellow of the daffodils, and the gangly forsythia bushes flowering in the yard, their slender branches punctuated by the sweet blooms. I remember a sun-warmed backseat and the peculiar smell of warm vinyl. Silver-gray vinyl.

I don't recall the details of the pilgrimage to the hospital, and I'm not even certain whether it was St. Joe's or Greater Baltimore Medical Center, but I remember being shown to the room, Mom with me every step, helping me change into the hospital gown, pulling my hair into a ponytail. Then finally, I found myself looking up into the concerned, cornflower eyes of the anesthesiologist, and two nurses, one with dark eyes surrounded by long, thick lashes that curled up into blond tips, the other with deep crow's-feet and a friendly slant. They asked me to count to ten. I guess they deemed me too young to count backward.

The black gas mask descended, and a sudden panic milled in my chest and behind my forehead like a swarm of bees, but I counted anyway. Something stoic resided in me even at three. I remember five but not six. I remember wanting so much to cry. I remember swallowing the fear. And then nothing.

That something stoic has stood me in good stead from time to time, like when Rusty had his heart attack at thirty, or when Lyra refused to breathe right after her birth. It doesn't negate the fear, mind you, but it sees me through with little outward hullabaloo. A force field, really, it fools onlookers into believing I am in control, steady and ready to do what needs doing.

Maybe it isn't stoicism, maybe it's just good acting. Whatever the case, it works for me today as I sit here alone in the surgical waiting room at GBMC hospital.

Rusty offered to come right home, but I told him to keep the kids at the park until dinnertime. They can't do anything, and Mom would hate it if she spoiled the day for them.

Unfortunately I called Brett in the thick of a discussion with Marcus. "Do you really need me there, Ive?"

"The ambulance is on the way, and I'm sure they'll get her right into surgery."

"Call me when she gets to recovery."

We rang off three hours ago. How hard would it be to pick up the darn phone? I'm sorry her marriage is falling apart, but this is our mother. Our only mother. Marcus is husband number three, and dear God, don't let there be a number four down the line. The family won't survive it.

Busy at the restaurant, Brian still calls me every thirty minutes. He's coming down after the lunch rush, and I'll actually be glad to see him. Loneliness heavies the air.

Because there was no such thing as outpatient surgery back in the sixties, Mom packed a suitcase for both of us, and she stayed overnight with me. After the descent of the scary mask, I remember sitting in the hospital bed and watching the nurse enter with a tray of that famed ice cream they bribe you with.

"You'll get to eat all the ice cream you want!"

Kids, easily fooled by dreams of endless sugar, fall for it. I did. They still do. After her tonsillectomy, Lyra looked at me, the knowledge of my betrayal narrowing her eyes. Yep, I used the same ploy, knowing firsthand she'd take one bite and push the bowl away. Nevertheless, doing so made it easier on me.

Mom unwrapped the flat little wooden spoon and pulled the tab of the cup top to reveal the smooth vanilla coolness inside. She tipped the spoon into the ice cream, dug up a heap, and held it to my mouth. Oh, that frozen sweet mass on my tongue. And then I swallowed. It transmogrified into a substance fiery and glassy and loud. I shook my head as though someone had slapped it from one side, then the other.

One lousy spoonful of ice cream. Great.

We lay in the darkness of the hospital room after watching reruns of *Hogan's Heroes, F-Troop,* and *McHale's Navy* on channel 45, and I remember docking my eyes on Mom's mass beneath the sheets of the bed next to me, hearing her breathing change as sleep took her. And it was good.

The next day an aide walked in, the memory of her as clear as yesterday's chat with Trixie about what it takes to be a nice girl. Short dark hair sprouted from her head, and white plastic hoops, three inches long and shaped like tear drops, dangled from her elongated earlobes. Pale pink lipstick blanched her lips, and Cleopatra eyeliner defined her snappy black eyes.

Mom, hair having reached the proportions of a mushroom cloud, stood near the foot of the bed adjusting the television set. She apologized for her state of disarray.

The woman waved a dramatic hand. "You look sexy! Down-right sexy!"

Mom laughed.

I'd never heard that word before, but I knew it was a compliment.

Nobody's said that about me for years. Even Rusty skirts his way around the word, telling me I'm pretty and sweet and attractive. Oh, dear Lord!

I reach into my purse for a stick of gum. They're packaged in such cute little envelopes these days. So many options. I remember the days of Wrigley's and Black Jack. And that Clove gum! That sure made a kid run and hide from Grandma. My grandmother liked Black Jack too.

Lou, swathed in a leopard-print throw, blows into the waiting room, a jangle of wooden animal-print bangles and gold chains. "Oh, Ivy, I came as soon as I could! Neil called my cell, and the message just came in an hour ago while I was with a client. These cell phones are so untrustworthy."

Now friendship looks like this.

"I brought you some lunch." She pulls a brown bag out of her tiger-print tote. "I stopped by the restaurant and got this from Brian."

I don't feel like eating. "Thanks, sweetie." I set the bag beside me.

"Promise me you'll eat it sometime today."

"I will. Thanks for coming over."

"Would I be anywhere else? Oh right, I brought paint chips with me. Now, I know you don't feel like looking at paint chips, but sometimes it's good to have something else to concentrate on at times like this."

She's right on both counts. "Hand them over."

"Naturally, I'd like to go a tad bold on you, but you'll never go for that, so I'm thinking of some of the new greens. You have to live there, so I'm trying to be sensitive."

"I like these, Lou."

"Honestly?"

"Yeah. This mossy color looks good. Which room is first?"

"I know you want a new couch, but I was thinking of doing the kitchen."

"Oh, Lou. The cabinets are horrible."

"Not if I lacquer them white."

"That's a lot of work."

"I'm up for it if you are, and you know Lyra will help."

"Definitely."

"And Ive-O, you've got to get rid of all those flags. I mean, I'm as patriotic as the next person, but as a decorating scheme, it's positively horrific."

"I'm sick of them myself." I glance at my watch. One thirty. "You'd think she'd be out by now."

"Are they going to do a replacement?"

I nod. "The nurse came out a while ago and told me. Everything's shattered. Socket too. Not surprising, with her osteoporosis."

"It's going to be a long recovery for her. And you."

Boy, she calls that with utter precision.

She reaches into her tote. "Because the self-possessed siblings won't lift a finger."

Boy, she nails that one too.

"Maybe they'll rise to the challenge."

Lou snorts and pulls out a nail clipper, getting to work. Lou's nails contradict her overall appearance. While one might expect a

French manicure or the latest polish, she keeps them unpolished and extremely short. Just like mine.

"Eat the sandwich, Ive-O."

"Okay, okay."

———

My cell phone rings. Great. "Ode to Joy" blasts into the waiting room, which now contains four other people besides me and Lou, who, by the way, convinced me that I needed a tile backsplash above the kitchen counters as well.

Sofa shopping with Rusty is just going to have to wait.

I rustle through my bag, searching for the blinking light. Yes, finally.

Oh no. "Hey Tony."

"Ivy. And how are you this fine day?"

"I'm in the waiting room at GBMC. Mom's in surgery."

"What happened?"

I offer the abridged version. Tony, practically a one-man show at the *Lavalier*, appreciates brevity. "So can you give me an extra day on my deadline?"

"How about tomorrow evening?"

"Okay."

"What's the topic?"

"Don't know."

"Terrific."

"Yeah, tell me about it. Hey, how 'bout an encore piece?"

"Nice try."

"You know, I don't make enough money for you to be so picky."

"It's why they keep me on."

"You're a tough taskmaster."

"No. You're a good columnist. Your readers look forward to what you have to say."

"Keep talking the bull, my friend."

Tony chuckles. "You can do it, sweetie."

Unfortunately, he's right.

———

My mom's never looked smaller than in that hospital bed tonight. Surely she hasn't shrunk that much since the night I stared at her form all those years ago, my throat burning a hole through my neck. By midnight, when I tiptoed out, she slept via drip, and I promised an early return. A foam triangle of mountainous proportions separated and steadied her legs. My inner legs itch just thinking about it. They'll send her home within the week. Along with the triangle.

As I pull out from the hospital, my cell phone rings.

"Mitch?"

"Hey Ivy. I just heard."

"Who told you?"

"Lou. I called her to reminisce, and she said your mom had the surgery today. You okay? You're not too tired to drive home, are you?"

"I'm already on my way. I'll be fine."

"Okay, I'll let you go, then. Just be careful."

"Thanks."

"And I had a really great time the other night."

"Me too."

Rusty's watching a movie in the living room as I enter the house. "Hey hon."

"Hi Rust."

He rises to his feet, surprisingly nimble for his size. That's the thing about Rusty, he wears it well. I guess. "I've got the kettle on and a chamomile bag ready in your cup." He kisses me. "Go get changed, and it'll be ready when you are."

"Thanks, sweetie."

The steps loom. So long and so steep. But I think if I can just get up there the rest will be easy. Inside the bedroom my favorite candle burns, and soft music flows from the CD player on the dresser. I just want to strip, climb in bed, and sleep. And I know Rusty well enough to realize this setup isn't about sex. He's trying to be needed.

I kiss each sleeping child, then wash my face, brush my teeth, and slip on my nightgown. When I emerge from the bathroom, tea steeps in my favorite mug on the bedside table. Rusty sits at the foot of the bed. "Let me rub your head, hon."

I go to him and feel his arms fold about me, and I go limp. Yep, I don't need to move now for a good long time.

Awhile later Rusty asks about Mom and brings me up to speed on the day at King's Dominion, how Persy finally stood tall enough to ride the Rebel Yell, how Trixie's nose burned red as the color Lou's dying to paint the powder room, how Lyra got her period for the first time.

Oh man.

"Really?"

"Yeah. I felt so sorry for her."

"It's like missing her first step or something."

"Sorry, hon."

"That really stinks. She okay?"

"Oh yeah. You know Lyr. Came out of the ladies' room, asked for a dollar and went back in. Of course, I was clueless, and when she came back out ten minutes later I asked her what she needed it for."

"What'd she say?"

"She said, 'I got *it*.' Just like that. *It*."

"That'd be right."

"That's what you say? *It?*"

"Uh-huh."

He laughs. "So anyway, she must've noticed the clueless expression I had on my face, and she leaned close and whispered, 'My period, Dad. I got my period.' She was as red as Trixie's nose."

"Poor girl."

"So is it really that big a deal?"

"Huge. You guys have it so lucky."

"I won't argue with you there. How 'bout that tea?"

How 'bout it? Men hate talking about menstrual things. I don't blame them.

"Get tucked in, hon."

I climb between the sheets and comforter and feel the egg-crate mattress pad accept my weary bones.

Two sips. All I can manage. Good night, newspaper column. See ya in the morning.

———

I awaken at three in the morning remembering when I first got my period. The last girl in my class. Right in the middle of church. I held Mom's large King James Bible behind me over the crimson spot as the congregation flowed from the pews and down the aisle. I made it to the bathroom unnoticed, turned my skirt around, and rinsed it, not very well, watching the pinkened water skip over the folds of cloth and down the drain.

Mrs. Tolsen helped me. She said little, but patted the wet spot patiently, over and over, using the entire supply of brown tri-fold towels from the dispenser on the wall.

"I'll go get your mom, Ivy."

"Thanks, Mrs. Tolsen."

She walked to the door, placed her gnarled hand on the push plate, then turned. "Darn that Eve." Then she disappeared.

Mom and I were the last ones to leave that Sunday, the warm, summer air removing all traces of the event other than the blood-ied panties at the bottom of the ladies' room trash can.

8

I seem to remember some old movie, perhaps an adaptation of *Dante's Inferno,* with people wailing and gnashing and clawing and committing all manner of sin, and Satan standing like an Egyptian captain, feet spread, hands on hips, with his head back and his mouth wide open in devilish laughter. He triumphs, souls writhe in torment, and all because of him…Him…HIM!

But these days, now that I gather in the years to my heart and have seen heartache as it ages, I think Satan laughs hardest at the quiet moments of humankind, those times when a person fails to recognize or receive the lavish grace and mercy sown his way. And there one sits at one's kitchen table alone, silent wreckage all around, lives destroyed or at best limping along. And nowhere to go from here.

Yes, I'm convinced Satan's laugh rings like a bell in the eerie quiet of destruction. He declares in smug satisfaction, "I have destroyed this person. I have taken the image of God within her and crushed it beneath my heel."

He'll have to stop laughing soon enough. Nobody wanders past redemption when God still loves us.

The alarm clock buzzes, and I quickly stifle its voice. Five thirty already. My column awaits. Rusty sleeps peacefully, and I let him slumber on. He'll have the kids all day.

I slip on a pair of boxers and a T-shirt, pull on some socks, and after setting the kettle to heat, I fire up Old Barbara.

Having self-absorbed siblings affords me the luxury of writing whatever I please in my column without fear they'll ever pick up the paper and read it. Today, I'm talking about being there for your family. I'll birth my frustration in print and feel much better before heading to the hospital. I'd hate for Mom's radar to start bleeping, alerting her to the fact that something's bothering me. At least not until she reads the back issues of the *Lavalier*, once recuperated.

The kettle screams, and I jump up, yanking it off the burner before it wakes up one of the kids. I don't need Trixie bugging me right now. I really don't. Love her. Love her better when she sleeps, her blankets swaddling her baby warmth, her cheeks blooming in the heat.

I'm awful.

I reconsider calling her by her full name, Bellatrix. Bellatrixes surely possess a more staid pattern of behavior. Bellatrixes never scream, "Wake up!" right in your ear at 6:00 a.m. Bellatrixes never remove all the laces on all their shoes and tie them end to end, then drag your favorite stuffed animal from childhood around the dirty yard. Bellatrixes go to bed early and wake up late. Bellatrixes play quietly with their dolls. Bellatrixes love vegetables.

Oh well, what can you do?

Oh, Trixie, Trixie. My baby. I do love you so. Maybe I need to pray more. For you. For me. For this broken little family.

———

Column number two comes as easy as microwavable macaroni and cheese. Mr. Moore's wisdom, simple and profound, generates plenty of fodder.

I'm on a roll. You know what gets me? How people justify their sin with some made-up ideology. Take the feminists for example. They wanted to have sex with everybody, get great salaries, and squeeze out children before the biological clock wound down—in other words, do whatever they wanted, whenever they wanted, with whomever they wanted, and curse the rest of the world. But who could do that and justify it on their own? No. They needed a movement. "We'll call it feminism. Yeah, yeah, yeah! And whenever anybody questions our actions, we can point to a higher authority than ourselves. We can get all high and mighty and act like this is all for the greater good. Stuff convention. Stuff the fact that someone else might suffer for our actions. We learned this in college so it must be right! Right?"

Feminist studies.

Look alive, girls! If you can't be a woman by the seat of your pants, you can't begin to claim the honors. That's what makes us who we are, we feline wonders, who, when suddenly falling from the heights, can twist, turn, assume a proper vista of the situation, and land on our feet. We are the ultimate survivalists, the potentates of practicality. We've lived that "Just Do It" slogan since the garden. Let's face it. As the original sinner, Eve was the one responsible for original sin, but Adam still takes the brunt, as in "In Adam all die." In this, I do believe the soft spot God feels for women shows itself. After all, we may bear our children in pain, but we also feel the first movements of that tiny parcel of humanity inside of us. We nurture and protect the very beginning of life. Somehow God entrusts us with this very thing, the most important act of being human. I for one am grateful.

I say, "You go, girl!" and mean it with the fullness of my heart.

I click Save and whiz this column and the other two off to Tony. My feminist readers will e-mail flames, and I'll love it. And now, with three in the bag, I'll be free to care for Mom next week. Thank you, God, for this bit of grace.

Can't wait to hear the phone call from Tony. I'd better start formulating my arguments right away.

———

I actually shower and dress before the crew awakens. As I try to cover up my dark circles, Rusty hums downstairs, and that telltale sputter awakens my nose to the aroma of the coffee. Now tea accompanies me through the wee hours just fine, but coffee is the great awakener. Something spiny and operatic swims inside it, something longing to bop you on the head and scream in your ear. I hurry through the rest of my "toilette," as my grandmother called it, to steal a few moments with Rusty. I've thought about Mitch way too much even with my husband home. I need to bolster myself, to attack the problem at its source.

He sits at the kitchen table sipping from a mug emblazoned with the name of some small recording studio in Nashville, maybe, or Memphis, the type of place that lays down the tracks of a gospel barbershop quartet. The popularity they've been gaining in this day and age of hip-hop and technopop amazes me. Rusty, a true performer, plays the part well. But at home he's so different, so placid and peaceful. I used to love that he saves that precious part of himself for us.

Keep talking him up, Ivy. Don't meander down the stupid path.

A mug, a packet of sweetener, and a spoon rest on a paper towel in front of the coffee maker. I reach for the pot. "Get a good sleep, Rust?"

"Not bad. Probably better than you did after all that happened yesterday. You doing all right, hon?"

I fix my drink. "Yeah. Sent three columns to Tony this morning, so that's off my chest. I'm going to toast an english muffin, then head on back to the hospital."

"Just sit. I'll get it for you."

I pull out a chair, take a sip of coffee, and hold my head in my hands. "You know, Rust, I'm going to have to bring her home here to recuperate."

"I figured as much. Hopefully she'll be out in a few days, and I can help you with the hard part."

"Brett's place would be so much better, with that guest room on the main floor, a housekeeper three days a week. But if I so much as hint at it, she'll blow up."

"She's having it really rough right now." He shakes his head. "Not that it excuses her."

Good boy.

"I know. I feel like I can't ask anything of her. I'm sure she's thinking, 'Why me? Why now?' as far as Mom's concerned, even though it won't really affect her one iota."

Rusty leans down and kisses my cheek. "It's a good thing Dorothy has you." Rusty calls my mom Dorothy, like she's more than just a mother-in-law, she's a dear friend. Which is true. If Mom and I weren't so close, I'd be jealous.

"Even if Brett did take her in, it wouldn't be for long, and she'd never let the rest of us forget her largesse. I don't want to be forever in her debt that way."

"I'm sure your mother doesn't want that either."

True. But right now, I'm sure my mom has yet to think of it. I'm sure she's awakened, felt the pain, and wondered when they'll unstrap that ungodly foam triangle.

"Darn that Marcus. Why now?"

"Bad things come in threes." Rusty sets the muffin in front of me. "Here you go, Ive. Eat up. You don't know when your next meal will be today."

"I hate hospital food."

"Well, hon, you can always get around that."

I take a big bite of the muffin for his benefit. He slathered on so much butter it literally drips down my chin and onto my clean T-shirt, the last clean T-shirt in my drawer.

Drat! Can't even one little thing be easy today, Lord? Well, maybe I can count that as the third bad thing.

Rusty sits down. "I have an idea. Why don't I go in for an hour or two this morning? Then you can come in around ten, and I'll take Trixie to the bowling alley. She's first up on the Daddy Date List."

"Bowling?"

"She's talked about nothing else since I got home."

Wow, that was a quick answer to prayer.

He points to the phone book atop the fridge. "I'll call the medical supply company and get a bed delivered."

"Thanks, Rust."

He needs to be home here with us. He's better at this stuff than I am. Lord, make him stay. Make him want to stay.

———

Mom sits up in the bed drinking a cup of tea. "Hello, dear!"

"Hi Mom."

"I'm so glad Rusty came. I was hoping I didn't have to eat breakfast by myself."

The tray still rests on the cart.

"Some breakfast."

"I know. I'm not on solids yet. Beef broth for breakfast. Whoever heard the like? And did it need salt. But they put me on the high-blood-pressure diet. I have high blood pressure. I never knew."

"Well, it's a good thing they've caught it."

"I suppose. But truthfully, ignorance would have suited me just fine."

"Maybe it's just due to the surgery. They would have caught it well before now." I scrape up a chair. "Well, you ate good."

"Rusty convinced me of the need."

"You'll need all the strength you can get for rehab."

"Ugh. They tell me I'll be out of here in four days, five tops."

"Good."

"Although I don't know how I'll make it up the steps to my apartment."

"You won't have to. Rusty's setting up the dining room for you. We're going to bring in a bed, and you'll be all set."

"Are you sure?"

"Of course." I wave my hand, hoping the words *nonchalant* and *Ivy* intersect flawlessly. "Piece of cake."

Piece of cake, my foot. Trixie will be all over her.

She sighs. "Well, that's one load off my mind."

"Good." I really mean that.

My father is a jerk. Mom put up with so much of Harry's abuse, she doesn't deserve to suffer through this without the support of at least one of us.

She pushes the tray farther from her. "I can help Lyra with her sewing. I've been wanting to sit down with her and do that for a long time now. There's just never been a good time."

"Well, you'll have plenty of that. And since Lyra's out of school for the summer, I'm sure she'll be glad for it. Rusty'll be there the first week you're home too. He'll look after things while I'm at the restaurant."

"Oh, Brian came by early this morning. I was so glad to see him."

Figures he arrived first.

"Good. He says he doesn't need me around today, so I'll be here all day."

My family abides by a set of screwy regulations. When somebody is in the hospital, it's of paramount importance that someone blood-related attend the bedside almost twenty-four hours a day. When my grandmother went in for heart surgery, Mom and Grandpop took turns at the vigil. I'd run in from my classes at Towson State around suppertime and sit with her while they had a bite down at the cafeteria. Heaven forbid they'd take an extra thirty minutes and head out for some decent food at a real restaurant, and not our restaurant either. I hope someday I don't end up in the hospital for long. The nonstop visitation would drive me crazy.

She sips the weak tea. "Ugh. This is horrible. I'd love a good cup of coffee."

"I'll call Brian and tell him to bring you one when he comes in after the lunch rush."

"Don't bother. He said he's got appointments this afternoon and tonight, which is why he came in so early."

I don't say what I'm thinking.

"I'll call Rusty. He can bring a decent cup by later on his way back from the bowling alley." Good old Rusty.

"Thanks, dear."

Rusty says fine. He'll drop off some Starbucks on his way to Persy's game.

"Oh man. I forgot about the game. I am so sorry."

"No prob, hon."

I hang up the phone.

"I'm going to meet Rusty down in the lobby a little later."

"Thank you, dear. I'm sure Brian would have come if he'd been able to."

"Mom—"

Oh, never mind. Let her think he hung the moon for now. She'll see his stripes in two weeks, three tops.

———

The phone rings at 5:00 a.m.

"Hey sis."

"Bri?"

"I can't get to the market this morning."

"Why? Are you okay?"

"I'm on my way home right now. I'll tell you about it later. I really need some sleep."

"Are you coming in for lunch?"

"I already called Matty. He'll run the kitchen."

"Are you hung over?"

"…"

"Okay, I'll take care of things."

"You're a peach."

"Yeah, yeah."

A verifiable peach.

No sense trying to get back to sleep with my blood churning and curdling this way. Rusty's whistle-snore warbles away, so I claim the wee hours for myself. Oh, God, give me strength. Make me a morning person. Please, please.

I've prayed this at least once a week for the past fourteen years. So far God has only given me the same answer He gave Paul regarding his thorn in the flesh.

I fix my cup of tea and settle in at the computer. I should work on a new column; Tony hated the antifeminist one, and I failed to convince him of its merits. But boy, did that feel good to write! I think I'll write about the insignificance of an organized pantry in the grand scheme of living. I'm going to write about the messy things of life, like love and family and watching your children become their own persons who will make many mistakes. One error they shouldn't make, however, is thinking they're better people if their pantries are organized or they can actually make it through a year of Bible Study Fellowship or a Beth Moore book.

I've never made it through either one of those, and the Lord knows I've tried. I want desperately to be one of those people God ushers gently aside for a time of rejuvenation and growth. But so far I'm still careening to the right on the Snow Emergency Route of faith. I don't just lean on the everlasting arms, I weigh them down. I wonder why God isn't sick of me yet, and for every situation I handle with grace, two bovine scenarios precede it. For every word seasoned with salt, four are covered in crushed aspirin.

So maybe this column will sit well with Tony. I hope so. He's such a gentleman, but I know that two blathering columns in a row might raise even his temperature a bit. And I'll ruin what little Christian testimony I have with him. God, I hope he doesn't think all Christians are like me.

Harry wasn't all bad. He didn't mind taking us to the movies. He loved movies. I think he secretly longed to play meaty parts on stage and screen. I can easily picture him as a great actor, especially in roles containing a large measure of feigned contrition. He proclaimed Sunday afternoons "our time." He'd pop popcorn on top of the stove, drizzle on the melted butter, shake on the salt, and sit with us watching channel 67's movie lineup. Movies like *Play Misty for Me* or *The Chalk Garden*. And you have to love those old actress names like Piper and Greer.

Bellatrix? Perseus? Lyra? What were we thinking?

He'd call up the steps, "Come on, gang! The movie's starting!" A trilling undercurrent in his voice twanged like a Jew's harp and betrayed his thought: if he didn't put in his time with us then, when he enjoyed it too, he might end up doing something horrible, like taking us to our swim meets or, heaven forbid, church.

Every Sunday morning Mom readied us all, and we slipped out early for Sunday school before my father woke up. At eight years old I got miffed at him for not attending with us. Would that have been so hard? It would have meant so much to Mom. But Mom, in her typical Mom fashion, said, "Pray for him, Ivy. He needs the Lord."

He still needs the Lord. All these years later, all these prayers later, Harry still repeats the same mistakes, and he still needs the Lord.

This fact alone keeps me from pulling the plug on him. I feel terrible about that, as if my relationship with him is transactional, a mere sales pitch for a close walk with almighty God and a one-way ticket to heaven. But it is what it is. And if tolerating my dad is only obedience to my heavenly Father, so be it. I see no other choice I am capable of carrying out.

Do I love him?

In the sense of "love your neighbor as yourself," yes, I love him. But do I love him as a daughter? Well, I take a pulse on that every so often, and today I'd have to say no. See, I called him and told him about Mom's accident, and he only said, "Tell her to cheer up and get well soon!"

Like some pathetic greeting card. I went so far as to ask him if he planned to visit her, and he only said, "You know me and hospitals don't get along, babe."

He only said. He only said.

And I hung up.

———

The replacement column's finished and off to Tony. Martha Stewart would hate it. An e-mail came through just as I sent my piece, so I take a few minutes to check my messages. Oh great. Angel again. An avid reader of my column, although I can't understand why she keeps skimming the lines. She never writes anything positive. You'd think maybe she'd try to live up to her name. Unless, of course, she's going for some apocalyptic being sowing destruction on the end-times survivors.

> Once again, Ms. Schneider, we disagree. I find it hard to believe that there is a human being alive with whom I can find no common ground. I always try to see the best in people, look at life through their eyes. Maybe you should try this yourself.

Yak. Yak. Yak.

Delete.

It's not that I don't care what my readers think, I really do. But I have a feeling Angel enjoys playing the part of devil's advocate. I don't know where she finds the time.

Next.

Lou sent pictures of various borders and wallpaper patterns for the kitchen. I like them all. How am I supposed to choose? Everything looks good, yet everything constitutes a change. I hit Reply and type, "Like them all. You choose."

She'll love that.

Next. Oh goody. I can have my male member enlarged. That keeps me up nights. And Viagra at sixty percent off. I can refinance from three different mortgage brokers or order refurbished ink cartridges at a much-reduced rate.

Who orders those things?

I scan the clock in the corner of the screen. It's late enough to call Brett to see if she'll sit with Mom while I man the restaurant.

"Ivy! How in the world can I? I mean, you're calling at the last minute, and at an ungodly hour, mind you. I do have plans, you know. I do have a life."

Oh, that's right. I don't have one. I forgot for just a sec.

"But Mom's going to be by herself all morning and most of the afternoon, then."

"Oh please. She'll be fine. She can't expect us to be down there with her every waking moment."

"You know she does."

"Well, it's too much to expect."

"What are you doing this morning anyway?"

"The girls have hair appointments, and we're meeting Marcus for lunch."

"Really?" Sound positive. Don't act needy.

"He's broken it off with that other woman."

"And you're taking him back?" Cloak the shock.

"It's the first time he's done this. I feel I ought to forgive him this once."

"Just keep your eyes peeled from now on."

"Don't worry! I forgive him. Doesn't mean I'll ever trust him a wink."

"Okay. If those are terms you can live with. I'll figure something out from this end about Mom." An idea interrupts. "Or, hey, can Rusty take the girls to their appointment maybe? And you can go sit with Mom? Or maybe the girls can drive themselves?"

I hold my breath. Please oh please oh please.

"Let me think for a sec. I mean, Rusty knows nothing about hair. And the girls will try and get away with some serious changes if someone's not there. I don't know, Ivy."

Think quick!

"Well, how about if you write down what's supposed to be done and he can give it to the beautician? Or…you can have her call you on your cell phone to get the scoop right from the horse's mouth."

I hear her nails tapping, probably on her mug. "Well, okay."

"Great! Just stay until lunchtime. Where are you meeting Marcus?"

"Over at the Towson House."

"Okay, and see? The hospital's only a couple minutes from there! I'll have Rusty drop Ashley and Margeaux off at the restaurant as soon as they're finished."

"Okay." I'm sure she's gripping the phone and shaking her head. "Thanks, Brett."

"Sure. But you owe me one."

What?!

She hangs up before I can blare an air-horn scream of frustration. I should let the yell fly anyway, but I'll be darned if I'll wake up those kids a moment too soon.

———

When did I become my mother's keeper? How did my shoulders end up as platforms for the rest of the family's feet? Brett's the oldest, the most idle, really. Shouldn't this be up to her?

Never mind. Heavenly rewards. Golden crowns to cast at the feet of Jesus. Of course, my attitude might render them nothing more than wood, hay, and stubble. But as an old friend of mine, a lady named Tanzel, says, "Praise God I'll be there to watch it burn!"

The e-mail harp chimes.

Mitch.

My breath catches in my throat, and I remember how he hugged me and hung on my every word. I remember his own pain and disappointment.

Hey Ive,

Didn't want to bother you on the phone. Things must be hectic. Just wanted you to know I've been thinking about you and your mom and hoping she's improving. You need anything, I'm here.

Mitch

———

Trixie sings in her crib. I should leave her be. She'll stay put a good half hour. I sit on the top step and listen. She inherited Rusty's singing ability, her tones clearer and purer than anything Evian ever could bottle. It's all I can do not to laugh, however. She's crooning a song off of Lyra's Good Charlotte CD. A song called "The Anthem."

"It's a new day, but it all feels old. It's a good life, that's what I'm told."

And how can guys that young already feel the way I do approaching my forties?

I feel sorry for little girls with teenage sisters. No "Mary Had a Little Lamb" or "Bear Went Over the Mountain" for Trixie. She sings mild punk music, Creed, and gospel rock. And the Beatles. Lyra's navigating a Beatles phase right now. Fine by me.

Rusty's voice joins her from the bedroom. "Don't wanna be just like you." Only he's harmonizing, and darn it if that little thing in the crib doesn't stick with the melody line. I can't wait to see the plans God's drawn up for my youngest.

I rush past Trixie's door before she can spot me.

Rusty smiles from where he sits on the edge of the bed shoving bare feet into loafers. Wow, I didn't even hear the shower. Must've taken it when I was on the phone with Brett. Or reading Mitch's e-mail.

My face burns.

He stands up with a groan. "So what's the game plan for today?"

I turn away and pretend to search my jewelry box. "You'll hardly believe where I have you going."

"Spill it, hon."

"How does a trip to the beauty parlor sound?" I turn around.

Rusty shakes his head at the whole arrangement, regurgitates it all back at me to make sure he understands, and finishes with, "I'm doing this for Dorothy and for you."

"I know, Rust. Thanks."

He hugs me, and because I must, I rest awhile. A very little while, because Trixie, having climbed out of her crib, crashes into us. Her little arms feel so good against my legs. "Mama! Daddy!"

———

I check my e-mail one last time before I leave for the restaurant. The cooks have everything under control, so I'm not too worried. Truth is, I don't obsess about the business. I never wanted my life to revolve around the place. I pictured myself building a writer's shed out in the backyard, à la Annie Dillard, with nothing inside but an old metal army-issue desk from Sunny's Surplus, a chair, a cot, an old Royal, and a hot pot for tea. I'd hang old quilts and art posters on the walls to hide the two-by-fours.

The short stories would come first, brilliant ones, of course, and then the novels, important ones that exposed an evil or lifted up a forlorn, heretofore uncelebrated segment of humanity. I would voice the plight of the downtrodden, the lame. I would champion their existence, honor their lives, and vilify their enemies. I would fight for justice. I'd have an important-sounding pen name like Margaret James or Anne Standish.

Yet I have to admit I get a kick out of the daily specials and enjoy being the first to taste a new dish, and I did write the descriptions of dishes on the new menu, no purple prose there. But I set my dream in the warming oven, hoping that someday, when Rusty's exhausted his dreams, when his gifts have depleted their present expression, my hopes will tap my shoulder and demand a proper audience. Every so often I pull up a password-protected file on my computer and gaze upon my lofty ideas, wondering which ones, if any, will find the daylight. Kind of like the survivors of the capsized *Poseidon* journeying from that grand ballroom up to the bottom of the ship's hull. "There's got to be a morning after." Yeah, that sounds like my life.

I check the new messages to see if Tony received the column.

Yep. And it's a keeper. What a relief. Certainly some columnists' initial offerings are perfect. Not mine. I've knitted this darn column for years, and one would think I'd eventually stop dropping stitches. Instead, each week unravels my confidence, and sometimes I look down at a mangy pile of knots and loops and wonder why I'm still at it.

Yes. He thinks it has "widespread appeal." Good.

Only two other e-mails. One titled, "Danielle says Meow!"

Delete.

The other, from my "Odd Fan," as Lyra calls her. Kirsten writes me more than Angel and always agrees with me, but something creepy laces her notes.

Dear Ivy,

I so appreciated your column this week! As always. You somehow say exactly what I'm feeling. By the way, I stopped reading your columns to Mother. They always anger her and she fears, with the way you encourage us women to be strong, that I'll end up leaving home and where would she find herself then? You're more of a feminist than you think, I gather.

I've begun clipping your articles out of the paper and decoupaging them to plaques. The wall surrounding my headboard is halfway full! Mother never comes up the steps, because, you might remember, she is an invalid and resides on the main floor. But your columns do so inspire me. If you ever need a copy of one, just let me know.

Spooky!

I hit Reply.

Dear Kirsten,

Thanks, as always, for your encouraging e-mail. I always love to hear from readers, especially those who agree with me! Best regards to you and your mother.

Lyra wanders in, bleary-eyed and looking cuter than Hello Kitty in pink pajama bottoms with little owls all over them. The T-shirt matches.

"Got a note from the Odd Fan. You're not going to believe this. Go ahead and read it."

She leans closer to the monitor. "Oh, good grief. Decoupage now?"

"Yeah. Guess the scrapbook got full."

"Still, you've got to feel a little sorry for her. Chained there to that invalid mother."

"At least they're rich."

I know exactly what house they live in, because Kirsten's described it to me. The large white Victorian sits nearby in Old Lutherville. The gardens are amazing, and Kirsten takes care of them herself, though the house looks like it's dying for a coat of paint. Naturally, I've no plans to divulge my own location, and I never mention the restaurant. I may be opinionated, but I'm not stupid.

I delete her e-mail. "Well, at least it's not from that guy down in Jessup."

Jessup houses one of Maryland's penitentiaries. Like anybody down there is penitent about anything.

"Most definitely." Lyra scratches her ankle. Poor thing suffers with eczema. "Weren't you supposed to be gone by now?"

"Yeah, I'm heading. Daddy tell you about the hair salon jaunt?"

"Uh-huh. We're all going. He's going to drop them off, and we're heading to the park."

"Cool."

"Some visit for Dad."

She's not saying it to be nasty. It's just the truth.

"Maybe you can wear Trixie out."

"Yeah right, Mom."

It's sad. While Lyra loves her little sister, she doesn't like her at all. This grieves me. It's unlike Lyra to take such a disliking to someone, but Trixie is a trial. I know this. I can't force her to reach out to her sister on that kind of level, especially when Trixie's behavior, lots of mean faces, and get-away-from-me-Lyries do nothing but antagonize her. Still, Trixie's only three. If these two had their own rooms it would make a big difference, but we can't afford a four-bedroom house, and honestly, the thought of moving all our junk, with Rusty gone to boot, is more frightening than finding Osama bin Laden in my attic.

———

Matty crosses his arms and stares at me like I'm intruding. I mean, yes, I do own this kitchen, actually. However, I've been around cooks enough to know they stake out their domain, and heaven help anyone who trespasses.

"Okay, I'm sorry I asked if the prep work is finished. So what's the lunch special?"

We stand out back. He smokes a Dunhill Menthol; I chew on a fingernail.

"We've got two. I went to the market this morning. Had some beautiful rockfish."

"Okay, rockfish. What else?"

"Garret's doing a blackened burger with Havarti and beefsteak tomatoes on seared sourdough bread."

"Mmm. I'll have one of those myself. And a taste of the fish, too."

He can't help but smile. Matty's got about three years of kitchen experience and ten years of attitude. He also possesses twenty years of charm. He wears the burn marks on his arms with pride. The battle scars of the kitchen professional. Garret awarded him the best one when Matty opened Garret's broiler to check on a filet of sole ready to burn. Garret grabbed a hot broiler plate and slammed it against Matty's inner arm, leaving a line the length of an unsharpened pencil and almost as thick.

"Okay then. I'll be out front."

"You'd better be. Sorry about your brother, though, Ivy."

"I'm sure he's fine."

"Yeah, but a DUI. Dang."

A DUI?!

Okay, I guess the butter on the T-shirt didn't count as number three after all.

I'm going to kill him.

Rusty's filled with a lot more sympathy than I am.

"Oh Ive. He needed a lesson, and this could be it."

"Rusty! He totally denied it was his fault."

"He's just scared."

"I hope so. I hope he's scared to death."

"Well, at least you had a good day at the restaurant."

Good. He doesn't want to talk about it either.

"Oh yeah. Those guys ran the kitchen like clockwork."

Rusty chuckles. "Anybody get a burn?"

"Nope. They behaved themselves."

He rises from the kitchen table where we're drinking a late-night cup of tea. "That just tickles me. I had no idea chefs behaved that way."

"They're very territorial."

"Well, maybe that's a good thing. Makes cooking macho."

Yep, still a very male profession.

"Thanks for doing all that today, Rust."

"Sure. You know, it's providential that this all happened when I was home. I don't know how you would have done it by yourself."

"Me either."

"You're a good woman, Ivy."

So stay home this time, Rusty. Get a job here and help me.

But I don't say it. Why?

Because apparently I'm not important enough.

I can't sleep. Big surprise there. Sometimes that's okay. Sometimes God uses those times to draw me into communion with Him. He reminds me that no matter what's going on around me—crumbling marriages, DUIs, broken hips—He's busy with plans of redemption. Not just for the people I love, but for me, too. He is the Great Physician, as so many people call Him. Able to heal not just physical troubles, but emotional, marital, and spiritual trials. He loves Brian. He loves Brett. He loves Mom. He loves Rusty and Lyra and Persy and little Trixie. He loves me.

God loves me.

A basic understanding of that overwhelming love grows inside me. God loves all His children. Even Harry.

The thought actually comforts me.

So I cast all my cares upon Him. Jesus told me to do that, to come unto Him. And if I don't, if I think He doesn't care about all this, I'm questioning Him and calling Him a liar.

It's tempting, actually, to hang on to trouble. And sometimes I succumb, pulling into myself, trying to convince myself I can handle my life just fine, fine, fine. In fact, sometimes I turn rather holier-than-thou about it, as if I'm doing God a favor by not bothering Him. How ridiculous, because in His omniscience, because He feels the pain of His creation, He's already bothered in a way. He feels the groaning. He knows our frame. He remembers we are dust.

I groan softly. Begging Him to work, to blow in like a cleansing wind, to stay true to His promise that He is not slack, that He will provide a way of escape, that all things work together for the good of those who love Him and, in that great omniscience, all those who will love Him. Brian will love God someday. Someday he will stand with the great throng and bow his knee with every knee and confess with every tongue that Jesus Christ is Lord. To the glory of God the Father.

I can trust Him. He is not a liar.

I lie in the dark stillness of my room, consumed by the brightness of His love, His purity, the cleansing fire of His wondrous mercy that will one day abolish all sin, all death, all rebellion. All unfaithfulness, all addiction, all pain, and all loneliness.

9

I remember the trunk of my mother's olive green Chrysler Newport. When we packed up for our family vacations, Harry actually stood our suitcases up in a row. Seven of them across the trunk, easily arranged. When the auto manufacturers reduced the area, the bickering began. Our first flat-trunked car being the Chrysler Cordoba, Ricardo Montalban and his Corinthian leather, and really, does Corinth even exist anymore? Mom was actually more spatially minded, but my father failed to see that, let alone admit it. Perhaps he would now. Who knows?

One day Mom pulled up to the house, the trunk of the Newport filled with red plastic ten-gallon water jugs. They stood politely together, like a line of red-caped troubadours patiently waiting to woo the princess. Mom recruited Brian to unload the trunk and haul the containers into the kitchen.

"What are we doing?" Brett asked Mom.

"We're storing up water."

"Why?"

"They're planning on poisoning the reservoir at Loch Raven."

Loch Raven Reservoir lay three or four miles from our split-level home in Lutherville.

I didn't think to ask who "they" were. According to the John Birchers, "they" were always up to mischief somewhere or other.

But here we are in the new millennium and no communist take-over yet. No doubt their attention has turned to the Middle East these days.

Mom filled the bottles, and Brian dragged several down to the lower level. The remaining two ended up in the front hall closet between the wall and a green vinyl vacuum-cleaner box with a hinged lid. Our closets were famous for junk. But this square box held moldering treasure galore: sweaters with rusty zippers, old tennis racquets I'd strap to my feet with yarn and pretend were snowshoes (Harry had a fit the first time I did this and ruined the strings), old hats, gloves, scarves, and a stuffed lamb with a tinkle bell inside. Oh, and my parents' duckpin bowling balls from their bowling-league days. Each had a little trophy on the desk in our living room. Mom's said: LAST-PLACE CHAMPS. I think they had more fun back then.

My father arrived home from his optometry practice that night, upset about something as usual. Mom clicked in from the kitchen on her high heels, spatula in hand. They never kissed hello. I think that stopped sometime before I was born. In fact, I've often wondered how I was even conceived. I hate to admit it, but Harry grew happier after he left.

"Dinner's almost ready, Harry."

Harry hung up his suit coat. "What the heck are these red bottles?"

Only he didn't say heck.

"Peggy Robinson got word they're going to poison the water."

And Harry said nothing. Even now, I wonder that he didn't ask who, or say a word further.

Now I know there were some things better left unsaid.

Maybe Harry got tired of being married to a nut. Maybe he got tired of living with a woman who lived in fear.

———

I shouldn't feel guilty, but I do. If only Mom would complain, I might feel vindicated about my inner grumblings. But she bears up under the rehab with a grim smile. She does, however, mumble at the demonic foam appliance she must keep between her legs. How in the world anyone can grab a single wink with that thing, let alone an entire night, mystifies me. But then I've never been a great sleeper. Have to have a fan running, total darkness, and my own pillow.

We brought her to our house yesterday. Brett mercifully drove her sedan, as Mom could just as easily climb the Matterhorn as climb into my Blazer right now. Of course, Brett will count this as having done her part for the next month, I'm sure.

And now that Mom's here, I can bet my life and the life of my children that I won't get any offers of help from my siblings. I hate seeing my mom like this, the woman who never traipsed outside without makeup and heels. I heard it all the time. "Your mom is so pretty. Your mom always looks so nice." She looks old, and I don't quite know what to do with that truth.

Brett's "on a second honeymoon" now. Marcus planned a trip to Aruba, just the two of them, next week. Mom, who never really trusted Marcus, admits mixed emotions, but believing in the sanctity of marriage and knowing the fallout of fidelity gone awry, she hopes for the best. I do too, I have to admit.

Mom has always been strong. Physically and emotionally. But when my father left, she told the truth, laying out his shortcomings before her children in a way psychologists would frown upon. She probably just didn't know what else to do.

She sat us in a line on the couch. I was twelve, Brian fourteen, Brett sixteen. She twisted her wedding band around her finger. "Well, Dad's gone."

"Where to?" Brett.

"With *her*."

Brett nodded and looked down. Brian cursed.

"Brian. Please." Mom.

I said, "Who's 'her'?"

"Janice."

"Why would he leave with a girl named Janice?"

"He loves her."

A hot flush filled up my cheeks. "Doesn't he love us anymore?"

Mom shook her head. "I don't know." She grabbed my knee. "But of course he'll always love you kids."

I began to cry. But he loved Janice more. Even at twelve I could do the math.

Mom sat beside me. "But I can tell you, I'm not going anywhere. We'll see this thing through together."

"He left before and came back." Brian.

"He did?" I asked.

They all nodded.

Mom put her arm around me. "I didn't think you were old enough to know those other times, Ivy. I just told you he was away at conventions."

It's not like Harry was ever close to us. An arbitrary melody in our lives, he sang his own descant at will, leaving the true composing to my mother. The sad part? As devastating as the news seemed to be, it ended up making very little difference in the day to day.

Dear God, if I die suddenly, I hope a tizzy erupts. I hope I'm that necessary.

Brian leaned forward. "But he may come back this time too, right?"

Mom stared him in the eyes, her own eyes drooping into her dark circles. "I told him if he left this time, I was done. That I'd never take him back again. He left anyway, Bri."

"So you've decided for us that we won't have a father around?" He bit his bottom lip.

Brett turned on him, a fierce glow in her brown eyes. "No. He decided he didn't want to be one, Bri. Big difference. Don't you ever say anything like that again! Mom's not to blame! Dad's a creep. Face it. He's scum!"

Brian ran from the room. A few seconds later, his bedroom door slammed shut.

"Brian makes me so mad." Brett.

Mom stood up. "It's okay, sweetie. He's got a lot to deal with. You all do. But we have to be a team or this isn't going to work."

Brett ended up in her room too, and I went grocery shopping with Mom, like we always did on Thursday afternoons. She said yes to everything I asked for, including the large, clear, glittery rubber ball that still lays in my nightstand drawer.

Well, I wish we tackled life that way now. Go team, go, and all that. As soon as Brett and Brian got their driver's licenses, they began carting me around to and from school, sports activities, and—when I reached ninth grade—my student internship at the *Lavalier*. I really should move on from that paper, but Baltimore holds on to me like Elizabeth Taylor holds on to her diamonds.

I suppose they feel they paid their dues on the front end of our odyssey. And maybe they're right. Maybe that's why I feel like I can't speak up. Maybe that's why I can't stand my father. I can point to that day we three lined up on the couch as the beginning of it all.

Well, time to get up and ready the kids for church. I haven't sat through an entire service since Trixie was thirteen months old and assumed the throne as the Robespierre of the nursery. No children's worker will assume responsibility for her, and I don't blame them one iota. At least she graduated from the baby section a while ago. Now she wreaks havoc in the twos and threes, where her peers are a bit more capable of defending themselves. She seems to gravitate to the boys, which only comforts me because if she hits them, most of them hit her back, and harder. She's learning not to hit. Still, I repeatedly catch her trying to whack the other kids over the head with one of the puzzles.

But during song time, she sits quietly, joining in with her sweet strains, until "I've got the joy, joy, joy, joy down in my heart" begins, at which time, she runs around in circles shaking her booty like a dancer in a rap video. Lord, help us all.

They don't sing that song as much as they used to.

I have a feeling Trixie will stumble through life misunderstood, and people will employ all sorts of guilt, shame, and bribery to turn down her volume to a more acceptable, conventional level. And a God-made piece of her will die. Somewhere, someday, a teacher, or several of them, will try to redefine her. And I'll become one of those harping mothers who knows her child is difficult but expects everyone else to deal with it. Maybe I'll homeschool her.

Or stick a fork in my foot.

I quickly shower and throw on some cover-up and blush. Thank goodness the smaller ones bathed last night. Hand off the toast, slip on the clothing, and they'll be set. Lyra, however, requires at least an hour to ready herself. Much to Baltimore Gas and Electric's delight and my checkbook's chagrin, she discovered the joys of long hot showers and feels the need to shave her legs every single day. Now I must ask myself, who is she doing this for? Lyra's never had a boyfriend, has never ever felt the need to like a guy just to like a guy. So why this penchant for leg shaving? Well, truly, it's none of my business. If she's one of those hyperhygienic chicks you meet every so often, the ones that wouldn't dream of going a day without a shower, so what?

As for me, the luxury of a daily shower seems more impossible than Rusty coming home for good.

We're off. Rusty's singing with the choir as well as performing a solo, so he's somewhat more quiet than usual. Earlier I heard him practicing in the shower a Keith Green song called "You Put This Love in My Heart." He tries not to sing barbershop unless the occasion requires it. I mean, nothing but tight harmonies and slipping and sliding from one note to the other all year long must bore him silly. He enjoys venturing out.

I actually administered a healthy dose of Children's Advil to Trixie before piling everyone into the car, which smells of the corned beef sandwich I left in here yesterday. Determined to hear Rusty sing, I figure she'll be out like a Quaker at the RNC before the second congregational song. She already looks bleary-eyed sitting there in her car seat, and I offer a prayer of thanks. Not that drugging your child really constitutes the best means of behavior modification, but Trixie has almost nothing in common with Spiro Agnew when it comes to bribery. Even pizza at the bowling alley holds no leverage on a Sunday.

Rusty wings off to the choir room for practice. Persy and Lyra migrate toward the Sunday school rooms, and I usher Trixie to her class, where I sit and monitor her every move and mutter. Right away she tugs on her teacher's slacks and displays the new underwear she's wearing for the first time today.

I let it go. Not worth it.

She's mellowing by the minute though, so I pull out a copy of *Confessions* and hold my own private Sunday school. I like Augustine's writings because the lifestyle he led before converting makes them all the more profound. Kind of like the apostle Paul. I mean, the man was murdering Christians, for heaven's sake, running coat check for stoning parties, and Christ still grabbed him by the neck scruff and swung him onto The Way. Augustine, well, he was a garden-variety sinner. Sort of the Colin Farrell of the fourth century: party boy, lusty fellow. But his mother, Monica, never stopped praying for him. So really, his writings also testify to her faithfulness. It kind of explains his hardnosed outlook.

Let's face it, everything circles back to us women. God gives life through us and trusts us to sustain the most valuable of His creations. We cradle the human soul made in His image. And when that soul emerges in its fleshy casing, we can expect Him to keep His promises. I shut the book and pray for Trixie as she heads toward the puzzles.

Sunday school's half over, and Trixie fades more quickly than a seventy-year-old during a boring sermon. I decide to carry her up to the sanctuary and rock her for a bit.

Just as I walk in, Brenda Burkendine approaches me. Oh great. Brenda heads up our women's ministries and believes that Priscilla's Gathering, which meets every Wednesday morning, answers all of life's ills. Maybe it does. I only went once and felt like a niggling spacer between healthy teeth. Honestly, our church attracts a lot of wealthy people, and either you fit in, or you're simply tolerated, loved "in the Lord," and not much else. I don't know why the poor, weird women don't see it. They're projects.

I'm so judgmental of rich people. I'm horrible. God loves them, too, and I'm supposed to but find it so hard. I'm jealous. It's that simple. When you grow up in spiffed-up clothes from the Salvation Army and your sister's hand-me-downs, which were outdated when she first got them, something grows inside you that's hard to extract. Maybe I should find some snappy, upstart congregation downtown. A church disguised as a wi-fi coffeehouse or something.

Brenda sees me and skids to a stop in her designer pumps, her designer handbag bumping against her designer jacket. She looks just like the character from some chick-lit book, but of course, she's older than that, has a husband, and all her accouterment is paid for. She employs a full-time housekeeper, holds no job, and still acts like she's busy all the time. Well, it's only because she chooses to be. It wasn't foisted upon her.

Why do I continue to come to this church with such a bad attitude?

God help me. I mean that.

Something's got to give inside me, or I'll become the bitter pill everyone around me is forced to swallow.

She tucks the sides of her perfectly colored and cut modern pageboy behind her ears. I'll bet those diamond studs weigh in at a carat apiece. "Ivy! I heard about your mother! How awful! Is she okay?"

"She's staying at our house now."

Nobody sent me any meals to help out like they did when you had gall-bladder surgery, even though you have a full-time maid. Not one person even bothered to call.

Her eyes crinkle in concern. "How about you?"

"Hanging in there."

"I'm sure it's hard."

Sure could use help in the baby-sitting area now and again, like that'll ever happen. "Yoo-hoo! Down here, everyone!" Yep, I've fallen through the cracks.

I adjust Trixie. "Hey, I'm almost done with the July newsletter. You sending me the article for Women's Corner?"

She sets her bag on the pew, her movement releasing a graceful puff of her perfume into the space between us. Really, Brenda is beautiful. Perfect. And she truly is kind. But while part of me yearns to be rich, kept, put-together, and able to choose my stressors, another part of me realizes I wouldn't trade places with her. Brenda can't have children, and for some reason she and John never adopted. But they travel all over the Third World trying to improve the lives of poverty-stricken kids. John's a surgeon.

Brenda will never feel her own Trixie snuggling against her breast and falling asleep, or look at a good report card and feel that candy-coated pride. Brenda won't cry at a daughter's wedding she paid way too much for, thinking it unfair she and John had to shell out fifteen thousand dollars (or fifty thousand with their finances) for someone to steal their baby right out from under them and move off to California or Europe or Thailand where she'd never get to know her grandbabies in a way grandmas should.

Now why can't I think this way right up front? Why does it take years for me to give people a break? Well, while it makes for good relationships, it does *not* make for good writing, and I find it hard to switch gears between my column and the everyday.

I need to work on this.

"So you doing okay, Brenda?"

"Oh yes. John and I are going through some changes. Good changes."

"Really?"

"Uh-huh." She nods.

I settle Trixie into my right arm.

"Look, Brenda, I'm not one of the needy ones. You can be honest with me. I can take it."

She sinks back into the upholstery. "Fact is, I'm scared to death."

And each honest word she entrusts to me changes me.

———

Lou slips in next to me before the service starts. "Guess what? Mitch got in touch with me, and we're meeting for lunch Tuesday, but only if you can come."

"So you've talked to him?"

"Yes. He really wants the gang to get together. What do you think?"

"I don't know if I can get out of work. You wanna come to the restaurant?"

"Absolutely! We'll make it late so you can join us. How about two thirty?"

"Sounds like a plan."

It's okay. Lou'll be there, right?

So many women feel removed from their husbands' callings. Their husbands march off to work each morning, sweating it out on construction sites, in factories, at garages; spending their days on retail floors, at computers, in boardrooms; trudging through silly meeting after silly meeting, putting out silly billing or payroll fires, or even making fabulous multimillion-dollar deals. But Rusty's gift, given to him by God, is something from which I can benefit directly. If I allow it.

Oh, the full, magnificent tones of his voice, the wide range, the emotion he taps in himself and pulls hand-over-hand out of those who hear him, all used to cause such an explosion of admiration and love inside me. I'd truly forget everything else as the song streamed into my heart and down into my soul.

But today, as he sings and Trixie misses his performance entirely, I only think about Tuesday's lunch.

You know, it's like this: how does a pastor's wife sit there and listen to her husband's sermon knowing he's really saying, "Do what I say, not what I do"? She must keep a mental checklist as he presents each point, silently grading his performance at home. Well, Rusty sings, "You put this love in my heart," and all I hear is Keith Green's old tune, "You can run to the end of the highway and not find what you're looking for."

And then he sits down next to me, the little wife. He rests his arm across my shoulders, flips open his Bible, and we read the scripture together off the same page. But the fact is, we're not on the same page at all anymore.

———

Mr. Moore inches his way up the path to his porch. His Bible hangs in a blue grocery-store bag from the hand that's free of his cane.

"Ivy!"

I slam the car door and run over. "Good morning!"

"Just getting back from church?"

"Yep. Rusty sang this morning."

"Hoo, that boy can sing. Mama loved to hear him sing."

I smile. "Remember when he used to come over and sing to her?"

"Oh yes. I certainly do."

"So how was your church?"

"A real blessing. Hearing about Jesus always is."

I need to remember that earlier on Sunday mornings. Like when I first wake up. I need to stop giving God my castoffs and acting weary even about that. I need to lift His name in my heart before I can lift it with my mouth.

I feel like the priesthood in the book of Malachi.

"You're a real blessing too, Mr. Moore."

"Well, praise the Lord, then, child."

"We're having roast chicken for dinner. Why don't you come on over? Rusty and Mom would be so glad to spend some time with you."

"I believe I will. Let me drop off these things and put on a clean shirt."

"You don't need to go to any trouble. It's just us."

He lays a hand on my arm. "My mama taught me to be respectful of the table, Ivy. Which really means to respect those sitting around it."

———

We drop Rusty off at the airport at seven. Life returns to normal.

10

I couldn't believe Brian agreed to meet me Monday afternoon. I needed to run out to Hunt Valley for shoes at the discount warehouse. If Persy's feet get any bigger, I'm going to send him out to sea.

So here we sit at Panera sharing a loaf of oat bread and a tub of jalapeño cream cheese.

"So tell me what's going on, Bri."

"Sis…"

"No, really. I'm not going to come down on you. I promise. I just want to know what's going on."

He sits back in his chair. "Same old. Dad's been calling me. Bugging me about a place to live."

"No kidding. He wants to come live with you?"

"There's no way I'll have that man come live with me."

I don't blame him. "What about his fiancée?"

"She dumped him."

"Big surprise there."

He reaches forward and slices off more bread. "He's about to lose the lease on his apartment and doesn't have enough for a security deposit on a new place."

"What about all that work he's been doing down in Canton?"

"Showed up too late one too many times is what I'm guessing.

Of course, he's got a ton of other excuses, and none of them are his responsibility."

Sound familiar, Bri?

An unused apartment molders in our basement, nasty now, creepy-crawly. It reminds me of a setting in a movie where the killer lies in wait for the tough but feminine detective who's frightened but moves forward for the good of society. But there's a bathroom, a bedroom, a living room, and a kitchenette. Only spiders and our junk inhabit the space.

Crud. There you go, then, Ivy. Save the day.

I spread some more cream cheese on my bread. "How did a man who lived with our mother end up with nothing of her rubbed off on him?"

"Meaning?"

"Faith."

"Oh."

"No, I mean it, Bri. It's like he doesn't think about God at all."

"Well, neither do I, if you want to know the truth, and I lived with her longer than he did. It doesn't make him a bad person, Ive."

He sits back in his chair again and stares at me. Crosses his arms. "..."

He blinks. "Yeah, well it's all okay for you, Ive. It does what it needs to do in your life."

I want to tell him my life isn't what he thinks, *I'm* not what he thinks, but something tells me to just let him keep going. So I stay silent. He fills it in, like we Starlings usually do.

"It's not that I don't believe in God anymore. It's just never done much good in my life. Practically speaking."

"How so? Just asking."

He turns his knife over and over between forefinger and thumb. "Do you think I haven't prayed to change?"

I shrug, trying to keep my expression open and accepting.

"Well, I have. And year after year, I just end up more like the old man."

Go, Harry.

"Ivy, it shouldn't be that hard for God to change one person who wants to change."

"Nobody can change on their own, Bri."

"I'm not trying to. I want help."

"Brian, remember that day when you were nine and you walked down the aisle in church?"

"Sure."

"Did you mean it?"

"I thought so. But look at my life now."

"It's nothing Jesus can't fix." I need to remember that myself.

He sets down the knife. "Well, maybe that's my problem. Maybe I just don't have the faith I need. I don't know if I even believe in all that anymore."

"So you want to change, but on your own terms?" I say this as gently as I can.

"Yeah, I guess. When it comes down to it."

"You want God's help, but not from God's places and God's people."

He scrunches his brow.

"Why don't you start coming to church with us?"

"If church was the answer, Ive, the world would be a better place than it is."

I can't argue with that. "Okay. I agree. I don't get much from church either. Scrap that idea. But Jesus and the church are two different things. How long has it been since you've read the Gospels?"

"I don't know if I've ever read all four books."

"Will you try?"

"I don't understand all those antique words, Ive."

I take a bite of my bread. "You should see the translations they've got available these days. Plain English now. Not all that KJV-only nonsense we grew up with. I'll get you one."

"It's your money. But don't expect much, sis. I think I'm a lost cause."

"Nobody's a lost cause."

Except maybe Harry.

My soul recoils at my own knee-jerk observation.

"How about coming over for supper tonight? The kids just got *Pirates of the Caribbean*."

"I've got a date."

"Bring her."

"Really?"

"Sure. Why not?"

Actually, I can think of lots of reasons, but sometimes you just need to go out on a limb, right?

———

I stop at the bookstore. Pick up a friendly translation of the Bible and pray. Dear God, let him show up tonight.

This prayer from the woman who can't wait to see another man at lunch tomorrow.

———

Okay, correct me if I'm wrong, but God really does have a sense of humor. Brian's latest girlfriend is a preacher's wayward daughter. Only Brian doesn't know this. I want to laugh myself silly, but I don't. When I headed back to the kitchen to fix some snacks, Danielle followed me in her clingy jeans and cropped top. The girl's abs ripple like you wouldn't believe. John Basedow, look out.

She pointed to the plaque over my kitchen door, which reads, *Home. Where each lives for the other and all live for God.* "We had something like that in my house growing up."

"Oh yeah?"

"My dad was a preacher."

"What kind?"

"Independent fundamental Baptist."

It certainly all makes sense now.

"That must have been tough."

She nodded. "I couldn't wait to get out of there."

"I grew up in a strict church. Needless to say, I don't go there anymore. No pants, no nail polish, Sister This and Brother That."

"Sounds too familiar."

"I didn't realize there's a whole big world out there in the church. It took me a long time not to feel guilty when I went to the movies!"

She laughed. "I'm glad to be past that."

"Can't blame you there, Danielle."

"Sometimes I want to go back, but I'm not willing to risk it. It took me years to stop looking over my shoulder for lightning bolts. Call me Dani, by the way."

"Hey, would you get the mayo out of the fridge? It's in the door."

"No prob."

Dani's about thirty, I think. Brian told me she's a trainer at Gold's Gym.

"You look great, Dani. How many hours do you work out a week?"

"Probably about thirty. But hey, it's what I do. If I had as many kids as you and had to run a restaurant, I'd be totally out of shape."

At least she didn't put a *too* on the end of that. "You have kids?"

"One. A little girl, Rosa. She's almost four."

"I bet she's cute."

"She's adorable. Best thing that ever happened to me." She hands me the mayonnaise.

"Nice nails."

"Thanks. What're you making?"

"Just some mustard dip. I picked up those little smoked sausages at the store."

"I love those."

"You're not a health nut?"

She grimaces. "No way. Now that's one thing I kept from my heritage. The ability to ingest large amounts of animal fat."

I like her.

"Know what you mean. My new church doesn't believe in potluck suppers."

"No way."

"Now, I ask you, what's wrong with a potluck supper?"

"I do miss the potlucks."

I spoon two parts mayo to one part honey mustard into a small bowl. "When I was growing up, there was this one lady, Sister Norma, and she made the most gorgeous fried chicken. First platter to be cleaned."

She picks up a sausage with a toothpick. "That was Brother Joe at our church. Now his wife, Sister Grace, she made a broccoli salad like you wouldn't believe. She sent me the recipe years ago, right after I got married, and darn it, I follow it religiously but just can't make it taste like hers."

"Brian wouldn't admit this, but I think he could trace his love of food to the church."

"I know I can."

"So what about your parents? They still active in your life?" I sure am nosy.

"My mom lives with me. She's calmed down a bit. Just a bit. More like she's resigned herself to the life I lead. Of course, she tells me she'll never stop praying for me, and I have to admit, sometimes that's a comfort."

I think of Mom. "Is she healthy?"

"Not at all. I'm taking care of her."

Sounds familiar. "Young child and ailing mother. I can relate."

"I know. It's why I didn't mind coming tonight. Brian says you're still really religious, which isn't my thing anymore, but I figured we'd at least have that in common."

"Yep, the sandwich generation."

"Never heard it called anything before."

"Yeah, well sometimes you're the lunchmeat and sometimes you're the bread. Right now, we're the lunchmeat."

She leans against the counter as I arrange sausages around the sauce bowl. "I think I'm spiced ham."

Ha! "I'm baloney."

"Better than head cheese."

"Who eats that stuff anyway?" I hand her the tray of sausage and grab the chips and salsa. "Ready for a little Johnny Depp?"

"Who isn't?"

That sure is the truth.

Brian yells, "Ive? Can you bring Mom a cup of tea while you're at it?"

"Okay!"

The kids are climbing all over him. Why don't I invite him over more?

"Thanks, dear!" Mom. In her voice a tremolo of excitement sings, and I'm happy for her. Maybe things will start turning around for the Starling clan.

Before I forget, I place the new Bible under Brian's keys. Not that I deserve to, for I know who I am and what I am. But if a sinner like me can't pass the buck on to God, then I really don't know my going-outs from my coming-forths.

━━━━

Oh my. I'm glad I checked the coffeepot before I went to bed. Mom set it up but without water and instead of setting the timer, she turned it on. I think I saved the pot, though. I also found a bag of chips in the fridge.

━━━━

The next morning I'm surprised to see Brian already at the restaurant. Excuse me, the bistro. He's pulling the bread and rolls for the day out of the freezer.

"Hey bro."

"Hey Ive. Nice little gig last night. Thanks."

"You've got a great gal there."

"Oh yeah. I'm going to do my best not to screw this one up."

"Bri, we need to talk about the DUI."

He stiffens. "Dani's getting me through it."

"I haven't told Mom."

"I didn't think you had. Thanks."

"Are you getting help?"

He turns to me. "I'm forty years old. It's my business, Ivy, okay?"

I want to tell him I'm worried that if he doesn't stop this stuff, I'll be the one picking up the pieces, but I can't. I've got to leave what dignity remains, not make this about me. Maybe inside of him a strength gathers, and he'll do the right thing on his own. I can't be everyone's savior, right?

"Got it. I'm here if you need me, Bri."

I pour my cup of coffee, pull out my devotional, and sit at the window table. It's raining today. But two thirty is coming!

─────

Flannery, our waitress, arrives a little early. She wraps her apron around her waist. "Listen, don't worry about a thing when your friends arrive. I've got it all covered."

"You don't have to do that. I'll just jump up when I need to."

"Are you kidding me? Hey, you don't get opportunities just to hang very often."

"Is it that obvious?"

"I hate to say it, but yeah." She looks at her watch, then leans forward. "You've got something stuck between your front teeth."

"Oh great."

Life can be so charming.

In the bathroom, I dig through my purse, put on a little blush and some fresh lipstick, and actually find a pair of dangling earrings

I threw in there months ago. They're too heavy, but I don't need them for long.

Lou's already sitting down at the table near the back corner. "Hey Ive-O!"

"Hi Lou. Want something to drink?"

"Just some ice water."

Flannery says, "I've got it! Ivy, what do you want?"

"A Coke?"

"Sure thing."

I sit down. "This feels weird."

"You've got yourself a gem there in that girl. I may steal her from you someday."

"Just wait until Rusty comes back home."

Lou rolls her eyes.

"Don't say it."

"Ive, when are you going to say what needs to be said?"

"Look, if he doesn't want to be with me, he doesn't."

"So what are you sticking it out for?"

"The kids."

Dear God. I actually said it out loud. In fact, I don't think I've even said that inside my own head before.

Lou reaches for one of the breadsticks Flannery sets down with our drinks. "Someone needs to give Rusty a good bop on the head."

"I'm in more than a pickle, I think."

"You have no biblical grounds to leave him."

"Believe me, I know. And I can't help but think, 'Is this it? Is this what I get from the wheel of life?' I mean, will my entire life be spent picking up the garbage so Rusty can do what he wants?"

Lou nibbles the breadstick, then sets it down. "Ive-O, that's pretty much life for most women if they'd care to admit it."

"It isn't for you."

"Neil is a simple guy. Artsy types are never simple."

"I should've tried harder to keep Tom Webber."

We laugh. Tom Webber still lives with his mother and manages a shoe store.

———

What was I thinking back then? I knew Mitch would have dated me had I given him the slightest encouragement. It wasn't like he was a geek. Mitch oozed coolness, athleticism, and smarts.

I observe him from across the table. Dressed casually in khakis and a madras plaid shirt, he laughs with such ease and speaks with such confidence and listens with such attention. What was that supermodel thinking?

Oh yeah. The supermodel. Even with this lipstick and these earrings, I'm probably about as close to her as Ralph Nader is to the presidency.

We reminisce and drink wine, and soon the dinner rush begins. "You guys sit. I've got to get back to work."

I hate my life.

An hour later Mitch stops at the register. "You've got a nice place here, Ivy. By all appearances, you've really done well for yourself."

"You too, Mitch."

He shrugs. "I've got to wonder if there's more, though. You know?"

"Yeah, I know."

He smiles with half of his mouth. "Anyway, thanks for the nice time. Tell Brian the food was great."

I jerk my head toward the kitchen door. "Peek in and tell him yourself. He'll be glad to see you."

A few seconds later I hear great peals of laughter ringing from the kitchen. Mitch seems to do that sort of thing, and though I try not to let it, my heart leaps, and I feel sixteen again.

11

B renda flags me down after I drop Trixie off at her Sunday-school room. "I've got the greatest idea!"

"Okay. Spill it on the way to the coffee maker. I had no time to fix a cup this morning."

She takes my arm, all high-school-like, and I've got to admit, I like it. I feel so starved for affection. And Rusty called yesterday and told me his normal September visit has to wait until Christmas. I said, "Whatever." And he didn't like that. And I didn't care.

After the talk with Mitch, I decided to start building a life without Rusty, and it feels great. Hey, he's chosen his path; now I've got to pick out my own if this is going to work. Or more to the point, if I'm going to survive. Nowadays I have to face the possibility that my marriage just might not make it.

"I've got a great idea for a new women's group."

Fabulous.

She pours me a coffee, the dear. "You know, you're not the only one caught between an aging parent and children who need raising. It's happening more and more."

"Yeah, the sandwich generation, they call it."

"I know. Isn't that cute?"

Cute? "Uh, yeah?"

"Your situation got me thinking. So I sat down and made a list—want to sit down? My legs are killing me. I packed boxes all day yesterday."

"Sure."

Our church built its own canteen. We take a booth.

"Do you know there are ten other women in your situation here at our church alone?"

"Really?"

"Yes, and that's just what I can come up with off the top of my head."

I really need to get more involved. "I had no idea." Too true.

"So I was thinking of starting a support group and calling it Club Sandwich! Isn't that cute?"

Oh yeah. Everything's so cute. Snap out of your mood, Ivy. Brenda loves you. "Definitely."

"So when's a good time for you?"

"I'm pretty busy. You know, Brenda, I don't mean to throw cold water, but the last thing our church needs is another Bible study group. What if we make it an outreach sort of thing instead? I'm sure there are women out there who need to know God's along for the ride if they'd just invite Him."

She knits her brows, licks her lips, then raises up. "You're right! Kill two birds with one stone!"

"Let's do this: let's put an ad in the *Towson Times* and go from there."

"I'm on it."

Oh great. One more thing.

———

Mom's hobbling around pretty well now. Rusty left three weeks ago, taking the bearability of June with him and leaving a July much in need of a fourth person "like the Son of God" to keep us from burning alive. No disrespect meant, just feeling confident that He'd come through for me if I needed Him as badly as Shadrach, Meshach, and Abednego. Thankfully, right now I'm doing okay, even though Mom still inhabits the dining room. Next week she finishes her rehab and will move back to her apartment. She insists on "ambling around on her own turf." And I don't blame her one bit. It will, however, raise the difficulty level for me. But not too much, the restaurant being down below. Brian's thrilled. He can just run up whenever he wants and still be the fair-haired boy. We've hidden the DUI from Mom. He says it was such a travesty there's no way any judge in a free country would convict him. He ended up with a slap on the wrist, it being his first offense.

How is it when I so much as look at someone cross-eyed I get the rug yanked out from under me, and DUI Brian just gets slapped on the wrist? And he thinks God's not helping him? He's just not aware how bad it could really be.

So anyway, Mom's none the wiser. I even lied for him when Mom asked me if something was bothering him. It gives me further cause to believe I'm not exactly "pure and undefiled, unspotted from the world." What did Paul write? What I want to do, I don't do. And what I don't want to do, I do. I'm telling you, that passage and the whole thorn-in-the-flesh aspect of the man humanizes him. If not for those passages, I just wouldn't relate to Paul at all. When Paul says, if you want to imitate Christ, imitate me, I think…good heavens! I can't imagine saying that about myself!

Lou visits the restaurant for lunch with none other than Miss Women's Ministry herself, Brenda. Man, I feel so sorry for her, yet admire her at the same time. She and John are selling everything, moving to a little rancher in Lutherville, and starting an orphanage in Mexico with all their money. So, yeah, she's excited. We're all excited. But she's still scared. And there are only two women in the church she can go to with veil removed, with face pale and soft in the stark winds of the unknown. Good old Ivy and Lou: real women with real problems and real people inhabiting their real world.

Personally, I could use a little fairy-tale existence about now.

———

Two o'clock. The rush scurried back to work, or carpool, or more shopping, dahling, a while ago. It tickles me how many diners show me their purchases, freely offering up the prices they paid, especially if bargains were pursued and won.

Lou hugs me, Brenda too, and I show them to my favorite table, right inside the kitchen. The staff congregates here during slow times, and sometimes a party will request it to make their dining experience more interesting. They don't request it more than a few times, obviously tiring of the cooks mercilessly burning each other. That's enough to strangle anyone's appetite.

"Have a seat. Would you like menus, or do you want to place yourselves in Brian's hands?"

"Oh, let's live dangerously." Brenda.

She looks great in a long, slender ecru dress with lace-up espadrilles to match. She recently had her hair cut off in one of those cute pixie dos with blond-and-red frosting. Now see? I need some style like that.

I stuff the menus back under my arm. "Seafood or beef or chicken? We may even have some pork tenderloin."

Lou requests seafood pasta, and Brenda says, "Pork works for me."

"Got it."

Club Sandwich

145

Brian's in the dish room, rooting around for his favorite saucepan, cursing the dishwasher, who's out back smoking.

"I've got Lou and a friend from church at the kitchen table. Lou wants a seafood pasta, Brenda wants pork. Do whatever you want."

"Cool."

He looks terrible.

"You okay, Bri?"

"Just a long night last night."

"Anything I can do?"

"I'll be fine."

I leave it.

Fifteen minutes later I'm sitting with the girls, and Brenda declares she'd like to be on the Schneider house redecorating committee. And truth be known, I like her ideas. Boy, does she know where to get good furniture cheap. I see a great couch in our future.

Before they leave, Brenda lays a pink envelope on the table, my name written in the center. "You're the type of woman who doesn't take time to be good to herself."

"Is it that obvious?" I say again.

"I told her that." Lou.

Pushing my bangs back—"It's true. When is there time?"

"It's only there if you make it." Brenda slides the envelope right up to where my arms rest on the table. "Go ahead and open it."

I slide a piece of glossy cardstock out of the scented envelope: *A Day at the Spa at Cross Keys.* Apparently I'm entitled to The Works. And the spa is near Brett's boutique. Maybe I can have supper with her afterward.

"Wow. This is amazing. Thanks!"

"Fact is, Ivy, the church hasn't been there for you, and I realize that. And I've been so caught up in the larger ministry I let you down. I'm sorry."

I laugh the awkward laugh of a woman whose tactless thoughts have been exposed. Did I say anything to Lou? "You didn't have to go to such an extreme to make up for it."

"Oh, I wanted to do it. Believe me, I know a good cause when I see one."

I need to be someone's cause. Dear God, I really do.

Rusty deserves the credit. He's a reader and brings all sorts of interesting books home to the kids, especially Persy, who loves mysteries of nature and ancient cultures, and *Calvin and Hobbes*.

Each day my son relates a startling find in his new book *Ancient Marvels and Mysteries*.

This morning I'm learning all about healing and medicine.

Persy shoves a picture in front of me of the upper portion of a skull and a large squarish hole cut into the temple.

"Persy, I'm eating!"

"Isn't it cool?"

I can only think, "No anesthesia! No anesthesia!"

Oh, forget this plate of eggs. They look too much like yellow brains. And why did I think ketchup was a good idea? Blech.

I hand him the plate. "Here, yellow brains and blood for breakfast."

"Cool!"

He sits down and flips to the next page. "Hey, they actually built up new noses by cutting a flap in the forehead, then twisting it around—"

"Persy! Stop it!"

"And they'd use big black ants for stitches. They let them bite into the folds of flesh, then they'd rip off the bodies leaving the heads—"

Lyra bops him atop the head as she sits. "Gross!"

An idea for a column erupts, one about those bozos who say the difference between genders is primarily the result of socialization. Those people must not have kids. Especially boys, who can fashion guns out of cutlery, toothbrushes, or a piece of pizza. And what about passing gas? This inherently embarrasses most girls, Trixie not included, and causes great amusement for the boys. Sometimes I wish these sociologists, psychologists, and scientists would stop trying to figure out what makes us tick and just enjoy the rhythm.

Oh yeah. Tony's going to like this one.

———

Trixie crawls up on my lap as I write my column. It's late, as usual. A summer storm just rolled through, and a cool breeze flutters the curtains at the opened kitchen window.

"Mama, I can't fall asleep."

"Why don't you just get one of my silky bras, lay on Mama's bed, and suck your pinkie?"

She places her pinkie in her mouth and grabs my thumb, running the pad of her index finger over the slick nail. I can't put her to bed. I need this as much as she does.

"Mama? Lyrie's mean to me."

"I know she gets frustrated with you."

"She hit me on the head today."

"She what?"

"She told me I was a bad girl, and God gets mad at bad girls."

Oh man. How did this happen? I know Trixie's a pain. But that was so mean of Lyra. Just so mean.

My heart hurts. I wish I could suck on my pinkie and feel better too.

———

"How's it going with the baby-sitting, Lyra?" Next morning, seven o'clock, we're both rubbing the sleep from our eyes.

"Okay, I guess." Classic teenage eye-roll. "Mom, Trixie won't listen to a word I say! And Winky's no help anymore. She's getting absolutely bonkers, if you ask me."

I'd noticed it too. "I know."

The coffee maker is destroyed from having tried to brew a pot with no water one too many times. And the burner's been left on too much for comfort.

She spoons sugar into her cup. "It's too much for me."

"I know. I'm sorry."

"If only Daddy—"

"Let's not go there."

"Not that I can blame him for staying away."

I don't want to ask what she means.

———

Rusty calls. "Hey hon."

"Hi Rust."

"Whatchya doin'?"

"Just sat down in the kitchen to fold laundry. You should have seen Persy this afternoon. He took the hose out and watered the mulch, then decided to unpot all my geraniums and put them in the beds."

"How'd he do?"

"They look great. You know that boy's got a green thumb. I'm going to the nursery tomorrow to get some pansies for him. He's loving that book, by the way. Getting more gross-out mileage out of it with Lyra than I'll bet even you thought possible."

Laughter. "How's Trixie girl?"

"Asleep. Finally. Mom gave her a Jolly Rancher stick at nine."

"What was she thinking?"

"That's the problem. Not much these days."

"Oh no. Going the kooky way of all aging Starling women?"

"I think so, although I prefer to think of us as eccentric. I don't know what I'm going to do once Mom moves back to the apartment. Lyra's tired of bearing the brunt during the day. Who wouldn't be? And yet I can't bring myself to put Trixie in day care."

"Pity all the other children."

I can see it now. Getting kicked out of day care after day care. Oh yeah, that would be great.

Rusty says, "Maybe you should think about it seriously."

At least he doesn't say *we*. That would be too much to take after a day like today. Two doctor appointments for Mom, and Trixie pooped her training pants right in the middle of the supermarket.

"How would we pay for it? We're almost hand-to-mouth now. And Lyra's starting high school this year. Hey, on a lark, I saw if she couldn't get accepted at Notre Dame Prep."

"Really? Why didn't you tell me?"

I feel my ire rising. "Gee, Rust, it must've slipped my mind." I stand to my feet and head into the living room and my new couch, which I haven't told him about either. I don't plan to. But what a time I had with Brenda and Lou when they brought a million swatches on rings big enough for a giant's nose. I'm not talking Andre the Giant, I'm talking *The Land of Canaan* or *Gulliver's Travels.* We settled on a simple, squarish sofa in a muted berry color with mossy green-and-cream trim. Lots of floral pillows that coordinate with the curtains Lou's sewing. Let's just say, we're going to be stylin' up a storm on Allegheny Avenue. Brenda's giving me tons of furniture she won't need when she moves. And it's the good stuff.

Rusty's voice escorts me back to the real world of how-could-I-forget-to-tell-you-that.

"Ive, we said we'd still make all these important decisions together."

"Look Rusty, I haven't enrolled her or anything. I'm trying the best I can. You can't be an absent father and husband and expect me to remember every little thing."

"Our daughter's education is a little thing?"

"Look, the point is, we can't afford day care, can we? Not with you gone."

"How would my being home make a difference? I wouldn't make any more money. In fact, I probably wouldn't make as much. And I'd still be working and unable to take care of Trixie."

"Well, then. Stand up to Marlin. Tell him you want a raise."

"I could lose my position."

"Aren't we even worth the risk?"

Dramatic sigh. "Okay, I'll ask."

"Thanks."

And now I feel indebted. Great.

Oh boy, here he comes. Harry in all his glory.

But he shuffles by the window this time, the Zig Ziglar gait gone. Shuffle, shuffle, head down. Mr. Wiggins, can I help you?

Aw, shoot.

My heart wilts, darn it. Why am I cursed with this terrible caring instinct? I'll blame Mom. She won't know the difference these days. I had no idea dementia could progress so quickly.

He swings the door wide, stepping in, stopping as his eyes adjust.

"Hey Harry."

"Hi Ive."

"Come on in."

"Thanks. Appreciate it."

The August heat follows him and soon dissipates in the air conditioning.

Only a few early lunchers assemble at one of the front tables, lingering over coffee and business conversation. The scream of a siren hits us as a fire truck bustles by. Hopefully a false alarm.

"Mind if I sit for a bit?"

"Nope. Go ahead."

I know he's in a bad spot. I should really stop this clipped speech, but I can't. Instead, I pour him a fresh cup of coffee and set it in front of him. "Just brewed."

"Thanks."

"No prob."

"Brian in?"

"Just went down to the fish market. Garret's here though. Want anything?"

His brows raise. "Um, yeah, sure. Fried egg and toast, okay?"

"Fine. Sure."

I turn back around, head into the kitchen. Garret preps for the lunch rush, slicing up tomatoes and onions and roasting red peppers on the open flame of the gas burner. Garret's our resident hippie. Long hair the color of dark honey curls in a ponytail down his back. Lots of piercings in his ears, and well, his eyebrows wing in a lovely way. I've always liked our rock-climbing, free-spirited Garret.

"My dad just came in."

One brow rises. "Wants a filet mignon?"

I laugh. "Fried egg and toast, believe it or not."

"I'm on it."

"Thanks, man."

I need to roll cutlery, but I stop. "On second thought, I'll make it. You've got enough to do."

"No prob."

I pull a saucepan from the shelf beneath the range and set it on to heat. He likes wheat bread, so I grab two slices from the fridge. Five minutes later, I set the meal before him.

"Tell Garret thanks."

"I made it."

Brows furrow. "Thanks, then?"

"Sure thing, Harry."

"Want to sit with me a bit?"

I shake my head. "Got to roll cutlery."

"Oh, come on, Ive. Sit with the old man. You can roll it here at the table."

I stiffen. Honor your father and mother that your days may be long. Okay then. But just for You.

Gathering napkins, forks, knives, and spoons, I pray for a wise mouth. My head usually knows what to do, but my mouth wills its own way around this man, God knows.

I set the items out across from him at the table. "So. Brian told me about your plight. I don't want to hear about the whys, Harry, but I will say I'm sorry you're out of work."

"Thanks, I guess."

"It's the best I can do right now."

"Then I'll take it."

"Good."

"How are the kids?"

"Not bad. I've checked out four day cares for Trixie, and none of them are what I'm looking for."

"Day care?"

"Yeah. Mom's beyond watching her now, and Lyra's really worn thin. Those two don't get along under the best of circumstances, let alone times like this. A fourteen-year-old shouldn't have to bear the brunt, you know?"

"I could sit in for a while."

"Oh, Harry. You and Mom under the same roof? I don't think so."

But I appreciate the offer. It's more than he's ever done before.

"Guess you're right. How's her hip?"

"Not bad." I won't offer more.

I start rolling napkins with a vengeance. Not to be prideful or anything, but I can go like a cat with its tail on fire with this stuff. What a skill. "Find a place to live yet?"

"No. I have to be out by Friday."

"That's only three days away."

"No kidding."

"We have the basement if you're interested." I knew it was slated to issue forth; I just didn't expect it to sound so glib.

"Oh yeah?"

"I'm not the most loving daughter, Harry, but I won't let you go out on the street."

"Okay. Appreciate that."

"But...we've got some house rules."

He bites some toast. "Shoot 'em at me. I can't be too choosy right now."

Did he actually say that?

"First of all, Mom can't know you're down there. Absolutely not. She doesn't deserve that kind of stress, okay?"

"Agreed."

"Second of all, you can't come up whenever you want. It's your apartment, and you'll come and go through the basement door around the side of the house."

"Won't she see me?"

"It'll be up to you to make sure that doesn't happen."

"I'll give it my best shot."

"Third, no women."

"I knew you'd say that."

"Then we understand each other more than I thought."

"What else?"

"It's a mess down there. For rent, you can fix it up. Other than that I won't charge you a cent."

"Got it."

I look up at him, and for the first time ever I feel extremely sorry for the man. I try to imagine finding myself in his circumstances at his age. I can't. How awful is that? And as macho and vivacious as he's always been, I think he's finally staring his own mortality, as well as his choices, in the face. Maybe he sees things a little more clearly now. Or maybe I'm giving him too much credit. I hope not. But I've got choices to make too. And I'll do the right thing. God will bless me. I'm hoping that's true. I really am. And am I fooling myself? Who's to say I'll have the strength to do the right thing day after day after day? I mean, so far so good today, and maybe even tomorrow. But next week? Next month?

"So when can we expect you?"

"I can pack up my stuff over the next two days. A buddy of mine has a pickup truck. He offered to help with the move."

"Okay, but this is the deal. Mom goes to bed around nine. You can't move in until ten."

He just nods.

"You need a couch?" I ask.

"Yeah."

"Okay, we just got a new one. I'll put the old one down there. It's not all that great."

"There cable hookup in the basement?"

"Harry!"

"Just asking, Ive, just asking."

"No, there isn't."

"Well, I know this guy—"

"Nothing illegal, Harry. Rule number four."

I'm done with rolling. I stand up and begin to gather.

"Good eggs, Ive."

"Thanks."

Trixie's dancing around the kitchen. "School! School!"

Day care really, but calling it school makes me feel better. Sort of.

I feel sick, in spite of Rusty's raise.

I found the perfect lunch box last night. Disney princesses.

A whole new world.

The final surrender.

Oh, baby girl. I'm so sorry.

Persy lays back on the couch, *Ancient Marvels and Mysteries* leaning against his raised knees. "Hey Mom. The people of Baghdad might have had electric batteries. Look at these jars."

I look over his shoulder. "Too bad they don't have those now."

He flips several pages. "Look at this figurine. Doesn't it look like a little jet?"

"Yeah. Wow."

"Found in an ancient tomb in Colombia. Wow, that's close."

"Colombia, bud. Not the District of Columbia. It's in South America."

"Cool."

I kiss his sweet cheek and finish dusting the room.

12

M om enters the kitchen as I work on my secret book, thinking maybe Candace Frost the agent will call me any day now.
"The sink is full of dishes, Ivy."
"I'll get to them."
"I never let dishes sit like that."
Huh? What's this?
"No. You were a great housekeeper."
"You were raised better than this."
Okay, okay!

———

Brett lets us in. She pads around wearing a pair of fluffy slippers. A robe cinches her waist. Still depressed, I bet. Brett's usually up and dressed by seven, and it's past ten.

The foyer of her home reminds me of something out of a movie. It's probably bigger than my living room and dining room put together. My entire downstairs, for that matter. Staircases curve up either side, and a chandelier from some Austrian crystal company dangles overhead. Marble, parquet floors, wainscoting, molding, tapestries.

"I've got *The Little Mermaid* ready to go for Trixie." Brett leans down and hoists her onto her hip. Man, she loves my kids. "Want to come back to the movie theater with Aunt Brett? I even made you some popcorn!"

"Popcorn!" Trixie yells, and Brett winces at the volume. The child is louder than Harry's old ties.

She heads back to the living quarters and says over her shoulder, "Coffee's on in the kitchen, Ivy. I'll be right in. Persy, you want to watch a movie or do the game system in the family room?"

"Video games, Aunt Brett!"

"All right!"

I have to admit she could teach me a thing or two on the art of being an aunt.

I clog back to the kitchen. Restaurant-quality everything, and I should know. Pouring a mug of coffee, I realize she's done the necessary in this whole Marcus situation. And in that, we're exactly alike.

"Thanks for letting us come over."

"I wish you'd come over more."

"Really?"

"Are you kidding? Let me pour some coffee, and we can go out to the breakfast room. Want to put in a CD on the system? I need something soothing."

"Sure." A nearby walk-in closet houses the sound system, the security system, and countless other who-knows-what systems. Maybe lighting? Indoor sprinklers? Lawn watering? Pool cleaning?

Black equipment stacked on racks winks green and red lights at me as I stand before a wall of CDs. Okay, soothing. Wow—a large collection of praise-and-worship music. Well, good. I thought Brett stopped caring about religion years ago. *Praise Strings.* An oldie goldie and definitely soothing. I choose *Praise Strings III.*

Now, finding the right apparatus.

I commence the great scan. Okay, certainly it would say *CD Player* on it, right? So, I begin up in the right-hand corner. Nope, nope, nope. My eyes lower. Nope. Nope.

Ah, there. I hope. Dear Lord, don't let me unwittingly summon the police and fire department curbside.

Thank heavens the music begins only a few seconds after I load the player.

I inhabit another world in this place. I have to face that. And I have to at least be happy for Brett. She had enough to deal with growing up. At least I had the cool factor going for me back then. She got made fun of all the time.

Brett's breakfast room is easily my favorite room in her home. So feminine and inviting. The table sits lower than normal, the chairs more like lounge chairs, comfy with lots of cushions and throws. Sunlight flows in, illuminating the red-and-yellow upholstery. Lots of bamboo, floral, and striped patterns. "It's so pretty in here."

"I love this room. Did you know I did this myself, Ivy? I didn't let the decorator touch this room."

"It's my favorite."

"Really?"

"Uh-huh."

I set down my coffee and sink into a chair. "Music okay?"

"Perfect."

"So tell me what's going on with you."

"The girls go back to school next week."

"Where are they?"

"Still asleep. Big night last night with friends." Her brows furrow, then clear. "Anyway, Marcus has been home every day by six. I'm thinking about selling the shop."

"What? Really?"

"Yeah. Maybe I need to devote more time to him. I'm usually gone three nights a week down there."

"I wouldn't argue against it." And I wouldn't. Maybe the reason she's never made a marriage work is because the shop continually wears on her. I mean, it seems glamorous, all the buying trips and window decorating, but it's hard work. I can't ever call my sister lazy, that's for sure. We know how to work hard, us Starling children.

"Really? I thought you'd think it was a bad idea."

"Nope." Maybe she'll spend more time with Mom.

"How about you? What's going on with you?"

"Well, that's what I wanted to talk to you about. I wanted you to hear this from me first."

"Sounds scary. You and Rusty okay?"

"How can we be anything but, when he's never around?"

"I don't know how you stand it."

Should I confide? She is my big sister. "Sometimes I can't, Brett. Sometimes I just want to break down and scream. Sometimes I do."

"I'm sorry."

"Yeah, well, that's just the way it is. Would it be wrong of me to insist he come home?"

"With all you're going through? No way. You're not a wife to Rusty, you're a support system."

"I couldn't have said that better myself. Well, anyway, I'm thinking about telling him that. He did get a raise, though. Now we can afford to send Lyra to IND."

"Notre Dame? She got accepted?"

"Yep." I am proud right now. I really am. "Got a bit of a scholarship, too."

"That's my girl. I want to buy her uniforms."

"You don't have to."

"I want to. Can we do a day of shopping together? Just her and me?"

"She'd love it."

"We'll go to the salon, too." A smidge of color returns to her cheeks. "So, what is it you have to tell me?"

"Well, Harry's moving in with us tomorrow."

"What?!"

"Into the basement."

"Mom'll flip."

"I told him she can't find out."

Brett begins to chuckle. "This is going to be funny."

"Yeah. Har-har."

She places her hand on mine. "You're a better woman than I am, Ivy."

"No."

"Really, you are. As soon as I sell the shop I'll get more involved. I promise. Maybe I can take Mom a weekend here and there too."

"I'd appreciate that." If I make too big a deal of it, I might scare her off. "So...show me those pictures from your trip with Marcus."

"Okay!" She's trying to sound excited, I think. But it's not fooling me. And she starts in on another vein of conversation.

The Little Mermaid ends, and we leave without viewing a single snapshot.

———

"What's that banging going on in the basement?" Mom stands at the stove grilling sausages.

"I've got a guy coming in to do some work down there."

"Why?"

"It's nasty. Maybe we could rent it out. Make some extra money. With Lyra going to private school and all."

She turns back to her task.

Well, it's true. Harry *is* a guy, right?

———

Lou and Brenda enter with paint cans, brushes, stirring sticks, tarps, rollers, and a general bustle of female goodwill.

Lou raises her hands. "Okay, this is it. Time to paint that living room! Brushes for all!"

They finished the kitchen last week. Harry's living with my flags.

"Even Trixie?" I smirk.

Brenda removes her blousy shirt to reveal a pair of paint-splattered overalls. "Of course. She can paint designs on the wall and we'll just roll over them. Think how much fun that will be for her."

Lou releases her load with a *plop*. "Persy, too. That boy's got an artistic flair for sure."

He'll probably draw trepanned skulls. Or Sonic the Hedgehog. Or a trepanned Sonic.

"How long do you think this will take?"

"With all of us? Three hours."

"Good. Brett's taking Mom out for lunch. They'll be back around three."

"Let's get started then." Brenda.

We all change into our scrubby clothes, congregate the furniture and pictures in the center of the room, and spread out the tarps.

Trixie and Persy go to work, and the pictures they paint are so adorable, painting over them is much like cutting into a pretty cake. We hate to spoil it.

Lyra paints the woodwork with a pristine, glossy white enamel. The effect of her painstaking efforts is sheer magic. The once drab, off-white space jumps into significance. The berry shade warms the room, and the couch springs into action, so to speak.

When all is back in place, I view the scene. Wow, this is *my* living room. "I love this, guys!"

"Naturally." Lou. "Would we steer you wrong, Ive-O?"

"Absolutely not."

Brenda heads toward the door. "Hang on, I've brought some stuff from the house, but I've got to get something in particular. You'll love it."

Two minutes later she reenters with a large wreath, burgeoning with color and texture, coordinating perfectly with the décor. "For over the fireplace."

Lou nods. I smile. And Lyra proclaims it all "Perfect!"

Lou, Brenda, and I sit out on the front porch, hot chocolate in hands. "So how's it going, Bren?"

"Sold the house. The market served us well. We'll be able to build the orphanage with the proceeds. The rest of our investments will fund the staffing and the running of the place."

Unbelievable.

"I think this is amazing."

"Me too, Bren." Lou.

Brenda takes a sip. "I think I've found a really cute little house in Lutherville. But Lou, I'm going to need your input. The kitchen needs to be redone."

"You got it, babe."

I really respect Brenda for laying it all down at the feet of Jesus.

"Please, hon, it's just temporary."

I squeeze the phone. "Rusty! How can you even ask this? Mom's still in the dining room as it is. Harry's sequestered downstairs. Where in the world am I going to put your father?"

Yes, Barnum and Bailey could do no better than this house on Allegheny Avenue. Step right up, folks! See the collection of crazy people assembled from the four corners of Baltimore for your entertainment!

"He can sleep on the bottom bunk of Persy's room."

"Persy hates the top bunk, Rust. It scares him."

Reuben Schneider's house sold more quickly than anybody expected. His condo at the retirement village won't be ready for six months, unless somebody there dies, and I refuse to wish that. I couldn't handle the guilt.

How did this happen? They talk about slippery slopes. Well, sister, buckle your seat belt and hop in for the ride, because we're going downhill and fast.

"What about your sister, Rust?"

"Leah? Oh please."

Another Brett in the family-responsibility department. Worse than Brett, actually. Leah's a mooch.

"Okay. But you owe me big time on this."

I mentally slide a bead across my imaginary abacus. Great. There's no way he can ever pay me back this much. I'm done for.

"Rusty? Will you ever come home for good?"

"..."

"..."

"Aw, come on, hon..."

"I thought so. Okay, tell your dad to come on over."

———

When Is Too Long Too Long?
By Ivy Starling-Schneider

How long do we give our husbands to come to their senses over any issue?

If I knew the answer to that, I wouldn't be writing a column for the Lutherville *Lavalier*. I'd be on *Oprah*.

———

My cell phone rings. I answer without looking at the caller ID.

"Tony!"

"Four lines, Ivy? That's it?"

"What do you think? I mean, I know it's gutsy to admit you don't have all the answers, but it's also refreshing, right?"

"I can't print this and you know it."

"Okay, okay. I'll send you something by tonight."

"Thanks."

The phone rings.

"Ivy, darlin'!"

"Mr. Moore!"

"Can you come over and give me a hand? I'm trying to clean out the refrigerator and just can't get the vegetable bin freed up."

"I'll be right there."

I stand at the door to the dining room. "I'm running next door for just a second to help Mr. Moore."

"You do an awful lot for that man. What does he do for you?"

What? "Mom, are you okay?"

"I just hate to see you taken advantage of."

"I'm not. I'm only being neighborly. Anyway, Trixie's two doors down playing."

How weird. I mean, back in Lutherville Mom wasn't exactly your friendly neighborhood Welcome Wagon type. In fact, she remained downright reclusive, our whole existence revolving around church and right-wing politics. No wonder our neighbors thought us wackos. But really now, I didn't think she'd be opposed to *me* reaching out and loving my neighbor as myself, etcetera, etcetera.

Mr. Moore's waiting at the front door. He swings wide the screen door. "Come on in! Back to the kitchen. You're a gift from God, Ivy!"

He sure sounds excited about pulling a vegetable bin out of the refrigerator.

"You had lunch yet?"

"No. I'm just about to make some for Mom and me."

He ushers me into the kitchen. "Surprise!"

A peach pie sits in the center of the table. He reaches out and lights the candle in the middle. "Happy birthday, Ivy!"

"Oh my goodness. I forgot today was my birthday!"

Thirty-nine years old. Good grief.

In a warbly old voice, he sings the song.

God, I love life sometimes.

13

I'm typing away for Tony, darn him. Mom enters the kitchen. "Look at that living room, Ivy. I feel like I can't breathe in my own home!"

"I'm sorry, Mom. The kids are still little and playing with toys. I just can't keep things straight twenty-four hours a day."

"When I got up this morning there were toys all over the floor. I stepped on a LEGO and thought I would scream. And with my diabetes, I can't take chances of injuries down there."

Excuse me for living.

"Okay, okay. I'll try harder. I really will. I'm sorry."

I'm on pins and needles all the time now. I mean, she hasn't lived here for years. Grandma and Grandpa owned the house. I know she grew up here and owns it now, but this is my home too, and has been for a long time.

She crosses her arms. "And I hate the new color of the living room. That dark berry makes it look half the size, and it wasn't a big room to begin with."

What do I say? I can't fight back. She's sick. And she was never like this before. It's the illness talking. It's the illness talking.

The illness talking.

Persy stands in the doorway. "Winky! *Hey Arnold!* is on! Want to watch?"

She turns toward him, and as her face swivels from me, I see it clear. "I love that Helga. She's hilarious!"

My son holds out his hand. "Come on, Winky. I've got a spot saved for you on the couch."

Rescued by a nine-year-old.

I call Lou. "Mom hates the color of the living room."

"Oh drat."

"Should I repaint it?"

"Let me think for a sec. How's everything else going?"

"Okay. I'm so tired."

"Got a solution. Why don't you offer to buy the house from her?"

Hmm? "Never thought of that before."

"With Rusty's raise, it would be a good investment."

I do the mental calculations. Day care. IND. A mortgage? "Maybe so."

"There you go."

"I hope I can find the courage to bring it up."

"You never know, she may welcome the idea."

"I'll run it by Rust."

Owning this place for ourselves. The idea attaches itself to me. I buzz off an e-mail to Rusty and continue this week's column, which is about honoring your parents no matter what your age. Or theirs. Man, it's so hard sometimes, though, when you feel you just can't do anything right in their eyes, and the vision you possess of yourself seems to deteriorate week by week. I don't care how old a woman is, when her mother criticizes her, it chips away at her self-confidence.

I send Tony the column, and e-mail comes in. Great, one from Rusty.

Hey Ive,

It's a great idea to buy the house. I've been wanting to do that for a long time, but, it being your family's place, didn't want to assume. Let's go for it.

Hey, I started on a diet and have lost twenty pounds so far. You'd be proud of me.

How are the kids?

Blah, blah, blah.

The closing music to *Hey Arnold!* begins, and I think, "There's no time like the present."

"Mom! Phone call! A lady named Candace Frost?" Lyra.

My so-called agent!

"I'll take it upstairs!"

I bound up the steps two at a time, race into the bedroom, and shut the door. "Hello?"

I hear Lyra's line go dead. I still haven't told anyone about Candace. I still can't.

"Ivy. I've got good news."

I arrange a pillow against the headboard. "Great."

"I found a smaller publishing house interested in your manuscript. It may need a little tweaking to fit their audience, but nothing you can't handle."

"What kind of tweaking?"

"Well, they cater to men, but they like the story idea. Can you change your protagonist to a man?"

Wow. A man? "I guess so. But half the story is about an unwanted pregnancy."

"Maybe he's got a girlfriend?"

"I'll make it work."

"Most of their books have a lot of violence in them. But if you can fit it into the plot line, it won't be gratuitous."

"Okay."

"And you'll have to write under a pen name. Or do your initials for your first name. Something like that."

"No problem there." I might be able to keep this a secret for years to come.

"I'll tell them you're interested, then we'll start talking figures."

"As in money?"

"Right. Leave that part to me, though. I'll get you as much as they'll possibly give."

As if I even believe that. I may be a novice in the publishing world, but not in the world in general. People hang on to as much of their money as possible.

The rest of the day I can't wipe the silly grin off my face. Dear Lord, please let this work out. Please please please.

———

Mitch Sullivan enters the bistro, three other men accompanying him. "Ivy!"

"Mitch!" Did somebody jump-start my heart?

"Thought I'd bring a little business your way. Got a table for four?"

"Absolutely. Some good lunch specials today. Brian and the boys went all out." I sound so professional and smooth.

I show them to a table in the back corner, private and perfect for business. "Can I get you all something to drink?"

Water. Water. Decaf. Coke for Mitch.

I fade into the background as I should.

And that's me, isn't it? Fading into the background. Hey! When did I become so obscure? The kids went back to school, which I can't believe starts in August these days. How horrible for them. Trixie's still at the day care down the street from the restaurant. Mom just moved back to her apartment with a Life Alert necklace around her neck, and Rusty's in Minneapolis.

Or is it Milwaukee?

I don't like that Mom's on her own, but I'm definitely glad to be out of the trajectory of her barbs. Honestly, Mom and I used to be so close. I hate this. I feel like I've lost her already.

I'm praying like crazy that she doesn't burn the place down around her.

Harry keeps to himself for the most part, and now that Mom's back home, I'm not on edge about that subterfuge.

A small breathing space surrounds me, and I should be enjoying it a lot more than I am. But I'm worried. About Mom, about Rusty, about Brett, not to mention my own family. Poor Trixie. A little boy named Brady has been downright cruel. I mean, we parents secretly like it when our kids get a taste of their own medicine, but enough is enough.

After the meal a lot of handshaking occurs, and everyone but Mitch exits the restaurant.

"When do you get off work?" he asks.

Whoa. "Three. Persy gets off the bus at three forty-five, and I have to be home by then."

"Bummer. Okay."

"Why?"

"Well, just have something I want to talk over with you. You still interested in freelance writing jobs?"

"Definitely. Trixie's day-care fees are killing me. Lyra's in private school, and we're thinking about buying the house from Mom."

"How about getting together tonight? Can you meet me for coffee?"

Yes! Yes! "It'll have to be late." I'll have Harry keep an eye on the kids. He can handle them sleeping.

"That's fine. You still live nearby, right? At your grandparents' place?"

I nod.

"How about at that Starbucks across from Greetings and Readings? It's more quiet than the one here in Towson."

"They got one there?"

"Yeah, just down from the Crack Pot."

The Crack Pot. Maybe we should meet there. It would be fitting for me. The place looks like a dump, but they make great seafood. Sounds just like me. "Okay. How about nine thirty?"

"Great. See you there."

Off he goes, all businesslike and professional and real. And there. Mitch in the actual flesh. I shouldn't compare him to Rusty. I shouldn't wish my husband were more normal. But I can't help myself. Yeah, Ivy, you thought being with the artsy type would be so cool.

Man.

———

As I hurry into the day care, the director stops me. "Mrs. Schneider?"

"Yes?"

She lays a hand on my arm. Oh no, here it comes.

"We had a bit of a problem with Bellatrix today."

"I'm sorry." One of these days, I'm just going to have "I'm sorry" tattooed on my forehead. It would make things so much easier. "What did she do?"

"Does she normally take her diaper off?"

"I wouldn't say *normally.*"

"Well, she did it several times today. All the toys are going to have to be disinfected, and there's a fee for that."

"How much?"

"Fifty dollars."

I root for my checkbook. "At least she didn't hit someone over the head today."

Unfortunately, the director doesn't find that at all funny.

Trixie runs into my arms after the transaction and kisses me all over the face. I kiss her back, and we smile at each other. She smells clean and sweet. I hold her hand as we leave and rest under no delusion that the staff isn't glad to see her go.

———

I've decided on a venti caramel macchiato. Whole milk, lots of sugar and fat. Yes ma'am. Mitch orders the same.

"You're my kind of gal, Ive. These women that drink skim stuff drive me nuts."

"Well, it's a special occasion. I'm celebrating the fact that I'm here as Ivy Starling, writer and friend, and nothing else."

"Great. Grab a couple of chairs, and I'll wait for the drinks."

I sink into a plush, mustard chair and close my eyes. I need more of these moments.

Mitch wears jeans and a heavy T-shirt. Still slender, he sports a nice flat stomach, a good tush. Fine red-blond hairs soften his arms.

I should flee. But he's just a friend. Nobody would blame me for feeling this way, if the feelings remain only that. We all experience unwanted physical attraction at times. Usually it's over men on television and movie screens. Sometimes it's for real.

I was a fool to let him go. He loved me once.

Keep it business, Ivy, and get thee behind me, Satan!

My own feelings scared me so much I purposely didn't comb my hair or put on lipstick. I mean, infidelity is a big sin. A big, big sin. And it's got to start somewhere right?

"So what's up, Mitch?"

"I'm thinking about starting a newsletter."

"Oh yeah? For international business?"

"No. It's an organization I'm trying to start called MOMS."

"Moms?" That sounds like something I know a little about.

"Yeah, actually, M-O-M-S. It stands for Mothers Off Main Street."

"And the purpose?"

"It would find jobs for women who need to work but want to stay home and raise their children."

"Telecommuting stuff?"

"Primarily. Bona fide assembly work, too. None of that envelope-stuffing malarkey. I've already contacted twenty major corporations who've agreed to participate."

"Makes sense. Less overhead for them. And did you actually just use the term malarkey?"

He laughs. "Yes, as a matter of fact I did. Anyway, the plan works for everyone."

"That's what you need."

He sips his drink. "Everyone needs a little incentive. So what do you think?"

His eyes are so deep. And he's sensitive and caring and wants to give back to the community.

He gets better and better every second. Lord, help me.

"Sounds fabulous."

"I've got a couple of people interested in doing research, and a lot more corporate ins. All you'd have to do is the writing and, if you're able, format the actual newsletter."

"What kind of circulation are you talking about?"

"Twenty thousand to start. But we're hoping to get a real Web presence going. And we'll definitely want to send the newsletter out by e-mail, too."

"Oh yeah. Absolutely."

"Now, let's get down to brass tacks. I'm figuring this is going to take you around four hours a day. If you're still the fast worker you used to be."

"I'm faster."

"I figured."

"Motherhood will do that to you."

"And you'll be our first placement. Get you out of that restaurant."

Wow. That's true! And Trixie out of day care. Although maybe I'll leave her in for a couple hours a day to get work done. Rusty'll take this as license to stay away, though, but hey, you've got to do what you've got to do. You can't sit around twiddling your thumbs getting angrier and angrier while the world passes you by and you age day by day, and my goodness, Ivy!

"Four hours sounds right. Probably a little more nearing press date."

"Of course. Let's talk money, then. You're an experienced writer, so how does four a month sound?"

"Well, that's a little low. I make considerably more than that from the bistro."

"More than four thousand? I had no idea it was doing that well! Good for you. I guess I could go up to four-five."

Four *thousand?* Keep your mouth shut, Ivy. Keep the shock from overloading your expression. "You've got a deal."

"Great. I'll have my assistant draw up the paperwork, and we'll get started at the beginning of September. Can we get the first issue out by November?"

"Absolutely."

He puts out his hand. I take it. We shake, and oh, how good the warmth feels. I hang on to it for a couple of seconds and squeeze. "I'm glad you came back home, Mitch."

He squeezes back. "Me too, Ivy."

———

"Now why can't they have a picture of these glass fortresses?"

Persy and I lay on the bottom bunk together. I have a rule. My kids can stay up as long as they want provided they are reading. This must be a great book. It's eleven o'clock.

"I agree, Perse. And if there are as many as they say, why not give us a look-see?"

"I know. Can we go to Scotland someday to see one?"

"I hope so. That would be really cool."

"Castles of melted rock." Dreamy-eyed boy, lost in some imaginary battle with an imaginary magic sword in front of some glass castle.

This is good. I can understand this conversation. When he gets going about Mario and Wario and Sonic and, heaven help us all, the legion of Digimon characters, I just nod and smile, nod and smile.

"Persy, how are you doing with Winky and all?"

"Fine."

"You know, the reason she acts differently sometimes is because she's sick. Deep inside, she's really the same old Winky."

"Okay. Hey, look at this huge mound in England! A hundred and thirty feet high! Let's read this one. Oh, wait a minute, look at this crystal skull!"

I guess we all escape in different ways.

This isn't going well.

Maybe it was too early. Maybe waiting until after the lunch rush to broach the house-buying subject would have proved more prudent.

"Just think about it, Mom. That's all I'm asking. I'm really not trying to take anything away from you."

"I'm just concerned about your brother and sister and their share in this."

"Well, we'll have to take out a mortgage. You'll get the cash, and you can distribute it to them."

She nods. "I feel a little queasy right now. How about some soup?"

"Okay."

"Maybe you can get your grandfather to come over and make a pot of his chicken dumpling soup."

What good will it do to remind her Grandpop's been dead for ten years?

"That sure is good soup, Mom."

I could use some myself about now.

———

Persy's laying in bed, *Ancient Marvels and Mysteries* resting on his chest again. I slide under the covers, settle another pillow behind my head. "I've got a present for you. Just something little." I reach into my front jeans pocket. "Here."

He accepts the disc of amber. "Is this what I think it is?"

"Yep. Remember that part in your book about looking at sunspots?"

"Yeah." His sensitive fingers run over the smooth surface. "Too bad it's nighttime."

"I know. But it's supposed to be sunny tomorrow."

"Cool."

"Don't you wonder what people thought those spots were when they looked at them for the first time?"

"I'll bet they thought the sun was burning out."

"And that some god was angry with them."

"That would be scary." He holds the amber up to the lamp on his nightstand. "It's a good thing God's not like that, isn't it?"

"Unfortunately, a lot of people think He's sitting in heaven, ready to zap us with lightning bolts."

"Like Zeus."

"Exactly."

"Bennie next door says his grandmother's always zapping him for all sorts of things."

"Makes Winky not seem so bad."

"I feel sorry for Winky. She was throwing up again, wasn't she? I heard her in the bathroom after supper."

"Yeah. She seemed to be fine when I drove her home, though."

"I hate it when I throw up."

"Me too, bud."

14

The phone rings at 11:15 p.m. Who in the world?

"Ivy, it's Dani, Brian's girlfriend."

Oh no. "Hi! Everything okay?"

"Well, not really. I'm here at the police station with Brian."

"Another DUI?"

" 'Fraid so. Problem is, my mom's home alone, and I haven't been able to give her her shot. She's also getting scared to be home alone."

"I understand."

"Rosa is with me, and she's exhausted. I just don't know who else to call."

"Dani, I'm his sister. Of course you could call me. What precinct are you at?"

"Towson."

Right around the corner. "Okay. I'll be right there. Go ahead and get you and that baby home."

"Thanks. You have no idea how much I appreciate this."

"Oh yes, I do. You shouldn't have to deal with his issues. You're not even related to him."

I hop in the car and begin dialing my cell phone.

Mitch meets me on the precinct steps.

"Thanks, Mitch. I didn't know who else to call. Lou's out of town visiting her mother."

"Glad to help."

"I just don't think I can handle Brian like this on my own."

We pay the bail. Well, Mitch pays the bail, and I'm humiliated. Here I was feeling all professional, and now I'm beholden once again. To somebody else, once again. How did I get so entangled in everyone else's webbing?

Brian's curses echo all the way down the hall. "I'm so embarrassed," my mouth mutters on its own.

"Don't be, Ive. He's still drunk. This has nothing to do with you."

"Thanks for saying that."

"It's true. You can't pick your family."

Brian pales when he sees us. "This was *not* my fault. I swear, Ivy. I only had one beer, and this guy stopped short."

Can you smell that smell? P.U., Brian.

"You rear-ended him, Brian. He was at a red light. Dani told me everything."

"Well, she's wrong! The wench."

"Just shut up, Brian. She doesn't deserve that, and you don't deserve a girl like her. Let's just go."

Mitch steps forward. "I'll drive him home, Ive. You get back to the kids."

I point in my brother's face. "If you're not at the restaurant for opening in the morning, I'm going to tell Mom all about this."

Another string of expletives. Yeah, yeah, whatever.

Mitch jerks his head toward the door. "Let's go, Bri. I'll see you home."

I run to the car, thanking God for Mitch, his kindness, and my new job. Yep, it'll be great to say good-bye to that bistro. Too bad I can't leave Brian behind with it.

———

"Look Brian, I don't want to hear your excuses. *Nobody* has two DUIs in less than three months and it isn't their fault. Were you drinking?"

"Yes."

"Were you driving?"

"Yes, but—"

"Then cut the crap."

"The officer, she had it out for me before she even stepped out of the car."

"Whatever you say."

"Thanks for bringing Mitch by."

"Well, listen, *you* owe him one. Not me. I'm done."

"What do you mean?"

"I mean, I'm done with you. Remember that day Mom told us she was done with Dad?"

"Yeah."

"Well, I'm done with you. And guess what? I got a job offer for over twice what I make here, and I can work at home. I took it."

"You're leaving the bistro?"

"Yep. You're on your own."

"What about your stake in the business?"

"You can buy me out whenever you want."

I turn and head toward the door.

His eyes grow. "You're leaving right now?"

"You got it. The toilet paper's in the bathroom, Bri. You can wipe up your own mess from here on out."

Oh, brother. What a horrible parting line!

I step onto the sidewalk, his string of profanities following me out the door. They call stuff like this tough love. I call it heartache.

Dear God, am I doing the right thing?

———

I call Mitch's cell phone.

"Hi Ive."

"Listen, I just wanted to thank you for being there for me last night. I don't know what I would have done."

"You'd have been fine, but hey, I'm glad to help."

"Lord knows I need it."

"So what's the deal with Rusty?"

Huh? "I wish I knew."

"Doesn't he realize what a lucky man he is?"

"Guess not." Okay, this is scary.

"I'm thirty-nine, no kids, no wife, and here he has a woman like you, and he turns his back. I just don't get it."

That makes two of us, although I can't believe Mitch is actually saying all this. "Normally I can handle it."

"Well, I'm here whenever you need me."

"Thanks. I appreciate that."

"I mean it. You shouldn't have to be doing all this on your own. That's not what marriage is about."

"Yeah, you're right. I just don't know what to do to bring him back home. I've thrown more hints than should be necessary."

"Have you ever just told him he'd have to choose between his family and his dreams?"

"I've never wanted to put it in those terms."

"Not ready to follow through if he chooses his singing?"

"Not yet."

"I can understand that. How long's he been on the road?"

"Three years."

"He doesn't deserve you, Ive."

My heart races.

———

I love my new job. I love my new job.

I need something like that to encourage me right now. Mom's slipping more and more. I hear about the past more frequently, finding myself in the world of the fifties and sixties. She really shouldn't be alone so much, but she refuses to entertain any other option. She's also canceled her doctor appointments. I can't drag her there by the hair.

The autumn light illuminating the leaves of the sugar maples outside falls across my kitchen table. September is my favorite month, just enough summer clinging to the air, just enough nip promising relief. Persy's turning ten today.

Mom saunters in, already here for the celebration meal. "I feel sorry for Trixie at that place all day."

"It's only three hours, Mom."

"I never did that to you."

"I was twelve when you and Dad split up. And I spent plenty of afternoons coloring at the table in the restaurant kitchen."

"Don't throw that in my face. I did the best I could."

"Precisely. And I'm doing the best I can."

I am, aren't I?

"Mom? Are you mad at me?"

"I just don't want to see you throwing your life away."

"What else can I do? I'm drowning, and there's nobody to help."

"So it's my fault then, is it?"

"Of course not. Here, I'll make us some coffee."

I used to be able to talk to my mother about anything.

15

Harry sits on my new couch sipping a mug of tea. "Your mother's still looking good. I forgot how pretty she is."

"Harry! Cut that out." I reach for the remote.

"Hey, a fellow can't be blamed for looking."

"Yes he can, if it's you…and her. And when did you see her anyway?"

"I saw her when she came over for Persy's birthday dinner."

"Did she see you?"

"Wouldn't you have found out if she did?"

The doorbell rings. "Hang on."

A Yu-Gi-Oh! character, Darth Maul, and Sleeping Beauty stand on my doorstep. They say nothing.

I reach into the bowl of candy bars. "You've got to say 'trick or treat' for these babies."

They mumble it.

"Oh, come on, you guys! You can do better than that!"

"Trick or treat!"

"Yes!"

I drop a full-size Nestlé Crunch bar in each pillowcase.

"Yeah! Full size! Thanks!" Darth Maul.

Love it. Love being the lady who gives out full-size treats even more. I am the Halloween Queen of Allegheny Avenue. Four jack-o'-

lanterns and a string of orange and purple lights set the tone on our porch. Lyra strung up gobs of cobwebbing, and Persy set out a speaker to the stereo that emits screams, moans, howls, and freakish laughter.

Two Power Rangers, Harry Potter, Jasmine, and a hippie girl hurry up the walk. I do the honors and wait while a father and a tiny angel climb my steps.

"Oh hey Bernie! Hi Lynnie!"

"Hi Ivy. How's it going?"

"Full house! Rusty's dad just moved into the basement."

"No kidding!"

"Never dull around here. Tell Debbie thanks for the soup last week. It was the perfect day. Those matzo balls were amazing."

"Mrs. Waxman makes it by the gallon. Every Saturday brings over a bucketful. We're glad to find homes for it."

I laugh. "We appreciate it anyway."

"She'll be glad to hear it. Hey, you'll have company in the whole parent thing. My mother-in-law's moving in in a couple weeks."

"Oh man."

Mrs. Waxman has already achieved more than her fair share of renown in the neighborhood, and she doesn't even live here. She'll yell at the kids if they're screaming too loud or playing in the street when she's ready to leave. And when she backs out that Lincoln, just watch it.

"We're already painting her room. I said we should paint it black, and Debbie hit me on the arm." He pushes up his small glasses. Bernie's a gem.

"At least she makes a good matzo-ball soup."

"Oh, believe me, we'll be eating well, that's for sure. Hopefully it'll make up for her personality."

"Tell Deb to call me. We'll have a cup of commiseration together."

"Will do."

They turn to continue the candy spree. He tenderly takes Lynnie's tiny hand and helps her down the steps. "Come on, angel baby."

I love the Meyers. They're such a sweet, decent family.

Deb's Jewish, but maybe she's not bigoted like some Christians I know. Maybe she'll join Club Sandwich anyway. I have a sneaking suspicion we're really going to need each other in the days to come.

The clock on our mantel chimes the hour. Eight o'clock. And the cutest gaggle of trick-or-treaters yet climbs the steps. A little pumpkin, a knight, and Lyra, dressed like a medieval princess, a costume she slaved hours over.

"Trick or treat!" The gusto almost blows my hair back from my face.

Now these kids know how to trick-or-treat. "Good job!" I distribute the goods.

Rusty's dad, chaperone extraordinaire, smiles. "Haven't done trick-or-treating in years!"

I love Reuben. Plainly, Rusty inherited his charisma from his dad. I step clear of the doorway. "Enjoy yourself, huh?"

"Yep."

"Want a cup of tea?"

"No thanks. Set up my coffee maker downstairs before I left."

Reuben's a coffee hound. I don't know how the man sleeps. Judging by the huge box of books he brought with him, I have a feeling he doesn't much. Oh, but the conversations we've always enjoyed, he and I, on such a variety of issues!

Reuben actually reads my column.

Lyra plops down on the sofa five minutes later, arms full of books, legs swimming in pajamas befitting Henry VIII. "Man, this new school is tough."

"It's a good school, Lyr."

"Yeah. But all these papers!"

"You can handle it, kiddo." Harry. I have to hand it to him; he's a lot more encouraging than he used to be.

"Thanks, Gramps."

She opens a volume of Shakespeare and sets to work. I admire her so much.

"Harry, how about a fire? You up to starting one?"

"Sure, Ive."

"I'll make us some tea."

The kitchen sits dark and clean. Only the hood light over the stove illumines the countertops. I turn on the burner and begin filling the kettle. Contentment warms this moment. The first newsletter will be mailed out tomorrow, and women will find jobs. My sweet daughter is getting a good education, and Harry stopped his prowling. For now.

"I have learned, in whatsoever state I am, therewith to be content," Paul wrote millennia ago, and I think, right now, I finally understand the meaning of the passage.

Mitch calls at ten. "Hey friend."

"Hi Mitch."

"Everything ready for tomorrow?"

"Yep. Went to the printer and picked them up yesterday. We'll head down to the post office tomorrow, and out they'll go."

"Got the copy you couriered over. Looks great. You really know what you're doing. Oh, and I found a good Web designer. We'll be online by the new year."

"Great."

"So how you doing?"

"Actually, not too bad. Harry's got a fire going, we're watching the news, and all is right with the world."

"Now that's what I like to hear."

"How about you?"

"Same as always."

"So how about you?"

He chuckles. "You're not going to let me get away with that, are you?"

"Darn straight."

He sighs. "I'm a little lonely, I admit. I came back to Baltimore hoping to renew old ties, and of course, everyone's busy with their lives."

"You know you can always come over here and hang out. Heaven knows we've got enough people to keep you company."

"Do you know how blessed you are?"

"I sure do."

We end the conversation, and I know that I lied. I stopped counting my blessings months ago, and isn't that a shame? But I can't appear needy to Mitch. Because if he picks up on it and offers more than a hand, I don't know what I'll do.

Trixie crawls into bed with me, her feet like winter. "Cold, Mama."

She snuggles into me, and I breathe in her scent. Oh, my sweet baby. And we fall back asleep. Just like that.

Brian's voice quivers with panic. "Get down to the restaurant, Ivy! The kitchen is flooded. Mom left her bathtub faucet running upstairs all night."

"Where is she?"

"In the dining room. Crying."

I run in ten minutes later and fold her into my arms.

"I had no idea, Ivy. How could I have done something so stupid?"

"It's not your fault, Mom."

We've all got to face facts now.

Man, I hate these family meetings. It's wrong sitting with Brian and Brett, Mom absent, while here in the bistro dining room we discuss her future. Workmen tear out the ruined carpet near the kitchen.

"If we put her into assisted living, we'll have to sell the bistro." Brian. "Her name is still on the deed with ours."

I shake my head. "That's not an option."

Brett. "I certainly have the space, but we're never home. Having a nurse come out means the same thing. There's no way she can afford that."

Even though Brett's sold her shop, she's still out and about all day long. Charity work now. Brett just can't slow down. She wouldn't be Brett if she could, I guess.

"We're chock-full here," I say.

My brother and sister both look at me.

"Maybe your new job is a godsend, Ivy. Did you think of

that?" Brett. "You're home all day. And Reuben's there quite a bit now too, right?"

I stare, undecided whether fear or anger is the appropriate response to that observation.

They stare back.

"Where do I have the space, guys? Trixie and Lyra share a room as it is."

Brian twiddles a napkin. Brett pretends to pick at a fingernail. Man.

Still, I'm going to make them work for it. I can keep my mouth shut too.

Finally, Brett. "Didn't you put her in the dining room when she was recuperating from hip surgery?"

"You know I did."

"Well?"

I decide. Anger. "So what you're saying, Brett, is that you have a freaking six-thousand-square-foot home with three empty bedrooms, and I have to lose my dining room? My fifteen-hundred-square-foot ramshackle house filled with six people—seven when Rusty's home—is the answer? Come on!"

Her lips tighten. "I can't commit to this, Ivy."

"You *won't.*" I turn to my brother. "And you won't either, right?"

"I just have a little apartment, Ive."

"How about when the work is done on the restaurant and Mom's apartment? Why don't you move in then?"

"Ivy! I can't do that. I do have a life, you know. I'm not what's best for Mom anyway. You know that."

"Can't you rise to the occasion, Bri? At least try? It's all I can do to hold things together as it is."

"No, I just can't. It's beyond me."

"What if *I* say it's beyond *me*, guys?"

Brett slams a fist on the table. "Oh, all right. Let's just put her in a home, and I'll pay for it! But is that what's best for Mom?"

Of course it isn't. She's not that far gone yet, and those homes are so sad. I can't picture her sitting next to babbling, demented people. It would break her heart.

But still. Brett's really being horrible.

I breathe deeply. It's up to me. It's got to be up to me.

Maybe Brenda's Club Sandwich idea was a good one after all. My thoughts flit for a split second to Debbie and Dani. I'm going to call them tomorrow and see if they'll join.

"Okay, I'll do the dining room over. But listen, you guys have *got* to take her off my hands sometimes. I can't bear all the responsibility. You both have cars. You'll have to help take her out for her shopping and prescriptions and doctor appointments and all."

Brett reddens. "Of course we'll help! You don't think we won't pull our weight, do you?"

No, I don't. But I say, "I sure hope it won't be the case."

Brian grabs my hand and squeezes. "You're the best, Ive. You really are. And, Brett, isn't it true? Ivy definitely has the best personality to handle this sort of thing. She's more caring and compassionate."

I can see Brett wants to contradict, but she realizes it would be against her best interest. She clamps her lips together and nods.

I want to tell them they'll owe me big time, but there are only two people I'm doing this for. Mom and Jesus. That's it.

Mitch and I meet for another late-night Starbucks conference. Still in his car when I pull up, he quickly hops out at the sight of me and opens my door.

Any idiot could see I've been crying all afternoon, and Mitch is no idiot.

"Oh Ive! What's the matter?"

The fountains of the deep bubble up once more. He crouches down on his haunches, reaches into the car, and takes me into his arms. And as I cry, feeling my life slip-sliding into a tailspin, he strokes my messy hair and mutters softly.

"It's okay, Ive, it's okay. Sh, baby. Everything's going to be okay."

ou stands in my living room. "That berry with the white woodwork is perfect. See, Ive-O? I told you to trust me."

"I still love it."

"We'll have the dining room looking like a bedroom in no time. Your mom's furniture is great. I'm thinking a nice plum in there."

"Nope, she hates dark colors."

"Hold on." She takes her paint chips and heads into the kitchen where Mom's sitting. I hear muffled conversation. Mom's always loved Lou.

She emerges. "How about a warmish lavender?" she asks.

"Whatever Mom wants. Can we install doors?"

"Sure. Will Harry do it, you think?"

"He'll have to. Mom will have a fit if she finds out, but I can't afford to hire somebody."

"How about your sister? She offer to help with the change?"

I cross my arms.

"I didn't think so. When are the others getting here?"

I look at the wall clock. "In ten minutes. I thought Brenda would be here by now."

"She's in Mexico! I forgot to tell you! They're breaking ground this week."

Very cool.

"Then let's get started as soon as they come."

Club Sandwich, here we come.

———

I'm glad I have this big couch now. Here we all sit: me, Debbie, Dani, and a lady named Krystal who answered our ad in the paper and actually showed up. Debbie's in the housewife uniform of jeans and a sweater. Dani looks like a hooker, and Krystal wears one of those fancy sweat suits only heavy African American women can get away with. And with aplomb. An amazing arrangement of braids and curls crowns her head.

Why can't I have that much sass?

I settle into the cushions. "Why don't we introduce ourselves and tell one interesting accomplishment or happening in our lives?"

"I'll start." Debbie straightens her jeans. "My name's Debbie Meyer. I have two children, Bennie, age eleven, and Lynnie, age four. My husband is Bernie. I was known as Chug-a-Lug in college, and I'm sure you can figure out why!"

Well, this is a good start.

"Ha!" Krystal. "I'm Krystal Percy. I've got one daughter, five years old, named Toinette. I'm a preacher."

Whoa-ho.

"Dani?"

"I'm Dani Hoskins. My daughter is four too, Debbie. Rosa keeps me from being wild."

Debbie almost chokes on her coffee. Danielle laughs.

"I'm a trainer at Gold's Gym in Timonium. My interesting accomplishment could well be the ability to tie a cherry stem in a knot, in my mouth, in less than five seconds. But with Chug-a-Lug here, I'll go a little more tame and say that my favorite TV Land show is *Family Affair*, and I actually shook the hand of Brian Keith when I was six."

Debbie sets down her mug. "I loved that show! And to think what eventually happened to Buffy! *Buffy*, for cryin' out loud!"

Krystal rolls her eyes. "Girl, I know. And that Jodie boy disappeared after *Sigmund the Seamonster*, didn't he?"

Well, we're really off to TV Land now. No prob. I know a little bit about each of these women and the people they care for. Krystal has a bedridden father and all that entails. Debbie's mother, Matzo-Ball Waxman, screams at her all day long. Dani's mother is as helpless as she is sweet. If they want to escape to TV Land, so be it. I'll go right along with them.

"And therefore I shall say to ye, 'Repent for the end is near!' "

What? Who?

I bound from my bed and run down the steps. Did Harry leave the television on last night? It sounds like one of those charismatic women preachers. But then again, "The end is near"? That's a bold statement for anyone to make these days!

"Turn from your wicked ways! Repent of your sins!"

"Mom?"

She stands by the fireplace, facing out, arms waving. Her skin shines an eerie gray in the light from the powder room. I realize she's losing weight. But her stomach has become so sensitive, and she eats sparingly. She doesn't look as full, and the skin on her arms hangs down as she flaps them, punctuating each word with a sweep. "Verily, verily, I say unto thee, except a man be born again, he cannot see the kingdom of God!"

The words of Jesus can't be wrong.

I walk carefully toward her. "Come on, Sister Starling. Testimony time is over. Enter into your rest." I mentally cross my fingers, slip my arm around her waist, and stroke the back of her hair.

"Thank you, my sister."

I guide her back to her bed and tuck her in. Grandma's wedding quilt snuggles her chin, and I begin to grieve afresh. I'm losing her day by day, and I'll be here for each of them.

Count your blessings, Ivy, count them one by one.

On my way to the door, I stub my toe on the dresser. I swear.

———

"So what do you want me to do about it, hon?"

"I don't know, Rusty. I'm just upset."

"Look, it's 4:00 a.m. here. If I could do something about it, I would."

"Forget it." Where's my Rusty? Who is this guy?

"It's just that I'm powerless. If you want me to feel guilty, it's working."

If I believed that, I'd be more gullible than Mom, who still thinks Brian is "the one who turned out so well."

"So how's the group?" I ask. The current tack is obviously not working. Let's talk about Rusty. It's all he's interested in anyway.

"Fantastic! The boss is working on a European tour."

"Really?"

"Yep. Spring. Babe, I've got to get some sleep. Big travel day tomorrow."

"Where you heading?"

"San Diego."

"I hear it's beautiful there."

Yep, it sure is. I've got to get a grip. I've got to get a grip.

"Mr. Moore? I'm sorry for calling at this hour."

"You okay, Ivy dear?"

"No. I need a good cry. And not by myself."

"You just come on over. I'll put on a pot of tea."

At first, I thought to call Mitch but decided no way. Too dangerous.

So I head next door, and Mr. Moore sits me on a lounger, puts a dining-room chair right up next to it. He sits next to me, holding my hand as I sob and sob.

God, I'm so sick of crying. I feel like such an emotional wimp.

The day-care director crosses her arms.

"Fifty dollars?" I ask.

"I'm sorry, Mrs. Schneider. But I think it would be in everybody's best interest if you found another center for Bellatrix."

"All right."

I gather Trixie and her effects, and we head out the door into the cold November afternoon.

"Mama! We going home?"

"Yes, baby. We're going home."

"Hi hon!"

"Rusty! You okay? It's the middle of the day?"

"Just thought I'd call and talk to the kids."

"Okay." I turn away from the mouthpiece. "Guys! Daddy's on the phone!"

They rumble in. Ten minutes later I chat with my husband. Or rather, he chats to me.

The audiences keep getting larger and larger. And people actually ask for their autographs now. Especially down south. Airplay like crazy on the gospel radio stations. On the bus, they slide the dial from station to station and catch a song or two with regularity. He never thought he'd be involved in something this big. It's like a drug, he hates to admit. But that's the case. Bringing joy to people, even if only for a little while, is incomparable to anything he's ever experienced. It's nice to support them like that, to offer help and hope and therefore, a little mercy. He's glad to do that for them. And thankful. And honored, even. See, Ivy? It isn't all about him. He's part of something far larger.

"And get this! Marlin gave us the news about Europe. Plans are finalized, and we leave after the New Year. Six months we'll be gone. I'm sorry it's so long, and I hope you won't flip, but who knows what kind of audience we'll garner over there? It could bring in more money than we've ever dreamed we'd have, hon. We can hire a nurse for your mom, put *all* the kids in private school, and maybe even add on to the house, a nice master-bedroom suite on the ground floor, a bed and bath for your mom. It's all going to work out beautifully."

I've got nothing left to say.

———

Okay, so now I really have to get to work on this novel. Ten grand for the advance, a third up front, which will pay for my kitchen renovation and Mom's room. Lou talked me into a new stovetop and an extra oven. Rusty will be thrilled, as well as Brian. I wish I could say my brother's tail rests between his legs, but no. That would be too much to hope for.

I fire up Old Barbara, buzz off this week's column, this time about taking advantage of our right to vote. Tony loves it.

Now. The book.

My basic story: a woman, pregnant, turns on her stalker, the father of her child, and the hunted becomes the hunter. What started out as a story of female empowerment will become another male-vigilante tale. But it's a break, and I'd be a fool not to take it.

Okay. Jane becomes Nick.

I have six months to revamp this sucker.

Chapter One

Jane was tired of looking in her rearview mirror.

Well, that's no good anymore. Universal change from Jane to Nick.

Nick was tired of looking in his rearview mirror.

Hmm, that doesn't work either.

Oh great.

———

Two in the morning and I've decided just to scrap the manuscript and begin again. Six months to write an entire novel, forty-eight columns, and six newsletters. Brian's trying to talk me into returning to the restaurant. "I'll even start reading that Bible if you do." No way. The boy's on his own.

Someone's behind is bumping down the steps. Persy enters the kitchen. "Mom, I don't feel good. My stomach hurts."

He looks gray.

"Have you thrown up?"

"No."

"Do you feel like you have to?"

He nods.

"Now?!"

He nods again and lets it fly. All over my lap.

An hour later he's tucked back in bed, we've read about more *Ancient Marvels and Mysteries,* and I'm so mad at Rusty I could spit. I didn't say "I do" for this. I thought a marriage meant mutual support, not this lone life of coping and trying and praying and grasping and sucking wind and hoping things will change.

I pray that God will change Rusty. I should pray He'll change me, but I'm scared to do that. I'm scared of what the answer will look like. And anyway, I'm not the one who left.

Sometimes I want to take Rusty up on his RV dreams. Leave all this behind. Say good-bye to Brian and Brett and Harry. Say good-bye to this life where I'm stretched so thin I can only do a half-job on everything. And then, poor Mom.

No sense in going to bed now.

I make a cup of tea and get back to work.

Will anyone close to me see that I need help? Will anyone notice that I give and give and get little in return?

Stop feeling sorry for yourself! That's what they'd say.

I turn on IM.

Mitch's button is lit up.

hi ive.

hi mitch.

you doing ok?

persy's sick.

poor kid. poor you.

i'll survive. you're sure up late.

yep. pulled out the old yearbooks, believe it or not.

no way!

yep. i'd forgotten we were voted king and queen for the
      sweetheart prom when we were juniors.

tom webber was furious.

what a geek, ive. why did you date him for so long?

looking back now, i just can't say.

if I'd have known you two would have eventually broken
      up, i'd have gone to school around here.

Oh Lord.

life never seems to work out like you think it will, does it, mitch?

I sit and wait and wait and wait for him to reply.
Finally.

maybe sometimes, though we can decide to go for it
    anyway. happiness, I mean.
and what makes you happy?

More time elapses. Then—

i think you probably know.
i'm still not ready to think about big changes, mitch.
i know, i know. but i'm not going anywhere. i'm not
    going to make the same mistake twice.

I change the subject, get back to business. But when we sign
off, I shut down the computer. My hands shake so badly I can
hardly type.

17

Christmas Eve, and here we all sit at the airport. Hard to believe it's been almost six months since Rusty's last visit. Trixie's beside herself, singing all sorts of carols. Lyra wears a new dress she designed and made. Persy feels fine now and presses buttons on his Game Boy. I took an old Demerol left over from Trixie's C-section and feel better than usual. Hey, you do what you have to do. And my head was killing me. I've got to start getting more sleep.

Here he comes. God, give me strength.

———

"Rusty! How did you afford something like this?"

The ring twinkles in its velvet box. A three-diamond sparkler. I've always wanted one of these. He takes the box, gently lifts out the ring, and places it on my finger. "I've saved a little here, a little there."

It's beautiful. I suspect his motives.

"Thanks, Rust. Hey, I think I smell something burning in the kitchen!"

I jump off the couch.

He stands up. "Hey kids! Let's play one of those new games you got!"

Did he hear me?

———

I didn't sleep with Rusty once during his entire visit. I blamed it on the novel. Yes, I confessed the venture to him, staying up late each night to work. It's coming along. I've set aside any delusions of grandeur and am shocked at how easily violence pours from my fingertips. Maybe it's not so surprising, considering my burgeoning anger. Thank goodness that tomorrow Club Sandwich meets. I need it these days. I hate to even admit that I've become a support-group kind of person. But with Mom up three times a night—another excuse to sleep on the couch—Brian's letting the restaurant slip down a slope to ruin with the most peculiar menu ever heard of, and Brett's marriage utterly on the rocks despite her selling the shop, I'm eager to hear about situations worse than my own.

Which is a bummer in itself. I can't even feel as sorry for myself as I'd like.

I try to keep clear of Mitch as much as possible. When he looks at me with those eyes... But business is business, and I can't avoid my boss completely.

———

Rusty leaves for Europe in eight days. For the first time since this circus began, I'm glad he'll be far away. Honestly, I used to think the kids would be better off with the visits. But now, I wonder. Is a fly-by-night father better than none at all? I wish I knew.

———

Poor, lonely Mitch stands on the other side of the door in the bitter January cold. He called thirty minutes ago, told me to turn off Old Barbara and get dressed.

"I'll take care of things at your house. You can just have a good time."

I don't know what I'll do, but hey, an evening to myself? I'm not stupid.

I open the door. "Hey Mitch! Come on in."

He holds out a ticket. "It's a ticket to that comedy you were talking about. At Towson Commons." He reaches into his pocket and pulls out a gift card from Starbucks. "And this is for afterward."

"What's all this about?"

"Consider it a belated Christmas gift. You've seemed stressed." He slips out of his parka and lays it across the back of the couch. "I know you, Ive."

"Is it showing in my work?"

"Not a bit."

Yeah. Nobody but Lou knows me like Mitch does.

Thank goodness he's a gentleman.

———

I'm crying through the entire movie. A comedy. I can't stand this. I feel guilty sitting here while they're at home. Mitch is probably at his wit's end with Mom. I need to get out of here.

———

"Home already?" Lyra asks as I let myself in through the kitchen door.

"I couldn't relax."

"Well, you can here. That Mitch guy is really neat. Winky loves him. They're in the living room listening to big-band music."

I set my purse down. "Really?"

"Yeah. That Glenn Miller is great. You'd really like it, Mom."

Fact is, I love big-band music. Maybe I need some old-fashioned swing to kick me up a bit. I enter the party room.

"Hey guys!"

Mitch. "What are you doing back already?"

"Couldn't sit still. Anyway, I hear there're big doings right here."

"Yeah. Dorothy and I are having a good old time, right Dor?"

She smiles. "You have a nice gentleman caller here, Ivy. Do your best to hang on to him."

"Mom—"

"Let it go, Mom," Lyra whispers in my ear. "She doesn't know her right from her left tonight."

"Have a seat, dear, and listen to records with us."

A turntable sits atop the television. Next to it, a stack of records.

"Where did all this come from?"

"I brought them with me." Mitch. "Thought your mom might like it."

"Oh, I do! Makes me feel like a girl again. The last time I heard 'Tuxedo Junction'…" And she's off on a story.

When Mitch leaves, I thank him. "How did you know what to do?"

"My grandma lived with us when I was little, remember? It was amazing how music soothed her. These are her records. I'll leave the turntable here for a while."

"Thanks."

This guy is just too good to be true.

We sit and talk long after the others retire to bed. And I unload. I can't help it. I need this so badly.

When he leaves, he holds me, and I just can't pull away.

Debbie arrives last, but she bears a coffeecake, so no prob. I start a pot of coffee, and the commiseration begins.

I take a bite of the cake.

The best coffeecake I've ever tasted roams around my tastebuds. Debbie laid down some pastry dough, obviously on a bed of butter, spread on a sweet cream-cheese mixture, and topped it with another layer of pastry, more butter, nuts, sugar, and cinnamon. It's still warm. Oh yeah.

I try to savor this moment, willing it to flavor the rest of the week.

I go for another piece just to make sure. Yep, the appetite finally kicked in after all these years, and I don't care. That phrase "fat and happy" must contain a grain of truth, and I think maybe I should try it on. Look at Rusty. The perfect testament to the adage. Although, I have to admit, he lost a lot of weight this past fall. Fifty pounds at least. He's still heavy, but a garden variety heavy.

Hmm. He sure didn't lose the weight for me. Oh, shut up, Ivy. Worries enough abound without those sorts of suspicions. But if I'm not above infatuation with someone who's not my spouse, who's to say he's above it either?

Krystal, who sailed in wearing a different wind suit, a nautical-themed silken delight, raises her hand. "Well, I'd like to start if it's okay with the rest of you all."

"Go ahead." Brenda. She also brought snacks, but healthy ones. Still, it's the thought that counts, right? Truthfully, I'm glad she's here, though this group has become something of a desirable sisterhood. Brenda's tranquillity and service-mindedness radiate outward, something desperately needed if everyone else's week mirrors mine.

Lou's here too. Even though her kids are all teenagers and her mother is fit and in better shape than all of us put together, she comes to the meetings. For me. Krystal scoops up another piece of Debbie's cake. "My father has been in the ICU for the past two weeks. He had a stroke right after Christmas."

"Oh, Krystal!" Brenda lays a hand on her knee. "How are you dealing with this?"

"I was all right the first few days. The family's been taking shifts. But as it wears on, I get so tired I can hardly stand up."

Debbie nods. "And then you can't sleep!"

"That's right! I fall into my bed and pray to God that tonight will be the night I actually get a good sleep, and then I toss and turn, toss and turn, my mind spinning along at a hundred miles an hour."

Brenda reaches for a baby carrot. "I know. When my mother was ill it was the same way."

"You took care of your mother?" I ask.

"For eight years. Eight long years. I thought it would be the end of John and me."

Wow. "How come I didn't know about this?" I ask.

"It was years ago. Before we moved up here."

How old is Brenda? I pegged her for forty-five, tops. When will I learn not to make assumptions about people?

She crosses her legs. "It was the exhaustion that made it so bad. When she'd have to go to the hospital, and I'd go down every day, I'd think to myself, 'All I'm doing is sitting around. Why do I feel so exhausted?'"

"That's right!" Krystal. "Some of the church women have been taking care of Toinette. I have a hot meal waiting every night, and you'd think I'd be revved up and ready to go. Instead, I drag myself around all day by the back of my own coat collar. And for some reason, my daughter has been so touchy. There's no pleasing her."

"I know how that is," I say. "The other day Persy looked at me like I was a slug when I asked him to bring his dirty clothes down for the laundry. Then, he dropped them at my feet and said, 'I have to do all the work around here.' It isn't any wonder. Children are a direct barometer of the mother."

Debbie. "What I don't think is fair is that we can't have a bad day. My mother criticizes me from sunup to sundown. 'Deborah Ruth'"—her voice goes down an octave and takes on a smoker's rasp—"'Benjamin has been coughing since yesterday and you haven't done a thing. I had you kids to the doctor's at the first sign of sickness.' 'Deborah Ruth, look at the shelves in this refrigerator. I raised you better than this.' Then Bernie comes home, looks at the state of the living room and the kitchen counters, and asks innocently, 'So what'd you do today, Deb?' Which I immediately interpret as criticism. I go off in a tirade at him, blasting all my frustrations, and he doesn't deserve that. I mean, how many men allow their mother-in-law in their own home, making trouble?"

"How do Bernie and your mom get along?" Brenda. "John and mine fought like cats and dogs."

"Oh, she's fine with him face to face. But when he's not home, all she does is criticize him. He doesn't make a lot of money, and we do have to scrimp and save. I cut coupons and do rebates, and she sees that as failure and selfishness because he's doing what he loves. I try to tell her that this is the life we've chosen, that money isn't everything, but there's no convincing her."

Krystal sets her fork on her plate. "What's his line of work?"

"He's a social worker." Debbie cuts herself another slice of cake. "So Mom gets me going, and my bad mood escalates, and soon everyone is grumpy. But if I keep a clear head and a smile on my face, things are much better. I'm telling you, it's too much responsibility."

"I know that's right!" Krystal raises a hand.

"How about you, Ivy?" Lou asks, darn her. I love her, but I'll jump into the conversation when I want to, thanks. I'll have to talk to her about that later.

"Mom's dementia is getting worse. She's probably got enough plaque in her system to choke the Alaskan pipeline, which is what they're attributing it to. I can't even believe the way she cooked when I was little. Fried everything."

"Lord, yes!" Krystal. "Don't even get me started on all that. It hasn't changed any at my church either. I've gained seven pounds since my father went in."

"Not unusual. Not at all." Brenda.

I tell them about Mom's nighttime preaching.

Krystal laughs. A fabulous throaty chuckle. "I'll bet I could get some pointers. My congregation needs a jump-start!"

"Well, come at 2:00 a.m., 4:00, and 6:00, and you'll get an earful."

"I don't know how you do it without Rusty." Debbie.

Krystal sets down her plate. "I don't have me a man either. Don't want one. Having one who won't stick around is for the birds."

Yep. She's got that right. "I'm on a rubber band, Rusty on one end, Mom on the other. And me and the kids are wobbling the length of it like amateur tightrope walkers. I can't let go of my responsibilities to Mom, but am I being an unsubmissive wife by not doing what Rusty wants? But how can I? Where would that leave my mother?"

Debbie. "Rusty should be doing the right thing here, Ivy. You're merely doing what you can to cope. If he was a man, he'd fess up to his responsibilities and come home. And what's this submission thing anyway?"

I raise my coffee cup to her. "Thanks for saying that."

"Well, we don't like to say stuff like that out loud for ourselves, so I thought I'd just do it for you."

I lean forward. "So do you make ultimatums? That's what I want to know. Would it be wrong to demand he come home?"

Krystal. "How long's he been out on the road?"

"Three and a half years."

She nods once. "Yep. You got a right. You absolutely do got a right."

18

Well, Nick the protagonist is fully engrossed in planning his retribution on Maximilian, my new evil genius. Ha! I can't write some seedy, one-sided villain. This guy oozes sex appeal, and he's trying to seduce Nick's ex-girlfriend, who's pregnant with their child. A marvelous plan, really, and Max's day looms. I still need a hundred and fifty pages, however, and a subplot or two would come in handy. Sadly, Nick bores me. Nice enough guy. I like him, but he resembles nothing more than a good yawn. Which has its place. Just not in a book. I mean, if Rusty were a yawn, we'd be doing all right.

It's Valentine's Day, and not one word from my husband in Glasgow. Maybe Valentine's Day isn't big in Scotland. Maybe no red-and-pink cardboard hearts reminded him of the occasion that's always epitomized our romantic life. A parade of dinners out, stunning flower arrangements, new dresses, and memorable times of intimacy dances before my mind's eye. Stuffed animals here and there. Picnics on the bed. Soft music. Or raucous music. Lots of kisses.

He hurts me. Can't he see that he hurts my heart? I sent an e-card earlier and a gift certificate to Starbucks online, since I know they litter the city streets over there as well. But no reply. Nothing.

Oh well, I have my dependable Nick here. An ex-Marine, naturally, and so patient. What might switch him over to a darker side?

Maybe he needs to be a father already! Maybe *that* child needs to be threatened.

Oh Lord, maybe I don't have the stomach for this after all.

And honestly, what male in my life can I use as a model for this character?

The phone rings. I check the clock over my new kitchen counter: 10:00 p.m. Yes! Maybe Rusty remembered.

"Hey Ive."

"Hi Brett." Drat.

"Listen, we've got a situation."

"What's up?" At least I know it's not Mom. She's sleeping in her room with Glenn Miller softly playing. Lyra ordered a bunch of CDs off of eBay and faithfully adjusts the player to Repeat every evening when she says good-night. Man, I miss my daughter. But finding the time to do anything special with her these days is akin to locating the exact shoes you have in mind to go with the dress you bought at an outrageous sale price. Brian's not in a state to baby-sit, and Mom obviously can't. Mitch offers all the time, but I can't bring myself to take him up on it. I feel much too close to him already.

And all Brett's promises to take Mom on her errands or to lunch have proved as fruitless as a pile of cherry-wood mulch.

"Brian's going off to rehab, Ive."

"What? When?"

"Tomorrow morning. His lawyer recommended it. They've been able to move things along slowly, and when they finally appear before the judge, it would be better if he was already working on his problem."

"Where's he going?"

"There's a place up in Cecil County."

"Live in?"

"Yes."

"How's he going to pay for it?"

"Well, he's not. I am."

Oh great. I mean, good. But oh great. "Are you sure you want to do that?"

"Spend some of Marcus's money? You'd better believe it."

"What does Marcus say about it?"

"He doesn't have much political capital with me these days. Did I tell you he's running for state senate?"

"Must have slipped your mind."

"He decided last week. I've got enough dirt on him to ruin him."

Why she's resigned herself to this kind of marriage, I don't know.

"What about the restaurant?" The renovations after the flood have been extensive. We're reopening tomorrow. Way to go, Brian.

"That's why I'm calling you."

I can't tell her I'm swamped with my book. I still haven't told a soul. "Brett, I have a job now. And there's Trixie to consider. There's not a day care in ten miles who will take her. Believe me, I know."

"It can't be helped. It's only for a month. You'll have to go back."

"I can't!"

"Well, what am I supposed to do about it?" she yells. "I'm paying for the blasted rehab *and* the lawyer! You haven't done squat for Brian."

"Guess I've been a little busy with *Mom*."

"Don't throw that in my face."

"I'm not trying to throw anything in anybody's face. I just can't do it."

"It would kill Mom to see that restaurant go down."

"She won't know the difference."

"I beg to differ."

"You would."

"What's that supposed to mean?"

"Let's just say you can afford the luxury."

"Look, Ivy. If you want Brian to have a job to come back to, you'll do what it takes."

If it was about Brian alone, I'd say no. But my family has owned this restaurant for years. And it's just a month, right? I mean, it's not like I'm heading off to sing around the world for years and years. And the truth is, somewhere down inside of her, Mom would know the difference.

One month. Just one month.

"Okay, okay. I'll make it work. I'm never getting any sleep anyway. What's one more thing?"

"Well, I'm not sleeping either. Does that make you feel better?"

Strangely enough, it does.

Rusty had better not send me a Valentine right now. And if he does, he ought to be glad he's not here because I'd ram the cheap thing straight down his golden throat.

I turn on IM. Mitch is on.

Always there for me.

I click on his screen name, and he responds right away. Poor Mitch. My Valentine by default.

———

Will Brenda be awake yet? Six a.m. already. Still too early? But I need help. I need someone to watch Trixie, and maybe the church women can pitch in. Why didn't I attend more of those Priscilla's Gatherings? Well, visit the widows and the fatherless in their afflictions and all. If Trixie doesn't count as fatherless, I don't know the meaning of the word.

I need my kids right now. I need the reality of them. I'll get them up early, make something special for breakfast. Pancakes and sausage. Oh yeah. Of course, they'll wonder who stole their mother and left Suzie Homemaker in her place.

Lyra first. The child sleeps with the covers completely shrouding her head. I don't know how she stands it, inhaling her own breath over and over. Maybe hers smells better in the morning than mine.

Kneeling down next to her, I lift the blanket off her face and rest my fingertips on her cheek. Oh God, I love her so much. I want the best for her. I want her to sail through life with no pain, no meanness, no trials, and yet, even the most simple person knows that we grow through pain. I want her to care deeply about life, but from which direction the winds of trial will blow, the winds that will deepen her roots and make her a human that bears the image of Christ, I can't say. For the winds will blow, I can count on that. I breathe out a prayer. "Dear God. Let them strengthen her faith, not destroy it." I groan inwardly for her sake, willing our family situation to change, knowing she needs a strong male influence right now. But who can fill that role? Brian? Marcus? Harry? Dear Lord, You've got Your work cut out for You.

I can only plead for her here in this silent stillness. I can only trust, something I've never been much good at, that her life will play out better than mine, that wise decisions won't be so hard-won.

I raise up, kiss her cheek. "Lyra, baby. Wake up, sweet pea."

She mumbles something and opens her eyes, none the wiser.

"Shower's yours."

Next stop, Persy. Oh man, this kid looks so comfortable when he sleeps. He's easily got the softest, thickest comforter in the house. And the little heater is still young enough to crawl into bed with and get warmed. I slide in between the covers and gather him into my arms and pray for him as well. Such a sweet, innocent boy, he plays with even the smallest child without a hint of their age difference, hardly realizes when others snub or abuse him. Just keeps going, playing his heart out, enjoying himself and his toys. Not that Trixie can't yank his chain. Oh boy. Lord, keep this sweet spirit inside of Him for as long as You will. I picture him committing those random acts of kindness the crazy bumper sticker talks about. Let that be so, Jesus. Please.

"Persy, buddy. Time to get up."

Nothing.

Man, I'd trade a sleep like that for my left foot these days.

"Come on, bud. Time to get ready for school."

The boy-angel stirs. God, I love him so much.

I roll out of the bed and nuzzle into his neck, kiss his cheek, and yank the covers off him. "Let's go! Your school clothes are all set out."

Trixie next. Obviously I can't climb into her crib, so I lift out her little body and take her into my bed. She's so lovely now, swaddled in slumber. The soft curve of her cheek, the unformed nose, the shallow U of her golden lash line. I close my eyes and breathe her in. My baby.

Count your many blessings, name them one by one.

What's this? The aroma of coffee tickles my nose. And sausage. Panic erupts. What time is it?

I lean up on my elbow.

Eight thirty?

Oh no!

I throw back the covers. Trixie's gone. Lyra should have been at school half an hour ago! And Persy? Oh dear. I see yet another tardy mark on the report card. Well, maybe I can drop him off first. Why didn't anyone awaken me? And I still haven't called Brenda!

The restaurant!

Man oh man. I'm toast.

Whistling wafts up the steps.

Harry?

Harry!

Dear Lord, please please please let Mom still be asleep!

Reuben rises from his chair at the kitchen table. Thank You, Lord. Harry's nowhere in sight. "Good morning, kiddo!"

"Hi Dad."

Isn't that a kick? I call Rusty's father "Dad" and my own dad "Harry." What a wacko world I inhabit. The kitchen smells so good. So breakfasty and homey.

"Where are the kids?"

"Harry took them to school."

"Trixie?"

"He took her, too. They're going to McDonald's for another breakfast. That one with the Playland."

"Man, that's great."

"I've kept a plate warm for you. I saw the pancake mix out, so I figured that's what you were planning."

"I was. I thought you were going out early to work out."

"Funny thing. I was planning on it, but my coffee maker went on the blink, and so I came up to make a pot. Lyra came in and told me you and Trixie were fast asleep, and I thought, 'Why not? She needs a break.'"

He hands me a mug of coffee, Reuben style. Tarlike. Slick and perfect for dissolving the hefty fuzz inside my head.

"Your timing couldn't have been better. I haven't slept like that in months."

"Good, then. So what do you have planned today?"

I tell him about the restaurant dilemma and my plans to call the church.

He waves a hand. "She's my granddaughter. Harry and I will tag team it."

"You sure? Harry's not very reliable."

"Leave him to me, hon."

Reuben is ex-Marine. Like my protagonist.

Bingo!

Nick Porecca just opened his eyes and sat up on my mad-scientist operating table. Oh yeah, I bet Reuben Schneider could kick some kind of butt in his time.

This'll be great. I can't wait to dive back into the chilly pool of words.

Oh yeah. The restaurant.

Okay, so if I tote Old Barbara to the restaurant and set her up by the counter, I should do fine. I throw on a skirt and sweater, grab my briefcase, and head on out to the grand reopening.

I call Matty. "Have you heard?"

"Yeah."

"Garret coming in today?"

"He's probably already there."

"Can you step in as head chef?"

"Sure."

"Can you go to the markets?"

"Uh-huh. No prob."

"Thanks, Matty."

"No prob."

Nine thirty. Ninety minutes to opening. I call Garret's cell.

"It's Ivy, Garret. I guess you've heard."

"Of course. Sucks."

"Yeah. Hey, you got enough there to round up a couple of lunch specials?"

"Sure."

"I'm on my way in right now."

I call my sister.

"Brett?"

"Hi Ive."

"Hey. You busy?"

"Very. Marcus is announcing his campaign tonight, and I need a new dress."

"Can you sit with Mom in the afternoon?"

"Did you not hear me, Ive?"

Oh great.

I don't know what to say, so I hang up. That'll provide her with some fuel for the next few days.

Once inside the restaurant, I nab the phone book and look up adult day care. It breaks my heart. Oh God, it breaks my heart.

Family First.

That looks nice. I make the call, gripping the phone, willing my insides to calm down. I shake.

A lady named Margaret knows how to ease my mind as I relate Mom's limitations. She invites me to tour the facilities and "bring your mother too."

I peep my head into the kitchen. "Is there a waitress on?"

Garret shrugs. I'm sure Brian and Brett didn't think about the schedule. I make a couple of quick calls, and no one answers. I leave panicky messages and hope for the best.

But I end up waiting tables for the lunch rush. Thank the Lord, the normal staff turns up for dinner. Except the hostess.

Figures. I call Reuben and ingratiate myself.

"Don't worry about a thing, hon. It's all taken care of."

Old Barbara's been flashing her screen saver for hours.

———

I made it through the day. The restaurant? Clean and locked up tight. Tomorrow Matty and Garret will completely control the joint, and I'm willing to take the chance for Mom's sake. One day won't kill us, and Mom's needs come first. Besides, being back there today only confirmed that I just don't enjoy the whole restaurant lifestyle.

Too much drama.

And drama? I thank God the mess in which my mother's children now find themselves remains a secret. Brian's two DUIs. My tenuous marriage, not to mention Mitch. And Brett? Well, at least one of us is out of the closet.

I met Mitch last night at his office to go over the latest newsletter. He walked me out to my car afterward, and he held my hand in both of his as he thanked me for my friendship. I felt so cherished.

I set the teakettle on and begin entering the final edits to the latest newsletter. Full steam ahead, because I accomplished nothing in the way of writing at the restaurant. Why did I dare even hope?

Mitch sent me some listings from an airline. They hook up their reservations-desk employees from home computers. An insurance company agreed to do their data entry the same way. And a computer corporation will provide the computers for these ventures. Fifty jobs just waiting for our ladies.

Now that's something to get excited about. I'll take it.

Mitch interviewed the CEO of the computer company, which will provide a nice item for the newsletter. I called one of the moms who hooked up early in the game with an automobile dealership; they hired her to schedule their service-department appointments. A very good thing. She'd never have made it out of the welfare system without us, she said. They're doing fine now. Just fine.

Mitch's voice held such pride and warmth last night when he told me about the success stories. I mean, he's really doing something for people, you know? I'm not just falling for those eyes. I'm falling for that heart. A heart that actually hears the hearts of others.

Okay, back to work. I can't think about Mitch. I've got to get a handle on this. I'm in a state of emotional adultery. I won't lie about that.

Glenn Miller's "Sunrise Serenade" gently imbues the night with soft brass sounds. If I don't get going, it'll be sunrise before I finish.

The kettle screams, and I jump to my feet. A minute later, Reuben appears.

"Heard the kettle. Any extra water in there?"

"Yep. Care to join me for a cup of tea?"

"Love to."

I take down a mug and string in a bag of Lipton.

"Can you put two bags in there, hon?"

"You got it."

He sits down at the table and moves aside a couple of papers. "I don't know how you do it all, kiddo."

I want to complain about his son, but blood is thicker and all that. "I'm going on steam, Dad. And thanks for all you did today. I'm glad Mom wasn't too difficult."

"She was great. We played cards most of the afternoon."

"How'd she do?"

"She trounced me!"

"Well, at least that's still left."

"And Trixie and I played Barbies and baby dolls. She's a real cutie."

I just nod, trying to appear as thankful I feel.

"If only that son of mine would come back home."

There's my cue. "I don't know how much more I can stand."

I set the mug in front of him, pleading in silence. Help me, Reuben. Help me not to sin so badly I destroy everything I hold dear.

He nods. "I know, hon. You know I hate to interfere. But would you mind if I gave him a call?"

"I'd welcome it."

"Where is he?"

"Great Britain still. I haven't heard from him in a week." I check the schedule I put up on the fridge. "York."

"There a number where he's staying?"

"Yes."

"What time is it there?"

I add five hours. "Four a.m."

"Give me the phone."

I grab it off the wall. "Go for it, Dad."

"Oh, believe me, I will. Cheryl and I raised him better than this."

Rusty's mom would weep if she had lived long enough to witness all this.

He reaches into his shirt pocket for his reading glasses. "Go on up and take a bubble bath, hon. I don't want you to hear this."

Father-son stuff. I shouldn't hang around.

———

I'm horrible. I eavesdrop from the bottom step, unable to help myself. I have to know what I'm up against when Rusty calls me tomorrow. If he calls me tomorrow. He might tell his dad to go jump in a lake and take me with him. Not much chitchat transpires before Reuben jumps right in.

"Are you aware that your mother-in-law is worsening?"

"..."

"What do you think you ought to do about that? Ivy's here by herself, and the kids… Dorothy is very, very ill. I know where you are, but this is a serious situation. How are you going to handle this thing, son?"

"..."

"Sure, I know you're out on the road, but with Ivy having all these problems, how do you think you can help your family?"

"..."

"It's not about money, Russell. The home front is in need of reinforcements. Ivy's taken a direct hit. She's trying to keep things together."

"..."

"What else do you think you can do?"

"..."

"I know you're working hard. But bottom line, son, is you're not here. You don't take the time even to call home. And Ivy's shouldering this burden, and I'm watching her waste away."

"..."

"Think about this, then: if you came back and Ivy wasn't here, and your kids weren't here, what would you do?"

"..."

"There's got to be something you can do around here."

"..."

"Sure, I can put out some feelers. Maybe you can go back to teaching."

"..."

"I know. All I'm asking you is to think about things."

"..."

"Love you, son."

Whew. He handled that well. Better than I would have. Now we'll have to see how long it takes Rusty to come up with a solution. If he really bothers to.

"Go take that bubble bath, kiddo!" Reuben yells.

19

Marty Bass rambles on and on about this "winter weather event" on channel 13. Everything's an event with the news these days, special graphics in the corner of the screen, a theme song. But I love Marty Bass.

A fine, freezing rain descends, and Lyra and Persy boogie down with the "school's canceled" dance, overtones of SpongeBob tingeing the melee.

I love snow days. Although it isn't technically a snow day. It's a "winter weather event" day. I do, however, whisper a prayer that ice won't coat the power lines and abandon us to the cold, silent darkness.

I hate that.

I check on Mom. She's awake.

"The kids are off of school today. Freezing rain."

"I hope they won't do too much running around. I'm not up to it."

I kiss her cheek. "I'll try to keep them quiet."

"It is my house, you know."

Tears prick my eyes. "Yes, I do know."

"I don't know if I want to sell it."

Disappointment jabs my chest. "Don't do anything you don't want to do, Mom."

I tiptoe up the stairs, lay on the bed, and lay in my own emptiness, bound in the chains of a woman whose life isn't her own.

———

Help me, God. Help me. Help me. Help me.

The once-freezing rain turns to drizzle by 10:00 a.m., and we are off to visit the adult day-care center.

———

Margaret of Family First reminds me of a retired gym teacher. Kind of stocky, walks by leading with her shoulders, not her hips. Her extra-short brown hair curls at the trim line, and a bit of gray sparkles in the sunlight now streaming through the large windows of the warm recreation room. "We do all we can to keep them happy and busy."

Sweet pictures decorate the pale-blue walls: families on picnics, mother and child walking the beach, folk art with no depth but lots of busyness. A middle-aged man plays the piano in the corner, "Red Sails in the Sunset" coloring the atmosphere.

Let's see: a Scrabble game in full swing, chess, a couple of puzzles, backgammon, crafts. An orderly enters bearing a tray of medicine cups all queued up neatly. "So you oversee their medication?"

"Oh yes. We take care of everything you'd do if they were with you at home."

"Everybody looks content."

"We find folks actually like being with people their own age. You'd be amazed at the connections. So-and-so knows so-and-so, and off they go, talking about shared experiences. It's never dull around here."

Yeah right, Marge.

"We arrange field trips for those who are capable. We go to the mall, take in a matinee sometimes, a play occasionally, concerts."

I squeeze Mom's arm. "What do you think, Mom? Is this some-place you could be for a few hours a day?"

She nods. Mom says little to strangers nowadays.

An older woman stands up and begins to cry. "I can't find my doll. I can't find my doll!"

"That's Eunice. She's a sweetie pie." Margaret doesn't explain further, which is good because it's none of my business. I don't want Mom's condition bandied about with strangers.

"It seems nice."

"We don't have too many people who remove their parents from our program. But to assure you, we do have a thirty-day trial period. If you find this isn't for you, you can stop Dorothy's enroll-ment without any penalty."

Good. And a lot can happen in a month, right?

———

Later on, after Lyra's ensconced in her room studying for a biology test and the little ones are asleep, I have to admit that God had mercy on me. Just knowing Rusty's aware of my plight and is at least ruminating on a solution has given me hope. And I refrained from sending Mitch any IMs. But tonight it felt like a fifties show around here. Garret called and told me everything was going well at the bistro and to relax, which, for a guy his age, I thought was incredibly mature and caring. I picked up a beautiful pork roast, browned it, and baked it slowly with apples and sauerkraut. The aroma put us all in a good mood. I made rolls and even baked a pie. We congregated around the table, Mom flirting with Reuben, believe it or not, and him patting her hand, smiling warmly. Trixie was at her cutest, and I made sure to seat her as far from Lyra as possible.

No call from Rusty yet. But I imagine him with his thoughts toward home. I have to. As usual, he's left me with no other option.

Warm baths for the little ones, bedtime stories, prayers, and they lay sleeping in their beds by eight thirty. Even *Ancient Marvels and Mysteries* proved too much for Persy, whose head kept drooping forward during prayers.

While I tended to them, Reuben cleaned up the kitchen, and I came downstairs to a humming dishwasher and a hot cup of tea. After I settled Mom in bed, Harry emerged and warmed up his plate in the microwave, poured a glass of milk, and told us about his job search. And I truly didn't mind his company. In fact, I felt genuine excitement for him as he talked about working at an optical center.

"You've kept up your license?"

"Yep."

Shocking. You just can't ever tell, can you? You think you've packed people neatly in a box, and they upend all your ideas about them.

"It's been good here with you, Ive. I've forgotten how precious a home life can be."

Precious? Did he ever once think that about our life in Lutherville?

Two months ago I would have made a crack. Tonight I just take it at face value.

"I want to be more of a help with your mother. Lord knows, I owe her that."

True, but…

"Let's introduce you slowly, Harry. Why don't you come for dinner tomorrow night? By way of the front door."

He nodded.

So now we sit here at the table. I work on Old Barbara, Reuben reads a James Clavell novel, and Harry tinkers with a crossword puzzle. More tea all around.

"Tomorrow morning's going to be difficult with getting the kids off to school and Mom to day care. Harry, can you drive the kids?"

"Sure thing."

"I'll drop Mom off on my way to the restaurant. Dad, you up to Trixie patrol?"

"Of course. I don't get the problem with that child. She's as good as gold for me."

"Just wait until the bloom wears off."

Harry laughs.

Reuben shuts his book. "I'll cook up breakfast as well. I enjoyed that the other day."

"You don't have to do that."

"Look. You've taken me in, and I'm no mooch. I can pull my weight, and what's more, I'll enjoy doing it."

"Thanks. I've got a box of frozen waffles and there's some bacon in the fridge. But waffles will be enough if you don't feel like really cooking."

"You got it, kiddo. We'll get through this somehow."

I smile. God's sent these two my way. Reuben I can believe. But Harry Starling sent by God? Go figure.

Okay, so I need to call Brett, and I'm dreading it so much I feel the nausea burbling in my throat.

She'll still be up. I am.

"Brett, it's Ive."

"Hey Ivy."

"How did Marcus's announcement go?"

"Fine."

"Find a good dress?"

"It was all right."

She must really be depressed. "I'll bet you looked great."

"I tried."

"I took Mom over to see one of those adult day-care facilities. She starts tomorrow."

"Oh."

"Yeah, I know. I just don't know what else to do, with the restaurant and all."

"Get that husband of yours home."

"Tell me about it."

I might as well just come out and say it. "I don't know how I'm going to pay for this, though."

"How much is it?"

"Two-fifty a week."

"So call Brett. Miss Moneybags. It's all I'm good for." Her voice, soft, quivers.

"Are you okay?"

"Not really."

"Have you thought about seeing a doctor?"

"Oh yeah, that would be rich. Marcus Forsythe, political candidate and husband of a crazy woman."

"You've got more on him. What are you doing tomorrow?"

"We have a coffee tomorrow night with some influential people, fund-raising and all that."

"Come by the restaurant during the slow hours. I haven't seen you in a while, and I miss you." I add that to subdue the rising hackles.

"I'll try."

"Thanks. It'll be nice. Have you seen the place since the work was done?"

"Not yet."

"You'll like it."

We're silent for a second, and then she speaks. "I'd give anything to sit in Grandpa's diner again."

"Yeah, me too."

"How did life get so complicated?"

I sigh. "I don't know. But it isn't just us. Maybe it's just the way it is these days. For everybody."

"Yeah, maybe."

"Okay, well, hopefully I'll see you tomorrow."

I tell her how much I love her. And I hang up with no promise of cash. But a heart full of sorrow is mine.

———

In bed, I begin to pray for everyone in one big, sweeping, generalized groan. Dear God, come in and work Your wondrous ways. We need You so badly. We need grace. We need mercy. We need Your loving hand.

Jesus died for me. A simple thought. I, a sinner, desperately in need of grace, had all I ever needed for the taking. Rusty sings a song called "Jesus and Me."

"Now it is Jesus and me, for each tomorrow, for every heartache and every sorrow."

Each tomorrow. Yep, that's what I need, Lord. Just tomorrow. Every day, just tomorrow.

"She loves Glenn Miller," I tell Margaret. "And I brought some of her favorite magazines."

"She'll do fine, Mrs. Schneider, don't worry."

"I can't help myself."

"It's okay. It's natural."

"And you'll call me if there's any problem?"

"You bet. Don't worry."

Mom looks scared.

"And sometimes, she starts preaching."

Margaret laughs. "I've seen it all."

I'm sure that's true. "I'll be by at 3:45."

"She'll be ready for you."

I check the week's menu list on the way out. Wednesday, Swedish meatballs and egg noodles. Good. Mom loves Swedish meatballs.

Brett's comment about Grandpa's diner set me to thinking.

I sit at the kitchen booth nursing a cup of coffee as Garret and Matty chop stuff. "So here's the deal, guys. I've been looking over the books, and as nice as running a *bistro* sounds, business has been slacking off. It's not that your food is bad, I love it. But for at least this month, I want to try running a couple blue plate specials. Meat loaf. Chicken-fried steak. That sort of thing. I also want you guys to dream up a burger menu. Standards. But put a few gourmet ones in there too. Shiitake mushroom teriyaki stuff, whatever."

Garret raises his brows. "Brian's going to freak."

"Brian's not here this month."

Matty smiles. "Hey, I like my job. We'll do whatever it takes to keep this place afloat."

"Great. Okay, then let's start it up next week. Can you have the new menu ready by Saturday night? I'll make them up Sunday and have them ready to go Monday morning."

"You got it." Matty's already dreaming. Garret, too. Good. It's smart to let these creative types do their thing.

At two o'clock, Brett slips in wearing a pair of jeans and a flannel shirt. And she's gained some weight. Which makes sense. She and I possess opposite coping mechanisms. My stomach closes up shop; she eats all day long. I give her as warm a hug as I am able to give. "I'm glad you came."

"I couldn't not come. I think I'm drowning and that I don't even have the right."

"Come sit down. I'm having Garret make you something special for lunch."

"You having lunch?"

"Yeah. How does a big sloppy cheeseburger sound?"

"Perfect."

"Blue cheese?"

"You know me."

I give Garret the order and sit back down with Brett. A check sits on the table in front of my chair. "Thanks, Brett."

"I'm sorry I gave you grief last night. I just can't seem to control myself these days."

Fact is, I still don't remotely want to be her, boss sound system and all.

"Apology accepted."

"How's Mom doing at the day care?"

"They haven't called, so I'm assuming everything's fine. I'm getting off here at three thirty, and I'll go pick her up. You ready for that coffee tonight?"

"Oh sure. I'll just sit there and smile and nod. Piece of cake."

Brett fills me in on the girls and the general state of her life. Her emptiness touches my soul. I can't find it in me to be upset that she's really no good to me. That perspective is from God, pure and simple.

"Let me pick Mom up," she says.

"You sure?"

"Yeah. I need to see my mother."

"You got it. Thanks."

Wow.

———

"Mom?"

She's crying. Glenn Miller plays, and her dim room feels chilly.

"Ivy?"

"It's me, Mom. What's wrong?"

"I was thinking about when I met your father."

No volcanoes at Harry's first public supper with us. Harry played the perfect gentleman, and we all kept the conversation light. Mom said little and played with her napkin.

"You want to talk about it?" I sit on the edge of the bed.

"Oh, I was just thinking about that day. Your father was coming down the street from some bar with a buddy, and I was sitting in the car with my friend Eleanor."

Uh-oh.

"And a fight broke out, nothing to do with your father, of course, but they didn't want anything to do with it. He and his friend jumped in the backseat of our car."

Oh man.

"I was wearing Chanel N°5, a Christmas present from my father, and do you know, Harry leaned up and said, 'You smell really good.'"

Only it wasn't "really good," it was "extremely good." And it wasn't her and my father, it was my grandmother and grandfather.

She finishes the tale. "Tell me about how you and that nice fellow Mitch met."

———

"Dr. Roberts?"

"Hi Ivy."

"It's about my mother. Her dementia is getting more pronounced. It's all been happening so fast."

"We need to check the arteries leading to her brain."

Mom's arteries are harder than James Carville's head. I heard that knee-jerk liberal on *What Do You Know* the other day and wanted to throw up. Rant, rant, rant. Rave, rave, rave. How did this guy ever become a celebrity? I mean, foaming at the mouth isn't exactly an attractive quality now, is it?

I should know. I'm doing it right now!

"What can be done?"

"Well, we can do a balloon catheterization on the arteries that aren't completely blocked. The problem is, I don't know how strong your mother's heart is. She does have that arrhythmia. We'll have to run tests to make sure the surgery can be done safely."

"When can we get this scheduled?"

"Is she HMO or PPO?"

"PPO."

"Good. I'll have one of the office managers call you and set up appointments for the testing. You prefer St. Joseph's, if I recall."

"That's right."

We exchange a few more details, and I hang up. Thank God for Reuben and Harry and their willingness to drive a car.

━━━

I want to ask Reuben if he's found any opportunities for Rusty, but if I do, he'll know for sure I was eavesdropping.

Rusty's sent some very interesting e-mails. Slipping little things into his remarks like, "not all it's cracked up to be," and "becoming increasingly disillusioned with life on the road" and "missing the milestones in the kids' lives." He's definitely relinquishing his hold on the singing business, and doing so in such a way as to save his pride. Reuben's a genius.

But a dark question overshadows my hope: am I beyond loving him the way I should?

20

Someone pounds on my kitchen door. At this late hour?
"Debbie! Come on in!"

"I can't take her one more second."

"I've got a fresh pot of coffee going. Tell me all about it."

She sits in Harry's seat, Harry, who's downstairs installing kitchenette cabinetry. Reuben sprang for a double sink and a range. I'll never get rid of Harry now, and maybe I won't want to. Trixie's really taken a shine to having these men around. They're so good for all the kids. Why didn't I realize until recently that asking for help isn't a weakness but a streak of brilliant savvy?

I set a mug of steaming java in front of her. "Now take a couple of sips, close your eyes, and relax for a minute."

"Okay."

I turn to pour my own cup and catch my reflection in the night panes of the back door. Turn away! Dear Lord in heaven, if that isn't depressing. My hair resembles withered grass. And my eyes are so sunken I look like I've started decomposing.

Debbie must be enjoying the stillness. Well, ten o'clock constitutes "late night" at our age. But according to Debbie, her mother night-owls every evening, wandering around, muttering criticisms. I check Old Barbara's screen. Page seventy-five of the novel. I've decided to tell my agent I'm bidding adieu to the male protagonist. Avoiding this conversation has been a mental pastime for the past few days, but the deed must be done. Tomorrow, I tell myself. But how to sell the idea?

Revolutionizing my original female protagonist from the timid librarian to a really beautiful, really built woman with a soft voice and a hard fist sounds ideal. And she can be mentored into this startling vision of roaring woman by some old, tired detective who's been tipping the bottle, who doesn't want to go on living and needs to care again, care about love and life and gag me with a spoon.

They'll love it.

Debbie's eyes open. "What're you working on?"

I can't lie. "It's a project almost nobody else knows about."

"Ooh, do tell!"

Hmm. I mean, maybe it's nothing more than a fairy tale. Maybe she'll laugh. Maybe not. Oh, whatever. I spill it all.

"No!"

"Yep."

"That's fabulous! Why aren't you telling the world?"

"That's the question, isn't it?" Truth now, I don't know why. The subterfuge appears extremely silly floating on open air.

"Well, I won't tell anyone, but if I were you, I'd shout it from the rooftops. A book contract? Do you realize how many people dream of that?"

"Sure. Everyone thinks they have a book in them."

"Yes, but only a chosen few have what it takes to get it out of them."

"You think?"

"You have a gift. I read your column."

"You do?" I'm stupefied. I mean, who reads the Lutherville *Lavalier* other than me, Tony, and my Odd Fan? And Reuben, I can't forget Reuben.

"Sure. I love it."

"Really?"

She laughs. "Hey, we're mothers, aren't we? And wives and care-givers. We have a great deal in common."

"Then why in the world didn't we start doing this a long time ago?"

"Beats me."

"Well, the back door's always open."

"It's a good thing to know."

I lean back and pull the coffeepot from the cradle. I top off our cups. "So you want to talk about your mom?"

"Nope. I thought I did, but now I just want to sit here, sip on a cup of coffee, and close my eyes while you tap on that computer."

"Works for me."

I continue working while she keeps her silence. Thirty minutes later she stands up, rinses out her mug, and kisses my cheek. "This helped more than you know."

"Then come over more often."

"You'll get so sick of me."

"Oh yeah, having someone sit at my kitchen table and sip coffee with their eyes closed is a real drain."

One hand on the doorknob, she asks, "Mind if I read what you've written someday?"

Surprisingly enough, I don't mind the question. "I'd be flattered."

"Thanks. Need to look outside myself, you know?"

———

Look outside myself. Look outside myself. When do I look out-side myself? Everything I do connects to me somehow. *My* job.

My kids. *My* husband. *My* mom. *My* restaurant (which, by the way, may escape the red-ink tar pit now that Brian's out of the picture). *My* sister. *My* church. Well now. This is a very interesting thought.

———

Oh great. An e-mail from my Odd Fan.

> Dear Mrs. Schneider,
>
> I hate to admit this, but I haven't been reading your column as faithfully as before. Mother took a turn for the worse, and I hate to admit this too, but when they took her away to the hospital, I sighed with relief.
>
> She passed away during the week between Christmas and New Year's, and I've been busy getting her estate in order.
>
> I read your column the other day about searching outside yourself for meaning, and I wanted to let you know that I enrolled at Towson State. I don't start until next September, but in the meantime I'm keeping busy. The estate was a mess, but there's nobody but me, and the house is paid for. All in all, however, I'm well-heeled with no friends. But I'm searching for some sort of community in which to learn and grow.
>
> Anyway, I haven't written in a while so I thought I'd just say, "Keep up the good work."
>
> Kirsten

Well, now. An unusual development. I bet Club Sandwich would benefit from some pointers from Kirsten. Her mother probably made Debbie's look like Mother Teresa.

I call Garret.

"Huh?"

Darn, I woke him up. Well, no wonder. It's 7:00 a.m. and he's twenty-three.

"I'm going to be in a little late this morning. You got everything under control?"

"No prob."

"Thanks."

I figure I'll head on over to Lutherville after I drop the kids off at school. Maybe I'll visit that lonely old stone house in which Kirsten seems to be growing like a tender plant in a spring sun. Gee, that's nice.

—————

Another good morning. Reuben fixed bacon-and-cheese omelets, and Harry bundled up Trixie for a trip to one of those new kids' swim clubs. She's a fish, that one, and we signed her up three mornings a week. Harry pours coffee into a travel mug, grabs the *Sunpaper,* and sits in the observation room. He acts like a grandfather now, and I'm not sure what to do with that. Each morning Reuben drives Mom to day care, then heads off to the club to work out.

I'm beginning to like this life. I'm beginning to think maybe Rusty should just stay away. That's a dangerous thought, though. Thank goodness Mitch has been traveling lately. At least I don't have to worry about those feelings, and the further I am from the day we reunited, the weaker they become. I'm starting to think most of our inner turmoil would take care of itself if we just let it.

Right.

I pull into the parking lot of the office building in which the

Lavalier resides, near the beltway, in quite possibly the ugliest building ever. Dark-brown brick, orange doors, and creepy lights. Who looked at the drawings and the architectural model and said, "Oh baby! This is a beaut! We'll break ground next spring!"?

The army-issue elevator rises at the pace of a bubble in King Syrup, but soon enough I sit before Tony's army-issue desk with a cup of army-issue coffee.

"It's nice to actually see your face, Ivy."

"Mutual. You lost weight?"

He chuckles. "Not as much as I'd like. Been through a kidney-stone ordeal. So what brings you here this fine morning?"

"I've been wondering if we might start taking the column in a new direction."

"Oh yeah? How so?"

"I'm tired of being angry. Does that make sense?"

He relaxes in his chair, folding his hands across his stomach. "Absolutely. Unfortunately, it doesn't make for good column writing."

"Well, hear me out. I think this really has potential. I'm thinking of a hometown-hero sort of thing. But about women. Regular women exhibiting quiet heroism every day."

Thoughtful, he rubs his goatee. "Where do you propose to find these women?"

"Are you kidding? They're all over the place!"

He holds up his hands. "Sorry!"

"So what do you think?"

"You'll end up sounding like one of those feminists, Ivy."

I indulge in a smarmy smile. "It's a chance I'm willing to take."

"Let's give it a shot. See what happens."

"Thanks."

Next stop, Kirsten the Odd Fan. Hopefully she's home.

A green Dodge Dart sits in the driveway. Maybe that's hers. Or maybe not. Maybe she spent some of Mother's dough and tools around in a Mercedes right now, hair in a scarf, cool sunglasses on her nose, and a tiny dog beside her, nose in the wind!

But no, a curtain moves aside as I traverse the brick walkway, a pretty white-lace curtain. Fits the house perfectly.

The door swings open before I can even ring the bell.

"Mrs. Schneider?"

My photo appears alongside my column each week.

"I hope you don't mind me stopping over like this."

If she's shocked to see me, she covers it well. "Of course not. How did you know where I live?"

"You described the house to me once in an e-mail. I grew up over by Ridgely Junior High School."

"You hail from Lutherville too?"

"Born and bred. Well, sort of. Towson too."

"Well, do come in."

She's very pretty, our Kirsten, slightly overweight. A pair of Levis hugs her hips, and a heathery sweater overlays a good-sized bosom. No makeup, but then, she doesn't need any. Her voice sounds like I expected, soft and musical. "What brings you over this way?"

"I got your e-mail this morning, and an idea came to mind."

"Would you like a cup of coffee? Or tea, perhaps?"

"Tea would be wonderful."

"Come back to the kitchen."

I follow her down the central hallway, gaping at the living room, the dining room, the drawing room, the music room, the sun room, and the den, and the antiques that fill them. "This is unbelievable!"

"These things are so old." She points to an old high chair in the corner of the kitchen. "My great-grandfather's."

"No kidding!"

"No. This house is truly a museum commemorating my dead ancestors."

"It's gorgeous."

"Funny, but I find it horribly depressing. I'm thinking about buying a sunny condo. Have a seat at the table." She grabs a cherry-wood box from the counter, opens it up, and presents to me a selection of high-quality teas. "What would you prefer?"

"Oh my. What's your favorite?"

"Hmm." She turns it around. "Nobody's ever asked me that before."

Poor dear.

Oh, good grief, I'm even starting to think like my mother.

"Mother didn't like tea at all. I kept this box and a hot pot up in my room. It was nice to be able to bring it out in the open. I just love good tea."

"Me too."

"Let's see. There's English breakfast, always a good choice. And green tea. I've got some loose green tea."

"Love to try it."

"I'll make up a pot!"

She scurries at top speed, moving like a little squirrel beneath a freshly shaken oak tree. She fills a large kettle, the water drumming against the bottom. I smell something fresh-baked too.

"I can't believe you're sitting here in my kitchen. I don't wish you to take this the wrong way, but your columns helped me through some pretty dark days."

"Thank you."

"No, the thanks are mine."

She's so normal.

She spoons tea into a ball, opens a cupboard that towers to the eleven-foot ceiling, and gently lifts down a Belleek teapot.

Sometimes in your life you know you are exactly where you were meant to be. I sit in that place, and man, it feels good. God's working right now, and I get to be part of it. Anticipation fills me.

"Our tea should be ready in just a few minutes. Shall I set out a plate of cookies?"

"If it isn't any trouble."

"None at all. I baked them earlier. I can't resist a good cookie."

Her educated tone surprises me. She must be well-read, having been cooped up with Joan Crawford all those years. "Do you like to read, Kirsten?"

"I love to read. You as a writer must love to as well."

"I used to read all the time. But I don't have much free time anymore. My mother is very ill."

"Oh dear. I'm sorry to hear that." And I can tell she means it.

"What do you like to read?"

"Of course, the classics. But I love women's fiction, the empowering kind. I need that sometimes."

"I'll bet."

She leans back against the counter. "It's funny, but we hear all the time about our chains being forged by men, and yet, with women like me, and I'm sure I'm not alone in this, it's other women who put us in the most severe bondage."

Hear, hear! "We do try to live up to expectations, don't we? Perceived or otherwise."

"I think that's the saddest thing. We find it hard to confront people and their expectations, and so we snap to, when maybe we're misinterpreting the masks they wear. Maybe they long to rip off their own masks as well."

"You said in your e-mail that you were seeking some community in your life."

"Absolutely." The kettle whistles, and she grabs it, pouring the boiling water into the fragile pot. I wonder how the delicate china handles the heat. Because it was made to?

I tuck that thought away. "Well, there's a group of women that meet at my house. We call ourselves Club Sandwich."

"That's cute."

I tell her the purpose of the group. "I thought maybe you'd like to come be a part."

"But I don't quite fit. I don't have children."

"But you know what it's like to live under scrutiny, to rise to unreal expectations."

She dips the tea ball up and down. "I didn't always rise to Mother's standards."

"Then you'd fit in even better. What do you say? They're awfully nice ladies."

"I've no doubt of that. When do you meet?"

"Every other Monday night."

"Are they all Christian ladies like yourself?"

"No. Most are. My neighbor's Jewish, and she comes."

"Good. I'm really trying to expand my life."

She pours the tea into a cup with a portrait of Bonnie Prince

Charlie on the side and sets it in front of me. Her cup is bright with pink roses.

"I feel like I've been shot out of a gun, Mrs. Schneider."

I wave my hand. "Please call me Ivy."

She nods.

"And it isn't any wonder, Kirsten. How old are you?"

"Thirty-two."

"That's when a lot of people say life begins." Actually, I believe it's forty, but that's not important, right?

She raises her cup. "To life, then."

"To life."

To life.

21

M y cell phone rings. I grab it from its resting place beside the cash register.

"What have you done with my bistro?" And a blankety-blank-blank-blank.

Stay calm, Ivy. Breathe, count to ten, do jumping jacks, whatever.

"Who have you been talking to, Brian?"

"Everybody. Not that you've called."

"You're a bonehead. There, is that what you wanted to hear? Because that's all I've got to offer. That's why I haven't called. I've been here, keeping your job alive, not to mention trying to do my own, while looking after three kids and three parents."

"I'm in rehab. What more do you want?"

"Nothing. In fact, I want nothing from you. And don't you dare get on your high horse about the blue plate specials. You were running this business into the ground with all your hoity-toity non-sense. We're doing a lunch business like you wouldn't believe."

"That's not the angle I was going for, and you know it."

I grip the phone. "Maybe. But I own a chunk of this business too. I do have an interest."

"Well, if Rusty was home maybe you'd be getting some, and you'd leave me alone."

Why do my siblings seem to think they can throw Rusty in my face?

"Oh please. Women aren't like men, Brian. And most men aren't like you. Now, are you done?"

"Not nearly. Who do you think you are, Ivy? The little sister taking over Mom's role? And I hear you're getting chummy with Dad these days too."

I'm going to kill Brett.

"You're the one that asked me to take him in!"

"I did not. I just told you of his circumstances. You took him in all on your own."

I punch the End button.

I head back to the kitchen. Lunch in full swing, Matty and Garret do the chefs' waltz. "Guys, what do you think about the blue plates?"

Garret checks on a pan under the broiler. "I like it."

"Me too." Matty. "Business has sure picked up."

"Bottom line." Garret.

"Okay, just making sure. By the way, the chicken croquettes are a big hit."

"Cool." Matty.

Garret nods.

So there, Brian.

Can somebody just beam me up to Mars?

I punch Brett's number into the phone by the register. "So tell me again what a great guy Brian was before Dad left."

"I know. He called me and complained too. Typical Brian. He can say all sorts of things about our lives, but heaven help us if we return the favor."

"He cussed me out royally."

"Me too."

"You? Why you?"

"Basically because I was trusting enough to answer the darn phone."

We laugh.

"Will we ever get to the other side, Brett?"

"Oh, we have to, Ivy. If we don't kill each other first."

———

Harry has dug out his saxophone, Trixie beats on a pot, and Reuben sings in a glorious baritone, which isn't surprising. Rusty had to inherit it from somewhere. Lyra strums her guitar, and Mom sways on the couch as they all take the A Train.

Persy plays his GameCube. Oh well.

It's funny how memory can be so selective. I remember Harry doing so little for us, but now I recall many nights when he played his saxophone to the old records, and Mom sang along, and Brian played his guitar, Brett her clarinet. I was Trixie in those days, banging away on a snare drum he traded for an eye exam.

That happened a lot, Harry giving services for whatever his patients might trade. Funny how I forgot that big bag of socks or sweet potatoes in his fist when he swung through the door at the end of the day, and the funny stories he told about the interesting folk who came his way.

"Boyd Horn was in today," he'd say every April.

"What did he say this time?" one of us would ask. And he'd scrunch up his nose to ensure the right nasality. I'll never forget this one: "Yes, Dr. Starling, my wife is fragrant with our first child!"

"Fragrant!" And we laughed and laughed.

Why did he leave all that? What did he run from? Or to? Somebody's not telling us something, and the truth is, maybe I'm better off not knowing.

———

Mom screams. "What's he doing in my house!" and points at Harry across the breakfast table.

"Mom? Harry's been here for weeks. Remember? He's been driving you to Family First sometimes."

Why am I doing this? Obviously, she's out of her gourd.

"Get him out of here! Please, get him out!"

Harry rises to his feet. "I'm going, babe."

"Don't you 'babe' me, you snake, you guttersnipe, you letch!"

Wow. Dorothy's inhibitions have taken their final curtain call. I feel sorry for my father, but let's face it, he's had this coming for a long time.

He beats it down the basement steps.

"Come on, Mom. Let's go to your room."

"I'm not done with my breakfast, Ivy, and I'll thank you not to browbeat me."

I bite my tongue but can't suppress a smile. It's good to see her out of her shell, even for an occasion like this.

Everyone finishes up quickly. The kids grab their book bags and jump into Reuben's car without being told it's time to leave.

"I don't want to go back to that place, Ivy."

"Mom, it isn't safe for you to be here by yourself."

"I don't care!" And she begins to cry. And I cry right along with her. Dear God, getting old is so frightening. I hope I just drop dead, still in my right mind, still healthy. Just drop dead and make it easy on everybody else.

———

Brett calls. "Brian's here, in case you were wondering."

"He's out?"

"Yeah. I picked him up this morning. He'll be at the restaurant tomorrow."

"What about his apartment?"

"Evicted."

"What about Mom's apartment?"

"I don't trust him to live alone yet."

"Well, he can't stay here. We're bursting at the seams."

"Did I ask you to take him in?"

"No, but I thought maybe you were hinting."

She laughs. The tension scatters. "I've got him covered."

"Thanks. Brian and I have never gotten along."

"No kidding, Sherlock. Well, you've got enough on your plate. I do realize that, Ive."

"Thanks for that, too."

I tell her about Mom's outburst.

"No way! That's hilarious."

"Yeah, it was a regular barrel of monkeys."

"Sorry, but you've got to admit he deserved that."

"You know, I thought it would bring some satisfaction, but I actually felt some pity for Harry."

"You don't know him the way I do."

I beg to differ, but I only say, "You're right." I'm not up to a brouhaha today.

"You going in to the restaurant?"

"No, the boys have it under control, and Mom refuses to go back to the day-care place. Luckily there was a thirty-day trial period that ends tomorrow. She's in her room watching a soap."

"Where's Trixie?"

"In there with her. Did I tell you she's finally potty-trained?"

"You must be thrilled."

"You have no idea."

"What do you have going this afternoon?"

"Mom's got a test over near St. Joe's."

"I'll take her."

"Really? Thanks."

"Marcus just has to know he's not all I've got going."

Hey, whatever her reason for doing this, I'll take it. "How's the campaign?"

"Fine. Lots of bucks coming his way. It's been busy, and it's only March. I don't know what it's going to be like come September."

"Well, I'll be home during the day. Come by whenever you like. Coffeepot's always on."

"I may just take you up on that."

———

Finding the female heroes of Baltimore County? Piece of cake. Mitch paved the way with this newsletter. I'm always talking to cool women. But this one came to me by another channel.

Women Wonders, Column 1
by Ivy Starling-Schneider

Mrs. Geneva Parker, born in 1930, whirls through life with the joy of a child. In her tiny home in Essex, she's raised ten children, six of them her own offspring, three brothers, and finally her sister, Elaine. Her parents died when she was sixteen. Forty foster children have since passed through her little cottage as well, mostly newborns, older children occasionally.

"I think newborns are better than candy! Sweeter. And let's face it, you don't want to kiss a peppermint drop! Of course some of those babies stayed on a little longer, and we had us a good time."

Geneva has directly impacted the lives of over fifty children. I had the privilege of sitting with her in the VFW hall up in Bel Air, where several of her biological children now live. Called the Geneva Summit, it hosted over a hundred people devouring pit beef and bay wings, drinking Coors or Cokes, laughing and kissing the cheek of the woman who held loving court in an easy chair set up by the water fountain.

The stories would take an entire issue of this paper to tell, probably more, but when I asked Geneva to name one thing she did that gave these children stability, her reply surprised all of us.

"Roller skating. No one left my house without knowing how to cross over at the curve, skate backward, and do a decent doubles skate."

How did that make a difference?

"If you can keep your feet beneath you wearing wheels and traveling on a slick wooden floor, you can keep your feet beneath you anywhere."

Club Sandwich

More memories flowed from those standing around.
They recounted times when Geneva took them skating,
held their hands, lifted them up when they fell, kissed their
hurts with tenderness. "Now get right back in there and try
again!" she always said, according to Leon, one of the foster
children, now thirty-five and a paramedic. Helping profes-
sions abound in the legacy of Geneva Parker: a doctor, four
teachers, a handful of physical therapists, a social worker,
even the town barber, who assures me his chair is a place
of refuge.

"We wouldn't be where we are today without this
woman," more than one of her kids said. And looking at
this kind-faced lady who still pats cheeks and hands, it's
clear the truth has been spoken.

Bada-bing, bada-boom. I send the column off with the file of
pictures I shot at that sweet reunion. Oh man, I like this so much
better. It isn't about me now. Not even remotely!

I found Geneva through Dani. She went to school with one of
Geneva's foster kids and was over there all the time herself. At the
last meeting of Club Sandwich, at which Kirsten was a big hit, Dani
told us, "This lady, Geneva Parker, was my saving grace. My mom
never has been well, and those afternoons I sat with Geneva, looking at old picture albums or watching a soap... I realize now that's
what kept me going."

"So your mother's always been ill?"

"Not physically, like now. But mentally."

"I had no idea!" Debbie.

"Yeah, it was pretty bad sometimes."

Krystal leaned forward. "Did she drink?"

"Yeah. Although I didn't realize it until I was older."

"Self-medicating." Krystal. "I see it all the time at church."

"Where's your dad in all this?" I asked.

"He died last year. They were both older when they had me. He was a great man, though. Unskilled, worked several jobs to keep food on the table. Unfortunately, that left my mom to me, and it wasn't long before the roles reversed."

"How old were you when that happened?" Brenda.

"About nine, I guess."

Debbie shook her head. "Tell me why life is so sad."

I had the pat Christian answer, but that night it didn't seem to apply.

But sometimes, like now, sitting at my kitchen table, Old Barbara fired up, writing about Geneva, a beam of light shines. If there were no pain, there would be no place for the Genevas of this world to work, to succor and heal and distribute the loving mercy God so longs to give us.

There'd be no doctors or nurses, no ministers, no social workers, no rescue-mission workers. We'd be missing a large bolt in the cloth of living, and we'd not be wise, for there'd be no lessons from which to learn.

22

My agent sounds doubtful. "They were pretty adamant about a male protagonist."

"But think Angie Dickenson, or *Charlie's Angels.* Okay, maybe *Charlie's Angels* isn't a good idea. But how about the *NYPD Blue* girls? They're realistically sexy and as good as any man."

"You may have to forgo the whole unwanted pregnancy angle."

"How about she already has a kid? She really needs to have a great reason to want to get this guy out of the way. And it would appeal to female audiences that way as well."

"That could work."

"Well, anyway, let me know. And if you can get me a couple of extra weeks on the deadline, that would be good."

"I'll feel them out. They may not schedule you for editing until after your manuscript arrives. It might be flexible."

"Thanks."

Man, I hope she's right. Just over a hundred pages in, Jane's doing some serious damage. If I was that Maximilian dude, I'd be shaking in my Tony Lama alligator boots.

———

Well, money's not bad right now. At least there's that. Between Rusty's salary and mine, we're doing better than we ever have. Brett

and I put our foot down with Brian and told him, as financial part-
ners in the epitome venture, we voted to keep the blue plate specials. He cussed us out, big surprise there. For the life of me, I can't
figure him out. Been through rehab, two DUIs, and still nothing's
his fault. At least he comes over to visit Mom more. But he left that
Bible on my kitchen counter. I cried, not because he's not reading
anymore, but because I failed to love him as I should. I think Dani
makes him visit, because she comes with him and sits in my kitchen,
and we chat.

I make her a cup of Irish breakfast tea tonight because it's Saint
Paddy's Day. She accepts it like it's the Holy Grail or something.

I'm learning a lot through Dani. I was raised to judge people by
their outward appearance. We had true hippie leftovers around in
those days, not the neohippies of these days. The grownups quoted
the it's-a-shame-for-a-man-to-have-long-hair verse with more regularity than the ocean waves. So let me digress: how does that verse sit
in the same book with John the Baptist and Samson? I'd like an
explanation. Anyway, we'd almost cross to the far sidewalk rather
than be sullied by a brush of the sleeve with someone "like that."

But Dani's a decent, loving human being. She cares deeply for
and about her mother and her daughter and even Brian, setting
herself aside. She gives far more than could ever be repaid, and she
doesn't complain half so much as I do. Dani lives the Golden Rule
far more faithfully than a lot of other Christians I know. In her,
the healing hands of Jesus do their work. Maybe she learned that
from Geneva. And so I'm thinking God's busy using people cast
aside by the religious establishment, and it's time I get with the program. So she wears tight jeans and goes to bars. So what? What
good are skirts and teetotaling in the fortress when a world is crying out for meaning and a little TLC?

I squeeze her hand. "Glad you all could come over tonight."

"Yeah, well it's better than being at the bars with all that green beer. Brian wouldn't do well there at all."

Rosa and Trixie giggle over something Brian's doing out in the living room. When the boy's on, he's really on. His deep laughter mingles with their baby voices.

"How's he doing with his addiction?"

"Hasn't had a drop as far as I know. We're together quite a bit now."

I sit down opposite her at the table. "Dani, I feel like I've gotten to know you on a whole new level with Club Sandwich and everything. Do you mind if I ask you a personal question?"

"Not at all."

"Well, I love my brother. I don't like him very much these days, to be honest, but he is my brother. And I've got to admit I've failed him in some ways. But do you really know what you're getting into with him?"

She nods. "I've been around, Ivy. You know that."

"He's an alcoholic."

"Yeah. I'm used to alcoholics."

"He may never change."

"I don't expect him to."

"Then why?"

She shrugs. "We all have our issues, Ivy. I've been a giver so long, I guess I don't want the pressure of being a taker."

"I'm not sure I understand."

"Well, you of all people should understand. What's the difference between a man being out at the bars every night or singing? He's gone all the same, right?"

"Right. You're absolutely right."

That stinks.

"How's your daughter?"

Her demeanor flowers. "Oh, she's great. Just great."

"Is she in day care?"

She shakes her head. "No. My grandmother watches her."

"Your grandmother's still alive?"

"Yep. Dad's mom."

"Thank God for her."

She lifts her teacup to her mouth, "That's what I say," and takes a sip.

———

Reuben and I wander the halls of a small Presbyterian school near Bel Air. Along the wide main corridor, bright and clean, children's coats and backpacks line up in a pliable row on their hooks. Laughter bursts from the third-grade room, and I peer inside. The teacher, middle-aged and more animated than any Warner Brothers character I've ever seen, spreads her arms wide, then talks about the Greeks and the Olympic Games. A little boy wearing oversize spectacles raises his hand. "Is it true they were naked?"

"Oh yes. And no girls allowed."

"All right!" he says.

"My boys would have loved that." Her smile bestows something good upon him.

A blond, curly-headed girl forgets to lower her raised hand. "You should see my little brother. He's always running around naked."

The class laughs.

The principal, Mr. Brandon, hurries us along with a laugh. "Classical education at its finest."

We peruse the drawings and projects tacked to the walls. Medieval castles. Roman temples. Latin tests. Impressive. Persy should be here. And they have a preschool. Perfect for Trixie next year. The very same year they're beginning a full-scale music program. I'd love to move up here. The countryside isn't far away, Starbucks and Barnes and Noble already inhabit the town, and Chick-fil-A is building nearby. Now I don't know about you, but that first bite into one of their chicken sandwiches is pure nirvana. Yep. I could go for this.

"Right now we just have music classes once a week, but we want to start a school band next year as well as a choir for those children who are so inclined."

"Russell plays several instruments." Reuben. "And his singing experience is bar none."

"His résumé is impressive. I wonder why he would want to even come here? A better endowed school would love to have someone of his caliber."

I say, "He loves children, though. When he wasn't traveling, he taught our own children quite a bit."

"When is he coming back into town?"

"Around Easter."

"Well, we'll hold the hiring process in check for him. We'd love to talk with him if he's interested."

We finish up the tour, thoroughly delighted, the peaceful atmosphere of the school pervading our hearts. We let Trixie explore the playground for a quarter of an hour to work off some energy.

"I like it here, Dad."

"Me too. It has *Rusty* written all over it."

"It would be a definite drop in income."

"Don't sweat it, Ive. If it's meant to be, it'll work out."

"And there's a church here too. I sure wouldn't mind starting over fresh."

"Well, just start praying, and we'll see where it leads."

Rusty's used the lack of opportunity here to keep on his current path. Maybe this will help. But I hate to get my hopes up.

Truth is, I haven't prayed about this enough. When is there time? Maybe I should pray to be given more than twenty-four hours in the day.

———

"I can't take you to the party, Lyra. Winky's not feeling good, Persy's sick again, and there's no one to baby-sit. Reuben and Harry went out to run errands and do grocery shopping and won't be back for hours. I think they're having dinner at the bistro."

Did I really just call it the bistro?

Lyra storms off to her room. "I can't do anything anymore!"

I remember the days when I just worked at the restaurant, ran everybody around, and thought, "It must be nice to be stuck at home, unable to go anywhere." I pictured the life of ladies like Marion Cunningham, waiting for Joanie and Richie to come home from school. Those women weren't overextended. They took care of their families, and that was deemed a worthy enough calling for one person. They also drank cocktails before dinner and used real cream in their coffee. They fried chicken in lard, for heaven's sake. Yep, that seemed like the life.

Today the world of the fifties just doesn't jive, because people are busy, busy, busy. It's the standard answer these days to "How are you?"

Remember when people would respond, "Fine. And you?"

Now it's, "Busy. I'm busy." People used to be expected to suck it up and not complain. They were fine, fine, fine. Now it's a sin to be idle. Heaven forbid we say, "You know, I was just lazing over a book today. And yesterday, too." Or "I sure did waste a lot of time surfing the Internet, and I bet I checked my e-mail a million times yesterday."

I know I'm guilty of writing one of my old columns in my head, but this irritating ruminating refuses to die. I miss the outlet, so I sit down and write out my blabberings to the beat of Lyra banging around up in her room.

I don't blame her.

Mom threw anger darts at me yesterday because I forgot to pick up her medication. But on my way to the pharmacy, Persy called my cell phone from school to report that he forgot his lunch. I swung into the Super Fresh and picked up a Mega Lunchable, delivered it to his classroom, returned home, and didn't remember the prescription until late this afternoon when I went to dole out Mom's pills.

I called Harry, who's greeting at the Wal-Mart in White Marsh and loving it. He decided not to take the job at the optical center so he'd have more time to help me out. He agreed to pick up the meds. But Mom's still mad at me. "You'd think it would be important enough for you to remember, Ivy."

"Why don't you ask Brian?"

"Honey, he's a man. He's got to work."

I keep thinking my hair is falling out until moments like these when I look down and see two handfuls in my own fists.

Rusty, Rusty, Rusty. If you don't send me more than a newsy e-mail, I'm going to tell you to just stay in Europe. Which reminds me.

I call the little school in Bel Air. "Mr. Brandon, please?"

They patch me through to the principal, and we exchange pleasantries.

"I'm calling to tell you that I don't know what I was thinking the other day. Russell's not coming back until the beginning of June. I guess I was so excited about the school my mind went to pieces."

"Understandable. It must be very difficult to have all that on your shoulders, Mrs. Schneider. Rest assured, we have no qualified candidates in the running as yet."

"Will you keep us posted?"

"Certainly."

Well, good enough for now.

I hang up, a picture of naked Olympians springing into my mind. Oh great.

The Lunchable made Persy ill. And I chipped a tooth. Will it ever end?

————

Reuben amassed his money long after Rusty left the barn. We'd been married five years, in fact, when Dad gambled on an unknown inventor of some widget I've never begun to understand that helps out the pharmaceutical industry, and struck not just gold, but platinum.

Rusty sold his plasma twice a week to get through college. In fact, once I found out you could go twice a week and get paid fifteen dollars a pop, we went together. Funny what you'll do when you're young and poor. But hey, fifteen hundred dollars a year paid for my books and a bit of tuition.

Rusty donned the lightest clothing possible and the easiest shoes to scuff off because if you weighed in under 167 pounds you only had to fill one bag. Even in winter he'd slip into his silky running shorts, tank top, and sandals.

We'd laugh and laugh, especially at the first-timers who arrived in jeans and sweaters. I had to give Rusty credit, though; his veins ran small and deep, but still he never missed a tuition payment. He also sang in sleazy clubs, but we won't divulge the details of when and where, or the famed incident of the overcoat and loafers. Let's just say he's learned a lot of lessons since then.

Dreams of all manner of grandeur propelled Rusty through childhood, Reuben told me. He entered talent contests at the school and usually won. He sang at weddings, bar mitzvahs, anniversary parties, birthday parties, you name it, once he lost the baby cheeks of childhood and could play the guitar well enough to accompany himself. It's one of the reasons I'm finding it hard to give the ultimatum. I know the steep road he traveled to get where he is today. Maybe I'm too soft, but if I found no compassion in my heart for the man, I'd be too far gone for any future with him.

Even with compassion, I'm still not sure we'll ever have a true life together again.

I'm driving Mom to her monthly appointment with the neurologist. She started having small seizures, the vacant-stare kind, a few days ago. I'm sure it's her hardened arteries. We've explained the need for surgery to her, a balloon catheterization in the arteries in her neck, but she refuses. I've tried to tell her a stroke is definitely coming if she doesn't, but she juts her chin out, shakes her head and says, "I'm tired of trying, Ivy. Can't you see that?"

"Trying what? Living? What?"

And then she clams up. Or starts preaching.

Well, Lord, if a stroke is coming, may it be one of diluvian proportions.

I feel guilty even praying that.

But if that's what she wants, so be it.

Have we kids really been that much of a drain on her?

Man oh man, Ivy. No wonder the poor thing's ready to go!

Sadder still, her few moments of lucidity are filled with sadness.

"And in such days there will be tribulations and trials, temptations and testings. Thus saith the Lord. Come out from among them and be ye separate! Those who stand firm to the end will be saved. Let us pray."

Mom bows her head, and Trixie, sitting in her high chair, claps.

"Dear heavenly Father…"

And off she goes. After her resounding, "Amen and amen!" I chuckle. I mean, there's only one other alternative.

Lyra casts me a look of loathing. "How can you even laugh, Mom? It's cruel and not the least bit funny!" And she pushes back her chair, grabs her dinner plate, and storms up to her room.

Persy's eyes are platters, deep blue platters, and they fill with tears. "Are you gonna die, Winky?"

She plops back down in her chair. "It is appointed unto men once to die, but after this the *judgment!*"

Persy breaks into a wailing sob.

I e-mail Rusty about the happenings at the supper table.

> I wish I was strong enough to handle our family alone, but I
> can't do this anymore, Rusty. I simply can't.

It's my last dignified cry for help.

I send it out and hope he'll be able to log on and find it wherever he is in France.

Until I hear from him I get to be a bundle of raw and bleeding nerves, if nerves actually bleed. I suppose I'm about to find out.

23

Mitch returned to Baltimore yesterday, and we're meeting for a late breakfast this morning at the Bel Loc Diner. I'm nervous about seeing him after this hiatus.

Reuben agreed to stay with Mom. In fact, they're working on a thousand-piece jigsaw puzzle of raising the flag at Iwo Jima. I feel like we've returned Mom to her childhood and wonder if it's really good for her. Reuben's so kind. He brews a pot of decaf for her and some regular for himself, and there they go. For some reason, she doesn't preach to him. She hums along to the music and places a piece every so often. Usually in the wrong spot. Reuben leaves it there.

Trixie's with me. I feel so guilty leaving her with her grandfathers all the time. We're heading to the duckpin bowling alley for a couple of games afterward. Mitch will just have to deal. If he's for women working with their children around like he says, he'll handle it just fine. Of course he will.

I order Trixie a grilled-cheese sandwich and myself a western omelet with a side of grits, remembering the days when our place served food like this. Oh, my grandparents. Mom's marriage and divorce must have killed them. Those two were one of those couples "meant to be together since time began."

I'm not sure how they did it. The lack of disagreements. The harmony. Did they sweep everything under the rug, or truly understand what was important and what wasn't? And if so, how? I search for these answers, and I search alone, and that ticks me off.

Mitch turns his old Jaguar into the parking lot. Good, he's smiling and singing to something. Probably an old ZZ Top song. He may be all polished businessman on the outside, but he still likes his rock-'n'-roll.

The stiff breeze of late March tumbles his curls as he slides into a navy sport coat. Khakis pressed. Button-down starched. No tie, though.

He hurries up the steps and into the diner. "Hey! Sorry I'm late. The 695 was really a bear."

"I heard on WCBM on the way over. Have a seat. I already ordered. I hope you don't mind."

"Hey Trixie! How you doing, sweet pea?"

She throws her crayons up in the air. "Hi! Hi! Hi! I got girl-cheese sandwich!"

If smiles bestow blessing, Trixie's one blessed little child right now.

"So how was the trip?"

"Great. Three more corporations signed on with another sixty jobs available for the next issue."

"I can't believe how this has taken off."

"Better than I ever dreamed. How's the May issue coming along?"

"Wonderfully. I've got two interview pieces—success stories—and I'm also working on an article about setting up a home office in a minimum of space for under fifty bucks. Everything but computer equipment. Reuben has constructed a prototype of the work area using inexpensive supplies from Home Depot and Staples. "

"Great idea."

"For June I'm writing an article on making the most of nap time."

"I like that. I'm more pleased than I can tell you with the job you're doing, Ive. Really topnotch."

"Hard to believe, eh?" I give him a smirk.

"Well, when you've known someone all your life, it's just a shock to see them turn into a capable, well-rounded adult."

I bark out a laugh. Me? Well-rounded?

"Don't be so hard on yourself. There are a lot of people who couldn't bear up under the pressure you do."

"Oh, I don't know, Mitch. People do what they have to do."

"No, they don't. And you know it."

"Okay, whatever. Let's talk about something else."

"I was thinking about coming over one evening this week for another forties night. You all up for that?"

"Sure."

"But I don't want you to come home early this time."

"Okay. I'd like to do a little shopping for Lyra. That kid needs a lift."

He twirls a fork between finger and thumb. "Having a hard time with all of this?"

"Yeah. I'm not sure what to do for her."

"She needs her father."

"I know." I turn to Trixie. "Can you go ask the waitress to bring us some coffee?"

She likes it when I give her big-girl jobs and immediately jumps down from the booth.

"You have every right to demand he come home."

"So everyone says. I sent out a cry for help two days ago, unmistakably clear, and I haven't heard back yet."

"Sorry."

"Yeah, well, whatever. He's probably in a place where he can't check his e-mail. I'm hoping that's all it is."

"Well, let's hope then. You know, though, I'll do whatever you need. You just say the word, Ive." He takes my hand. "I've always loved you. All these years."

"Even during the supermodel years?"

"Especially during the supermodel years."

"Why is it, Mitch, that givers and takers always end up together? Why can't two givers end up with each other?"

"That's one of the mysteries of the universe, Ive."

"The yin-and-yang thing."

"Yeah. We just both happen to be a couple of yangs."

Boy, he said it.

Still nothing from Rusty. I'd like to say I wait in a sea of calm. But I've swum in my own tears for the past few nights, because it comes down to this: either he loves us or he doesn't. And I don't have the confidence in him, or in me, to think we'll ever swim to shore without drowning first. And then what? Divorce? There's no biblical grounds. He hasn't been womanizing. As far as I know, he's been extremely faithful in circumstances under which many a man would falter. Music or us? That is the question.

"It's now or never, my lo-oooo-ve won't wait!" streams from the department-store sound system.

If that isn't the most royally stupid song ever written. Love always waits, doesn't it? Well. That is not the thought I needed to have. It's always back on my shoulders somehow.

I flip through racks and racks of junior clothing. This stuff looks trashier than Woodstock II after the crowds left. No wonder. Look at these tops! The larges are no bigger than my thigh, which means headlights galore in these things. The skirts hang about eight inches long and go all the way up to size 16. Now I don't know if it's just me, but a size 16 should know better than to wear a micro-mini. I mean, yikes!

Oh, but the longer skirts look cute, romantic, and totally Lyra. I pick out three, and a rack of loose poet blouses catch my eye. Perfect. Some of them are sheer, but I'll pick up a couple more bra-tank tops. Tights would be good, and a new pair of shoes. I decide to get her high heels with a lower platform. Shoes sure are cute these days.

After choosing Lyra's clothes, I decide, why not? Why not get something new for myself?

Problem is, all the stuff in women's wear looks like old-lady clothes. But I manage to find a new black shirt, a lime-green velour sweater, and a pair of sexy boots. Oh yeah.

Not having heard from Rusty now for six days, I figure I have to start doing things for me.

————

The party is in full swing as I pull up to the house. Tommy Dorsey's "Boogie Woogie" plays, and shadowy figures behind the sheers move to the beat. Dancing now? Well, we should call this the Tropicana or something. Fine by me.

I lug the bags into the house, and to my surprise, there sits Kirsten on the couch, clapping and swaying to the music. Reuben and Mom execute a very docile jitterbug, while Harry seethes in the armchair. Classic.

"I'm back!"

Mitch looks up from the crossword puzzle. "Hey Ive! Have fun?"

"It was great. Thanks."

Kirsten jumps to her feet. "I hope you don't mind my being here. But I called, and Mitch here answered and invited me over."

"Of course I don't mind. You having a good time?"

"Oh yes! Your family is so animated."

I laugh out loud. Yes, that would be us. "Well, you're welcome anytime."

Reuben guides Mom into her chair and swings by, grabbing Kirsten in a dance embrace. With surprising grace, she steps to. My heart spins.

Harry is practically one with his armchair.

"Harry, come on out to the kitchen for a minute, will you?" I ask.

He follows me in. I hand him a small bag. "For you."

"No kidding."

"Go ahead and open it."

He reaches into the bag and pulls out a cigar. "Hey! A Punch Gran Cru!"

"Yeah, well, you haven't had a cigar in a long time."

"Thanks, kid."

I kiss his cheek.

He looks down, his hand suddenly shaking. "I'm sorry, Ivy. I'm sorry for what I've done to you."

"Thanks, Harry."

"Can I give you a hug?"

"Sure."

He reaches out, and I place myself in his arms, and they squeeze me tightly into the strong, bony warmth of him. He's an old man.

Oh God, my father's an old man! And I find I cannot move out of the embrace; I find it's something I've needed for a long time now and just didn't realize it or even dare to hope for it.

"You're hugging that man!" Mom yells at the doorway. "You stay away from her, Harry Starling!"

Dad stiffens, then he touches my hair. "It's okay, Ive."

———

"Mom, you can't buy me off with these clothes." Lyra picks up her geometry book and flips a page. The music still jumps downstairs.

"Buy you off? Is that what you think I'm doing?"

"Isn't it?"

"No, Lyr. I just wanted to do something nice for you, to let you know I realize you have to put up with a lot these days."

"I could have made this stuff for half the price."

What happened to my daughter?

Persy wails from his room.

"Go ahead!" she says. "Everybody else is more important anyway."

"That's not true, Lyra. I don't know what—"

A louder wail.

"Just go, Mom. I'm busy."

Persy decided to sleep on the top bunk, only the Lord knows why, and there he lies on the floor.

I fold him into my arms, and I cry with him. Nothing's broken on him. I wish I could say the same about myself.

———

Everybody but Mitch is gone.

"Ivy, you can't go on like this."

"I know. I don't know what else to do."

"You heard from Rusty yet?"

"Nope."

We sit on the couch, drinking hot chocolate.

He clears his throat, sets his mug on the coffee table, and takes my hand. "You've got to accept some responsibility in this, Ive."

"What do you mean?" I try to pull my hand back, but he tightens his grip.

"No, don't pull away. Listen to me. Your marriage isn't normal."

"Like I don't know that."

"It isn't even acceptable abnormal."

"What else can I do?"

"That's the point. You're doing too much."

I feel the blood rush to my face. "Come on, Mitch. Who do I slough off? Mom? The kids? My job? What?"

"Ivy, you're going to end up in a very bad place. Lord knows, I wish it was in my arms. And I'd wait for you forever if I knew that at the end of it, you'd be with me. But I can't see you slipping down more and more. And it isn't just you who's suffering."

"What do you mean?"

"Lyra opened up to me. We had a real heart-to-heart. Now if she's having a heart-to-heart with me, basically a stranger, things aren't what they need to be."

"So what do I do?"

"Let Rusty go. If you won't do that, at least give him the ultimatum. You're starving, Ive. You're a beautiful woman who's going to waste, and I can't bear to watch it."

"I'll think about it."

"You've been thinking about it for a long time."

I stand up and grab our mugs. "I'll get us some more hot chocolate."

When I return from the kitchen a movie plays on the television. *Tommy Boy.*

We laugh and laugh. Mitch rubs my shoulders. "I'm sorry if I was harsh," he says, his breath on my neck.

It feels so good to be touched. I close my eyes. I should tell him to stop, but I can't. I just want a warm touch, that's all, just a warm touch.

When I awaken, I'm covered by a quilt, the television is dark, and I decide I'll think about life tomorrow.

———

All mothers dread the day when they lose that connection with their child, when they become not so much an enemy as a nuisance and a stranger. Maybe I made a wrong decision in enrolling Lyra at that new school. Maybe going with all those rich girls has given her unrealistic expectations.

But the day has come, and she's turned her back, and I stand there looking at the fine shoulder blades that formed inside my own body; I watch the silky hair swaying against the nape of her lengthening neck, and it is as though I'm looking through a viewfinder.

She turns from her place at the counter, cup of tea in hand. As she sits down at the breakfast table, I say, "Lyra, I just—"

"I need to study for my geometry test, Mom. Can this wait for later?"

"Yes, I guess so."

So what do I do now? How do I tear down this sudden wall between us?

Still no word from Rusty. Not one word. If I ever thought I was in despair before, I obviously didn't understand the meaning of the word.

———

Brett's late-night call comes at eleven tonight. "I've got news about Brian's case."

"Okay."

"Well, at the preliminary hearing they couldn't get the judge they wanted."

"Lenient on DUIs I'm guessing."

"Exactly. So they requested a jury. His trial's set for two weeks from now. Maybe we should be there as some sort of support to him."

"..."

"Ivy, he's your brother. This is one of those times when families need to stick together."

"When is it?"

"March 20, 10:00 a.m."

"I'll be there."

I pop on the IM and chat with Mitch. Tell him Brian's news. He says he'll be there that day too if I need him.

You know, I don't know what I'd do if Mitch was more aggressive with this thing. Wait. Yes, I do. I'd be sleeping with him. I'd be warm and wanted in a man's arms. But he's a gentleman, and he's waiting for me to make the first move. Thank you, God. With the way my life unfolds around me, I'm not one to really make moves. I just let everyone else's moves run me down like linebackers.

Mitch is right. I need to do something about my inability to say no, my willingness to allow Rusty and my siblings to live their lives baptized by my sweat and my tears.

———

Lyra fumes as I relay the news about Brian at breakfast the next day. Man oh man, did Reuben make some good scrambled eggs. Put in a little garlic powder and some muenster cheese.

"I don't understand him," she says. "How could anybody be so stupid? And he's such a good cook, too!"

"Unfortunately the one doesn't have to do with the other," I say.

Harry shakes his head. "I've got some amends to make."

"He's forty-one, Harry."

"Doesn't matter, Ive."

I wonder what it must be like to be my Dad's age and suddenly have a spotlight glued to your forehead illuminating all your mistakes. I have some regrets, naturally. But overall, I can't imagine too much is going to come back to haunt me. Of course, all parents must say that, take some kind of inventory, and hope for the best. And if you do commit some major error, you pray that your children will forgive you, that they will realize when they have kids of their own that you did the best you could.

———

I tiptoe halfway down the basement steps.

"Harry?"

"Hang on, Ivy. I'm getting into my pj's."

"Okay."

Reuben's out with a few old friends, listening to jazz at some club downtown.

"Come on down, babe."

I descend the remaining steps. "Hey, this looks nice down here! Sort of a tribute to the sixties."

He laughs. "Your old couch is a nice touch."

"Yeah. It actually looks good in this setting."

"Can I offer you a beverage?"

"Sure."

My grandparents' old refrigerator stands in the kitchen area. A soft light emanates from the hood above the new range. "Wow, this is great."

"Yep. A regular old man's place." He opens the fridge. "Want a soda?"

"You got Coke? I have a lot to get done tonight."

He reaches in and pulls one out. "Your wish is my command. If I remember correctly, you like it straight out of the can."

"Yeah, that's right."

Neat.

"Have a seat."

This couch feels great down here. Why did I ever get rid of it? I don't feel a spring at all. "Harry, I need to talk to you about something."

"Sure."

"First of all, I'm glad you're here these days. You've been a big help."

"I'm trying, kid."

"I know, and I appreciate that." Okay, this next thing is going to be tough. I sip my soda. "I want to say something else, and it's going to be hard. Let me just gather myself."

"Look, Ivy, if you want me to leave, I understand. I've got a buddy up in Parkville who has a spare room—"

"No, no. That's not it."

"Oh. Okay. Well, that's a relief."

"I just wanted to tell you that I…that I, well, I forgive you. I do."

His eyes open wide, and they suddenly fill with tears as he drops his head and begins to sob. Deep and groaning.

"I'm sorry, Ivy. I'm so sorry for what I did to this family."

And he continues to cry. I reach out and pull my father to me, and even though I find I cannot cry, I feel and feel and feel, and something inside me, something bitter and hard, liquefies, empties out of my soul, melding with his tears.

24

I still can't bring myself to call him Dad, though. Plus, that would be confusing with Reuben around. But things feel different this morning. Lighter. Yet more significant.

My shower feels more fulfilling, I find a stylish new combination in the offerings of my closet, and my cup of tea tastes like a cupful of vacation. A Reuben special, two bags at least.

Lyra trounces into the kitchen, a smile on her face. "Good morning, everyone! Morning, Grandpa. Morning, Gramps."

"Want a cup of tea?" I ask.

"Most definitely. I've got a history test today."

"Cup of tea coming up." I'm dancing a fine line here, trying to be upbeat and supportive without assuming we're chums again. Maybe it was just PMS yesterday.

Reuben sets breakfast out. Hash browns with ham and cheese and a bowl of scrambled eggs.

"Oh man, Dad! That looks great."

He smiles. "I do a nice breakfast if I do say so myself."

We sit down. Trixie prays, and we fall to.

Harry pulls me aside after everyone's trekked upstairs to brush teeth and fetch backpacks.

"Ivy, do you think your brother and sister would be open to a heart-to-heart with the old man?"

"I don't know. They're pretty bitter."

"I figured."

"But it doesn't hurt to try."

"Yeah, I guess not. The hard thing is getting them to agree to even meet with me."

So far, Harry's stayed away during Brian's visits.

"Give them a call. It's got to start somewhere."

He nods.

A few minutes later, he heads out with Trixie to the swim school.

———

Mom's sure been sleeping a lot these days, and she gets winded so easily when she's up. With her diabetes, her neck arteries, and everything else, she's literally falling apart like an old set of draperies—dry rot here, fraying seams there.

I remember her young, a skinny thing running around that restaurant with the coffeepot, chatting up a storm with all the regulars who have since either died or become casualties of Brian's menu. My favorite customer was Stu Leonard, a salesman for the Comoy Pipe Company. When he'd make his run to Fader's Tobacconists in Towson, he always stopped in for breakfast or lunch and displayed some of his more choice wares. Grandpop smoked a pipe now and again, so he and I would join Stu, oohing and aahing over the polished briarwood.

Stu, sitting there in his checked jacket and dark wool pants, said many times, "One thing I've learned over the years is that everyone needs to relax."

"That's what a pipe will do, yessir." Grandpop.

And I've thought about that conversation many times over the past ten years, when I've taken no time to do anything just for me. But always, some new responsibility would emerge, like another child or a traveling husband or now a sick mother. That spa certificate of Brenda's, crammed in a kitchen drawer somewhere, comes to mind.

"When will it be my turn?" I ask God and immediately feel selfish, considering my blessings. But sometimes I'd just like to take a class in something ridiculous, like clogging or upholstering. I know I'm not the only woman who feels this way.

And then there's that pesky woman in Proverbs 31 who raises the bar for all of us. I mean, who is that woman? Her husband sits in the gate and praises her?

Okay, so Rusty's never home either.

She riseth while it is yet night, and her candle goeth not out by night?

Okay, that part sounds like me, but I'm sure she included a better attitude in her repertoire.

Maybe I need to give myself more credit.

Ten thirty a.m. and Mom hasn't yet called out or emerged from her bedroom. I planned a nice lunch. She loves chicken salad, so I bought a rotisserie chicken at the grocery store, some green grapes, and a bag of those purple tortilla chips, the purchase of which demands a complete paradigm shift. Toasted english muffins, some cookies for dessert, and we'll all be set once Harry and Trixie come home. Harry will have to leave for Wal-Mart, but I'll pack a nice lunch for him to take along.

Harry Starling's rising to the occasion. Good for him. Good for me. Good for God. This is more of a miracle than anything I've ever seen in my days upon the earth.

I raid the fridge for the salad ingredients, wondering what I'm going to do for dinner tonight. A knock vibrates the back door.

I straighten. "Hey Debbie! It's unlocked!"

She opens the door. "Krystal's with me."

"Great! I'll put on a pot of coffee. Can you stay for lunch?"

Krystal blows in with the March wind, but today she wears a spangled sweater and a pair of black palazzo pants. Dang, she looks good!

"I love your haircut, Debbie!"

Her dark blond hair, freed from its normal ponytail, now brushes her chin, and downy wisps surround her cheeks.

She blushes. How cute. "Krystal talked me into it."

"You two been getting together on the side?"

Krystal takes a seat at the kitchen table. "Yes. This one's a life-saver. I'm surprised you haven't seen my car."

I have no idea what kind of car Krystal drives, but I'm afraid to admit it. "Well, that's great. So did you just come from the salon?"

Debbie sits down too. "Yep. We went together."

"We did. I said, 'Girl, you've got to keep yourself fresh, or else you gonna get bogged down in the swamp of life.' And now that I've met Mrs. Waxman, I know just what a swamp that is. That woman is a piece of work!"

The coffee begins to trickle. Who wouldn't benefit from such a surprise? I could use the break. Debbie continues to amble over a few nights a week just to sit with her eyes closed, and although I don't know much more about her than I used to, a deep connection's developing. I provide her peace, and her quiet presence extends me the same. She also likes the novel so far, which I can hardly believe.

I start pulling chicken meat from the bones. "How's your dad, Krystal?"

"Got out of the hospital yesterday and is at Kearnans for rehab. He'll be there for about two weeks."

"Is he coming back to your house?"

She blesses us with a deep, bosomy sigh. "That right there is my dilemma. Even with rehab, I don't know how I'm going to care for him. But the thought of putting him in a nursing home just makes me want to cry. We've all heard the horror stories. And my father is just the sweetest little man. Wouldn't hurt a bedbug."

"Maybe your family could take shifts being there with him," I say.

"Maybe, but you know, it's always been my father and me. When my mother passed, it was just me and Dad. I have a hard time letting go." She picks a white hanky out of her cleavage and dabs her eyes.

Debbie squeezes her hand. "That's totally understandable."

I get the mayo out. "I know it's coming soon with Mom."

"What was she preaching on last night?" Krystal.

"The book of Revelation. Had me scared out of my socks."

She shakes her head. "Can't make heads or tails out of that book, and Lord knows I've tried."

Debbie. "I'm not too familiar with the New Testament. That's the apocalyptic book, isn't it?"

"You got it."

"Pops up in movies a lot. It's always interested me, the end of the world and all that. The Torah doesn't speak much on it."

"But we all feel it, don't we?" Krystal.

Debbie nods. "I can't imagine what Bernie would do if I started reading the New Testament. But it's always intrigued me."

"It's interesting reading." Krystal again. "Good advice for living. Of course, you can't beat Proverbs for that."

"I love the proverbs!" Debbie.

I nod. "Me too, except for that pesky woman in thirty-one. Who can live up to that?"

Debbie stands up. "Tell me about it! I'll get out some mugs."

"Thanks." I continue mixing the chicken salad. My mouth is already watering.

"Your Mom is something, Ivy." Krystal smiles. "A good woman to raise you all like she did."

"None better. Speaking of which, I'd better check on her. I haven't heard a peep all morning."

Krystal tucks her hanky back in her bosom. "You go, Ivy. We'll hold down the fort."

"Coffee's almost done. Help yourself."

Reuben brought in a new coffee maker, one of those BUNNs with the chamber that keeps hot water at the ready twenty-four hours a day. And there's a hot water spout too. I brew a cup of tea in an instant these days, which I need because Big Jane and Bad Max are burning up Old Barbara now. Thank goodness the publishing house realized the merit of my vision.

Inching open Mom's new door, I whisper, "Mom?"

No response. I push it open fully.

Oh dear Lord, not again!

How did I not hear her fall? She lies on the floor, her head against the bed frame. Blood pools near her, glistening on the matted sprouts of her iron hair. Her nightgown twists around her trunk.

"Mom?"

I run across the room and jostle her. Dead weight. A bottle of Lubriderm is lying on the floor. Her feet glisten. She must have slathered her feet and then… I feel my heart begin to pump, the adrenaline rushing forth. My hands shake.

"Mom?" My voice louder. "Mom!"

I hear footsteps rushing down the hallway.

"What's wrong?" Krystal.

"She fell."

"Is she breathing?" Debbie.

I lean forward and hold my palm near her mouth. "Yes, thank God."

Debbie leans forward. "Mrs. Starling!" she yells.

Nothing.

"Dorothy!"

Still nothing.

"Call 911," she says.

Krystal turns. "I'll do it. What's the house number?"

I tell her.

"All right." She hurries toward the kitchen. "Jesus, help us!"

Debbie touches my arm. "Where are your washcloths and towels?"

"In the bathroom closet, right off the hallway."

"Okay."

She comes back in with a folded hand towel. "We shouldn't move her. Here, apply direct pressure to that cut, and we'll try to stanch this bleeding on her head."

"I'm glad you're here."

"Ten years in the ER."

Debbie grabs the blanket at the bottom of the bed and starts to arrange it around her. "Let's get her comfortable and modest. Do you have her insurance information?"

"Yes. I'll be right back. Here." I hand Debbie the towel. The gash slices across the crown of Mom's head. Jesus, help us!

I locate my purse by the steps and start rummaging, my hands vibrating like a jackhammer now. Okay, Ivy, deep breath, calm down, calm down, deep breath, deep breath. I close my eyes.

There's my wallet.

Debbie emerges. "She's still out."

Krystal sidles up. "They're on their way, baby."

"Thanks, you guys." And I feel tears prick my eyes because they're here, these precious new friends. "What time is it?"

"Almost noon." Krystal.

"My father should be back any minute. Make sure Trixie doesn't see this."

Krystal nods. "I got that job. You and Debbie stay in here with Dorothy. I'll let the paramedics in."

Debbie sits on one side of Mom, holding up a fresh tea towel. I sit on the other. She strokes her arm. I stroke her hair.

A bustle sounds in the hallway how much later? I don't know.

Krystal opens the door. "Right in here, gentlemen."

The EMTs file in, and the paramedic leans down, asking what happened. I give him my hypothesis. Debbie speaks in medical terms about the state of her head.

The questions begin: Who found her? Has anybody moved her? Is she on any medications? Basic medical history.

They check her airway, her breathing, her circulation.

Debbie interprets as they look for injuries, examine the gash on her head, check her eyes for pupil reaction, and do a neurological survey for involuntary muscle response by running a key down the bottom of her foot.

"Let's start an IV; D5W TKO, and hook her up to a cardiac monitor," the paramedic says. He consults with the trauma center. This all seems like it's taking too long. Doesn't she need to get out of here?

"Immobilize her for transport."

They strap her to a board so as not to compound the injury, Debbie tells me.

"We're taking her to Shock Trauma by ground transport," he says.

They wheel her out on the gurney and heft it up into the ambulance. I hear the driver talk about the Golden Hour, that they'd achieve it with Mom. "One hour from time of call to the trauma center." Debbie whispers.

This is it, I think. This truly is the beginning of the end. I'm still shaking, darn it. Control yourself, Ivy.

The driver pulls away from the curb, turns on the lights and the siren, and speeds around the corner.

Dear Lord. I watch the empty street. I can't move. I can't move.

Dad pulls up with Trixie. My feet finally respond. I run over to the car window and explain. He whitens.

"Debbie's driving me over to the hospital now. Krystal's staying here to watch Trixie. Can you leave a note for Reuben to pick up Lyra from school when it's over?"

"Will do." He removes himself from the car. "Is she going to be okay?"

I shrug. "I just can't say, Harry. They couldn't bring her around."

"I'll call Wal-Mart and tell them I won't be in."

"Thanks."

"I'll keep things going here."

"Can you call Brett and Brian?"

He swallows. "Will do."

I know I'll hear about this. "Why couldn't you have called me, Ivy? Why did I have to hear this from him?"

Well, it's not about them today, and that's final.

25

I call Tony on my cell first and tell him the next column will be late. Of course, he understands because he's Tony. Mitch next. I explain.

"Of course it's okay, Ive."

"This issue is almost finished. Just one more article to write. But I'm not sure when I'm going to get that done."

"Just give me the info, and I'll see it's finished. You said she's going to University?"

"Yes. I'm on my way now."

"I'll meet you there."

"You really don't have to."

"You're my friend, Ivy. It's what friends do."

"I guess I'm just not used to this."

"Well, it's time you got used to it. Now hang up and concentrate on the roads."

"My neighbor's driving."

"Then concentrate on you."

I call Lou next. She's coming down here as well.

I am blessed. I'll tell you that right now. Dear God, just be with Mom. Please let it not be too bad. And if we could find a close-by parking space, that would be great too.

University Hospital towers above me. How does the staff not get lost within this maze?

We find the underground garage across the street. Down, down, down we go.

Debbie finally pulls into the first free space. "You okay?"

"Still breathing."

"I'm sure they've brought her around."

I climb out of the car. Debbie tucks her arm in mine. "Let's go."

We start off at a normal pace. And then, before I realize it, we are running. I run with hope down deep and dread on top. Scalp tingles, feet burn.

We tend to think about faith as some ethereal matter of the soul abiding on lofty plains of eternity, or the singular behavioral betterment of a person. But if that's all faith consisted of, I'll tell you right now, it would be a cup half empty.

But it's like this: God sent His Son in human form, who was, as the scripture says, "tempted in every way" like we are. In all ways. Am I tempted now to lash out in anger at my siblings, my husband, the bottle of Lubriderm, even Mom? Yes, I am. Am I tempted to say to God, "Thanks, God. Like I really needed this. Like Mom really needed this." Of course. And I have.

But Jesus, though completely God, inhabited the stuff of this earth. He was probably teased to no end at school as the goody-goody of the class. His brothers and sisters probably said, "Get Jesus to do it. He won't mind," and He'd come in from a game of stick-ball to help with the ironing. Perhaps He was the quiet kid who flew through childhood under the radar. Maybe He was a lonely boy. He experienced heartache and never sinned. Lore tells me He lost Joseph sometime before His earthly ministry began. Surely that was a sore time in His life, the death of the man who endured suspicion for the sake of Mary, who secreted Him off to Egypt as a child, set up shop presumably, and lived in a foreign land until He could return safely to Israel. Surely they worked side by side in the carpentry workshop, Joseph's strong, gnarled, scarred hands gently guiding young Jesus's hands, teaching them a certain coordination He would need in His ministry: a mixture of strength and tenderness, to heal the blind, lift up the lame, carry the children, and reach out as He preached the good news that the Kingdom of God was upon us.

Did Joseph die suddenly, or did he waste away in sickness? Perhaps he was injured and lingered for several days. Did Jesus sit with His brothers and sisters, His mother Mary, and grieve that the end of this precious man was near? Did His pulse quicken even though He knew what was to come and when? Yes, I think so, because He felt what we feel.

For this reason I can feel angry as I sit here, and throw it upon His shoulders. Because He knows my frame, because He remembers an eternity ago when He created me in His mind, my soul can rest in His arms. Pie in the sky? Call it what you want. This is when faith grows feet that carry us through the briars of the earthly journey. This is when we cry out, "Even so, come quickly, Lord Jesus," because this thing called dying isn't natural. We long for the day when He abolishes sin and sorrow and death itself forever.

I bounce my thoughts against the baseboards of the waiting room in time with the ticking clock.

———

Brett rushes in. "Where is she?"

"They're still working on her."

"I was shocked when Dad called."

"I'm sorry about that, but I had to get going. Oh, Brett, it was awful!"

"It's okay. I was so scared driving down here." Pale and bloated-looking, she peels off her wool shawl. "So do we wait here?"

I nod. "Hopefully Brian will be here soon."

"He's giving instructions to the chefs, and he'll be right down."

"How did he feel about Dad calling him?"

"Furious. I chewed him out."

"Thanks." Fear swallowed my anger about an hour ago.

"Dad basically told me what happened."

I fill her in on the details. "I don't know what they're going to find. I'm sure they'll be doing a CAT scan. They said it will take a while."

"Well, I told Marcus to count me out of all activities for the next week."

"I'll bet that felt good."

"If it wasn't because of Mom, it would have."

That's true. I'm a boob. Everything feels so fuzzy.

Lou and Mitch arrive at the same time, warm hugs and encouraging words at the ready.

Lou plops down next to me. "Brenda's in the middle of the closing on her big house. She said she's praying and that she'll put you on the prayer chain at church. She said don't worry about meals, the church will be bringing dinner in for the next few days."

Krystal bustles in thirty minutes later and tells Debbie to go on home, she'll hold the fort. Reuben's got the kids.

"Can you get a ride home, Ivy?" Debbie.

"I'll take her." Brett.

With a soft kiss on the cheek, she leaves us.

Brian arrives. "Thanks a lot, Ivy."

I sense Lou and Mitch and Krystal all holding their breath. Brett stands up. "Knock it off, Bri. You are so full of yourself. Sit down."

I allow her the big-sister role. What's more, I'm grateful.

She sits back down. "Better yet, why don't you go down to Donna's and get us all a latte?"

He stalks out.

The boy really is a prime candidate for Jerry Springer. I swear Trixie's more mature.

————

His name is Dr. Smart. How reassuring. He doesn't look like your typical doctor, more like a football player: stocky build, blond crew cut, wide feet. The Johnny Unitas of Shock Trauma.

We sit with him in the waiting room. Brian and Brett and me. It's eight o'clock.

"Piecing things together from her medical history and the CAT scan, we've found she experienced a small stroke."

Brett sucks in a breath.

"She's actually fortunate it wasn't larger, with the plaque buildup she has."

"She didn't want the angioplasty," I say.

"She needs it done, and the sooner the better."

"I don't know how to convince her."

"Do all you can. She needs to have this done." He flips a page on his chart. "She's been experiencing dementia?"

"Oh yes. Getting worse and worse."

"And she's diabetic."

"That too."

"Well, we think that her dementia is coming from her lack of kidney function."

Wow.

"Her creatinine levels are extremely high. Has she been nauseated recently?"

"She's definitely lost interest in eating and has been throwing up occasionally."

"That's probably why. She needs to begin dialysis."

Can anything else be wrong?

"All right."

"We'll get her started right away, and I'm scheduling the angioplasty for tomorrow morning. Dr. Merritt is a good man. He'll be doing the procedure."

"Can we go in now?" Brian.

"Certainly. She's sleeping."

"Did she ever come around?"

"Oh yes. She was asking for her children." He smiles, blue eyes crinkling. "Go on back."

———

Thank God she's breathing on her own, deep and peaceful. At least there's that. Brian stands here shaking, and Brett cries. I'm sure they have regrets. We all know that the major responsibility for ailing parents always falls to one child, and the others continue to live their lives seemingly unscathed. But at least a few what-ifs must find their way in when your mom is lying there and could die, and you didn't find the time to stop in and chat or have a cup of coffee. Maybe her time in the hospital will afford them the opportunity to display their mettle, to acknowledge Mom's place in their lives. For her sake if not their own. And Mom will think they're so great.

In my heart, I resent this. I'd be insane if I didn't admit it. After I've done the majority of cooking and laundry and running around, they'll simply sit by her bed and even the score. But for Mom's sake, it's better.

Brett's different these days. At least she says thank you to me. But Brian's never once sat me down and said, "Ivy, I know you bear the brunt of the family burden, I know I'm not capable of dealing with this, so I want you to know how thankful I am for you."

That's never going to happen. He thinks that because I live in her house, I deserve all I get.

I take Mom's hand, punctured by an IV. "Let's hope that angioplasty does the trick."

"I know." Brett. "And the dialysis. Especially if it clears up the dementia. It sure would be nice to have the old Mom back."

Brian continues to sniff. "I've got to get out of here. I can't stand this."

He turns, and I lay a hand on his arm. "You did fine at St. Joe's, Bri."

"That was just a broken hip. We could lose her, Ivy."

"I know. Look, go on ahead. I'll call you if anything develops."

If I want him to play nice, I should do the same. And honestly, I pity him right now more than I ever have. No wonder he drinks like he does.

Brett kisses his cheek and pats his back, and off he goes. Maybe Dani will talk him into coming back.

"To tell you the truth, I'm sorry about Mom." Brett. "But I can't say I'm sorry I can't accompany Marcus these days."

"It must be tiring." I rub Mom's arm. Maybe, somewhere in her subconscious, she can feel the love.

"It's more than that."

"That doesn't sound good. What is it?"

"I'm suspicious of his motives for running."

"Marcus? I always thought he was a committed Republican."

"I did too. Obviously not dyed-in-the-wool like us Starlings. It's a power trip. Pure and simple." She begins to rub Mom's other arm. "I see a man for sale. Corporations meeting with him, other special-interest groups. All trying to buy his allegiance. So how can I support that?"

"I don't see how you can."

"I mean he's obviously not going to take a stand for what he believes."

"If he really believes anything."

"Exactly."

"Have you talked with him about it yet?"

"I've tried. It's like talking to a brick. He's decided he wants this bad."

"So if he can't have another woman, he'll woo the political whore."

"Exactly! That's exactly it, Ivy. Either way, I'm left on the outside. Maybe that's what he wants. And here I thought maybe we'd actually have a decent politician in Annapolis. How foolish of me."

Hmm.

"So do I tell him to go on without me? That I can't support his campaign?"

"What do you think you should do?"

"Seems to me I don't have a choice, not if I want a real relationship. It's the beginning of the end."

"The beginning?"

"That's true."

"Let's go get a cup of coffee."

"Sure."

We head down one of the many glass elevators to the atrium and Donna's Coffee Bar and Restaurant. She orders a triple latte, whole milk. I get a tea.

We sit at a table overlooking the atrium, glass walls towering above us. "I'll support you in whatever you do."

"I don't know how much more of this life I can stand. I feel like I've lost myself, Ivy. I don't even know what I'm supposed to look like or act like anymore. I'd rather go it alone than play the trophy wife beside a plastic man."

See? I could have it a lot worse. Maybe there's something to be said for being stuck in a quagmire.

"Why don't you come stay with me for a few days? We can run to and from the hospital together. You know, mutually support each other during this trying time."

"Those are good words. Marcus will go for that. And it'll give him an easy explanation for why I'm not standing by his side." She deepens her voice. "My wife asks for your prayers as her family goes through this trying time surrounding the illness of her mother."

I kiss her cheek. "Why don't you go home and pack a bag, and I'll meet you at my house? You can bunk with me."

"That'll be nice."

My house will soon burst if anyone else comes to stay.

It's kind of nice, though, isn't it?

Mitch walks into Mom's room.

He kisses my forehead but doesn't let it linger. Disappointment mixes with relief.

"How's our Dorothy?"

"Tomorrow will be a big day for her." I point to the large machine by her bed. "They're dialyzing her now."

"I was on my way home from a dinner with a potential business partner."

"Really?"

"Yeah. Still keeping a few irons in the fire. You going to be okay?"

"I have to be, right?"

He rubs my arm. "I'll be back tomorrow."

We talk in the coffee shop for an hour. He builds me up, tells me I'm more woman than he's ever met, tells me he's so proud of me. And at the end, he leans forward and kisses me. And I kiss him back, and dear God, what am I doing?

I run from the shop, accompanied by the hollow thumping of my heels and my guilty conscience.

Enough, Ivy. You've had enough.

—

Oh great! Brett went home, and there went my ride. I call home. Harry's on his way. He asked if it would be all right if he came up to the room. I said sure and meant it. Anything to keep the memory of that kiss at bay. I could use a dad right now.

All these years later, I still dream that my parents will get back together. Can you believe it? In my heart, I really wouldn't wish that on Mom, but that little girl who sat on the couch and heard her father was gone for good still thinks, "What if he came back to stay?"

How stupid. I'm almost forty, for crying out loud.

He enters the room, hat in hand, looking older than I've ever seen him. His gnarled hand smoothes his ruffled gray hair. "She's sleeping?"

"Yeah. She woke up for a few minutes earlier and asked where she was, then went back to sleep."

I go over the doctor's plans and my own for convincing her to get that angioplasty. "Do you think I'm doing the right thing by insisting on the procedure?"

"It's your call, Ivy."

"But what do you think?"

He lightly taps the bed rail. "Second chances are never a bad thing."

"You ready to go?"

"If you'd like."

I slip on my coat, tuck my hand in his arm, and we walk out together.

"I haven't been here in years, Ive. Sure has changed."

Let's hope that's a good thing.

———

I fire up Old Barbara and begin my column. It's not like I'm going to sleep anyway. The notes I took during the phone interview, hitched up with some modifiers, conjunctions, and decent verbs, provide me with an easy write. I send it off to Tony.

Oh, this woman was such fun! I hope I can meet her in person someday. All these women I'm meeting are people I'd like to be when I grow up.

The phone rings. Krystal.

"Hey baby. How you doing?"

"Pretty good, considering."

"Got you all on the church prayer chain."

"Thanks. It's what we need."

"It's what we all need. Now you shut down that computer and get some sleep. I'll tell you, you have to really take good care of yourself now. Eat right, too. You may not feel like eating, but make yourself. Fruits and vegetables, chicken, fish, meat. God's food."

I smile. I need a mama right now. "Will do. I just need to e-mail Rusty, and I'm off to bed. I don't have high hopes for a good night's sleep, but it's worth a shot."

"Drink a cup of warm milk before you go."

"Does that really help?"

"It sure can't hurt. Good night, baby."

Man, that felt good. When people care, it makes all the difference in the world. When this is all over, I'm going to behave differently.

Dear Rusty,

Mom had a stroke today. She's in Shock Trauma down at University. Needless to say, I need you, Rust. Please come home. If you don't come for this, don't bother coming back at all.

I can't risk a full-fledged affair with Mitch. My defenses are crumbling beneath the stress and the loneliness, and it will happen if I don't do something. I need my husband to love me. If he loves himself more, then good-bye.

I click the Send icon. Another e-mail arrives.

Ivy,

I'm sorry. Forgive me. That will never happen again. I trust our friendship won't suffer. I'm still here for you.

Mitch

So now we wait. I thought the hip operation was bad. But this! Well, I keep imagining them poking up into her neck with a coat hanger, dislodging the Drano-worthy plaque. And then those particles swim on up to the brain, tumbling in the flow, getting stuck in a gang, stopping the blood, and *whammo,* another stroke, only larger and more merciless, and she doesn't die on the table, oh no, she ends up unable to talk or use the left side of her body, and there'll be diapers to change, Ensure to buy, nurses coming in and out, baths to give, and, dear God, how will I do this?

Brett shuffles her feet.

"Did I just say all that out loud?"

"Uh-huh."

"I swear, I'm losing it."

She flips through a magazine. *Guns & Ammo.* Now who left that here? Oh well, she's not really reading it anyway.

"Brian's not coming until later."

"Brett, how do you do it? How are you so longsuffering with him?"

She shuts the magazine and lays it on the end table. "Do you remember Brian before Dad left?"

"Not really. He played a lot of baseball, I remember that. Boy Scouts, too. And I remember he'd play Life with me sometimes."

"He used to sing a lot too. Like when he was raking the yard, or emptying out the dishwasher, or doing homework."

I shake my head. Don't ever remember Brian singing.

"Remember when he stopped going to church?"

"That I do remember. Harry told Mom it was time to let him make his own decision about religion. But that was before he left, wasn't it?"

"Yeah, which makes it even more rich. I saw things you didn't, Ivy. I know it seems like we're always saying that, that we're almost throwing it in your face, and I don't know why I do that."

" . . . "

"Fact is, you've paid your dues on this end of the deal. Which is way more than we can say about Brian."

"Then how can you remain so close to him? Give him excuse after excuse? I mean, I love him because he's my brother and I have to. You love him for who he is. Which amazes me."

"He's not so bad when you get to know him. Unfortunately, by the time you were old enough to get to know him as a human being, he was too far gone."

"Maybe it's true. Maybe you do have more reason to be mad at Harry than I do."

"I don't know. But I saw what he did to my brother. That day Mom told us? Remember sitting on the couch?"

I nod.

"It was like a light bulb turned off in Brian. And Dad flipped the switch. No doubt in my mind."

"Yeah. I can see that."

"At the same time, you had to grow up with a mother who was never home, drowning in your schoolwork, your sister running you around, and yet you always did so well. And let's face it, you've made the best of your marriage, you have a great career, great kids, and you've carried the ball with Mom."

"Sometimes I feel like I'm about to die."

"I know. But I want you to know, Ivy, I think you're the most kindhearted, decent person I know."

It's been so long since I had a good cry. I feel my eyes begin to fill, and Brett reaches out. I'm done for. She smells so nice.

I lift up my head later. "Do you think you'll ever be able to forgive Harry?"

"I'm going to have to, aren't I? I mean, really, do I have an option?"

"No."

"Have you forgiven him?"

"Yeah. He's living in my house. It was either that or go around mad all the time."

She smiles. "Thanks for putting me up, by the way. I slept better last night than I have in months."

"I gave Rusty the ultimatum last night."

Brett grabs my knee and squeezes. "Good. Good for you."

———

"Hey Lyr."

"Hey Mom."

The connection isn't good. She sounds so far away.

"How's everyone?"

"Okay. Is Winky okay?"

"She's not out of surgery yet. Trixie driving you nuts?"

"Gramps thinks she's getting sick. And I agree. She's been sitting on the couch with him, sucking on her pinkie, and her cheeks are as pink as they can be."

Oh man. "Lyra...I'm sorry about all this. I'm sorry I haven't been the mom you've needed. I'm trying to do my best, but unfortunately, it's not good enough for anyone."

"Mom, I know. Don't worry about it. It's okay. I'm fine."

"You sure?"

"Yeah. It's going to be fine. Gramps and Grandpa are taking us to the fairgrounds after Winky gets out. They're having a car show there. You know Persy and cars."

"That'll be nice."

"So we're fine. Don't worry about a thing. Oh yeah! I forgot. Dani and Uncle Brian came by. They went into Winky's room and cleaned up everything. Took the sheets home to wash, polished the furniture, just everything."

"That's cool."

"I really like Dani, Mom. I know she wears those, well, *you know* type of clothes, but she's really sweet."

"I agree."

"And guess what?!"

Wow, she's back with a vengeance. Great! It's nice to have my daughter back. Hopefully she'll stay a long time.

Poor Trixie, though.

"I got my interim grades. Straight As!"

"Way to go, sweetie. I'm so proud of you."

"Yeah, well, anyway, just wanted to tell you. You want to talk to Gramps?"

"Absolutely."

"Hi Ive." he whispers.

"How's our baby?"

"Lyra found the Children's Advil. She just fell asleep."

———

Dr. Merritt pulls off his surgical cap, revealing a rumpled head of straight, dark hair finely lined with gray. "It went fine. None of the arteries were completely closed, so we were able to do the procedure. You should see a real improvement in her."

"Thank you, Doctor." I reach out to shake his hand.

"You're welcome. I'll fill Dr. Smart in on everything, and he'll be getting with you. In the meantime we'll be moving her down to ICU. I don't know which room yet."

He takes his leave. Brett and I pull out our cell phones and begin to make the rounds.

———

I sure wish I had an Internet connection here at the hospital. I'm dying to check my e-mail, having no idea how Rusty's going to respond.

You know, I thought I had it in me. You hear about women who can support their husbands in difficult career choices that take them far away for long periods of time. And then, when the man retires, the couple rides away into the sunset together to spend the rest of their lives at ease, enjoying and appreciating each other's company.

But perhaps they find they have nothing to say to one another anymore, and they separate, and those years of forbearance, of setting the teeth and swallowing hard, meant absolutely nothing.

Fact is, "It is not good for the man to be alone."

If God saw that, why shouldn't I? Why shouldn't Rusty?

The dialysis machine cleans Mom's blood, whirring and twirling its parts, blood-filled tubing jumping around a bit. And she's sitting up in her bed watching *The Lawrence Welk Show* on public television.

"You know, girls, I actually feel hopeful. I haven't felt that way in a long time."

Brett leans forward and takes her hand. "The doctor says if you take good care of yourself, you'll have lots of years ahead of you."

"I'd sure like to see the grandchildren all grow up."

"Me too, Mom," I say.

"Do you remember when you girls used to do duets together in church?"

"Oh yeah." Brett clears her throat. "Ready, Ive? How about the HASH Chorus. Got your alto on?"

"Ready when you are."

She begins, her clear soprano ringing truer than ever. "This world is not my home…"

I join in on the harmony. "I'm just a passin' through. My treasures are laid up…somewhere beyond the blue."

We sing softly, hymn after hymn, chorus after chorus, and Mom drifts off, sleeping soundly as we tiptoe from the room, homeward bound.

Brett shakes her head. "Good grief. All those songs seemed to be about dying and going home to heaven."

"I know! Do you think she realized it?"

"Let's hope not!"

I take her arm, and we chuckle as we set foot to the ugly carpeting.

26

Brett turns onto Allegheny Avenue. "That was a good day, wasn't it, Ive?"

"Far better than I dared even hope."

"She sounded so good, didn't she? Had that lift to her voice I haven't heard in months."

I've got my mom back. I've got her back. "I know! I think I should keep her at the house, though. Don't you? With running to dialysis three times a week."

"That's up to you. You think you'll be okay?"

"Oh yeah. Harry'll drive her. He's become a regular chauffeur these days. He and Reuben."

"So you think he'll stay?"

"I want him to."

We stop at a red light.

She looks at me. "You know, I've been thinking a lot about what we discussed earlier. I think I'm going to try and make a go of it with Dad. I'm not getting any younger."

"Me either."

"And I figure, when he goes, either I tried or I didn't. But I'd like to think I have more inside of me than this."

"Don't we all, Brett?"

"Yeah, well, 'only one life' and all that."

Mom's favorite poem. "Only one life, t'will soon be past. Only what's done for Christ will last."

A few minutes later we pull into the drive. Out by the front walk a cab idles. The back door opens, and someone climbs out from inside. Tall and not so heavy as he used to be.

"Rusty!" I scream, scrambling out of the car before it comes to a complete stop.

He quickly slips the driver some cash and runs toward me. I slam into his great warmth.

He came home.

Oh, dear Lord, he came home.

My knees buckle, and he holds me up, saying, "It's all right, Ive. Everything's going to be okay. I'm sorry, hon. I'm so sorry."

"I can't believe you came back."

"Marlin was really angry. But I told him, 'We go around singing gospel songs, and you want me to forsake my family in this time of crisis?'"

"What did he say?" I place a few teabags in my favorite pot. We're letting the kids sleep through. Awakening to find their father home will be an exciting surprise.

"He said, 'If any man come to me, and hate not his father, and mother, and wife, and children, and brethren, and sisters, yea, and his own life also, he cannot be my disciple.'"

"What did you say?"

"I told him I didn't think that was exactly what Jesus meant."

"So do you still have a place with the group once this is over?"

"I doubt it."

"I'm sorry."

"It's not your fault. Besides, I got an e-mail from Lyra a while ago that worried me. She's being made fun of at school a lot, did you know that?"

"No!" I fill the pot with steaming water. "She hasn't said a thing!"

"She said you've got enough on your plate."

"No wonder she's been so edgy. I thought it was me."

"She's got a lot to handle."

"I can't wait to see her face when she sees you."

He smiles. "I didn't get any supper on the plane. Is there any lunchmeat?"

"Sure. I'll make you a sandwich."

"No mayo anymore."

"Got it."

Rusty's looking good, I have to admit. "How much weight have you lost?"

"Seventy-five pounds."

"Really?"

He pulls a loaf of bread out of the drawer. "Yep. I've got another forty to go. I'm thinking about joining Dad's gym and going with him in the mornings. I'm feeling like I'm at the point where I can start working out again."

"I won't complain about that."

He grabs the turkey, mustard, and sandwich pickles from the fridge. "I'll make an appointment tomorrow to go interview up at that school."

"You'll like it there. It would be a great place for Trixie and Persy."

"It'll be lean for a while until I get a job."

"We'll make it somehow."

He fixes his sandwich as I pour the tea.

"You know you're going to have to give me a little time, don't you, Rust?"

He nods. "Yeah."

"I'll have to get to know you all over again."

"I've got some trust to earn."

"Yeah. I'm sorry."

He places the second slice of bread on the meat. "Ive, I'm the one who left. Bottom line. I just thought we could make it work."

"But 'we' was really 'I.'"

He doesn't argue. Rusty never does when he knows he really blew it. He sits down and begins to eat.

"Rusty, I just want you to know that I really wanted a divorce. In my mind, I was thinking it would really come to that. It's not fair if you don't know how serious this all is."

He looks me in the eye. "I know."

"I didn't want to give you an ultimatum. I shouldn't have had to. And that's still ticking me off. You really didn't miss us enough to come home on your own."

"You're right."

"You didn't value us higher than yourself."

His eyes drop to his mug. "So am I basically on probation?"

"Yes. I have to see for myself that you love us. Now, let me get you up to speed on Dorothy." Man, I need a subject change.

———

I rinse my cup out in the sink as Rusty sets up the coffeepot for the morning. "Brett's staying here, Rust. She's up in our room."

"That doesn't sound good. Marcus up to his tricks?"

"The campaign, his new mistress."

Rusty shakes his head. "Guess I can't judge him there, can I?"

"So we can pull out the sofa bed down here, I guess. Brett can take it tomorrow."

"I'll go get it ready. It's 5:00 a.m. by my body clock. You coming to bed?"

I've got a lot to do, naturally, but I'm so worn out concentration isn't a possibility. "Yeah, I'm ready to turn in."

Fifteen minutes later, Rusty's snoring away, and I'm numb, but this is going to work. It has to. I have no other option that's good for the kids or even me. If I fell in love with him once, I can fall in love with him again.

Falling in love? That seems a bit juvenile. I'd even settle for that lovely, worn-in shoe feeling. Yes, that's what I want to have with Rusty. I want to walk in rhythm down the aisle of the grocery store. Call his cell phone to tell him to pick up dinner at KFC on the way home. Watch a sitcom. Eat popcorn. Buy him his favorite soap. I want to repeat the same old stories, eat the same holiday dinners, and spread mulch. I want to grow old together, our relationship as warm and taken for granted as morning sunlight through a kitchen window.

———

"Daddy, Daddy, Daddy!"

Whoa! My eyes burst open.

Persy's jumping all over the bed, his voice raised to full volume.

I slept through the night without waking up once. I feel great.

I hear a bump from upstairs, and Lyra rumbles down the steps, sleep already far from her eyes. "Dad!"

Trixie slides down next, her behind thumping on each stair. "Daddy! Daddy!"

And soon they're all snuggled together around us, the king and queen of the sofa bed. Giggles and shouts explode, tickles and pokes draw out more laughter. I can choose to make it now. I can choose to get through today, and perhaps tomorrow as well.

Fifteen minutes later. "Okay, gang, get dressed for school!"

"How 'bout a day off, Ive? Just this once?" Rusty.

The kids cheer. I look at them. "Why not? In fact they're moving Mom down to a regular ward today. Maybe you can bring everyone down? It'll cheer her up."

"Sounds like a plan! Come on Trixie-girl, Daddy will get you dressed this morning."

"I'll help Grandpa with breakfast." Lyra.

"Can I play GameCube?" Persy.

I sit up straight. "Let's go."

Brett makes her appearance. "Rusty!"

"Brett!" He climbs out of the bed. "Hey girl!"

They embrace.

"You are a sight for sore eyes! And look at you. I think I picked up the weight you dropped." She reddens.

"Are you kidding me? You look great. Just how a woman should look. Did you know Marilyn Monroe was a size 12?"

That's Rusty for you.

———

My ear actually sweats up the receiver, the lineup of calls has been so extensive. Krystal. Debbie. Lou. Brenda. Not Mitch. Not yet. Dani, then Brian, who is crying and crying, now Dani again, who whispers into the phone, "He's stoned, Ivy. I have no idea where he got it."

"Oh no. What's he on?"

"He got Darvon somewhere. I think he raided my mother's medicine cabinet."

"You're kidding me."

"I wish I was. So anyway, he's in no shape to go to the bistro today."

"I'll call the guys."

"Thanks."

"Hey, it's not your problem, Dani. You want to bring him over here?"

"No. I have off today."

"I can't thank you enough."

"I've chosen this path with Brian, Ivy."

"For the life of me, I can't figure out why."

"It's like Mick Jagger says, 'You can't always get what you want, but you get what you need.'"

"You're too nice for this."

"Fact is, Ivy, I'm not very nice without it."

I still don't understand. "I'm going to keep this from the others."

"Good move."

"Dani, do you love him?"

"Funny as it may seem, I do."

We part. And I wipe my sweaty ear with a napkin.

———

Brett slides into the driver's seat, and we're off to the hospital.

"I'll get out of your hair tonight, Ive."

"You don't have to leave. In fact, why don't you stay in Mom's room? Brian and Dani have it all cleaned."

"No, thanks. I can't run away from the man forever. But I needed a break, and this was good."

"You're always welcome."

"Well, I may take you up on it, but let's hope I don't have to."

"Have you been going to church at all?"

"No. And I know I should."

"Why don't you meet us on Sunday? Then we can go down to the hospital from there. If Mom's still in."

"I may just do that."

I have no idea how Brett's situation is going to play out. Maybe she'll decide to make it work no matter what. Maybe she's more afraid of being alone than living with Marcus.

———

What a day! Mom was sitting up in bed, eating her liquid diet, enjoying a cup of tea when we walked in.

Rusty and I relax on the couch now, talking with VH1's *Behind the Music* in the background. I love the Metallica episode for some reason. But this one is about Nirvana, which just doesn't do it for me. I mean, I feel sorry for Kurt Cobain, sorry that he was so lonely and depressed. Something about the boy always made me want to mother him. But his music never reached my soul.

"How you doing, hon?"

"It was so nice to kiss her cheek and watch the smile come to her lips, Rust. It's like she's on her way back to us."

"I sure hope so. Dorothy needs to have more time with her grandchildren."

"You know, difficult as she could be with me, she's never taken it out on the kids. Not like Mrs. Waxman."

"Lyr was telling me about that. I don't know how Bernie and Debbie can stand it."

"Me either." I tell him about Debbie's late-night forays into our kitchen.

"Hey, whatever works."

"I hope you didn't have delusions of coming back to Beaver Cleaver Land."

"Face it, hon, it never was really fifties around here."

I hug a pillow to my chest. "Mom looked better than she has in months, don't you think?"

"Well, I guess I wouldn't know. But it was good to hear her laughing. I think the kids were a boost."

We're riding a high wave. And a little voice whispers, "Enjoy it while it lasts."

Oh, shut up.

———

I let myself in through the back door, completely ready for a cup of tea, bless Reuben and the new coffee maker. Instant gratification has become more important than ever now that my days run hither and yon. Whatever hither and yon means. I need to start making supper, but first, a moment of decompression.

Lyra bounds into the kitchen. "Stop!"

"What?"

"I'll make that. You've got to get ready."

"Ready? For what?"

"You'll see. Go on up. There's a surprise on the bed. We've been busy all day. It's been so much fun. Hurry!" She pushes me gently. "You don't have all day, Mom!"

I slip out of my coat, hang it on the back of a kitchen chair and run up the steps. On the bed an outfit is all pressed and ready. A new outfit.

"You all go shopping today?" I yell.

Lyra appears at the doorway. "Yep. Look, a new pantsuit. Isn't it great?"

A double-breasted gray affair, a cream camisole for underneath, and my new boots at the ready. "Wow."

"Come on into the bathroom!" Brenda?

"Brenda?"

"Yep. We're going to do your hair."

I walk in. "What are you doing here?"

"Used to be a beautician." She smiles and holds up a pair of professional-looking shears.

This woman never ceases to surprise me.

"Let's get started. We don't have time for a proper color job, but I brought an all-over rinse that will just take a few minutes. Put this cape on."

"Great."

Forty minutes later she's snipping away, and I examine myself in the mirror, all pink-skinned, eyes glistening. Lyra leans against the doorframe, smiling, arms folded across her chest.

"Where's Daddy, Lyr?"

"That's a secret!"

Brenda digs her fingers into my hair and fluffs. "Isn't this fun? I love surprises and makeovers, and when you put the two together it's the best."

"I won't fight against it. This is great, you guys. Thanks."

"Don't mention it, Ivy. I was glad to do it. I've cut back on so many of my activities, I was thrilled when Lou called."

"Lou's in on this?"

"Most definitely." Lyra.

The blow-dryer begins, and I watch in fascination as a bona fide hairdo develops before my eyes. Chin-length, lots of fluffy layers, and that rinse colored all my white hairs to platinum.

"I can't believe it's me in that mirror."

Brenda wields a round brush as thick as Trixie's thigh. "Wait until we do the makeup."

"Oh, Mom. This is going to be great."

After Brenda puffs and spritzes my hair, she grabs a makeup case—not a bag, a case—opens it, and lifts out several trays. Now this is a woman who knows how to take care of herself. Which reminds me. I have yet to glory in my day at the spa.

"I hope you don't mind if I use my own makeup. Trust me, it isn't old, and I'm very careful. I always use fresh sponges and applicators."

"See, Mom?" Lyra turns to Brenda. "I swear, Miss Brenda, Mom's using stuff that's at least ten years old."

"It's not quite that bad, Lyr."

She crosses her arms in the other direction and gives me the stare.

"Okay, maybe it is."

Brenda just laughs. "Now turn away from the mirror so you can get the full effect when we're done."

I can't tell you how nice it feels to be pampered like this. I don't ever remember anyone doing something like this for me.

"This sure is the life."

I close my eyes and savor.

Youth skips with me down the front steps, and oh, I feel sassy in this fresh outfit, dreamy haircut, and high-heeled boots. And sexy too. Now I haven't felt sexy in years and years. I think sometimes, when we start having kids, we forget to feel sexy, or we feel guilty feeling sexy, or most likely we're too darn tired to feel sexy. It's just too much work, and all those actresses and models have so raised the bar on sexy, it almost takes the faith of a thousand mustard seeds for the rest of us to even begin to compete. Don't even get me started on those extreme-makeover shows.

But tonight I'm cute, I'm sexy.

And it only took three of us to get me there.

"Oh my!"

A beautiful silver Mercedes, Brenda's car, idles by the curb. Lou, dressed in a blue pantsuit, climbs out.

"You guys!" I turn to Lyra and Brenda and wave to Lou. "This is so great."

She whisks around and opens the back door nearest the curb. "Your carriage awaits, my lady."

"This is too much!"

"And exactly what you all need." Lou.

"Thanks, you guys!" I wave to the group gathered on the porch. Harry, the kids, Brenda and Reuben. Mr. Moore waves from his porch, and Debbie from hers.

I sit down and swing my legs into the leather interior. Lou slides in and closes her door. "Ready, Ive?"

"For what?"

"How about a nice dinner without the kids?"

"Who masterminded all of this?"

"Who do you think?"

"Rusty and Lyra."

"The woman's a seer."

"So where are you taking me?"

She flits her gaze up in the rearview mirror. "Now do you really think I'm going to answer that?"

"Never hurts to ask."

Five minutes later, she steers the car onto the beltway, and we chat about décor, Mom, Brian, her husband Neil, who's taking up boxing in middle age and isn't that about the dumbest thing you've ever heard, a man his age pounding on people, and what is it supposed to mean, who's he trying to impress, who's he trying to *kid* is more like it, don't you think, Ivy? Her son, a boy named Atticus, believe it or not, is trying to get a scholarship at Loyola High School for next year and looks like he may just succeed. And that's really great, Lou, I mean that. He's a good kid.

She turns onto I-95 North.

"So we're heading out of town?"

"You bet. I sure wish Neil would do something like this for me. But he's thickheaded. Nice guy, but thickheaded."

"Maybe that boxing will thin things out a bit, shake things up."

"One can only hope."

"The trees are starting to sprout leaves."

"Yeah, isn't it nice?"

"I love that soft green mist."

"Me too. Smells good outside too."

My history with Lou has anchored me. I see that now. We can talk about the small wonders of life and not feel at all silly.

I wonder if she knows about Mitch and me.

More chat, about everything but that. And it builds up my heart to be with her, to just be Ivy Starling and nothing else.

We keep going north, past Bel Air, past Aberdeen, and finally Lou clicks the blinker before the Havre de Grace exit.

"Havre de Grace? I love Havre de Grace."

"Me too."

We head down Union Street, gorgeous old mansions from Federal to Victorian sitting comfortably amid trees older than any of the town's inhabitants. She pulls up by the curb in front of the Silver Inn.

"Remember how we used to come up this way for Sunday drives? I've always loved this house in particular."

The Silver Inn sprouts turrets and spindles and porches, and no two windows are the same size. Painted like a Victorian lady in white, greens, and reds, it looks ready for Christmas though it's only April.

"Did you tell Rusty about this place?"

"Yep. You'll have to tell me all about it! Maybe I can get Neil to bring me here."

"Ha."

"Yeah, I know."

"You know, he's not all bad. I mean, he makes a mean Irish stew, you know? And he loves you."

"Yeah. But then, how could he not?" She presses a button on the door handle and all the locks disengage. "Go on in and tell the desk clerk you're here. I'll be taking the car back to Brenda."

"This was great, Lou."

"I sure had fun."

I reach for the door handle.

"Uh-uh-uh. I'll get the door." She pops her door open.

I feel my face redden, but oh well.

She lets me out and gives me a hug.

"Thanks, Lou."

The desk clerk smiles after I tell her my name. "You're in the Brady Cottage." Her bright pink lipstick shines in the dim, antique lighting.

"Our own cottage?"

"It's gorgeous. Now, head out that back door there and down the walk, and it's the first cottage on your right. You have a gentleman there waiting for you with a bottle of champagne."

———

We sit at a table for two at the Crazy Swede. A delicate vase of baby roses perches to the side; a small candle lends its glow.

At the cottage we drank the champagne and he held me in his arms as we watched a movie. That was it. No tryst. Nothing spicy. Just warmth.

Now that was a smart step on his part. Maybe hope truly exists for us.

"So what'll you have, hon?"

I skim the menu. Brian deserves credit. He's a fine chef, and nothing on here compares to his offerings, but the restaurant enjoys a fine reputation in Havre de Grace. Seafood is always a good choice in Maryland.

"The stuffed flounder, I think."

"You want to split the entrée and get a couple appetizers?"

What? Man, he's really serious about this weight-loss business. "Sure. How about the fried calamari as one?"

"And the crab dip?"

"Sounds like a plan."

I relish this moment. Surely it's one most couples take for granted, but I think that's gone forever for me, simple things like ordering at a restaurant together, or driving to church in the same car. And maybe that's fine. Maybe the last three years can be turned into a good thing. Maybe we'll be better off in the long run if we appreciate each moment, recognize each act for the true gift it is.

"When do you think your mom will get out of the hospital?"

"In a couple of days. She's sure been lucid. I think it'll be fun having her around the house."

He gulps down his water. "Old Dorothy is a good gal."

"Thanks for coming home, Rust."

He shakes his head. "Why I was so content to leave you and the kids behind, I don't know. I'm still trying to figure that out."

"We've done a lot of growing up since then."

He winks. "Hopefully I'll catch up soon."

Rusty and I have always gotten along so well. And maybe that was part of our problem, neither wanting to make demands. But now we know, don't we?

"I need to ask for your forgiveness, Ivy."

"And I need to give it."

"I'm sorry."

And I forgive him. Not that I truly have a choice, but still, I want to.

"That's settled then," I say. "Where do we go from here?"

"Down the road, babe. We just go down the road."

We give our order to the waitress.

"So what made you want to start losing weight, Rust?"

"It took three people to get me into a wet suit when we sang in Florida. I've never been more humiliated in my life."

"Oh, sweets."

"Plus, there's a reason to stick around as long as possible. I mean, the kids haven't spent enough time with me as it is. It would be horrible to go that young."

"Well, sometimes it just takes something like a wet suit to get us started."

Or an illicit kiss with another man.

"I feel like taking the kids bowling," I say.

"That was out of the blue."

"Let's do something as a family. There's Rock and Bowl at Parkville Lanes tonight. Goes till midnight."

Ninety minutes later, ten o'clock, we're marching down the steps and into the bowling alley that sits beneath a sixties strip mall. Lyra's skin practically sings arias, she's so excited, but still a girl's gotta be cool. I can see it in her eyes, though. Times like these are rare.

We pay for shoes and find our lane. Persy checks out all the bowling balls in hopes of finding the perfect one. Trixie holds her crotch and yells, "I gotta go!" Music to my ears. I whisk her away to the ladies' room.

When I return to our semicircular collection of seats, two huge sodas, a bag of popcorn, and a large box of Mike and Ikes are waiting.

And the crier in me tries to push his way out, but I shove him down and begin to laugh.

The principal folds her hands on her desktop. Neat, unpolished nails, no rings. Hair folded in a bun. Crisp suit. A little too much red lipstick.

I say, "You send your child to a private school hoping they'll escape, even somewhat, the torture of not fitting in."

"It's why we have uniforms, Mrs. Schneider."

"She's miserable. Are you aware of the cliques here?"

"We certainly don't encourage it, but girls can be ruthless."

"Not for my money. I can send Lyra to public school for free for this kind of treatment."

Rusty leans forward in his chair. "We don't wish to pull her out, Ms. Zoll. We just want to know, at this point, that Lyra has an advocate."

She sighs. "Give me the names."

I rattle off the worst offenders. The cruel ones.

"I'm not surprised. I'll talk to some of the other students and see if they've had the same problems."

"I'm sure you'll have no trouble finding them. According to Lyra, they've singled out two other girls."

"Who?"

"Jenny. Clarissa."

"Oh my. That's so unfortunate. They're such nice girls as well. Such good students."

"Thank you," I say.

"Will we be hearing from you, then?" Rusty.

"Of course." She stands up and offers her hand. We stand up and shake it. "Thank you for coming to me."

I grab my bag. "Well, it is a parochial school. I figured you wanted your students to behave in a kind manner."

"We surely would hate to lose Lyra."

Rusty holds my hand. "But we will pull her out if it doesn't stop. And naturally, we'll expect the utmost discretion from the faculty and administration on this matter. If those girls realize this came from Lyra's direction, it will be terrible for her."

"I agree. We have ways of working behind the scenes, Mr. Schneider."

"Thank you."

We take our leave, walking in the spring warmth to the car.

"Wow, Rusty. I'm so glad you were there. I don't think I would have come on so strong at the end like you did."

"She's our baby."

I put my arm around his waist. "Yeah, she is."

"Whatever we do, we can't tell Lyra we did this. She'd flip."

Stealth parenting. Ain't it grand?

27

Nurses and doctors mill in and out of Mom's room. Brett and I start to run.

"What's wrong?" I ask.

Dr. Smart gives orders to a nurse: cc's of this and that.

A nurse with cropped red hair and a freckled face touches my arm. "Your mother is having a heart attack. Come in."

"Mom?"

She lies on her side, face screwed in pain. "Oh, Ivy. I've never felt anything like this before."

Another nurse looks up from where she stands by Mom's back. "Would you like to come massage her here between the shoulder blades?"

Brett turns whiter than a sugar cube.

"Yes!" I take her place and rub in a circular motion.

"It helps," the nurse says.

The doctor on call fills us in on the details, most of which I don't understand. All I know is my mother is having a heart attack and I need to massage her back.

"Oh, girls," Mom moans.

"We're here, Mom. We're here," I say.

And I pray silently, dear God, dear God, dear God. Oh, dear God.

They've taken her down for a heart cath. I didn't sleep last night. Nothing. Poor Rusty tried to sit up with me, but he only lasted until about three. Lyra got up at five to study, and we sat at the kitchen table together, drinking Coke straight out of the can, me tapping at Barbara as Lyra rustled pages, punched buttons on her calculator, and sighed.

Getting old is such a crime. That's simply all there is to it. Dear God, let me go quickly. That's all I ask. Again. I think I'd take five or so fewer years if I could say, drop dead, or get hit by a truck or a train so that people could say, "Well, it's obvious she was dead on impact. She didn't know what hit her." I don't want to know what hit me. That's it exactly.

I don't care how great a Christian you are, nobody *wants* to die if they're still young enough to multiply their age by two and get a truly achievable age. It's not so much the leaving of this earth, our lives, or our skin, it's the actual process.

What happens, really? What's it really like to die?

I wonder if Mom's thinking these thoughts, or if she's fooling herself like the rest of us that it couldn't possibly be just around the corner.

Now, dying in one's sleep surely is the best. I'll bet if we could choose our deaths, ninety-eight percent would pick that. My Grandma died in her sleep, and it was a blessing. She'd deteriorated mentally, thinking *Eyewitness News* was coming to film her as she sat on her toilet. No wonder we figured Mom was simply losing her mind. The women in my family should jingle when we walk, we have so many loose screws.

I glance over at Brian, who sits with us in the waiting room. He always looks so suave in his leather jacket, his up-to-the-minute haircut, his European shoes. Not the slinky, Italian European shoes. The orthopedic, Swiss-looking, I'm-earthy-but-hip European shoes. But today he's pale, clammy instead of cool. I think he's still taking painkillers.

"Do you think she'll die?" he asks.

"Not today. But this can't bode well for the future. First the diabetes, then the stents in her neck arteries, the dialysis, now this."

Brett roots in her purse and pulls out a tin of mints. "I think we have to face facts, guys. Her days are numbered."

Brian runs from the room.

"Get us another coffee while you're at it!" Brett hollers. "He's going to have to face this, Ive. For Mom's sake if nothing else."

"I think he wants to change. I really do. He just can't do it on his own, and he can't trust in that vengeful God we grew up with."

"Yeah." She opens the tin and holds it out. I take a mint and place it on my tongue. "It's taken me years to get over Him. Well, not Him, Him. Just the Him they said He was."

"Scary as it sounds, I understand that exactly."

We turn back to our magazines, the clock moving forward. I've learned in hospitals and doctors' offices to take the time they estimate for the procedure and multiply by two. Some family of bikers monopolizes the television with Spike TV.

"What's going on at home, Brett?"

"Same old. I put my foot down. Told Marcus I couldn't personally support his campaign. I mean, don't I have the right to live by my own code? And do you know what that rat said?"

"What?"

"He said, 'Well, as long as your mom is sick, at least we have an excuse.'"

"What a pig."

I shouldn't have said that.

"It's true. What did I ever see in that man?"

"Don't blame yourself for that. He was charming and settled. This is a midlife crisis."

"You think we can weather this?"

"If you want to."

"What if he doesn't?"

"I don't know then. You can't force him to stay."

She grins. "Maybe I could push him out in various other ways."

I laugh. "Make his life miserable?"

"I wouldn't be the first woman to do so!"

"You won't, though."

"I know. The Starling in me hangs on till the last hurrah."

I squeeze her knee. "It's a good thing, Brett. Then you know you did all you could. Just make a nice home for him, and do whatever you need to do to feel fulfilled yourself. Maybe it'll free you up to love him again."

She raises an eyebrow. "I'm glad Rusty's home, though."

"Me too."

She puts her arm around my shoulder; I put my arms around her waist and we sit there together. Dear God, I love my sister so much.

Harry enters the waiting room awhile later. We've sipped the lattes Brian dropped off before going who knows where. After the coffee, we shared a bag of Kettle Chips, two packages of Swiss Cheese on Wheat, and a sleeve of Caramel Creams. We looked at the copy of *Teen People* hanging about, and for heaven's sake, is this what Lyra's been reading? Perused a *New Homes* booklet as well as the *Apartment Guide.* Then, much to our chagrin, we were subjected to Spike TV's *Sports Illustrated Swimsuit Issue Special,* and how embarrassing is that? Brett kept muttering, "I have got to start losing some weight." I ate another Caramel Cream. But hey, that's what the bikers want to watch, and I'm not about to get up and switch it to something else. I don't want to end up in surgery myself today.

Harry nods once to the head biker, a very skinny guy with a black Fu Manchu mustache and acne scars, then turns to us. "Hey girls."

"Dad!" I jump up. "Have a seat. She should be up soon. The doctor'll give us the scoop."

He kneads his cap. "Hey Brett."

"Dad."

"Brett, can we go for a walk?"

She stiffens but nods.

"Okay, Dad. Let's go."

My nerves jump. I called him *Dad* too.

———

Dr. Merritt enters the waiting room, pulling off his surgical cap, then rearranges his mountain of hair. Harry and Brett are still out. Lots to say, I'm sure. Stuff I know I just don't want to hear.

"Well, she's finished and in the recovery room. You can go in after we talk."

"Great. How did it go?"

"There was a lot of blockage. But we were able to put in two stents. I think we can treat her medically."

"No open-heart?"

"As of this point, no. Two arteries are ninety percent blocked. We'll see how she progresses."

"Would it be better to just go ahead with the surgery?"

"In some cases I'd recommend that. But after all she's been through, I'd hate to take that chance right now."

I feel the tears pricking my eyes.

He notices, bless him.

"This is always hard on the family," he says. "Believe me, I know."

"You've been through this?"

"Yes. My own mother sure had her trials."

"Has she passed away?"

"Two years ago."

"I'm sorry."

"I understand you're the one who cares for her."

I nod.

"You're doing a fine job, Mrs. Schneider. She speaks very highly of you."

My heart swells.

"She should be able to go home in a few days. We'll be starting her on some heart medication, and she'll certainly have to watch her diet, limit her cholesterol."

I nod again. Nod, nod, nod. Doctors must feel like they do nothing but talk to dashboard ornaments. "She's always had a hard time eating low fat."

Now he nods.

And I nod.

And he clears his throat, and we say our adieus, and I sit back down, exhausted.

The publisher hates my new story line, Candace Frost told me. On my cell phone, she sounded full of regret but hopeful. I told her I wanted to write a memoir. She said fine. Even if it stinks it'll be better than writing nothing.

"And you never know, Ivy. It may actually end up as a winner."

She has to say this. She's my agent.

"Can I keep Jane?"

"Yeah. But they want a sexy name. And Maximilian needs to be just plain evil."

Oh great.

Club Sandwich sits around my living room. We've all got our chosen seats now, and every week we set our fannies in the same places.

"Can I go first?" Krystal.

"Go for it." Debbie.

"Well, I'm just praisin' the Lord this afternoon. Help is on the way!"

I cut myself another piece of Debbie's cinnamon cream-cheese coffee cake.

"My Aunt Prisma is coming up from North Carolina tomorrow! God bless that woman."

"Great news!" Dani.

"Tell me about it. Aunt Prisma can make a bedbug feel at home. I've never met a woman quite like her. So if you've been praying I find me some help, the answer is here." Krystal takes another slice of cake too. "Now, Ivy girl, you been through the mill lately. How's Dorothy?"

"She's sleeping in her room. I can't believe she's home."

"How's the trek to dialysis?" Dani.

"With Reuben and Harry around, and Rusty too, we've got it covered."

Debbie. "We can't do it alone."

Krystal raises a hand. "Amen to that!"

Debbie grabs the hand. "Thank heavens for you all. It's good to have neighbors and friends."

Now this is what I call a support group!

"How's Mrs. Waxman these days?" Dani.

Debbie rolls her eyes. "You know, I'm not sure why we brought her to live with us. She's perfectly capable of caring for herself."

"Maybe you got to give her the boot." Krystal laughs, *ha-haahh!*

"No joke. I'm considering it."

"Really?" I ask.

"Better believe it. I can't subject my kids to this for no reason."

"You got that right." Krystal.

Brenda sits up straight. "You're right, Debbie. They're the most precious gift a woman can receive."

We're silent for a moment. Reverence is deserved. For as much as we complain about being sandwiched between two generations, we wouldn't have it any other way.

Kirsten speaks up. "Give her the boot, Debbie. You really need to keep your sanity as long as possible. Because you can bet every last dime you have that she'll be back!"

At the end of the meeting Reuben enters the living room.

"Wow, Dad, you look spiffy!"

"I'm here to pick up my date."

"Your date?"

Kirsten raises her hand. "I believe that would be me."

"No way!"

Well, what do you know. Could anything be more fabulous?

Rusty walks in from the kitchen. "Call us if you're not going to be home by midnight." He slaps Reuben on the back.

Krystal claps, lets out a hoot, and gets her praise on. "Thank You, Jesus! Thank You, Jesus!"

28

Summer arrived dressed up in cool breezes and gray skies. Mom went to dialysis three days a week, lay exhausted from dialysis the other three, and so each Sunday proved to be the good day. We loved it, churching it together, family dinner afterward, Dani dragging Brian along, Brett joining the gaggle. She ended up going to a small church filled with hippie people that meets on Friday nights and shares communion as an actual meal and feeds the homeless and takes in prostitutes. Sometimes you just can't hazard a real guess, can you?

I'm thinking about going there myself!

I suppose I always imagined something big had to happen to mature my brother, but it wasn't that way at all. It was a little exercise trainer and her daughter.

We buried Dani's mother in July. A suicide. Overdose. Dani cried, and Brian became strong because somebody finally needed him to.

Dani turned back to God, and her daughter Rosa loves going to Sunday school. She and Trixie became little buddies, playing with Lyra's old Barbies and dress-ups. I swear, a revolving front door would have been a good investment here on Allegheny Avenue. But I loved it. Rusty did too. When Reuben's condo was finished, we all tried to persuade him to stay, but living with Harry? Well, what old man wants to live with another old man longer than necessary? He and Kirsten are planning a Christmas wedding, so the condo's up for sale, and he'll move into the big house in Lutherville afterward. Kirsten farmed out most of the family antiques to cousins she barely knew. Rusty and I are the honor attendants! I can't imagine being a matron of honor at my age, but Kirsten didn't keep in touch with her schoolmates. We've had so much fun planning this wedding, Lou and Brenda in on it, Lyra volunteering to make the favors, Brian taking on the catering. And Krystal's officiating after Debbie sings a solo. That woman can sing like an angel. Not that I've ever heard one, but I can't imagine anything sounding prettier.

Brett's still crossing her fingers that Marcus will lose in the primary. Even the girls don't appreciate their stepdad's newfound obsession, which does give me hope for them. Actually, Ashley's thinking about majoring in special education. Brett's thrilled. She said, "That sounds like something Lyra would do!" Which thrilled me. Ashley loves their new church, or "gathering" as they call it.

Autumn wheeled around the corner a few weeks ago. Skidded, more like it. I felt like summer had just begun.

The family left for school a few minutes ago. Rusty took the job at the school in Bel Air, and so he totes Persy and Trixie along. Harry's off to Wal-Mart, lunch pail in tote, working in their optometry office there now. I've been doing the newsletter for almost a year now, and Mitch is more pleased with each issue. Somehow our friendship has been able to pick up where we left it before that locker-room kiss all those years ago. Funny how one small moment can grow into something so momentous years on down the road. I have to give him credit for hanging in there anyway. If I were him, I'd have moved away. But Mitch stays, working on cars, finding people jobs, and traveling his life away. I'm praying God will send him a good woman.

Maybe Krystal?

Now that would be a trip! I'll have to make a mental note.

Trixie hasn't pooped her pants in two months, Persy stopped burping out on the athletic field, and I actually redeemed my day at the spa before it expired. Some victories are small.

In my darkest hour, I didn't realize it could be this good. But somehow God manages to redeem even the most wounded of families.

I don't know how He does it, only that He does.

I sit down at the kitchen table with a fresh cup of tea. Mom's still asleep. Thankfully she's on the afternoon shift at the dialysis clinic. The early morning time slots were torture.

I pull up the file for my novel. Almost done. I'm entering the edits I've made on hard copy, and boy is this the most tedious task imaginable. Having no idea how the publishing house will like it, I pray hard but still imagine copious rewriting. All part of the job, Candace assures me. Jane—excuse me, Lauren—and her baby ride off into the sunset, just the two of them, with fifty mil of Maximilian's money. Maximilian meets his fate when he collides with a live wire, a stainless steel sink, fifty gallons of water, and a rare porterhouse. The steak had nothing to do with his death. It was a bit of symbolism I used throughout the book.

They've titled it *Busting Heads.*

I've taken a pen name.

Man, this tea sure tastes good this morning.

Okay, time to get started. Enter changes on manuscript, write column, finish article for newsletter. There are plenty of great women in our world for those savvy enough to recognize them. Fact is, we're too busy comparing ourselves to one another to appreciate our sisters' accomplishments. But hey, when one of us succeeds, we are all lifted up. I guess you can say that about humanity in general as well.

The back door rattles beneath a knock. Debbie.

"Come on in!"

"Hey Ive."

"So, is the deed done?"

"Movers came this morning."

Wow, she looks horrible. Face blotchy. Old forest green sweatpants. Ratty flip-flops and a tattered Ron Jon's T-shirt.

"I'll fix you a cup of tea. How do you feel?"

"You got scotch?"

"That bad?"

She plops down on a kitchen chair. "Why does it have to be like this?"

I pull down a mug. "Some people just give us no choice."

"She cussed me up one side and down the other."

"I am so sorry."

"Was I right to do this?"

"Definitely. She'll be fine at the retirement village. It's nice there. Maybe she'll even make a few friends."

"*My* mother?" Deep sigh. "I feel just awful doing that to her."

I drape a teabag over the edge of a cup and hold it under the hot tap. "Debbie, she did it to herself."

"My head knows that. But my heart…"

I hand her the cup, which she white-knuckles. "Your kids should always come first. It would be one thing if she couldn't take care of herself. Now just close your eyes and sit. You don't have to talk or do anything."

"I liked your book, Ivy. I even liked the chase scenes."

"Thanks, Debbie. Now just sit and be."

One side of her mouth lifts slightly. "I can do that here, you know. I think it's the only place I can."

How cool.

―――

After many postponements, Brian, at the urging of his lawyer, finally pled guilty to the DUIs. They suspended his license for two years, put him under supervised probation for the same amount of time, and laid a hundred hours of community service on his shoulders. He's teaching cooking to underprivileged high-schoolers in a community center downtown.

They say folks never change. But if that were true, we'd be a whole lot worse off. *Some* folks never change. That's true. *Most folks never change* might even be correct. But maybe those around them don't let them, or even encourage them to try. I find myself feeling more and more responsible to be like God, that is, to look for places in need of redemption and do what I can. It may not be much, but sometimes a little help is all that's needed. And then God, who made all that supper out of a few loaves and fishes, does the same thing with my pitiful offerings. I think if we had to do it all, we'd just call it quits before we started.

I call Brian on his cell. "Hey bro. Can you bring Dani and Rosa over for dinner? Mom's hankering for your crab cakes. I've got all the ingredients."

"Should she be eating crab meat?"

"No. But I can't say no. She's been so good lately."

"I'll see if Dani can, then call you back. I'll come by myself if she can't. Can somebody pick me up?"

"Absolutely. I will."

It's like this: I'm standing by a switch that will turn off the electricity he's frying in. If I don't move a muscle, I share in the responsibility. Oh, a lot of people will tell you differently. Let each man be responsible for himself and all. But I don't believe that anymore. God put us on this earth to help each other out. I've been reaching for that switch more and more. Rusty convinced me it was the right thing to do.

"Man, those were good, Bri." Brett wipes her mouth. She heard rumors of crab cakes, and there she was!

Rusty took the kids for ice cream a few minutes ago. It's just me, Dad, Mom, Brett, and Brian. I don't think anyone realizes the significance of this gathering. And I'm scared to point it out or someone might leave.

Dad's made amends. Oh, Mom doesn't trust him any more than Elizabeth Taylor's next groom will trust his new bride, but she's decided to forgive. She told me yesterday, "I can't die in that state."

Which scared me to death.

I place a bouquet of cutlery in the sink. "Let's just let the dishes soak. I'm up for a good game of Boggle. Anybody else?"

"I'd love to play!" Mom's hands flutter.

That seals the deal.

I gather paper and mismatched writing instruments and pull the game down from the living-room cabinet, and soon the letter cubes are clacking with vigor, and pages of the dictionary are flying. Of course, I ended up with a crayon! But at least it's a pink one.

"Unbox?" says Brian to Harry. "Dad, I've never heard of that word."

"Me either." Me.

"Well, if you can box something, you can unbox it."

Brett. "Dad, people just say, 'I'll take it out of the box.' I've never heard anybody say, 'Hey Joe, will you unbox those widgets?' "

"Oh, let's give it to him." Mom. "Life's too short. I should know."

Well, nobody can argue with her on that.

Harry waves a hand. "Forget it. Your mother's right. Life's too short. I've never heard anybody use the word unbox either."

I make us tea. We drink together.

We even laugh.

"Whew! I feel winded!" Mom stops walking halfway across the church parking lot.

"You okay, dear?" I hold her arm more tightly.

"Just give me a second. Oh, look at the trees, Ivy. Aren't the leaves gorgeous right now?"

"I think they're at their peak."

"I'm glad I got to see this again."

Autumn in Maryland can be breathtaking, especially after a dry summer. Our skies may not be huge, but their blue resembles a deep aquamarine gemstone that sits behind the mosaic of warm leaves: ruby maples, garnet oak, and many colors of topaz. I'm seeing life through Dorothy's eyes lately, and the fleeting perspective affords me a breathtaking view, bird's-eye, pregnant with urgency.

"Oh, I'll bet you'll be around to see it next year too."

She only smiles.

"Mom, do you want to die?" I can't even believe I asked it.

Rusty comes up. "You okay?"

"Mom just needs a little rest. Go ahead and get the kids settled in their classrooms. And you get to go with Trixie today. I went last week."

Well, not everything can be perfect! Poor Trixie. Life as the family thorn must get a little sorrowful at times.

"I do want to go on home," Mom says. "I've been thinking about signing a Do Not Resuscitate order, Ivy."

I feel my heart sink. "Oh, Mom. Really?"

"Yep. I know it sounds drastic. And after all my years in Right to Life."

"Well, it's your decision. And certainly it's not something I'd be comfortable deciding for you."

"I'd like to make that decision while I still can."

"Okay."

"Can you talk to our lawyer?"

"Sure, Mom. I'll do that."

———

I cry for two hours in Rusty's arms. From eleven to one. He cried with me part of the time but stayed awake. Finally, I arose and kissed his cheek. "Go to sleep. The fall concert's coming up soon. You need your rest."

I bundle myself up in a sweat suit, grab two sleeping bags, and lay outside on the hammock. The aroma from the evening's fires in the fireplaces around the neighborhood swaddle me. Autumn's stripped the trees halfway to bare, and I stare up at the glimmering stars in between the dying leaves as they fall from their branches, kiss my face, caress my hands like a mother's fingers, and recline softly upon my covers.

Brian and Brett meet me at Starbucks.

"I know you've got bad news, Ivy." Brett. "I can see it on your face."

"Well, it's not bad in the sense that Mom's got something else wrong with her."

Brian sits back in relief.

I pull the DNR out of my knapsack. "Mom's going to sign this. She asked me to have the lawyer draw it up."

"What is it?" Brian sits forward and takes a pair of reading glasses out of his shirt pocket. When did he get those?

I tell them.

Brett nods, and so does Brian, but I see him begin to breathe in shallow bursts. I lay a hand on his hand. "It's okay, Bri."

He closes his eyes.

"Just breathe slowly, sweetie. Deep breaths." Brett.

We let him collect himself, and Brett's eyes look into mine, and we gather strength from each other.

The barista calls out our order. Brett jumps up. "I'll get those."

Brian looks up after a minute of silence. "I don't know how you do it, Ivy."

"Thanks."

"Here we go!" Brett distributes the drinks, then sits back down.

I fix my tea.

Brett stirs Sweet'n Low into her skim latte. She has dropped a few pounds.

Brian drinks an espresso straight. I sure wish I could do that.

I fiddle with the plastic lid. "The question is, guys, do you want to come home with me while she signs it?"

"Does she want us to?" Brian.

"I think she wants to explain."

Brett. "Then we'll go." She faces my brother. "Right, Bri? Can you do this for her?"

He nods, turns white.

"Thanks, you guys."

Brian wipes his eyes. Poor little Peter Pan. "Do you think we'll ever really need to use it?"

How can I lie to him? "Yeah, unfortunately I do."

———

Mom's eyes glisten. "I have so little control over my life as it is, kids. I just want to be able to say that I don't want heroics. I want God to take me when He wants to take me. If my heart stops, then I'm counting that as His will."

"But what about us?" Brian's words don't surprise me. And surprisingly, they don't anger me. He has a right to speak his mind at a time like this.

"You're all doing well. Brian, you have Dani. Rusty's home. And Brett, you've become your own girl, something I've been waiting years for."

Brett touches her arm. "Thanks, Mom."

"Oh no. It's true. I'm just glad I stayed alive long enough to see it."

"You sound like you're going to die tomorrow." Brian.

"If God wills it, I wouldn't complain."

It's scary when your mother starts "getting her house in order." Because we all have a clock within us, a windup variety, and we all feel in our souls when our springs are loosening whether our brains realize it or not.

"So you all understand why I'm doing this?"

We do.

"Then hand me the pen, Ivy."

I hand it over, its battleship weight slowing my hand.

Her signature is shaky and scrawly, and I remember the days when she laid it down in turgid boldness upon the back of my report card or my permission slip to the zoo.

"Here. It's all set."

I take the paper from her.

She sets both hands upon her knees. "Now. I would like to watch *White Christmas* together even though it's only October. Do you all have the time?"

And of course we do.

It's been a year since Rusty started losing the pounds, and he's down to his fighting weight, if he was a fighter, that is. Which he's not. He's a lover. Oh, baby. He's even got biceps these days. Okay, he's always had biceps. Even I have biceps. You can just see and feel them now, and when he holds me, or rocks me in his love, I steal a look at those arms and the warmth in my stomach grows.

I've got to say, the man has really been proving himself in every way possible.

Now we Christian women get a bad rap when it comes to sexual reputation. But most of those sex studies usually reveal that we are the most active, satisfied group of women out there. And believe me, after years of getting in bed and crossing my fingers in hopes Rust was really asleep, I'm glad to desire him again. That's really a gift from God. I know it sounds almost freaky, but, well, I'm right. And that's that.

Now, if I would just pray harder about being so darn opinionated, who knows how far God would take me?

Covenant Presbyterian School loves him. The teachers, the administration, the staff, the parents, and especially the kids. A little tow-headed first-grader named Henry calls him Mitter Wusty Neider. We called him that for weeks.

"Mitter Wusty Neider! Time to eat!"

"Wake up, Mitter Wusty Neider, it's time to get ready for school."

"Hey, Mitter Wusty Neider, can you take us out for ice cream?"

My favorite: "Come over here, Mitter Wusty Neider, and give your mother-in-law a buss on the cheek!"

One night as Rusty sat on the edge of the bed taking his socks off, he said, "I thought I was adored out on the road. It's nothing compared to the love I feel from these kids."

"And you get to love them back."

"Yeah. That's exactly right."

I thank him once again for coming home.

He thanks me for drawing a line in the sand.

And we'll continue to have this conversation as long as we need to.

Tonight, everyone but Rusty and the little kids are sitting in the audience in the school auditorium. Even Dani and Brian, who looks decidedly better these days after another stint in rehab—his idea this time. Thank You, Jesus, the courts took his license away so he can't get into more trouble that way. Some people just need their options reduced.

The students file into the gym and step up onto the semicircle of risers.

Rusty holds up his hands for quiet, lifts them higher, and the children begin to recite Psalm 8.

"O Lord, our Lord, how excellent is thy name in *aaalllll* the earth."

Trixie's little singsong soars above the others, her pink face earnest, believing every word. Persy's lips are moving too, which is a miracle. He used to just stand there with this blank look on his face at his old school.

For the rest of the evening, Rusty coaxes song and scripture from their innocent lips. "From the mouths of infants you have ordained praise."

On the way home, Mom stares out the window, then turns to me. "You're doing a wonderful job raising your children, honey."

"Well, thanks, Mom."

"I mean it, Ivy. You're a fine mother."

One more weed picked from her garden. My heart is sore.

———

And so it was that while watching her favorite sitcom, *Becker*, Dorothy Starling breathed her last. It had been a great day. I made shrimp salad for dinner, homemade rolls, and coleslaw. She ate better than she had in months. The Christmas tree winked in the corner, and she said, "You know, Ivy, I love those old-fashioned lights you used this year. They cheer a person right up, don't they?"

"And kids really like colored lights, don't they, Mom?"

She nodded. "You know, I think I'd like a cup of tea."

"I'll make us both one."

Becker came on in all his grumpy glory, and Mom laughed and sipped her tea. About twenty minutes in, she set down her cup, laid her head on a pillow against the armrest of the sofa and said, "That Becker sure is a jerk!"

We laughed together.

The television doctor showed his true stripes, however, and sat by the bedside of a woman in intense pain from bone cancer, or something. I have trouble remembering these days. I'm a little fuzzy now, and guess I will be for a while.

A strange raspy breath came from between Mom's lips.

"Mom?"

I tried to rouse her, but she failed to respond. I checked the carotid artery in her neck—nothing. Shone a light in her open eyes. Achieved no pupil response. Held a mirror up to her mouth. No fog laid itself upon the shiny surface. I tried it all. I tried to find some sign of life. I tried.

I called 911 and dug the DNR out of the drawer.

"Rusty!" I called softly up the steps. "I need you."

He hurried down.

"Mom just died."

"Are you sure?"

I nodded.

"Oh, Dorothy." His eyes filled up with tears, and he walked over to the couch, knelt down beside her, and kissed her cheek. He laid his head on her still chest. "Oh, dearest Dorothy." He looked up and took my hand. "You okay?"

"I think so."

And he held me in his arms, and we knelt down together on the living room floor and wept without a sound.

I wiped my nose with the back of my hand. "The paramedics will be here soon."

"I'll call Brian and Brett. Do you want me to wake up the kids?"

"Not yet. I think I'll just go sit with her until the paramedics come."

"You do that, hon."

And so I gathered Mom into my arms for the last time, positioned her head upon my chest, held her cooling hand in mine and kissed her hair over and over again until the paramedics arrived and took her body away from us forever.

We were made to live forever. This I know. We were made to be reconciled with our Creator. This I know. And so death is not the final battle, but rather, it is the beginning of the way life was always meant to be.

Are you looking down, Mom? Do you see me now? Do you know I'll always miss you?

G'night, Mom. I love you.

I set my alarm, turn off the light, and wait for tomorrow to come and life to begin all over again.

About the Author

Lisa Samson lives in the Baltimore area with her husband Will and their three children. She's presently homeschooling—an adventure in and of itself—and learning just how much she doesn't know. To find out more, visit her Web site: www.lisasamson.com. And to learn more than you ever wanted to know about her life and times, check out her blog, www.lisasamson.typepad.com, or Will's blog, www.willzhead.typepad.com.